THE
LAST SHROUD

DEREK BIRKS

DEREK BIRKS

This is a work of fiction.
Names, characters, places and incidents
are either the product of the author's imagination
or are used fictitiously, and any resemblance to any
persons living or dead is entirely coincidental.

Published by Derek Birks

ISBN- 978-1-910944-17-2

THE LAST SHROUD

To my daughter, Katie, for her enthusiasm, encouragement and support throughout the writing of this series, and for her patience in steering me through the process of cover design.

Acknowledgements

I would like to acknowledge the debt owed to Rob, for editing this book and in particular for his constructive suggestions and astute observations and also to Katie for producing such a great cover design.

Cover acknowledgement: The images of a pollaxe on the front cover and the Middleham Jewel on the back cover are courtesy of York Museums Trust.
http://yorkmuseumstrust.org.uk/:: CC BY-SA 4.0

I am also grateful to Paul Baker for his tour of the Barnet battlefield and his insights about the battle. Paul conducts walks both in Barnet and London. His website can be found at: http://www.barnetwalks.talktalk.net

Finally, as always, I must thank Janet for her long-suffering support - not least in exploring with me no fewer than three battlefields during the preparation of this book.

DEREK BIRKS

CONTENTS

Part One: A World of Blood   7

Part Two: A Place by the River   131

Part Three: The Rule of Law   239

Part Four: Rebellion   315

Part Five: Kingdom Lost   351

Part Six: Kingdom Found   409

Part Seven: Rebels and Brothers   481

Author's Note   559

Historical Notes   561

About the Author   567

DEREK BIRKS

PART ONE: A WORLD OF BLOOD

DEREK BIRKS

THE LAST SHROUD

1

26th July 1469, near Banbury

"How has it come to this?" asked Will Herbert, Earl of Pembroke.

Ned Elder stared down from the ridge on Edgecote Hill to the valley below where thousands of men were arrayed. "Warwick… and the Duke of Clarence," he replied.

"Even I can't quite believe that, Ned. Much as I'd like to blame Warwick for all the ills in Christendom, I can't see him provoking a revolt in the north - surely it threatens him too? And their leader is a certain Robin of Redesdale - why Warwick and Clarence aren't even in England."

Ned sighed. "I promise you, Will: if they're not, they very soon will be."

Pembroke surveyed the rebel army. "They look well ordered, Ned."

"Oh, trust me, they will be," said Ned, unable to keep the bitterness from his voice. It was not even a year since the events at Yoredale Castle. All that blood and sacrifice had done no more than delay the inevitable.

The rebel archers released their first arrows.

"It begins," said Pembroke.

There was a terrible fascination to it, watching the cloak of death smother the summer sky. The arrows fell thick upon them, rattling helms and striking armour like hailstones, piercing visors, punching through leather and burrowing deep into flesh.

Pembroke's army, exposed upon the eastern ridge of Edgecote Hill, had little response to offer against the storm of arrows. A handful of archers let fly, a few cannon roared forth smoke and flame, but they could not halt the slaughter.

Ned stood motionless beside Pembroke as men fell all around them. He made no attempt to dodge the arrows. Let death strike him in the forehead, or the mouth, or take him straight in the eye. If this was to be one battle too many, then God would decide, not he - and if God had no more time for him, then so be it.

The smoke that swirled about him could not mask the cries of the wounded, but at least it hid from the rebels the carnage their archers were inflicting. All too soon, though, the pall - and the illusion - would disperse. Not for the first time, Ned turned to look behind them back down the hill towards the south west. There was still no dust in the distant fields, no glint of sun on sallets and no hint of foot soldiers hastening up from Banbury to their aid.

"Blood of Christ!" shouted Pembroke.

For a moment Ned thought the Welshman was hit, but one look at his face reassured him. Pembroke was just choking with impotent rage. Ned turned his attention to his own men. Hal fidgeted close by and Ned found a grim smile as Bear planted a large hand upon the youth's shoulder to still his nerves. The waiting could kill you on its own - for if you weren't careful death came as a relief. He said a last silent prayer for his wife, Maighread, and the child she was carrying. He prayed too for his young son, John, who he barely knew but hoped to know better.

The arrows still fell, but not so thickly. Pembroke's cannon stuttered into silence and the smoke began to drift away down the slope.

"That's that, then," said Pembroke. "Out of powder

already - and where in the name of God is the Earl of Devon?"

"Your man's been gone long enough to ride to the sea and back, let alone the few miles to Banbury," said Ned. "I'll send one of mine."

Pembroke swayed involuntarily as a bodkin arrow scraped past his armoured shoulder.

"No, Ned, don't send a man; you go," he said. "Without Devon's archers we'll bleed our lives away up here. You take your fifty horsemen and drive his five thousand archers here to me!"

"I came to fight, my lord," Ned argued, "and, God knows, you need every man!"

Pembroke thumped a metal fist hard into Ned's breastplate. "Your few horsemen will make little difference on this hill. I need Devon's archers far more than I need you!"

He bellowed a string of commands which were relayed along the ridge where his Welsh spearmen stood. He seized his pollaxe from a page and took a pace forward. There was a ripple of movement all along the ridge as every man followed his lead. Pembroke bowed his head for a moment then turned to Ned.

"Get me those archers, Ned."

Ned gave him a curt nod but Pembroke was already on the move, cajoling his spearmen as he led them down the hill into the valley towards the advancing rebel host. Ned wanted to go with them but Pembroke was right: without more men, they would be overwhelmed.

"Bear, mount up the men!" he ordered, the words catching in his dry throat.

Ned's horsemen needed little encouragement to take to their mounts. They descended the gentle slope to the south west at breakneck pace, the fierce cries of the Welshmen echoing behind them from the far side of the hill. Ned had fought Welsh men at arms himself… a lifetime ago at Mortimer's Cross. The poor bastards might be heavily outnumbered but they would fight like men possessed. They would not be beaten easily and, if he moved swiftly enough, he might yet come to their aid.

Before they reached Banbury, they met Pembroke's lone messenger returning.

"Is the Earl of Devon on his way?" cried Ned, as the rider slowed.

"The earl's still in Banbury, my lord," gasped the man, lost for breath. "He says he'll come… with all speed."

Ned looked ahead towards Banbury. "Well? How far off lie his men? Are they close?"

"No, my lord, not very-" Ned's angry stare paled him. "The earl's men are all afoot and still south of the town. I fear…."

"Where's the earl?" barked Ned. "Is he at the castle? Speak man! Your comrades are being butchered whilst your words idle in your mouth!"

"The earl is at an inn… by the high cross… in the market place, my lord. He's waiting for his men. I think he moves… without much haste, my lord."

Ned cursed loudly. There was no love lost between Pembroke and Devon - the two lords had quarrelled violently the previous night and now the royal army was split into two warring halves. He must bring Devon's archers to the fight or the day would be lost and that was just… unthinkable.

"Go!" he ordered the messenger. "And tell the Earl of Pembroke that I shall persuade Devon to move faster - or I'll whip the damned archers there myself!"

He urged his horse forward, knowing such a ride could finish some of his mounts. They had been ridden hard from Corve Manor the day before and were still exhausted. They were poor enough beasts for battle too - but all an impoverished lord could afford.

When they reached Banbury town Ned saw from a small cloud of dust to the south exactly where Devon's army was.

"They'll never make it in time, lord," breathed Hal.

"Don't doubt Welsh valour, Hal. Will Herbert and his brother Richard are mighty men at arms and their spearmen can hold out longer than you might think."

"Yes, lord," said Hal, looking far from convinced.

"I know," said Ned. "They'll be hard pressed - and even if I can persuade Devon to move his archers we still may not arrive in time."

"What can I do, lord?" asked Hal.

"Well, now we know how far off the archers are, why don't you and Master Croft go back to Edgecote? When I return you can quickly tell me how the battles goes for I'll have no time to stand and think."

"Yes, lord," said Hal, clearly relieved to be doing something useful.

"And watch for our return," said Ned. "We'll come by the track south of Edgecote Hill!"

"We'll be ready, my lord. But I pray you'll not be too long."

§§§

It was not difficult to find Humphrey Stafford, Earl of Devon, in Banbury. Ned passed the great covered cross in the market place and recognised at once the gold Stafford livery of several men at arms lounging near the Red Lion inn. Humphrey himself was lodged inside with several more of his retinue.

Ned threw open the door and found Stafford holding court, seated at the far end of a long table with his captains arrayed before him. Ned had met Stafford before and did not care for him much. He would rather be dealing with Will Herbert. Herbert was a byword for bluntness and could start an argument with a passing horse, yet Ned preferred him to the wily Stafford. Neither man was especially popular with his noble peers since both had been raised up by the new king with what some regarded as indecent haste.

Humphrey Stafford glanced up at him but continued chewing on a piece of bread.

"My lord?" said Ned.

Stafford swallowed his mouthful and regarded him briefly. Untroubled but watchful, Ned thought. This man was no-one's fool.

"Do I know you?" asked Stafford, as he cast his eyes about the table for the next morsel to consume.

"We've met," said Ned. "The first time was in the battle south of Wigmore Castle. I'm Ned Elder."

Stafford looked up again at that. "Lord Ned Elder? Well, we are honoured, are we not, gentlemen, to be in such a heroic presence?"

He glanced around his comrades with a smile that degenerated all too swiftly into a smirk.

"Did you not hear Pembroke's cannon?" asked Ned.

"Pembroke?" said Stafford, looking puzzled. "Oh, Lord Herbert, you mean. Of course. Forgive me, but I can't keep pace with all his new honours."

That was rich, Ned considered, coming from Stafford who had only held the Earldom of Devon for a few months. He almost said so but contrived to keep his opinions to himself.

"Herbert needs your archers."

"Does he?" asked Devon. "Surely he can deal with the northern rabble alone. He didn't seem to value my men very highly last night."

"He needs you to join him," said Ned, struggling to keep his voice even.

"The rebel army would have to be several thousand strong even to come close to Herbert's force. Where in

God's name would such a rebel army come from?"

Ned's mind raced back to six months earlier. He knew exactly where such a northern army might have come from.

"Herbert's scouts talked wildly of thousands yesterday," continued Devon, "but I very much doubt that. In any case, Herbert has thousands of his own Welsh pike men. He should be able to despatch a few rebels and send the rest home with bloodied heads."

Ned thought he might strike this man if he spoke to him for too much longer.

"I've seen the rebel host myself," he said, "and it does number several thousand!"

Stafford frowned at him. "I don't like your tone, Lord Elder, and I don't believe I need answer to you for my actions. If you're so keen to join him, I suggest you go and do just that. I'll make my way north, as his grace the king requested, at my earliest convenience. Now, if you don't mind, I'd like to eat without interruption. This is an excellent local cheese - you should try it, my lord."

"Pembroke sent a man to ask for your help," persisted Ned.

Devon's face darkened. "He sent a common Welshman to command me to come... and he'll need to ask in a more civil manner if he wants my five thousand archers!"

"And what if Pembroke's force alone is not enough to stop the rebels?"

"Enough of your barking demands! Go to Lord Herbert yourself and leave me to break my fast in peace. My archers won't be here yet a while."

Ned snatched out his dagger and plunged it hard into the table close by Devon's right hand.

"I tell you this, Humphrey Stafford, it is no rag tag army of untrained rebels that Pembroke faces. It's an army raised for the Earl of Warwick and I don't recall that Warwick counts either you or Pembroke amongst his friends. So you'd better make sure you win - or your glistening new title won't last the month! Think on that - and think upon it swiftly!"

Ned could have said more, much more, but he did not. Instead he stalked to the inn door and then turned to Bear.

"Help the good earl to finish breaking his fast," he ordered.

Bear nodded and effortlessly upended the long table where Stafford sat, sending every item on it plummeting towards the earl's chest. Then he released it to the floor with a crash and followed his master out, leaving a speechless Humphrey Stafford to contemplate the contents of his lap.

§§§

When the Earl of Devon emerged from the inn not long after, he seemed a quite different man. He bellowed orders to his captains and they hurried off to meet the irregular columns of archers which were now skirting the northern edge of the town.

"Lead on, Lord Elder," called Stafford cheerfully across the market place. "Let us go then to Lord Herbert's aid!"

As Ned well knew, Stafford's words were meant not for him but for those in the market place witnessing his departure. What they would see was the noble Humphrey Stafford going to the aid of a comrade in the service of his king.

"Pray God we are in time," muttered Ned. But his worst fears were soon confirmed as the Earl of Devon's archers advanced at snail's pace. Ned's mounted column was soon half a mile ahead.

"Keep a sharp eye behind us," he told Bear, glancing back to check that Devon was still following.

Ned's grasp of the terrain around Edgecote Hill was poor. He had only glimpsed it when he arrived at Pembroke's camp in the gloom of the previous evening. All

Ned knew was that there were hills all around them and the rebel approach that morning had taken Pembroke by surprise since it came from the nearby village of Thorpe to the south east - hardly the direction from which they were expecting the northern rebels to come.

Ned halted his men where Hal and Croft waited on a patch of ground overlooking the field. In the valley below them to the east a fierce struggle raged across a stream.

"Lord Herbert's pike men pushed back the first rebel attack to the river," reported Hal, "but now they're struggling to hold the riverbank."

"Their line grows thin, my lord," said Croft.

Ned could see for himself that the Welshmen were starting to buckle under the sheer weight of numbers against them.

"Have you seen any rebel horsemen, Hal?" asked Ned.

"No, lord - but they could easily be beyond the hill - Thorpe Hill, I'm told. We'd not see them from here."

"No, we wouldn't," agreed Ned, studying the land that undulated away to the east. "And once we're down in that valley, we'll not see much beyond it either."

"Should we wait for Devon's archers then?" asked Hal.

"Aye, Hal, we should, but if we do, another hundred Welshmen will die." He shook his head. "If we wait any longer Pembroke will be routed. We'll have to risk it."

He quickly gathered around him the half dozen men he called his captains.

"Let's keep it simple," he said. "We ride down into the meadow, cross the stream and cut along the rear of the rebels, raking them with spear, sword and axe. We seek to weaken them, spread alarm and force them to fall back. But we don't stop! If we're brought to a halt, we'll be hemmed in and… well, just don't stop."

He gave his captains a few moments to pass on his orders and then set off down the incline towards the valley floor. They carved a furrow through the ripening grasses and then splashed across the stream onto the rebel held bank. There the dread sounds of battle greeted them: the cries of fighting men and the steely exchange of blows. Ned drew out his sword and glanced at Bear on his right hand. He could not resist a smile at the giant Flemish warrior, with his massive war axe in hand. Once a mercenary, he had served Ned loyally for the best part of ten years. If there was an irresistible force amongst mortal men, then Bear was it.

"An Elder, an Elder!" roared Ned and others in the column took up the cry. Thus, well before they reached the enemy, shouts of warning went up. Some of the rebels turned to face them; others backed away and fled as Ned gouged a bloody path into their left flank. Many of the rebels in the rear had yet to be involved in the desperate fighting across the stream and the sudden attack caught them out.

Beside him Bear wrought carnage as the mounted column drove like a keen blade through the rebel host, slicing it in two. Ned knew they must crush the enemy's fragile resolve speedily for in battle the smallest mistake or accident could herald disaster. Thus it proved, for when a horse went down the deadly charge soon began to slow, as riders became enmeshed in the falling, churning mass of men in their path. Despite Ned's intention to ride through, he was forced to a halt by those who could not flee fast enough. Once he stopped, others less timid tried to hack at his legs or those of his horse to bring him down. The more he tried to turn aside, the more trapped he became.

As he hacked down at the close press of men around him he saw some all too well, their blood-smeared faces screwed up with anguish or rage. Amongst them all, one face caught his eye for a brief moment. The face was only a few yards away but half-obscured by the man's helm. A pair of dark eyes bored into him with a look of shock and Ned shrank back. He knew those eyes - he would never forget them - the eyes of a man who should be dead.

Suddenly a pike slid off Ned's arm and struck the side of his helm, knocking his head back. Bear joined him and drove aside the men around him as a wolf might scatter sheep. Ned looked in vain to catch sight of the face again but it was lost in the crush of retreating men.

"Lord!" bellowed Bear, shaking him from his distraction.

"I'm alright!" cried Ned, moving his head gingerly. Together they rode forward once more. In the stream the Welshmen cheered their arrival and took heart, stepping forward to press their opponents back. Many were trapped between Ned's horsemen and Pembroke's spears. For a time the slaughter continued until the remnants of the rebel army scattered up the slopes of Thorpe Hill or fled over the ridge to the east, which brought another roar of triumph from the Welshmen.

Ned dismounted and Pembroke clapped him on the shoulder with a bloodied gauntlet.

"Good timing, Ned!" he shouted. "It seems we shan't have need of Devon's archers after all."

"Perhaps not," replied Ned, "yet they are on their way all the same - it'll take them a little longer on foot."

He stared at Pembroke in admiration. "I thought to find you dead," he mumbled.

"Never mind me, Ned. You look shaken yourself."

"I'm well enough," he replied.

Though he casually dismissed Pembroke's concerns, he could not dislodge the image of Thomas Gate from his head. Thomas Gate, who had brought such ruin upon him and those he loved. Thomas Gate, whom the Earl of Warwick assured him would be killed. If Ned had any lingering doubts about who was behind the rebel army, they disappeared with that glimpse of Gate, for he was always Warwick's man.

"When we've rested our men," said Pembroke, "we should head north and drive what's left of these rebels towards the king at Nottingham. We can break them between us - hammer and anvil, Ned, eh?"

Ned gave a weary nod. "I shall be glad to aid in the rout," he said, but his thoughts dwelt only on the pursuit of one particular rebel.

He led his horse down to the stream beside which lay the bodies of the fallen. It was never a welcome sight to see so many men laid low, their torn flesh still weeping blood into the water. He had thought such chaos to be behind him years ago - after all, what was the point of crowning a new king if that king was no more able to keep the peace than the last one. He stared at the trodden down grass and broken rushes in the bloody water at his feet - so many years gone by and still the blood flowed. He walked his mount further upstream to join Hal and some others of his men.

"Losses?" he asked Hal.

"God has smiled upon us, my lord: only two dead and four wounded - though one of them like to die, I fear. Bear tends the wounded now."

"Hal, you didn't notice anyone you knew in the rebel host, did you?"

Hal shrugged. "I didn't have much time for looking, my lord. Did you see someone?"

"Aye, I thought so - perhaps. Someone from the small army raised at Yoredale."

"That army was broken in the winter, my lord - all but destroyed."

"Aye, all but…" said Ned.

"Take time to rest, my lord," advised Hal.

"I've barely done anything requiring rest," scoffed Ned.

"It's the horses that need the rest!"

"Yes, lord," said Hal, "I suppose…"

He stood awkwardly, avoiding Ned's inquiring glance.

Ned gave a heavy sigh. "Did my lady wife have cause to speak with you, Hal, before we left Corve Manor?"

Hal gave a nervous laugh. "Lady Maighread is a generous soul, my lord. She told me she would pray for our safe return."

"And?" prompted Ned.

"Nothing else, lord…"

Ned put his hands on Hal's shoulders and looked him in the eye. The younger man looked away again. "And?" enquired Ned once more.

"She entreated me to… bring you back safe, my lord."

"My head is fine, Hal," he said sternly. "It does not ache at all. I have ridden at the charge, I've taken a blow from a pike and still I am fine!"

"That's good, my lord. I didn't doubt it."

"Did my lady… entreat anyone else?"

"Well, lord… Bear, I think…" mumbled Hal, "and perhaps Croft… and several others, I dare say…"

Ned shook his head. "So my men believe me to be but a frail husk of what I once was. That should help me a great deal!"

"The lady-"

"The lady weakens my lordship," said Ned softly.

"Not with me, my lord - nor the others."

"Yet if I hesitate in battle will you think my old head wound has returned? Will you lose attention to your own part of the fight? It's a dangerous thing, Hal, when men look twice at their leader."

He left Hal and wandered back towards Pembroke, but before he reached him there were ironic cheers from some of Pembroke's men as the vanguard of Devon's archers at last were sighted on the high plateau to the south west where Ned had begun his charge.

Ned gave a rueful smile. Devon would swell their numbers for the coming chase at least, though at the speed they moved it might be Lammastide before they arrived. The column of archers came to a halt on the crest but showed no sign of advancing further. What was the Earl of Devon playing at now? Still reluctant to join his rival, Pembroke, he supposed.

Other cries drew his attention then, cries of warning. He swung his gaze to the south east where he saw that the rebels had reformed on Thorpe Hill and were now advancing down its slopes once more towards them. How had they managed that?

"To arms!" bellowed Pembroke. "To arms!"

Ned hurried back to Hal where he had left his horse and swiftly remounted. Bear was already growling orders and the rest of the men mounted swiftly. The Welsh spearmen wearily picked up their weapons and formed a line on the banks of the stream. Ned cantered across to Pembroke.

"Where would you have us, my lord?" Ned asked.

"Take position on our left flank, Ned. I think you might try the same move again: crossing the stream and attacking their rear."

Privately Ned doubted that the rebels would be as vulnerable to such an assault a second time. Yet it seemed the best use of his mounted men.

"If Stafford gets a move on then we can rout this host for good," urged Pembroke. "I suppose he's waiting for every last one of his men to climb the slope!"

"I doubt he'll hurry," said Ned.

Pembroke laughed grimly. "Well, if he's late, he'll lose all the valour of the victory - and you may be sure the king will hear of it!"

Ned did not doubt it for Pembroke would not be slow to use Devon's reluctance to his own advantage later - but first there was a battle to be won. Ned led his troop of men at arms away from the stream and they dismounted in the meadow below Edgecote Hill, well behind Pembroke's men. By doing so he hoped to keep the rebels guessing about when and where he would strike. The opposing army was more numerous than he had expected. These rebels were no unruly mob; they were organised, resolute and they seemed to have leaders who knew what they were doing. Thomas Gate, for one, was no novice on the field of battle. Ned scanned the approaching ranks but the distance was too great to make out their banners.

"Hal, Bear, Croft!" He called his most trusted men to him. "These men we face are from the north… I fear we may make war against an old enemy. I think I caught a glimpse of Thomas Gate earlier. I could be mistaken - but watch out for him nonetheless."

Hal glared back at him. "If he's there, lord, I shall mark him out - you may be sure of that! I will take the memory of his bloody banner to my grave."

"So shall we all, Hal, but keep your wits clear. The struggle won't be so easy this time."

"And still the Earl of Devon stays on the hill, my lord," observed Hal. "He's just beyond bowshot..."

"Aye," said Ned, staring to the south. Then the roaring voices reached a crescendo and there was a mighty crash as the rebel line clashed with Pembroke's on the west bank of the stream. Ned's eyes turned once more to the field before him. The Welshmen withstood the first wave of attack and threw the rebels back into the stream, but as more men at arms pressed forward through the water, the spear men began to give ground. Ned noticed that the rebel leaders had kept some men armed with pikes in reserve. They hung back from the fray, as if daring him to intervene. Even so, they were on foot and few in number. His own men, being mounted, would still have the edge - if he judged it well.

"Croft," he said in a low voice. "A word, if you please."

Croft was barely twenty-five years old but he was one of Ned's most experienced men. Ned quickly outlined what he intended and then sent Croft off to choose his men.

In vain he looked to Pembroke for a sign, but the Herbert brothers were embroiled in a close struggle. He gave a nod to Hal and Bear. "Mount the men," he ordered. "We'll aim for their left flank again to draw the reserves that way but this time Croft will take half our number across to their right."

"Crush them between us!" said Bear, looking well pleased at the prospect.

Ned led them down into the stream and once again their presence brought a great clamour from the Welsh spearmen who pressed forward with renewed vigour. He rode across the water and noted with satisfaction that the rebel pike men who had hung back were now rushing to block his charge. With perfect timing, Croft sheered away behind the Welsh line to cross the stream on the rebels' right flank.

Ned grimaced behind his lowered visor as the rebel pike men hesitated and, at the last minute, several broke away to meet the new threat. Ned's sword battered aside a pair of pikes and then traced a bloody arc through the first rank. Beside him others rattled their long spears against the pikes to turn their sharp tips aside and thrust at the defenders. With his visor down, Ned could not see how Croft was faring on the far side, so all he could do was press forward in blind hope. Bear was suddenly alongside him once more and they forced a way through. The rebel reserve began to fall back in disarray.

Ned raised his visor and saw Croft ahead, unscathed, and his horsemen savaging the rear of the rebel centre. The manoeuvre had worked better than he could have hoped. The Welshmen now fought their way into the middle of the stream where the fallen began to pile up. They were going to win the day: it was time to seek out Thomas Gate.

"Lord!" Hal was screaming at him.

Ned turned sharply in the saddle but under him his mount shuddered, a pike buried deep in its chest. Ned braced himself for the poor beast to rear up but it did not. It merely gave a snort of blood and collapsed beneath him. Ned was pitched forward onto the pike man struggling to disentangle his weapon. Ned landed on him with some force and both men were slow to rise onto their knees. Ned still had his sword and leant his weight upon it. The other man abandoned his pike shaft and got to his feet first. He drew out a short sword and stabbed at Ned who was too slow to bring up his own weapon. The sword stopped mid-thrust, however, for Bear had calmly buried his pollaxe in the back of the assailant's neck.

"Lord! Take my horse," said Hal, swiftly dismounting.

"No, I'll fight on foot!" declared Ned.

Pembroke's brother, young Richard Herbert, was almost alongside him having fought his way through the rebel line, his armour slick with blood.

"Nicely done, Lord Elder!" he shouted with a grin. "We shall make short work of these northern outlaws now."

Ned frowned. "Have a care, Richard. I was a northern outlaw once!"

Richard Herbert grinned again, lowered his visor and proceeded to hack his way back through the rebel lines towards his brother. Ned scoured the line in search of Thomas Gate. Bear and Hal had both dismounted and flanked him as he entered the fray.

"Watch for Gate's banner," he snarled.

The field was now no longer two battle lines but a tangle of melees across the stream. In such a broken field Ned acknowledged few peers and the rebels scattered before his sword. Somewhere there, he knew, he would find Thomas Gate.

"Lord!" Hal laid a warning hand upon his arm, something Ned could not remember ever happening before.

"What now, Hal?" he said. Maighread's interference had a lot to answer for.

Hal pulled him round by the arm to look behind them to the east. He stared at the low ridge beside Thorpe Hill and caught the glint of armour in the midday sun.

"Who in God's name are they?" he murmured. "Hal, get a horse and ride closer. Try to make out their colours."

Ned stood off the relentless clamour of battle and watched Hal ride off. He dared not commit his men any further until he knew who was coming up behind them. So he did what he had never done before with a battle raging around him, he hesitated. Bear remained beside him ready to send to Hell any man who came close but Ned's eyes remained fixed upon Hal. He watched the young rider come to an abrupt halt and then wheel his horse around to gallop back towards them.

Sweat dripped down the inside of Ned's helm; it ran down his cheeks and into the corners of his dry mouth. He tried to discern from Hal's manner whether the news was good or ill, but could not. Hal would bring his tidings as fast as his tired mount allowed. Ned glanced up towards the Earl of Devon on the high ground to the south and saw that Stafford had yet to commit his men. What in God's name was he waiting for?

Hal was shouting but he could not make out the words over the din of battle in his ears. Hal was almost upon him when he learned who was approaching the field from the east.

"Warwick!" cried Hal, "the bear and ragged staff of Warwick comes!"

It struck Ned like a blow from a mailed fist yet he had known from the first that the rebel army was Warwick's. It should come as no surprise to learn that the earl himself had finally come over from Calais to take charge of it.

"To horse!" he bellowed. "Hal, we must tell Pembroke how it stands."

Then he realised he did not have a horse. Bear waited with him while Hal gathered several horses and the men regrouped around them. Ned mounted swiftly for Warwick's vanguard was barely a hundred paces away now and coming on with all speed. He had no need to tell Pembroke for the earl could already see for himself.

"Lord!" yelled Hal, pointing up to the Earl of Devon's men. Humphrey Stafford had at last made a decision and his archers were on the move. But they were not coming to Pembroke's aid; instead they were hurrying away to the west.

In that moment Ned knew the battle was lost. Fired by anger, he bludgeoned through the knot of men contesting the centre of the stream, with his horsemen following close behind. He made straight for the Herbert brothers who were rallying their men around them. The rebels at the stream fell back ten yards to reform their line and prepare for the fresh men to join them. It seemed as if all the combatants held their breath as they waited for the first wave of Warwick's men at arms to arrive.

Ned reached the blue and red standard of William Herbert and cried out: "Warwick has come!"

Pembroke raised his visor. "We can still prevail, my lord!" he declared, bullish as ever.

"They are too many! And that coward, Devon, has run!" cried Ned.

"If we flee now my men will be cut down as they run and none will reach their hearths in Wales," argued Pembroke.

"Aye, very well then," said Ned, "we'll fight on…"

"No, Ned, I'll fight on a while, but you will not."

"I'm not leaving this field a second time today!" retorted Ned.

"You must get to the king. His grace may have force enough to come to our aid."

"I'll send a trusty man to the king and stay here with you!"

"It must be someone known to his grace," insisted Pembroke. "Someone whose word he'll trust at once. You must go!"

"I will not!" roared Ned. "In God's name, I cannot!"

"Warwick's numbers can't yet be that great," said Pembroke.

"Warwick will have half the Calais garrison with him!" argued Ned. "And Clarence's retainers too!"

Pembroke shook his head. "We don't know that - it may just be Warwick's van. We'll see if we can force them to pull back, or hold them off till nightfall, then slip away westwards."

"Nightfall is many hours away, Will."

"There's no more time to argue, Ned." Pembroke clasped his hand. "Take your men and find the king!"

Before Ned could make answer the rebels crashed into their line once more and all discussion ended. For a few moments Ned stood his ground. Then he swung back up into the saddle and wheeled his column of riders across the stream once more. There was no guarantee they could even escape the field for he had no idea what other bands of rebels might be lying in wait.

They tracked north, eyes watchful for any hint of ambush but all they saw were tenants working their land. A bloody battle might be raging nearby, but the war these farmers fought was against dearth in winter, and it was fought with plough and scythe not sword or pollaxe. Some fields were already ripe for harvest and the harvest must be gathered in, at all cost.

He glanced back towards the valley where the Herbert brothers and their Welsh levies would be hard-pressed.

"God's blood!" he railed at the heavens. He hated abandoning the Welshmen but if Warwick himself had truly taken up arms then the king had to be told. If his grace already knew that the rebels were near Banbury there was a chance he might even be close by.

When they had ridden some miles, Ned thought it safe to slacken their pace, to spare the mounts. Only then did it occur to him that he had missed his chance once more to punish Thomas Gate. He brooded in silence as they continued slowly north-east but they found no sign of the king. It was not a pleasant journey: several men were wounded, some of the horses were lame and the bitter taste of defeat lingered with them all.

"Hal, Croft!" he said. "I want prickers all around us; I don't want any more surprises."

When Hal had carried out his orders he returned to ride alongside Ned.

"Lord?"

"Aye?" said Ned, with a wary glance at the archer. "Lord what?"

"Do you know where the king is, my lord?" enquired Hal.

Ned sighed. "Oh aye, I do, Hal. He's somewhere between here and Nottingham…"

He met Hal's horrified expression with a blank stare.

"What if we… miss him?" asked Hal.

"Then we're all going to be very… disappointed, Hal."

"What of my lord Pembroke?" asked Hal.

Ned shook his head. "I'm afraid Pembroke's finished, lad," replied Ned. "We had to find the king at once for there to be any hope."

Hal nodded and blew out his cheeks. "Christ's Blood…"

"Blood of Christ, indeed…" said Ned.

By the late afternoon they entered what proved to be a large wood and after a mile or so Ned called in his scouts. One by one they reported gloom upon more gloom.

"A column of horsemen heading north, not far behind us," said the first.

"See their livery?" asked Ned.

"Could be men of Clarence," offered the scout.

"Aye, and it could be a troop of dancing bears! Next time be certain!" snapped Ned. "What about to the east?"

Another scout spoke up smartly. "A few bands of men on foot, my lord. The nearest… a few miles east of us."

"Heading?"

"Some south, my lord, some east…it's a bit of a … muddle."

"Aye, it is. Very well, take your rest for now."

He dared not risk blundering into a larger hostile force.

"Lord," whispered Hal, "do you remember this wood?"

"I don't believe I'll ever forget it," acknowledged Ned. "What brutal fate has brought us back to Whittlewood Forest, do you think, Hal?"

"At least it's a big forest…"

"Aye. We'll camp here," he announced.

Bear gave him one of his solemn stares which on this occasion meant: are you sure that's what you want to do, my lord?

"Some hours before dark, lord," Hal observed.

"Listen. We're in Warwick's own country. We won't find many friends around here and I don't want them finding us first either. This is as good a place as any to rest. We've plenty of tree cover and there are streams nearby - and some game. We might last here a few days…"

Hal gave him a bleak look. "A few days?"

Ned lowered his voice. "Aye. Hal, we could spend the rest of our lives riding around in circles searching for the king. We know nothing, so if we're to find him, we must go carefully. Choose three men - good men - and send them out on our best mounts. They're to ride for no more than a day and then return here. They're to rest their horses often or they'll not get back at all. One goes north-west to join the old road towards Leicester, another north towards Northampton and the third further east to cut onto the road to London. They must seek news of the king: his progress - any news or rumour is better than what we have now."

"Very well, lord," said Hal, moving to go.

Ned caught his arm. "They must be careful, Hal, secret - and make sure none wear badges. Tell them if they're not back after three days, we'll have gone."

Hal nodded. "Lord… can we stay hidden here for three days?"

"I hope so, Hal. You'd best pray we can."

"It surely won't take too long to find the king - I mean, he must be travelling with a large host, my lord?"

"I thought that, but now I'm not so sure, Hal," murmured Ned. "If he has such a great host, then how did the rebel army get past him?"

2

29th July 1469, in Whittlewood Forest

It was a warm night, with a moon as large and white as a nun's wimple, washing its light over the horses amongst the trees. They had remained hidden for three days and nights in the woods, where the small stream gave them enough water and they hunted a little. Ned studied the silvered forest. He had men out there watching for any approach, if they were still awake. Their predicament should have been enough to keep any man wide awake, for Ned had little doubt that there were enemies all around them. Yet some men always found sleep easily and he envied them for it. Bear, as always, was still awake and close by, leaning against a large oak. Ned felt sorry for the tree, bearing such a heavy load.

Ned had not slept much since Edgecote. All he could think of was Pembroke's men being cut to pieces in that stream. He could not be certain, of course, but he could see no other outcome. Nor was he out of danger yet. If Warwick caught him again, there would be no escape this time. Gate too came into sharp focus in his head, prompting a faint throb of pain. Another chance missed to take down that murderous villain.

God, or good fortune, had kept them safe so far but it could not last and whatever happened now they must move on in the morning. Ned remained watchful, nervous, as he waited for his scouts to return. Three young men, three good men.

The first horseman to return passed with great slowness through the woods from the west. It was Tom, known to the others as 'Horse' - an unfortunate nickname but yet apt in so many ways. Tom looked exhausted. Ned glanced up at his long face and Tom shook his head at once.

"No news of the king, my lord," he reported, "but plenty of others around - mostly under Warwick's banner and hundreds on the road to Northampton. If the king's near there, he'd better be in force or he'll be taken for sure."

"Very well," acknowledged Ned. It was not exactly unexpected.

"There's some other news, my lord…" said the scout.

"Well?"

"Lord Pembroke and his brother were taken at Edgecote, my lord."

"Do you know where they're held?" asked Ned.

"Not held, my lord… beheaded… a day or two ago at Northampton."

Ned gave 'Horse' a nod and a gentle pat on the shoulder.

"You've done well," he said, trying to hide his shock. Even by Warwick's standards, executing men who were loyal to the king was a long stride towards outright rebellion. No matter that Pembroke had sent him away, Ned felt he had abandoned the Welshmen at Edgecote and he knew he would carry the guilt with him to his grave.

The second scout returned in the early hours with no attempt at stealth. He rode into the camp and fell from his horse at once. Bear lifted him up and Ned saw that he'd been wounded in the back.

"Crossbow bolt!" the man spluttered. "Passed through, I think."

"A gift from whom?" prompted Ned as Bear ripped the man's shirt and probed around the wound.

"I think the Duke of Clarence's men - ah, mother's blood! Be careful, Bear!"

Ned forced himself to wait until Bear had staunched the wound.

"So, tell me who or what you've found," said Ned.

"Some men of Clarence, my lord, but they are mostly Warwick's."

"Where?" asked Ned.

"Some in Northampton, others are on their way north, south - all ways, it seems."

"And the king?"

"I heard nothing of the king, my lord," said the scout.

"What happened to you on the way back?"

"I chanced upon the ancient track to the north but many men were travelling upon it. I asked a few too many questions…"

"How far are we from the road?" asked Ned.

"We're very close… too close to stop here much longer, my lord."

Ned left Bear to finish tending the man's wound and walked to the eastern edge of the trees. There was already a trace of colour in the sky there. He knew they had to move: but which way? He was still missing one of his scouts and it was clear that their enemies were all around them.

He had travelled the road his scout had crossed before, making his way south from Coventry to Stony Stratford - Watling Street, Spearbold had called it. But if the king was on it he'd have been taken by now and the news would be on every man's lips. The king was known to be in Nottingham, but Watling Street did not go through Nottingham - he was sure of that. He tried to imagine where Nottingham was - and failed. Nottingham was just a word to him, not a place. Yet surely by now the king would have left Nottingham in any case. It was making his head throb again.

The scout who had yet to return was sent east. To head east was Ned's worst option - west would take him nearer to home, to Corve Manor where Maighread would be waiting. Going east would close off the way home, yet if the king was making for London…

He had wasted three days and still he was not sure. This is the time, he thought, when your grizzled old adviser puts his arm around your shoulder and gives you his considered wisdom - pity he didn't have such a man with him. They were all dead now, except Spearbold, who was back at Corve Manor, and Ragwulf, who was most likely still in Yoredale with Eleanor.

So, he was on his own and if he guessed wrong he would likely condemn all his men to death in Whittlewood Forest which had nearly killed him once before.

"Dear Lord," he muttered under his breath, "please guide my thoughts and lead me to my king…"

They left on the cusp of dawn and rode east as swiftly as they dared. With fresh horses Ned hoped to put some distance between his own men and the numerous bands of Warwick's rebels. Very soon they crossed Watling Street, but it was mercifully quiet and they pushed on eastwards. Once more Ned put out prickers to scout all around the column.

They found the third rider, Will Hog, several hours later. He had almost got back to them - almost, but not quite. His mount wandered nervously with the rider clinging to his mane. The horse's flanks were covered in blood for Will had been cut about more than a little. Ned thought at first he was already dead but the young man's eyes fluttered open briefly.

"Thank God," said Ned.

"The king…" Will whispered and then fell from his

horse.

Several men leapt down to lift him up but he was already gone.

Ned shook his head. Another man down and yet he knew nothing more.

"The king… is what? Dead? Coming? Fleeing? Still at Nottingham? By Christ, I don't need riddles… not now!"

He stared down at Will Hog's torn corpse. Not just another man lost: another good man lost.

One of his prickers thundered in. "My lord! An armed host is coming up from the south - a hundred at least."

"How fast do they move?" asked Ned.

"Not fast, my lord - but steady…" replied the scout. "They lie behind us now, but they'll overtake us sometime after noon."

"Bear, see to Will's body," said Ned. "Come on! Let's hope Will found the king on his journey. Hal, can you follow his tracks?"

"Ground's a bit hard in places," said Hal.

"Can you follow them or not?" snapped Ned.

"I'll try, lord," murmured Hal and he set off, slowly at first and then it seemed with more confidence. Ned nodded his silent approval: Hal was a better tracker than he believed. Ned wanted to move with caution but he was all too aware of the forces gathering around him, pressing him to move on. If he did not keep ahead of them, he would not bring much of a warning to the king - assuming he found the king. Yet by now, after three days, perhaps the king had already heard news of the disaster at Edgecote.

They followed Will's tracks until they came to a river bank and from there it was clear that the scout had followed the river northwards. Ned had no idea where they were and as the day wore on he was beginning to despair. They were keeping their distance from the pursuing host, but only just.

THE LAST SHROUD

In the late afternoon the tracks left the river and, a short while after, a large village came into view. Ned breathed a sigh of relief. For there, flying above a large house, was King Edward's sun banner and outside some men at arms gathered on a village green bathed in golden sunshine.

"Thank God," he said. "Thank God - and thank Will Hog who must have seen the king's banners."

It was such a peaceful scene it was hard to imagine that there was anything amiss in the land at all. But as they approached there was a flurry of movement and a few cries of alarm.

"Christ's Blood! They're a bit nervous…" said Hal.

"They are not many," said Bear thoughtfully.

Ned led them slowly in single file into the village so as not to cause any further alarm.

"Water the horses, Hal, then fan out facing south," said Ned. "I've not forgotten we've someone following us. I'll go to the king."

The village boasted several large houses but Ned simply made straight for the one bearing the king's banner. When he dismounted a small cluster of men at arms blocked his path at once but, before he could persuade them to step aside, a loud voice boomed from the threshold.

"Let him pass! God's Horn! Ned Elder! Whatever next? We should have guessed that a fistful of terrible rumours would toss Ned Elder our way!"

"Will Hastings!" cried Ned, much relieved to find his old comrade. "And where exactly is this place?"

Hastings embraced him warmly. "This is Olney, Ned. Now, come and tell us if what we've heard is true or not! His grace will be much cheered to see you safe. Though in truth, he'll be glad to see any man he can call friend!"

Hastings took Ned up a long flight of steps and into the chamber at the top. There, crammed into the small space, sat King Edward IV, his brother Richard of Gloucester and

Anthony Woodville, Lord Scales, the king's brother in law. At a desk along by the wall sat two clerks.

"Ned!" The king greeted him enthusiastically. "It's good to see you! We've heard some worrying tales these past few days."

Anthony gripped Ned's arm in greeting and young Gloucester gave him a lazy nod.

Ned could see there was no point in further delay. "Your grace, the news is very bad indeed: the Earl of Warwick and… your brother, the Duke of Clarence, have taken up arms against you. They've joined the rebel host - in fact… they are the rebel host."

King Edward looked shocked for only a moment.

"Ah, then at least some of the rumours are true," he replied sadly. "But what of the armies of Pembroke and Devon? Have they mustered?"

"Aye, your grace," replied Ned, "mustered and scattered. Pembroke's men fought bravely. He bade me leave the field near Banbury to come to you."

"And what of Stafford?" asked Edward.

"The Earl of Devon fled the field without fighting…" said Ned grimly.

King Edward glared at that. "Yet Pembroke may still have triumphed?"

"That was three days ago, your grace. I've had worse tidings since: he and his valiant brother faced the axe at Northampton."

"On whose authority?" demanded Gloucester.

"The power in the land is Richard Neville, Earl of Warwick, your grace…" said Ned.

The king gave a weary sigh. "Well, many men warned me, Ned - not just you. Yet, still, I did not believe it. And Clarence has joined him too? Ah, well. He wanted the Warwick inheritance. I thought I had discouraged him enough there."

"Your grace, there are armed rebel bands everywhere," said Ned, "and one only a short distance behind us."

"Lord Scales," ordered the king, "you should go now. Go to your sister, the queen, at Norwich. See her safe to Westminster."

"Your grace!" protested Scales. "I can't leave you - you've few enough men as it is!"

"Too few to make a fight of it, Anthony. I don't think my cousin, Warwick, will harm me - yet. But if you're taken, he'll certainly have your head."

When Lord Scales took his leave, Ned followed him outside.

"God speed, Anthony," he said, clasping his friend's hand.

"Let's pray God watches over us all," said Scales. "I've had no news yet of my father and brother."

When Ned returned upstairs to the king he found the clerks were busy drafting letters.

"Ned, is there anything else you can tell us?" asked Hastings.

"Aside from the fact that your enemies are very close by..."

"Northampton is only a short ride away," said Gloucester. "Are you certain?"

"Brother," said the king, "if Ned Elder thinks it to be so, then that is enough for me."

"We should deploy our men at arms around the village edge and put archers in every house," said Gloucester.

Edward shook his head. "Ned? What do you think?"

"You don't have enough men, your grace - not nearly enough. By morning a few more of them will have drifted away. Of course, it depends what you want to do, but..."

"We'll fight our way out!" declared Gloucester. "However few we are, every man here will give good service, your grace."

"Indeed, Dickon," agreed the king, "I'm sure of it but I think Ned's point is that it would be their last act of good service… and in a vain cause. We'll make plans tonight and try to slip away at dawn - south to London."

He sounded resolute and determined, Ned thought sadly.

"Your grace," he said quietly, "I don't think we shall have tonight…"

The king stared at him for a moment.

"Then I'd best think further upon it, Ned. Go and take some rest whilst you may. I shall have need of you later."

§§§

A few hours later Ned walked along Olney's silent street deep in thought. It was not an especially long street but he continued for a further hundred paces or so where a rough track wound southwards. The full moon was gone now leaving a mere glimmer of silver and he peered uncertainly into the stand of trees where his men were camped.

"How does the king?" a low voice enquired, startling him for a moment.

"Hal?" he whispered. "Where are you? I can't see anything."

Hal emerged from the trees, a lighter shadow now against the many darker ones.

"All's quiet here," said Hal.

"It's even quieter in the village," said Ned, "since the good people of this shithole of Olney have barred themselves in their homes and all but the last few of the king's men have deserted him."

"The cowards!" said Hal.

"I don't know… Warwick must have thousands under his banner by now - too many to fight."

"What then, lord? We flee… again?"

"His grace has already sent most lords away - only Hastings and Gloucester remain."

"And you?"

"I'm still at the command of his grace. I trust we're keeping a close watch on the road from the south?"

"We're spread thinly, lord. Croft is on the south road and Bear is prowling through the western fields. God help any man that runs into him this night."

"I want to know as soon as there's any approach," said Ned.

"Perhaps they'll wait till morning," suggested Hal.

"If you could capture a king, Hal, would you wait till morning?"

"I'd not thought of capturing a king, my lord…"

In the darkness Ned could not resist a rueful grin.

"I'll be with the king," he said and retraced his path back into the village.

Will Hastings met him in the street. "Every last man gone!" he complained. "Whatever happened to loyalty?"

Ned shrugged. "You must pay a higher price for it these days, Will. You still have some men though? And Gloucester?"

"Some, a few personal men, but neither of us was expecting this. We didn't bring many retainers with us. God's horn, Ned! We were supposed to be on a royal progress, not a battlefield!"

"Well, there'll be no battle here," said Ned.

"I came to fetch you," said Hastings. "His grace is asking for you."

Ned gave a tired nod and went up to the king's temporary chamber which was brightly illuminated by a dozen or more candles. Ned wondered idly who would be paying for those. He found the king dictating to both his clerks at the same time. How he managed to keep two letters in his head at once, Ned could only wonder. The king motioned Ned to sit down whilst he finished with the clerks.

"This is Secretary Hatteclyffe, Ned. He's been working very hard this evening. Are we finished?" he asked Hatteclyffe.

"Yes, your grace," replied the secretary.

"Well? Seal them, man," urged the king. "We've little enough time!"

Ned watched as Secretary Hatteclyffe applied the King's signet seal.

"Now Ned, I'm sending you away - as I have all the others that Warwick has no love for. I must play his game now for a time. It'll be a waiting game, Ned, but I need allies, strong allies who can strike for me when the time comes. I want you back in the west, but not at your small manor near Ludlow. I'm sending you south of there. One of these letters grants you the manor of Quenhull on the Severn and the castle that stands within it."

"I don't know it, your grace…"

"No reason why you would but it's one of the few places I can give you down there. Both Clarence and Warwick are strong there and with Pembroke's power broken, Warwick will hasten to strengthen his grip on south Wales and the west. If it goes badly for me, then it will also be hard for you, but Quenhull is very strong and well-placed. If need be, you could hold it for months."

"And the second letter, your grace?" asked Ned.

"That is your authority under my seal… to raise men, to fortify…anywhere you choose… to oppose my enemies howsoever you can. It gives you my trust, Ned, my absolute trust."

"I'm honoured, your grace," said Ned.

The king grinned. "Of course, if my head ends up on a spike you might as well use the letters to wipe your arse…"

He opened the lid of a small chest on the table. Inside were several bags, one of which he took out and tossed into Ned's hands.

"Your tasks will need paying for but that should help," he said. "There's little point in Warwick having my coin as well as my person. Most of the rest will go with Will Hastings and Dickon - thank God for one loyal brother at least…"

Feet sounded on the stairs and Hal appeared in the chamber doorway. He looked uncertainly from the king to Ned and back again.

"Spit it out, Hal!" ordered Ned.

"Your grace, my lord… there are men on their way into the town… village?"

"Form the men up before the house -" Ned said.

"No, Ned!" interrupted the king. "That's your signal to go. There can be no fight here and you'll do me much better service in the west."

Ned hesitated and Hatteclyffe handed him the two letters wrapped in a leather pouch.

"Will you argue with me?" asked the king. "Come. Embrace me and then get thee gone!"

Ned took his leave of the king and Hastings then, clutching the letters and the purse, he thundered down the stairs after Hal. He wondered whether he would see King Edward again but he must look now to the task he had been given. In the street outside all his men were ready and mounted. Bear had called in the scouts.

"Whither, my lord?" asked Hal.

"Whichever way gets us out of here alive!" said Ned.

"We'll ride straight into them if we go south," Croft told him.

"Let's not then," agreed Ned. "We should be going west in any case."

"Many men to the west," announced Bear.

"Very well, north then - due north, avoid Northampton and then turn west towards Coventry. We might just thread our way through."

"With God's help," added Croft, though Ned was not so sure that God would be so keen to help him much more.

44

3

4th August 1469, in the Cover Valley in

Yorkshire

Eleanor Elder dozed contentedly outside the cottage, drinking in the scents and sounds of summer. Bees hummed around the flower heads, a pair of blackbirds scratched in the long grass and from the nearby forest came the rhythmic echo of Ragwulf's axe upon oak. She fancied the stroke of his axe matched the lazy beat of her heart and smiled a guilty smile.

He had been away in the morning, further up the Cover valley, and she had picked up her sword for the first time in months. He would be furious with her but the feel of the hilt against her palm reminded her of all that she had once been. When she drew Will's old blade from its worn, stained scabbard, she found the edge was bright and keen. That brought a smile too for Ragwulf must have honed it.

Now she was tired - glowing with rude health - but tired. He had told her to rest but had she not rested for months whilst her wounds healed? She hated having to sit still - God's blood, she would waste away from all this rest. She knew he worried about her and, now that her belly swelled with his child, he worried all the more. She would do all she could to allay his fears: she had been careful this morning not to overdo it… just a few guards, a few moves, a little exercise with a blade in her hand, feeling its balance, its weight… And it felt good, this guilty pleasure.

Ragwulf would change her if he could. So here she sat, outside the tumbledown cottage where they squatted, obediently taking her ease in the warmth of the sun like the lady he wanted her to be. She breathed in deeply the rich meadow grass infused with the sweet fragrance of… She sighed for she didn't know what it was infused with. Emma would have known, would have named it six different ways.

Her eyes flicked open: something had changed. Not the bees, nor the blackbirds… but the ring of the axe. Ragwulf had stopped. Well, he was allowed a well-earned rest too. Soon he would return and find her at ease. She smiled, closed her eyes again and drifted into sleep.

"You're getting fat, my lady."

Eleanor blinked open her eyes and stared up at him, her rugged and battered husband of five months. A fire flashed in her eyes but she grinned. She could not help it when he called her 'my lady'.

"You're right, husband," she replied, "as in all things…"

"You're only going to get fatter too, sitting on your arse all day."

"I swoon to hear your wisdom, lord," murmured Eleanor.

"The woman I married would have struck me already with the flat of her sword," said Ragwulf.

"The woman you married would have struck you with the edge of the blade!" retorted Eleanor. "I can barely lift a sword now…"

There was an awkward pause.

"And how would you know that?" he asked.

"I… I happened to … pick it up this morning…" She winced at her lame reply.

"You just happened to pick it up from where I'd hidden it?" said Ragwulf.

Once more she could not suppress a grin. "You didn't

hide it very well - and you've kept a keen edge upon it."

"Not for you…" His voice was gruff.

"But it's my sword!"

"You don't need it any more, Ellie. You have me." There was sadness not anger in his voice.

She stood up and wrapped herself around him, laying her head upon his shoulder.

"And I'm glad I have you… but I was not born to cower behind a man - and you know it. You knew it when we wed…"

"Once you had to fight to live, I know that, but you were born a lady of gentle birth. Be a lady again. You've no place in a world of blood and death."

Eleanor fell silent for a moment then she cupped his face in her hands to look him in the eye.

"I'm told my mother was a wild, wild spirit, who courted danger at every turn, who never took a safe step when she could find a reckless path. There's a little of her in Ned, but I have all the rest of her fire in me. A world of blood and death is where I belong, where I thrive and even your love can't change that."

"Your mother, Lady Katherine, died young, I heard," said Ragwulf.

"Aye, she did."

"What about your child? Other children we could have?"

Eleanor smiled. "My mother had no trouble giving birth… and neither do I - this is not my first remember… Just let me be what I am. You should be sparring with me, helping me to get strong again. My wounds are all but healed…"

"There'll be no sparring whilst you're with child."

She pulled away from him, bristling. "Do you think carrying a child makes a woman weak? It doesn't - it makes her fire burn all the brighter. I fought Edmund Radcliffe when I was carrying my son Will - and he's a strong boy!"

"Hah! And you nearly died, Bagot told me!"

The memory passed like a shadow across her face. "Aye," she said, remembering. Then she smiled suddenly and hugged Ragwulf to her. She couldn't be angry with him for long.

"I'm only so soon with child," she whispered in his ear, "because you couldn't wait to put your wicked seed into me."

"I don't remember any reluctance on your part," said Ragwulf.

"I'm a dutiful wife…"

"I do recall you moaning a lot though…"

"From the pain of my wounds!" she protested.

"It didn't seem so at the time…"

"Well… does the church not teach that a child comes only if a woman is pleasured?"

"Is that the only bit of the church's teaching you know?"

"It's the only bit I care to remember," she said with another grin.

"I swore to Ned that I'd keep you safe," he said.

"Don't try to put me in a cage," she said softly.

"No, if I did, you wouldn't be you. But, please, for my sake, don't forget where we are."

"I used to ride these valleys and forests without a care, without fear. We've been here in the Cover valley for months. Everyone knows we're here. And they know us well enough. We shouldn't be afraid."

"Afraid? No, but don't forget that most folk who thought well of the Elders went south to Corve Manor with your brother. Some of those that remain were Radcliffe tenants… and will ever be so. Ned destroyed Yoredale castle, now some men and women have no work, no place… Don't expect their thanks…"

"Surely many such men will have gone south with the rebel army, with their so-called captain, Robin of Redesdale?"

"Aye, I suppose, for now."

"You think we should we go to Corve then?" she asked.

He gave her a resigned smile. "We've stayed here too long, lady. We should be leaving for Corve soon or your brother will be wondering what I've done with you."

"More likely he'll be worried about what I've done with you!" she said. "And if I stay here much longer I shall look like a sheep!"

"Can I trust you to leave your sword alone for a while?" he asked.

She kissed him on the cheek. "A little longer - but only to please you."

"What mischief would you root out if I wasn't here to look after you?"

"Hah!" scoffed Eleanor. "When have I ever needed looking after?"

He looked her in the eye, the swiftest route to her heart. "All the time, lady. All the time."

She bit back an instinctive response, knowing he was right.

"Well, when I next need saving, I swear to you, you'll be the first to know."

She looked around and smiled: the cottage was a filthy hovel yet she had been content and the forest she had loved since childhood was close by. She would hate to leave this place, the peace of it, with the bees bustling from flower to flower and the blackbirds skittering about.

"Perhaps we should just stay here," she mused.

Ragwulf held her eyes with his. "You're right," he said, giving her a broad smile. "If the lady wants to wait awhile, then we shall wait."

Eleanor was still smiling at him when an arrowhead

burst through his chest and spattered her face with blood. The force of the arrow knocked them both to the ground. She lay shivering, with Ragwulf on top of her. She struggled to hold his weight, her eyes fixed on the black and bloody arrowhead that dripped her husband's blood onto her breast. She tore her gaze up to his eyes and they stared back at her. He was alive, still alive… She held her breath, blinking away tears as the light in those sparkling eyes slowly faded. She let him lie upon her until the arrow point pierced her skin.

"No!" she screamed, rolling his lifeless body off her. "No," she whispered.

She rose to her knees and it was then that she saw the three men step out of the forest. They began walking down towards her, casual and unhurried. She stood up, her face twisted with rage, gulping in deep breaths. Her legs felt too weak to support her. She could not fight three - not even at her peak - and certainly not now. And there was the child…

4

4th August 1469, at Ragwulf's cottage in

the Cover Valley

Eleanor stared at the oncoming men then forced herself to look down at Ragwulf. By the time she looked up again the three men were much closer. She searched their faces, seeking some hint of regret in their expressions, some sign that she would not be harmed. But they just looked so pleased with themselves… pleased that they had murdered her man. Now she must throw herself on their mercy - if mercy was to be had. It was her only chance. They might abuse her, but she might still live and her child, Ragwulf's child, might still be born. What other choice did a woman have?

They strode towards her now, sheathing their weapons. The archer was unstringing his bow. She watched their cheerful, confident faces - faces that seemed only to taunt her. Somehow the daughter of Kate Elder could not bring herself to embrace surrender so easily. She could not fight three men, but she might wound three. She glanced down again at Ragwulf, at the ugly hole in his brave body.

"Be with me, my love," she breathed. Then she cleared her mind of grief and hardened her heart to pity. Her fate now would hang upon instinct - instinct and heart.

When the three men were only a few yards away she threw herself down upon Ragwulf's body, sobbing pitifully.

She lay there until the attackers stood over her. It was a risk, for they might spit her where she lay. But it was a small risk, for she knew men. They had seen her stark red hair and her full breasts. They had drunk in the sight greedily and they had sheathed their weapons.

"Get up!" one of them ordered.

"What do you want with me?" Eleanor cried, her voice tearful, pleading. She clung tightly to Ragwulf's body, the hilt of his long knife digging into her stomach. Rough hands seized her around the waist. She resisted at first but two strong arms wrapped around her to prise her loose.

"Come on, lady, don't be a trouble!" warned her captor.

She came up fast then, swift and deadly as an adder, plucking Ragwulf's knife from its sheath and raking it across the stranger's throat. The other men were close but they stepped back in shock at her sudden strike. She felt slow, though, too slow, as she pushed her bleeding victim back into one of the others.

"Murderers!" she screamed.

Keep moving, she told herself, that's your man down there lying in his own blood! Her blade swung around. The nearer man was drawing his sword. She aimed at his thigh but stumbled forward, missed her target and sliced open his leg along the calf. He cried out, his sword caught in his belt and she ripped the knife up into his groin. Then she wrenched it out and he screamed, clutching at the wound as blood trickled through his fingers. He lashed out to seize her ankle but his bloodied hand could not hold her and she gave him a kick in the ribs.

The third man, the archer, had disentangled himself from his dying comrade and was backing away towards the trees. With desperate fingers he was trying to string his bow.

Eleanor stalked after him. "Do you fear me?" she railed, her heart thudding as she pursued him.

THE LAST SHROUD

She was five yards away when he managed to string his bow. The blade in her hand was still dripping blood. He fumbled an arrow from his bag, but dropped it as he continued to retreat up the slope. He snatched out another shaft and nocked it, raising his bow at the moment she pressed her knife against his chest. She leaned forward, so that the point of his arrow rested against her breast.

"Do you fear me?" she whispered. "You should, for you're a coward and you've put your craven arrow in the back of a brave man."

His arrow trembled against her as she looked into his terrified eyes, aware of the sweat running down his grimy face.

"You should fear me," she murmured, "for I am a she-wolf with not an ounce of mercy left within me…"

He stared back at her wide-eyed and his whole body began to shake.

"I'll cut your heart in two, as you have cut mine," she breathed.

"Lady, I…"

She thrust the knife with all her strength up under his ribcage. He staggered back, loosing the arrow high over her shoulder and letting fall his bow before he slumped back into the lush summer grass. Eleanor left the knife lodged in his chest and took a step back. She watched the blood pump from the wound and then, when he lay still, she dropped to her knees, drained… empty.

Somehow she made her way back to where the others lay. Ragwulf, the father of her unborn child, was still dead. Her bloody efforts had not somehow brought him back to life. The man she had wounded in the leg and groin tried to get up as she approached. She eyed him coldly for a moment but realised she had abandoned Ragwulf's weapon. He crawled towards her. She lifted her kirtle and reached for the knife nestling against her thigh. Amelie's knife was a small blade but most fitting for revenge.

She knelt down beside the wounded man. He mumbled curses at her so she stabbed him in the chest. Still he breathed, so she stabbed him again… and again, hot tears stinging her eyes and dribbling down her cheeks. And when finally her anger subsided she lay down beside Ragwulf.

She lay there, grieving in the blood and dust until sunset. In the crimson glow she lifted her head. Then she sat up and examined her hands, encrusted with dried blood. There were no tears in her eyes when she stood up and glared at the heavens.

"Five months?" she cried into the darkening sky. "Is that all the joy I'm allowed?"

She should have known that God would not forgive her so easily, but did He not tire of punishing her?

"You vengeful, spiteful God!" she screamed. "Must I still atone for cursing that putrid shit of an abbot at Coverham? You know he deserved it, the spineless little turd - and I'd do it again! What more do want of me? Do you want my child too? Well you can't have it! Do your worst - you shall find me more than ready…"

§§§

She spent the night outside beside Ragwulf's stiffening corpse. She had not expected to sleep but exhaustion claimed her and she did not wake until dawn. Her limbs ached and her kirtle was damp from the dew. She got up and walked to each of the assailants in turn, kicking each one. It seemed she could kill three men after all…

She must leave. She knew it… but the suddenness of her loss left her almost paralysed. She wanted to ask questions, to understand why they had been attacked but Ragwulf would want her to run. She had been lucky and he would want her to save herself, save his child. So, flee she must. She bent over his body once more, touching the arrow head with her fingertips. It was hard, it was real; it was death.

Once her mind was made up, she stayed at the cottage only long enough to give her husband a crude burial - and that was hard enough. Her hands were cut and bleeding by the time she finished piling up stones. Then she gathered what few belongings she had left and headed up the Cover valley with their two horses.

She tried to recall the last time she had been alone, completely alone... just a woman with blood on her hands and a child in her belly. A woman fleeing, without knowing why or even from whom she was fleeing. She wondered if Warwick's hand had guided the attack, yet he was known as a man of his word. And what possible threat could she or Ragwulf pose to the great earl? Besides, he was not at Middleham... she had heard that. Perhaps Ragwulf was right and there were enough local men who had no love for the Elders.

Mostly she followed the river but in places the water course passed through steep gullies and she was forced to leave it. Much of the upper valley was still forested so, where she could, she rode among the trees. As she climbed towards the valley head, the tree cover thinned and eventually disappeared. This was the most dangerous part of her journey, exposed for all to see for miles around as she crossed the uplands. In more prosperous times this had served as high grazing land but now she saw only a few sheep. She saw no man, either ahead or behind her, and in the late afternoon she crossed over a ridge into the valley beyond.

The setting sun lay ahead as she looked down at the golden sliver of water far below her - the river Wharfe. This was the extent of her local knowledge to the west and only once before had she caught a glimpse of this river. She eyed the low sun thoughtfully. In the high country, even now deep into summer, scores of hillside becks trickled down through steep gills towards the Wharfe. There was a bank that ran for some distance from east to west so she followed the line of it, keeping the bank on her left hand as a guide. But once darkness fell, she knew it would be foolhardy to continue her journey. She must find somewhere for the night, perhaps a shieling or abandoned cottage, or some other relic of past wealth.

She was so intent on scanning the hillsides around her that she did not see the girl. She must have been crouching or hiding in one of the gills close by and when she suddenly stood up, Eleanor's mount shied away and reared up. Eleanor flew back over the mare's tail and thudded hard into the ground. She landed on her back and, when she lifted her head, there was a stab of pain. She felt dizzy, so she lay back down again.

When she came to, it seemed darker. How long had she lain thus? She remembered falling and now she was lying on the grassy, uneven ground… and she was not alone, for she could hear the girl sobbing.

"Come here," she ordered.

The girl crept out of the gloom. "I'm sorry," she said with another sob.

"Stop your weeping," growled Eleanor, "it's me lying here, not you."

"I didn't mean to startle your horse…"

"Aye, I'm sure," said Eleanor wearily. "Come then, girl, help me up!"

The girl hurried to her side and held out a thin hand. Eleanor gripped it and the girl was evidently stronger than she looked for she soon had Eleanor sitting upright. Her head felt sore and a brief exploration of her scalp left her fingers damp with a smear of blood. She was dimly aware that her ankle hurt too.

"What are you called, child?" asked Eleanor.

"Mary - but I'm not a child! I'm fourteen years…at

least…if not more so … I'm a woman now."

It was said with pride but Eleanor thought Mary might find that being a woman had a few drawbacks.

"Well, young woman, did you see where my horses went?"

"I think they ran off back into Coverdale. That's where you've come from, isn't it? Coverdale?"

"Shit!" Eleanor shook her head. "You'll be the death of me, you foolish girl."

"It's Mary…"

"Well, Mary, without my horses - and what was on them - I am lost…"

"You're not lost - I know where we are!"

Eleanor gave a bitter laugh. "Wherever we are, I am lost…"

"What shall I call you?" asked Mary.

Death, thought Eleanor, call me death. But instead she said: "Call me Ellie."

"Is that short-"

"No more questions!" snapped Eleanor. She stood up and at once her ankle gave way, throwing her off balance. Mary swiftly gave her an arm to lean upon. Eleanor groaned, but not in pain and grimly took Mary's hand. The girl was slight but wiry and managed to give her a surprising degree of support.

"I could take you to our garth," said Mary.

"There's a family at your garth?"

Mary gave a shrug. "Aye."

"Then take me somewhere else, somewhere I can't be found," said Eleanor.

Mary seemed about to ask more questions but thought better of it and just nodded.

Eleanor wrapped an arm around her shoulder and Mary guided her down the slope in the darkness.

"Take care," warned Mary, "it's stony… and wet… and

a bit slippery..."

"Where are we going?"

"Somewhere I go when I don't want to be found," replied Mary.

5

7th August 1469, at Middleham Castle in Yorkshire

Middleham was eerily quiet, thought Robert Radcliffe, as he dismounted at the east gate. It had been a long, hot journey and he slapped some of the dust from his clothes. He passed under the gatehouse into the familiar castle yard and nodded to the stable boy who came out to lead away his tired mount. The gate could do with some repair, he noted, by the look of the rotten timbers at its foot. Still, by contrast with the pile of rubble that was Yoredale Castle, it looked wondrous. Yoredale Castle - now there was a running sore - and one he hoped could now be dealt with.

He smiled then, perhaps for the first time in months. He had done it: he was back with only a few scratches and the earl's grand scheme had worked as if wrought by the good Lord himself. The king's loyal councillors were defeated or dead, the king himself was taken and the kingdom was firmly in Warwick's hands. And he, Robert Radcliffe, had done it - well, played a great part in it. In his role as Robin of Redesdale he had led the Yorkshire rebels that crushed the earl's enemies. The man who was Thomas Gate was gone now, forgotten - just a distant memory. Now he could use the name he deserved, his father's name. Robert Radcliffe's star was rising.

Soon the earl would bring King Edward north and an army of hangers on, clerks, priests and the like, would descend upon Middleham like a plague. Until then, he was master of the place and he intended to make the most of it.

He strolled past the new north gate towards the west range where his chamber lay but, as he passed the steps to the northwest tower, a stocky figure emerged from the shadows to meet him.

"Brace?" he nodded to the man.

Brace was a necessary evil and every lord must have such a man. The earl had many servants at Middleham but it was often Brace who made things happen. It seemed sometimes that he knew every man in the shire and he most certainly seemed to know everything that took place in Yoredale and around Middleham.

"Lord…" Brace began. He looked troubled and if Brace looked troubled then Robert had learned that one should be careful.

"Better we talk in the privacy of my chamber," said Robert and walked on with a brisk step into the west range.

"Close the door," he instructed as Brace followed him into his chamber.

"Well then, what is it?" asked Robert.

"My lord, there's been a death in your absence - in fact several deaths…"

"I suppose that these deaths are not from old age nor fever?"

"No, my lord."

Robert sat down. He felt deflated, apprehensive now. "What's happened?" he asked quietly.

"Eleanor Elder's husband, Ragwulf, is dead…"

"Killed?"

"Aye, lord."

"By all the saints!"

Robert knew there were some who resented the Elders,

blamed them for the destruction of Yoredale Castle. It occurred to him that Brace might be numbered amongst them. Did Brace have a hand in it, he wondered?

"Do we know who did it?" he asked.

"Aye, because they're dead too," replied Brace.

"Ragwulf killed them?"

"We're guessing, my lord, but somehow he must have fought them off before he died, though…"

"You doubt that…" said Robert.

"From his wound he died quickly and Lady Eleanor was gone."

Robert sighed. "It's not beyond her," he murmured.

"But she's just one woman…"

"Well, Master Brace, I should say that there's a growing heap of corpses that thought just that before she gutted them. Still, she can't have gone far…"

"I've already got folk out searching Coverdale for her," said Brace. "We'll hunt her down."

Robert shook his head. "We're not hunting her down, Brace! We're not mad dogs. But we must certainly find her and make sure nothing else happens to her."

The last thing he needed was for Lady Emma's sister to be butchered by some grudge-bearing local whilst he stood by and did nothing. Better if he found the wretched woman and brought her to Middleham so that she would be waiting for Emma when she returned.

"There's some would not offer her such charity, my lord," said Brace.

"Well you'd better find her then! Look further afield! I've brought back plenty of men so get them scouring the head of the valley for her. It'll give the idle bastards something to do. Left to themselves, they'll wreck this place. Get them searching the forests and hillsides - and be sure they know not to harm her! Offer coin for the man that finds her. Send men into every vale. I want every man, woman and child looking for her."

"As you command, my lord."

"What about the dead men?" asked Robert.

"I've dealt with it, my lord." Brace gave a stiff nod and left.

It was not a promising start, thought Robert, and he dared not falter at the first hurdle if he wanted Emma. Yet how easily was he drawn once more into deception and violence? He needed her with him if he was to put aside his past and take his rightful place in the county, uniting the Radcliffes and the Elders. He knew Emma could be his… despite all that had passed, all the blood. There was a connection between them, he was sure of it.

He worried about Brace, but he would need him to force the search. The man might play him false for such men could be dangerous tools. The world was full of such butchers just now but in the future he must find better, more reliable agents… men who knew how to spill blood but also when to stay their hand. For now though, he needed Brace.

6

8th August 1469, in the Cover Valley

Hal led them slowly in single file along the Cover valley. Only a dozen men but Bear, thank God, was one of them. When Lord Elder returned safely to Corve Manor, he was surprised not to find Ragwulf waiting for him with Lady Eleanor. Since he could not delay the king's business, he was forced to send others in search of the missing pair. Take a dozen men, Lord Elder had told Hal. Pick the twelve hardest, fiercest bastards I've got, because you're more likely to need them than I am.

Posing as a band of mercenaries in search of an employer, they headed north. It seemed a long ride to Yoredale and, when they arrived, they found a shire crawling with fighting men. Robin of Redesdale's army, it appeared, had been sent back home. Some returned to the fields, belatedly helping to harvest the summer corn, but others, armed and bored, loitered in the villages.

There were even some camped by the ruins of Yoredale Castle and that had been a shock. Hal had gone there first, a sort of pilgrimage… a reminder of what he had lost. Finding the place occupied by the soldiers' sprawling camp disturbed him and he rode past swiftly. He knew they must keep clear of such men and for that matter most of the Yoredale folk since he, or Bear in particular, might be easily recognised. And now they were in hostile territory, for nowhere were the Nevilles stronger than the Cover valley and the lands nearby.

Hal's belly was rumbling but it was only partly hunger; mostly, it was worry. Ned Elder had given him command of these men and put trust in him to carry out an important task but his pride was tempered by fear that he might fail.

Ragwulf's cottage must be very near now, chosen for its safe and secluded position well up the valley where few went without good reason. Hal's task was straightforward: escort Lady Eleanor and Ragwulf down to Corve Manor, but Hal had learned through experience that nothing about Lady Eleanor was ever easy.

He held up his hand to keep the others in the cover of the trees and began to pick his way down the slope. Almost at once, he came to a halt. There was a lump in his throat as he stared in disbelief at the burnt out cottage. He could not bring himself to move and he soon found Bear beside him. They sat motionless on their mounts for a moment longer.

"Shit..." said Hal.

They rode down to the heap of large stones and charred timbers that had once been a cottage. Hal noted that the small animal pen nearby had also been wrecked, its wooden posts even pulled out of the ground. He swept an anxious glance around the whole area; the damage looked at least a few days old, perhaps more. They dismounted and began to examine the remains.

Bear said nothing as he picked amongst the rubble and then wandered in widening circles around the building. Hal followed him, making his own attempt to interpret the many footmarks and other signs he found. There was clear evidence of some bloodshed and in several places it was still possible to see a discoloration on the dry ground. It was only when they poked around in the cold ashes inside the crumbled cottage walls, that they discovered the blackened corpses. There were three, more bone than flesh, but Hal was certain they were all too large to be Lady Eleanor. Perhaps Ragwulf - the thought alone chilled him.

Finally, their exploration led them to a heap of stones not far from the cottage. They stood together and stared at it for a while, then went closer and Hal gasped. It was a grave. Many of the stones were quite small and had been disturbed, either by man or animal, to leave part of the body exposed. There was no mistaking who it was or how he had died. Hal almost wept to see how the body had been gnawed at and torn.

"I never thought to find this…" he said.

Bear said nothing but his face was dark with anger. They had been close, Bear and Ragwulf.

After Bear had examined the corpse, he went back to the cottage and began lifting the heaviest stones he could find. Hal could not see anyone or anything shifting the stones that Bear carefully laid down to repair Ragwulf's tomb.

Hal tried to piece together what he had seen but there were so many tracks all over the ground around the cottage that it was nigh on impossible to interpret them with any confidence.

"Cast about for tracks," Hal called up to the others, but even as he said the words he realised it was hopeless. They would find tracks alright, but there were just too many. Whoever had been here last had come in force: that's all the tracks would tell him.

"There's a trail leading upstream!" shouted one of his men.

Hal's instructions were clear: pick up Lady Eleanor and avoid being noticed; if Lady Eleanor had already left for Corve, he was to follow on. His visit was to be swift and invisible. His lord had not suggested what he should do if Ragwulf was found killed and the cottage put to the torch.

"We'll follow the tracks up the valley and see what we

can find," said Hal, pulling himself up onto his horse.

He rode swiftly up to the others and one look at their puzzled faces did little to help his fragile confidence. Bear clapped him on the shoulder and edged past him to lead them off, following the tracks to the south west. Hal gave a last glance back to the cottage in the clearing and then followed the others. After only a few miles he gave up all hope of tracking Lady Eleanor. As he feared, the tracks through the woods beside the river Cover were too numerous to distinguish and, since it was already late in the day, he called a halt and took his men back down the valley, keeping a watchful eye out for any others.

With the trail cold, he needed help. Lord Elder had told him only to seek the assistance of Canon Reedman if he was desperate - well, he was desperate and, if he was to find Lady Eleanor, then the white canon at Coverham Abbey was his only hope. The white canons were not always closeted away behind the stone walls of their abbey, but rather they were regular visitors in the villages and hamlets of the dales. Perhaps Canon Reedman could give him something to go on and, better still, the abbey was not far away. Nevertheless, Hal decided that a dozen armed men arriving at the abbey might be rather intimidating so he left all except Bear to make camp in the woods a few miles further up the valley.

A long narrow lane led to the abbey gate and to Hal's surprise he found a few armed men camped even near the abbey walls. Surely that could only happen with the Abbot's approval. Many of them wore faded badges depicting the Earl of Warwick's bear and ragged staff and their mere presence made Hal feel distinctly ill at ease. For all he knew, some of these had been with Robin of Redesdale's army at Edgecote. He was glad once more of Bear's immense presence beside him.

At the abbey, the gatekeeper regarded them with

undisguised distaste through the small sliding hatch set in the gate.

"What's your business here?" he demanded.

"Our business, fellow, is not your business," replied Hal. "We seek a few words with Canon Reedman."

"What do you want with Canon Reedman?" asked the gatekeeper.

Hal sighed. "We seek his blessing and his knowledge."

"Canon Reedman's a busy man, set upon God's work," said the gatekeeper. "He can't waste time talking to such as you."

Hal thought about a blunt response but kept his temper. "Tell him Hal is here. He'll see us."

"Hal? How do I know who you are?" argued the gatekeeper.

"You should have been here a few months ago," he said. "You'd remember me well enough then."

"Well, I wasn't!"

"Just go and get Canon Reedman!" ordered Hal. "Is that so much to ask?"

The gatekeeper hesitated for a moment. "Well, you'll have to wait until after Compline," he said and slammed shut the sliding panel.

Hal glanced at Bear uncertainly. "I suppose we'll wait out here then," he muttered.

Bear shrugged. They dismounted and sat down by the gate. At the far end of the lane, a few men still loitered.

After a while Hal got up and paced around in a wide circle whilst Bear sat impassively. It would be getting dark soon and surely Compline must have ended long ago. The canons would be retiring by now. He was about to rap on the great door again when there was a scraping and it swung open.

They were not to be invited in, however, and it was Canon Reedman himself who stood on the threshold. He looked older, though it was not so long since Hal had last seen him. Reedman smiled at him.

"We must talk out here and we don't have long for the abbot is in residence," he said, "and he has a long memory. Whilst he's here, no-one with any connection to the Elders will be allowed to set foot inside. Walk with me whilst we talk."

"It's good to see you once more, canon," said Hal.

Again Reedman gave a rueful smile. "I'm pleased to see you're still alive, Hal. Have you found peace yet from your loss?"

Hal shook his head. "I'll never find peace, canon. Wherever I go, Agnes will go with me…"

"And is her constant presence a comfort to you?" asked Reedman.

Hal looked at him sharply and then shook his head. "No, canon, she stays to remind me that I failed her."

Reedman nodded. "And have you sought solace in prayer through a priest or confessor?"

Hal shook his head. "No, canon, but I'm not here to speak about me."

"Then how then can I help you? Perhaps one of your friends is sick?"

"No, canon, it's not your physic I need. We came here to take Ragwulf and Lady Eleanor back home to Corve Manor."

"Ah…" Reedman paused for a moment to study Hal's face. "How much do you know?"

"I know that Ragwulf's dead from an arrow through his back!"

Reedman stared at the ground. "He was a good man…"

"What happened to Lady Eleanor?"

"I don't know, Hal…"

"Well someone must know! What about her sister, Lady Emma?"

"Lady Emma hasn't been at Middleham for months. A sudden… privy departure - the Countess of Warwick left with her two daughters and so of course Lady Emma accompanied Lady Anne."

"Very well, but what about Lady Eleanor?"

"I know nothing more than you can see with your own eyes," said Reedman.

"What do you mean?"

"Everywhere you look, Hal, you'll see men. They've been straggling back into the villages all week - some with mounts, but most footsore and weary. For a few days they did very little - glad to be back home I should think - but now? Do you know what are they're doing, Hal? They're searching, searching for her. And that tells you that she's not yet been taken."

"Yes, that's well, but it doesn't help me find her," said Hal.

"Be careful, young Hal, for whoever wants her has the power to command all in the shire."

"Warwick?"

"The earl has not been here for months but one can only guess that the search has been ordered upon his authority."

"I don't know where to start," murmured Hal.

"All I can tell you is that her horses were found up the Cover valley a few days ago - the men who found them were quite excited but they must have found nothing since. There were two mounts with all her goods on them - strange. She wouldn't have left her horses, would she?"

"No, she wouldn't! And she could ride as well as any man…"

"She's a survivor, Hal. She believes that God has forsaken her, you know, but I'm most certain she couldn't have endured all she has without His divine help. We must pray that He continues to watch over her. I wish I could help you more, but…"

"There is something else, canon. We fought against some of these men a few weeks ago and Lord Elder thought he saw Thomas Gate."

"Impossible! I was there when the earl gave his word that Gate would be executed."

"Yet… Lord Elder knows Gate well. I don't see how he could be mistaken."

"In the blur of battle, Hal? Gate is dead. I'm sure of it."

"Well, perhaps… if you do discover him in these parts, you'll send word to Lord Elder…"

Reedman nodded. "It's unlikely… but if I do, I shall make it known to Lady Emma when she returns."

"Farewell then, canon."

"I shall pray that God will guide you in your search, Hal."

Canon Reedman turned and then paused mid-stride. "One thing… the abbey owns grazing land in much of Coverdale and into Wharfedale beyond it."

"How does that help?" asked Hal.

"The abbot has just given his permission for men to search the Wharfedale lands."

"So, they're widening the search…"

"God speed your task, Hal," said Reedman and with a nod of farewell he went back through the gate.

Hal mounted his horse, deep in thought, and set off along the lane.

"So?" asked Bear. "What do we do?"

"We go hunting," said Hal.

7

9th August 1469 before dawn, at

Middleham Castle, Yorkshire

Robert Radcliffe sat alone in his chamber, pondering his choices. He had not slept much. He had expected Brace last night and now Brace was very, very late and time, as always, was important. He was not privy to the Earl of Warwick's plans. He did not know whether the captured king would be held at Warwick Castle or brought further north to Middleham, to the Neville heartland. Nor did he know when Warwick would return - and it mattered, because he must find Eleanor Elder before Warwick came back to Middleham. Her presence was, after all, sanctioned by the earl and, whilst he might not weep too much if she was dead, he would certainly blame Robert if she went missing. Brace, however responsible he might be for what had happened, was unlikely to feel Warwick's wrath.

A fist thudded against his chamber door. Robert snatched open the door and pulled Brace inside.

"Are you trying to wake up the entire household?" he hissed.

"I thought the matter was urgent," said Brace with a shrug. "I've been riding around Coverdale all night."

"Aye, it is most urgent," said Robert. "How goes the search?"

"I've men scouring the dales - we think she's gone to ground somewhere in the Wharfe valley. It shouldn't take long to find her, lord."

"Soon, I trust. It's already been days!"

"The price on her head helps, lord."

"Not very much, it seems," retorted Robert. "You should have found her by now: she's alone and on foot."

"I've got scores of men after her."

"Aye, but Brace…"

"Lord?"

"Remember: she must not be harmed," said Robert. "You understand me?"

"Aye, I hear you."

"I want word sent to me as soon as she's found," ordered Robert. "At once! The earl could return at any time."

"Lord…" Brace hesitated.

"What?"

"Another matter… there's a group of mercenaries riding through Coverdale."

"Hah! Only one group? I should say there's more than that," laughed Robert. "You can't move for them!"

"Aye, lord, but in this… one group there is a very large man at arms… a giant of a man. One or two of my men say he was at…"

"…Yoredale Castle," said Robert softly. "The one they call Bear… Could it be him?"

"I believe it could, lord," said Brace.

Robert's mouth felt dry and he could feel the sweat rising on his forehead.

"Are you suggesting that Ned Elder is here?" he asked, his voice a whisper.

"Lord Elder has not been seen but this… Bear fellow… is his man, isn't he?"

"Where have they been so far?" asked Robert.

"They were seen at the cottage then, like us, they tried to track the woman - and failed. Then they went to one of the white canons at the abbey."

"Canon Reedman," breathed Robert.

"How did you know?" asked Brace.

"Because he's a damned meddlesome old canon who is close to the Elders and far too close to Lady Emma!"

Robert gather himself. After all, what had he to be worried about? He had an army of men around him. All the same, he had hoped that Ned Elder might have fallen at Edgecote. Though Ned was Emma's brother, Robert could see no hope of reconciliation with him. Ned Elder would want his head and if he was in Yoredale then it would complicate matters a great deal.

"Keep a close watch on these mercenaries," he told Brace, "and find someone who knows what Ned Elder looks like. Let's see if we can be sure."

"Aye, lord."

He seized Brace by the shoulders. "If he's here, I must know at once!"

"It will be done, lord," said Brace.

Robert released the man and turned away. "Aye, well go and do it then."

8

9th August 1469 before dawn, in

Wharfedale

Eleanor was awoken by the patter of raindrops. She shivered and wrapped her cloak more tightly around her. This was the coldest hour when dawn was close by. As long as it was dry, she was comfortable and they had been blessed with a succession of fair days. It seemed that was over now and Eleanor suspected that the residue of dried shit that littered the ground would smell appalling with a sprinkling of rain upon it.

She had grown accustomed to the abandoned shieling; come to regard it as safe. Nestled at the foot of the ravine, it was certainly well hidden from view and its walls gave her enough shelter from the wind. In places they were broken down so badly that only a heap of moss-covered rubble remained and in one corner two young saplings had taken root.

Mary had taken care of her well, bound up her ankle and brought her food. She fetched water for her from the noisy beck which bubbled and splashed nearby. She also brought a little more straw each day so that Eleanor lay on at least a thin covering of it.

She gently rubbed her belly where the child lay. It would be a son, she decided. Ragwulf would have a son once more, even though he would not know it. She almost gave birth to the child there and then when a shadowy figure ghosted in front of her and squatted on the ground.

"Good Christ, Mary!" she breathed. She gave a sudden grunt and smiled as the baby kicked inside her. Ragwulf's son was awake too.

"Was that the babe?" asked Mary.

"Aye, would you like to feel him?" whispered Eleanor.

Mary nodded at once and moved in closer. Eleanor took Mary's cold palm and winced as she pressed it against her swollen belly. There was a reassuring kick and Mary gasped as she felt it. She stayed there and rested her head on Eleanor's breast. She was a sweet girl yet, Eleanor reflected, she was not usually here before the sun…

"Why are you here so early?" she asked.

"Oh, shit, I forgot why I came!"

"What's happened?" demanded Eleanor.

"Men - there's men everywhere in the village!" said Mary.

"What men? Whose men?"

"Men from Yoredale, men from Coverdale, men from Middleham… men from all over the shire - men looking for you!"

"I should have gone on days ago," said Eleanor.

"You couldn't - not without a horse. Your ankle wouldn't bear you."

"That's why they've come up here. They know I must have passed through here… or else I'm still here."

"But there's so many of them…" said Mary. "What did you do?"

"What did I do? It isn't just what I did… it's who I am. We stayed there too long… and he's dead because of it - because I was too content to leave…"

Mary remained close beside her: silent, thoughtful. It seemed the girl did not scare too easily.

"They're offering such a price on you, lady," murmured

Mary.

"Are you tempted?"

She felt Mary bristle at that but the girl made no response.

"Will you help me to get away then?" asked Eleanor.

"Tell me what you did."

"They killed my husband," said Eleanor in a quiet voice, "so I killed them…"

"How many?" whispered Mary.

"Three… I killed all three of them - and then I fled."

Mary was silent once more.

"I'm sure you're shocked… that I've killed," said Eleanor, "but if you're going to help me you should know: it's not the first time…"

The sky was lightening. She must move on swiftly or risk being trapped where she was.

"If I help you," asked Mary, "will you take me with you?"

Eleanor laughed. "Hah! Have you not heard what I've done? Believe me, child, you should stay as far from me as you can!"

"I told you, I'm fourteen," replied Mary, "I stopped being a child long ago."

"But you live in a garth with your kinfolk…don't you?"

"Kinfolk? Aye, I do. I live with my uncle and aunt."

"Then stay here with them. Why in God's name would you want to come with me?"

"Why?" asked Mary. She slipped her shift off one shoulder and showed Eleanor her back. Even in the thin dawn light, Eleanor could see the dark bruises.

"So? You've been beaten? Well, so was I - and I deserved it most times."

"My uncle doesn't beat me… he favours me."

"That's good surely?"

Mary looked her in the eye. "He favours me with…

touches - and my aunt beats me for it. Do you think I deserve it?"

Eleanor frowned, though it was not the first time she had heard such a story.

"So, take me with you," begged Mary. "I could help with the babe. And you wouldn't beat me..."

"No, I wouldn't beat you," said Eleanor, "but I'd most likely get you killed."

"You need me," said Mary. "They'll be out this morning, looking..."

Eleanor shook her head. She had no weapons save her small knife and that would not be enough. "Where can we go?" she asked.

"Further up the valley - north into the forest... Langstroth Chase. It's your only hope."

"But I need to go south..."

"Go south then," said Mary, "but you'll be taken by noon."

Eleanor scowled at her. It would soon be light - with or without Mary, she had to move. She stood up, rubbing the stiffness from her legs and putting a little careful weight on her right ankle. It was still a little sore - running might be difficult...

Mary got up too and pulled her boyish cap down to cover her ears because suddenly the rain fell harder. Large, full drops began to hammer down upon them.

"If you come," said Eleanor, "we go south."

"Aye, alright," agreed Mary. "We can make our way by and by down to the river on the far side of Kettlewell. There's a bit of woodland there... we might lose them... if we can get there, but this rain won't help us."

"Well, let's not stand around getting any wetter!" said Eleanor.

Mary grinned, her face already streaked by rainwater. "By Christ then, lady, let's go! It won't be easy now; there are becks and falls and deep holes…"

She held out her arm but Eleanor slapped it aside. "Save it for when I need it!" she said.

Mary shrugged and headed out of the enclosure with Eleanor limping behind her. Mary moved nimbly across the slope and at once Eleanor knew she could not keep up such a pace.

"Wait!" she cried.

Mary stopped and turned to face her, the rain streaming from her.

"It looks rough ahead," said Eleanor.

"We must keep to the steep ground for now, lady," explained Mary, "or we'll end up either close to the watch tower or down in the village."

"Which village?"

"Kettlewell - you don't want to go there, lady. That's where most of the men are sleeping!"

"Alright," said Eleanor, "but I'll need your arm if you expect me to climb like a goat…"

Mary grinned and waited for her, extending a hand. Eleanor accepted it without a word and they stumbled off over the unyielding terrain. Soon Eleanor felt the ache in her legs and a searing pain in her ankle. But they were making some progress and Mary too was breathing hard. She was just beginning to believe they might endure the ordeal, when the rain came on even heavier. It seemed that a relentless rain squall was descending upon them.

Eleanor's spirits plummeted but Mary seemed a little encouraged. "At least they'll never pick up our tracks in this!" she cried. "God watches over us, my lady!"

"Aye, until God remembers who I am," murmured Eleanor.

Mary chose to ignore her bitter response and carried on, half-dragging Eleanor with her. Every beck now seemed swollen to a torrent and every rock became a jagged blade.

They tripped or slipped with every step, snagging their feet on roots and tearing their clothes upon rocks or wiry branches of scrub.

A waterfall blocked their path so Mary dragged her higher still to ford the beck above it. Wind and rain tore at their faces as they fought their way into the gushing water. In the middle of the beck Eleanor lost her balance and staggered against Mary, clutching at her shoulder.

"Are you trying to kill me?" screamed Eleanor.

"We must keep going, lady!" Mary implored her.

"How much further?" Eleanor raged. "Blood of the Virgin! I'm with child, you know!"

"We daren't stop, we'll be washed away!" the girl wailed.

For a moment they stood facing each other with the angry water swirling around their ankles. Then Eleanor shook her head. "Get on then!"

Mary nodded, seized her hand and stepped towards the far bank. Eleanor moved with her but Mary's foot slipped and her legs were swept from under her. She yelped as the force of water tore her from Eleanor's grasp and carried her over the falls.

"Mary!" Eleanor hurled the word after her, limping towards the edge of the fall and flailing a hand at the nearest rocks for some grip.

"Good Christ!" Her fingers slid in vain across green, slimy stones and she fell backwards. Pain knifed through her back and ice-cold water washed over her. She lay wallowing in the water, scrabbling for some grip as the torrent tried to prise her from the stony bed. Slowly she was driven forward and, by the time she found a secure hold on some sturdy roots, her feet were dangling over the drop. She gulped in deep breaths. Her first thought was for the child. The water was up to her waist - he might be drowning for all she knew. And where was Mary?

She sat up as far as she dared and peered down where

the fall crashed into a small rocky pool. It was not far, but far enough. She expected to see the girl's broken body, another bitch to the slaughter, but Mary was not there. She was a determined little brat - perhaps she was still clinging on below the overhang which Eleanor could not see.

"Mary!" she shrieked into the wind, but no sudden hand appeared reaching for hers. She had warned the girl: sooner or later, travelling with an Elder brought only death. Eleanor sat back in the water, numb to the pummelling of its cold fists. Perhaps she should just let the fall take her too; after all, a river had nearly killed her once. How God must be having regrets about that!

The child kicked her and at once she moved, some primal instinct forcing its way past all other thoughts. She threw a hand at one of the larger rocks and levered herself towards the bank. Then she took a firm grip on another rock by the water's edge but as she shifted her weight, the relentless stream dragged her feet around over the drop once more. Fear seized her heart: Mary was gone, but she still had to save herself… for the child.

She was still on her back, better to protect the babe, for she could feel sharp fragments of rock cutting into her. She tightened her hold on the rock and pulled herself towards it, inching her body along. She winced but at least she was moving. Then a hand clamped onto her left foot and she screamed.

"Mary! I hope to Christ that's you - else it must be the devil himself!"

She half-turned and saw the thin wiry fingers wrapped tightly around her ankle. She was relieved but she could not pull Mary's weight up on her foot alone, nor could she reach her as long as she clung to the rock. I hate water, she thought, and this is the last beck I'm crossing, ever.

She tried to think. She could always kick off the girl's hand… but she did not. Instead she released her hold on the rock and shuffled around in the stream on her bottom. She could not move her legs with Mary still hanging from one of them. The weight was forcing her left calf down onto the rocky shelf and the pain of that alone needed to end…very soon. She bent forward to reach for Mary's hand. It was not so easy when you were carrying a child.

"Hold on, Mary!" she cried, panting for breath. She edged forward until the hand on her ankle was almost within her grasp. She gritted her teeth and touched the hand with her fingertips. A little more, just a little more and then she smiled with relief as her hand closed over Mary's.

"Won't be long!" she shouted.

A branch coming down the beck struck her squarely between the shoulder blades and sent her spinning over the fall.

9

9th August 1469 after dawn, in Upper

Coverdale

Hal studied the track ahead through the light drizzle. Scores of men must have passed along it in the past few days, scavengers after Lady Eleanor's blood. If Ragwulf could be killed then she was still at risk. He urged his mount forward and the rest picked up their pace to follow him along the rocky terraces that would take them onto the brown upland slopes. The rain began to fall more heavily, driven into them by a swelling north-west wind, but Hal pressed on harder, praying that Lady Eleanor was long gone.

They joined a walled track, an old droving route he assumed. Above them towered rock faces, great oblong blocks of stone, dripping wet. Soon the track was crisscrossed by rivulets of water, washing down a slush of animal dung and mud. His horse suddenly skidded and stumbled on the wet, stony ground. He reined in a little, hoping they could make better speed when they reached the open moorland pastures.

Long walls, broken down in places, stretched at right angles from the track across onto the grazing land. He could see a few sheep far away, in the lee of the walls, waiting out the storm. The folly of sheep had truly been much exaggerated for they at least had the sense to seek shelter. His cloak was already soaked when he crested the highest part of the pass and was buffeted by even stronger winds. The horses neighed in alarm as they were driven sideways by the force of the gale.

Hal stared down into the Wharfe valley but could make out nothing through the rain. Close by, steep gullies disappeared down into the valley carrying becks swollen into gushing waterspouts. Outcrops of rock crouched like cowering beasts amid the lashing rain. Hal could see no hint of shelter and the nearest trees were very likely miles away down in the valley bottom.

Bear pointed back into Coverdale but Hal shook his head. "We're not going back!" he cried. "Ride on!"

The ground was treacherous, strewn with sharp rocks and spongy green patches brimming with water. Their nervous horses slipped in the mud and shale as the riders tried to urge them on down the steep slope. One mount slid down on its side, shrieking in panic, and threw its rider off. Another put a hoof into a deep hole and plunged forward onto its chest.

"Dismount!" shouted Hal, "dismount, or by Christ we'll lose them all!"

They calmed the horses by walking close beside them, leading them down from the highest ground, but even the men began to lose their footing. By now they could see only a few yards in any direction. When they found a gully with some shelter from the wind, Hal called a halt. They would just have to wait it out, like the sheep.

They waited for most of the morning until the wind and rain began to ease. Hal stood out in the rain, trying to think. He reflected that plans always seemed a lot less hopeful when it was raining. He had been shocked to discover from Canon Reedman how many men were hunting for Lady Eleanor. It was a wonder that they had not yet found her.

But then Lady Eleanor was no ordinary woman, it was true.

"She must have come this way," he said aloud, "she must have!"

"But, Hal," said Bear, "the lady could be far away by now."

Hal was in a muddle. "Even if we find her, Bear, we'll be surrounded by the host of men sent to hunt her down..." he muttered.

Bear pointed down into the valley to the north. "Much forest to hide in."

The strong winds that had brought the storm were blowing the dark rain clouds away to the east and now the shroud of rain was lifted, an extensive forest was revealed higher up the valley.

"Yes, but if she got away, she'd go south."

"With no horse?"

Hal nodded. "All the same, we'll go south."

By about midday the rain stopped, though heavy cloud suggested that more was brewing in the west. They picked up a worn track which wound down the hillside and led them towards a small village below. Without the storm Hal knew the hillside would have been full of men searching for Lady Eleanor but the storm had kept the searchers indoors. Any local taverns would likely be heaving with men at arms. They rode on down to the valley floor but Hal drew them to a halt beside the river Wharfe before they reached the village. Grim-faced, he surveyed his disgruntled band of men at arms and took a deep breath.

"We'll find a tavern and dry ourselves out," he told them. "But keep your wits sharp! I've no coin to waste on you getting drunk - and watch what you say... As far as any man knows, we're men for hire joining the search. And let no man here seek any quarrel!"

These were some of Ned Elder's hardest men and they would root out trouble with ease if left to themselves. John

Long, Will Black, Walter Close: such men were always just a few words away from a fight.

He led them along the river bank into the village past several cottages and soon enough came across a low-roofed tavern. There were a lot of horses tethered outside and his men looked at him expectantly.

"Ride on," he said, "it's too crowded."

He passed by the noisy building, hoping there was another. He would certainly look foolish if there was not. The men at arms with him had no doubt been surprised when Ned Elder put Hal, a mere archer, in command. They accepted it but he was well aware that they would not tolerate many mistakes on his part. Thus he was relieved to find another tavern at the far end of the village by the river. In truth this one was hardly less busy than the other but it would have to do.

They dismounted some yards further on and left their horses in a stand of trees.

"Bear, you'd best stay with the horses," Hal said, "and John Long, you stay here too. I don't want you starting a fight out of nothing, so keep out of trouble. We'll send out some food for the pair of you."

Long muttered an oath but remained with Bear whilst Hal and the rest trooped towards the building. It was not much of a tavern but simply a large cottage no doubt pressed into use by an enterprising villager. Men milled about outside and a burst of raucous laughter greeted him when he squeezed through the open doorway. He was obliged to force his way through the throng of ale drinkers in search of someone who might be the owner of the tavern. He noticed at once a predominance of Neville badges which, though it was no surprise, hardly boded well. The sooner they were out of the Wharfe valley, the better.

When they discovered the landlord he regarded them doubtfully but showed little reluctance in accepting Hal's coin in exchange for some bread, cheese and ale. The long table in the centre of the narrow room was already occupied by a crowd of noisy patrons. The Elder men at arms stood apart and drank their ale in silence whilst Hal attempted to learn something from the landlord.

"We're in the hunt for the Elder woman," said Hal.

The tavern keeper grinned at him. "You've all come to Kettlewell to look for the same stupid bitch as all the others, eh? Well, I hope you don't find her for a few more days, because I'm doing very well out of this search!"

"You might not be so cheerful when our coin runs out," observed Hal. He looked around at the landlord's clients.

"I know it won't last. Anyway, if she's still in this valley, you won't find her alive - I'll tell you that much," he said. "She'll have fallen down a ravine somewhere and broke her neck. No. She's gone on or she's dead - that's certain."

"But… if she was still alive, where would you look?" asked Hal.

"Hah!" replied the tavern keeper, "You're not the first one to ask me that! I'll tell you what I've told all the others: if I was going to look, I'd be looking in the forest."

"Why aren't they, then?"

"Well, in the past you didn't go into Langstroth Chase without a damned good reason. Plenty of foresters in there would put an arrow in you before they'd ask your business. The chase is the king's forest but it's the Percy family what runs it. Years ago no Neville man would enter that forest unless they were looking for a swift end - 'cos God knows, they'd get one!"

"You said 'in the past' but what about now?" asked Hal.

"Well, look at all of you men at arms - the Percies can't match that. They've had their day. The Earl of Warwick's the power in this valley now - isn't he?"

"Indeed," agreed Hal, "it seems that he is. Perhaps we should take a risk then with those foresters."

THE LAST SHROUD

"I dare say you won't be the only ones now," said the landlord, "for you're all running out of places to look."

§§§

Hal breathed a sigh of relief when he shepherded the last of his men from the makeshift tavern. It was mid-afternoon but the rain had thankfully moved on. He returned to the horses expecting to find Bear and Long half asleep but they were very much awake and Bear was holding a leather bound bundle of items in his large paw.

"What's that?" asked Hal.

Without a word, Bear unwrapped the bundle.

"Well?" urged Hal and then he too fell silent as his eyes fixed upon the blade of a craftsman's sword. It was a highly polished blade looked after by a man who knew weapons well and it was a sword Hal had seen many times - one of a pair of swords wielded with the utmost skill by his friend Will Coster. Will was long dead now and one of his swords lost, but the other belonged to Lady Eleanor - until now.

"Where did you find it?" he asked.

Bear pointed to the string of mounts tethered alongside the tavern. "We should find who took this," he said.

Hal sighed and stared at the crowd around the tavern door.

"Perhaps… but we're not going back in there. Whoever found the sword can have no more idea where Lady Eleanor is than we do. Keep the sword and the rest of the bundle safe for her. I was going to say we'll bed down here for the night, but if we do you can be sure someone's going to come looking for that sword."

"Let them come," growled Bear.

"No!" replied Hal, surprising himself with his vehemence.

The others too looked up at his harsh tone.

"Yes, mind me now," he said, "and remember what our task is. We don't seek a quarrel; we seek Lady Eleanor. If blood's to be shed, it will only be shed to save her."

They stood in a ring around him in silence and he felt their doubting eyes upon him.

"What next then?" asked John Long.

Hal had been asking himself the same question.

"Hal?" prompted Bear gently.

"We'll ride upstream towards the forest and stop at the first hamlet we come to," said Hal.

"Up the valley?" asked Bear.

Hal nodded. "That's right - I don't think… I don't think she made it out of this valley and if not, then the best place to hide is the forest. The forest is governed by Lord Percy. The feud between the Nevilles and the Percies is well known - and since we are no friends of the Nevilles, let's see if we can find some allies amongst Percy men."

10

9th August 1469, in Wharfedale

Eleanor struck the pool hard, the breath torn from her lungs as she plunged in deep. Somehow Mary's arms were wrapped about her and the girl clung on as the water drew them down into the pool. Eleanor tried to keep calm, knowing that very soon they would bob up again to the surface and she could snatch a breath. But they did not rise again. The water kept tugging them down and down, sucking them further into a dark void. Her chest ached, empty of breath, and she felt every bruising blow as the current dragged them along walls of rock.

Suddenly they were thrown against a ledge and the water washed over and past them. The torrent had tossed them on the ledge. Eleanor managed to gasp in some air before another surge of water struck them and almost swept them away. Eleanor scrambled out of the water and dragged Mary after her. She could not stop herself shaking at first but Mary was not moving at all. Eleanor rarely wept. In fact she despised women who wept, but she was weeping now.

"Mary!" She shook the girl roughly and then thrust her down on her stomach, forcing her to cough up some water. Eleanor held her as she choked in some short breaths. After a while Mary was quieter and breathing more easily.

A yard away from their ledge the river still surged on down into a black hole in the rock below them. She had heard of such holes in the rocky terrain of Yoredale, but never seen the inside of one. As the beck flowed over the fall it had dragged them underground. Far above them there was a dim glow of light through the cascade of water - too far above their dark, cool ledge.

Mary stirred against her. She could feel the girl's small, hard breasts through the thin linen shift against her shoulder. Mary blinked open her eyes.

"Welcome to the shit hole," said Eleanor.

Mary sat up and stared at the dripping rock walls around her and the stream rushing by.

"I thought I was dead," she murmured.

"You are dead," replied Eleanor flatly, "you just don't see it yet."

"I knew a lad who fell down a hole up here…"

"And did he get out?"

"No… we never saw him again…"

"As I said…"

"But the water goes on down there," said Mary, "perhaps it comes out somewhere further down."

Eleanor regarded her coldly. "How many springs have you seen coming out of these hillsides?" she asked.

"I don't know… scores and scores of them."

"And how many came out of a hole bigger than your head?"

Mary turned aside and made no reply.

"How many?" Eleanor knew her voice was harsh - knew it had to be.

"None," said Mary quietly. "What's to be done then?"

"I can give you a swift end if you want it - I still have my knife…"

"There must be another way!"

"Aye, I can dash your foolish brains out against the rock!"

Mary said nothing in the face of Eleanor's raw anger.

"Or you can wait here and die very slowly. Plenty of water to drink, so it'll take a while."

"We should pray," said Mary.

"You pray if you like, but I couldn't," replied Eleanor. "I don't think the Lord wants to hear from me - and I've certainly had enough of Him!"

Mary frowned and began muttering a prayer.

"You can't just pray anyway," scorned Eleanor, "you need a priest to pray with you or God won't hear you."

"Isn't that up to God?"

"So you're going to sit on the damned ledge and pray until you starve to death?"

"You said there was no hope," said Mary.

"You don't give up just because someone tells you to. Do you think I'm just going to sit here on my ever-fattening arse waiting to die a slow death? Do you think I would let my unborn son die without at least trying to get out?"

"So you're going to risk it?"

Eleanor gave a bitter laugh. "What's to risk? We're dead anyway!"

"It'll be even darker down there," murmured Mary, "and colder… and there'll be sharp rocks to cut and bruise us."

"Perhaps not all so sharp," said Eleanor. She took Mary's hand and rubbed it on the rock wall below the water.

"It's quite smooth…"

Eleanor nodded. "I think the water must wear it away. So we'll probably not be cut to pieces - just drowned…"

Mary stared at her in the gloom. Eleanor put her hand on her belly, feeling the child, Ragwulf's boy… the last of his blood. God was cruel. She slid to the edge of the rock and dangled her sodden boots over the water.

Mary shifted to sit beside her. "Will you hold me as we go down?" Her voice was trembling and Eleanor reminded herself how young the poor girl was - but not too young to die.

"Aye," she said softly, "we'll go together. Hold on tight and we'll keep the child safe between us. Now, take a few deep breaths and then the deepest breath you've ever taken in your life."

With a final look up at the distant watery light, Eleanor filled her lungs, took Mary in her arms and they jumped off the rock together into the rumbling column of water and down into the darkness.

11

9th August 1469 late afternoon, in Wharfedale

They entered the forest late in the day, with Hal leading and Bear at the rear. Though the rain had stopped hours before, water still dripped from the branches when the wind rustled the summer leaves. Hal strung his bow and his hand rested on an arrow half out of his bag. All the men were watchful, aware that foresters - whether Percy men or any other - would not take kindly to incursions. Yet it was a brave forester who would declare war on a dozen heavily armed men - even in his own domain. And if the tavern keeper was to be believed, Hal's men were unlikely to be the first to search for Lady Eleanor in the forest. That they were being observed was certain for if anything moved in Langstroth Chase the foresters would know of it. Nevertheless, they were allowed to continue unmolested.

They must have ridden for several miles before they discovered the first hunting lodge. It was a large timber building, gated and enclosed by a sturdy wooden palisade. Hal dismounted and walked his horse towards the gate.

At once a surly voice called out: "Mount up again and ride on!"

The sound echoed around the trees and Hal could not

tell whether the voice came from within or not.

"I have business with the head forester!" he announced, continuing to the gate.

An arrow thudded into the timber by his head and at once his men had their weapons out.

"Sheathe your swords and put up your bows," ordered Hal quietly.

They did so, though not without a show of reluctance and they remained mounted in the small clearing by the gate, watching the trees warily.

"We've had enough of your kind these past few days," declared the voice. "Now ride on!"

"We're not those men," replied Hal, knowing he must now gamble with all their lives. "We're no friends to Richard Neville's dogs!"

But only silence greeted his words, a silence that threatened to last all afternoon. The horses shuffled restlessly as the silence lengthened. Bear dismounted and joined Hal before the gate but nothing more was said and no further arrows were loosed at them. Then the wooden gate opened a few inches and Hal found himself facing a forester with an arrow nocked in his bow.

"You can come in," he said, "alone - and leave your weapons outside."

Hal glanced at Bear who was shaking his head.

"I'll learn nothing out here," said Hal and handed his bow to Bear. "Wait here - and don't kill anyone while I'm gone."

He passed through the narrow gap and the archer lowered his bow to drop a bar across the gate. The man was alone.

"There's only you?" said Hal.

"There's others outside - where your men are," replied the forester. "Now, what do you want?"

"We're looking for Lady Eleanor Elder-"

"You lied then!" snapped the forester, raising his bow once more. "You're on the same path as all the rest!"

"No!" said Hal. "No, we're not! Because we're here to save her, not capture her!"

The forester studied Hal carefully but kept the arrow pointed at his chest. "What's this lady to you?"

"She's my lord's sister. I serve Lord Ned Elder."

"I've heard of the Elders and the Radcliffes... and the misery they brought to the dales."

"That was not the Elders' doing," said Hal.

"Aye, well so you might say."

"Have you seen the missing lady or not?" asked Hal.

The forester shook his head.

"Will you help us to find her?"

"Why in God's great name would I do that?" declared the forester. "If you want to argue with scores of Neville men over this lady, more fool you. I'll look upon it with pleasure, but I'm not joining you. I owe nothing to any man except my master, Lord Percy. I protect and defend his forest and his rights and my foresters will do only that."

"If you won't help us, will you at least not hinder us?"

"That would depend on whether you break any forest laws... such as hunting deer."

"We have to eat, man!"

"You don't have to eat in Lord Percy's forest."

"I've enough coin to pay you for a brace of deer."

"It's not about payment! It's poaching and I'm sworn to stop it, not charge folk for it!"

"Yet you collect fines, don't you? Let's call it a fine. When was the last time Lord Percy counted the king's deer?"

The forester hesitated for the first time.

"Listen, we're not your enemies," said Hal, "nor are we your lord's enemies..."

"Very well, but I want no coin; I'll have payment in

kind: your men can help keep the Neville men out of the forest. I've only a dozen foresters left in the whole of the chase and if scores of men come in, I can do little to stop them."

Decisions, thought Hal - how in God's name did Lord Elder ever decide what to do for the best? In this case he could see no other choice for he needed the foresters on his side.

"Very well," he agreed, "but only whilst we search for Lady Eleanor. Once she is found, we'll leave."

"Hah! If she's found, you'll all leave!"

"My men wear the pale blue badge of the Elders. Make damned certain your men know that we're their allies!"

The forester nodded. "You can spend the night here if you wish - at least I'll know where you are."

§§§

The next morning dawned brighter and Hal took his men out into the woods early, sweeping southwards in a broad arc round to the eastern fringe of the forest. A night under cover and a hearty meal had worked a miracle with the men at arms and their spirits were visibly lifted. He was glad of it for they would need sharp reflexes and all their wits if they were to survive this day. It was not long before they met the first of the Neville searchers and Hal recognised several from the tavern in Kettlewell.

It was a large group of a score or more and he was relieved he had deployed John Long and Walter Close on his flanks for they were handy with a bow.

"Spread out," Hal ordered, "and mark you: take your lead from me."

The column of men rode up to them but Hal could tell at once that no one man was in command. There were clearly several parties that had joined together to enter the forest, no doubt feeling more confident with greater numbers.

"Ride with us," invited one of them, "I'm sure we've a common purpose."

"Perhaps we do," replied Hal, "but we prefer to keep our own company. You take a risk by coming here into the forest."

There was laughter at that. "No risk," answered another, "a few shit-headed foresters won't trouble us."

Hal was already regretting his easy compliance in agreeing to help the foresters.

"Even so," he said, "this is the domain of Lord Percy…"

Hal saw the ripple of concern spread across many faces.

"Do you serve Lord Percy then?" asked one.

"We would not see the forest laws broken here," said Hal, treading as carefully as he dared. "Take care that you pass through the forest without trouble."

They were puzzled by his stance but seemed more concerned to continue their search than become involved in a needless argument and for that he was grateful.

Hal nudged his mount forward to lead his men through the column. He nodded to several as he passed and hoped his men would follow his example. He breathed a sigh of relief as Bear passed through at the rear and then there came an angry shout from behind him.

"Hold!"

Hal stopped and turned as did his comrades. One of the riders was staring at Bear's mount and another was now blocking his path.

"Christ's Blood," muttered Hal, "someone's noticed Lady Eleanor's damned sword."

"Hold! Hold!" Several of the Neville men now took up the cry.

"Move aside!" Hal shouted. "I shan't tell you twice!"

It was already too late though for swords had slid easily from their scabbards.

"Walter! John!" Hal cried. In the blink of an eye the two men at arms blocking Bear's path were down. Another reached for the bundle slung behind Bear's saddle and lost his arm to the big man's axe. Any hope of a peaceful encounter had vanished and Hal was forced to draw his own sword if only to defend himself.

The archers chose their targets with care and moved among the trees, constantly changing their positions. Hal wondered at how many arrows the pair could loose but then it dawned on him that a few of the foresters must have come to their aid. So they should, he thought, since we're doing their work for them. He angrily swatted away a sword thrust and veered towards Bear. They must make common cause to rally the men - he had fought enough such skirmishes to know that the greatest enemy was confusion.

"An Elder, an Elder!" he bellowed. "On me! On me!" He had watched Lord Elder do it countless times…but he was no Ned Elder and his men either wouldn't, or couldn't, go to him. But no man dared ignore the mighty Bear and he now took up Hal's cry. Hurtling through the trees he swept aside men and horses leaving a trail of broken bodies and blood upon the leaves.

Within a few moments most of Hal's men joined Bear to form a wedge bristling with steel. Bowmen were still picking off slow moving targets and the remainder broke south and fled out of the forest. One or two of Hal's men began the chase.

"Stand here!" declared Hal angrily. "We don't need to pursue them."

Bear rode up and clapped him on the shoulder. "Well done, Hal," he said.

"But for you, I'd have lost them," admitted Hal bitterly.

Bear nodded. "They'll learn to trust you, Hal."

It did not seem very likely from Hal's point of view but he was grateful for Bear's loyal support. The archers came in and several foresters followed with broad grins on their faces. That was all well and good but taking on Neville's men would not help Hal find Lady Eleanor. All the same, his men looked pleased with themselves too and he could not begrudge them that for they had not begun the quarrel.

"A small victory perhaps," he told them, "but now we have made more enemies and, if we ever find Lady Eleanor, we've just made it much harder to get her out alive."

Bear gave him a warning stare and he added: "You fought well though. Is any man hurt?"

Three of his men had received wounds and one had to be taken back to the forester's stockade.

"We must find Lady Eleanor today and we can't afford many more of these fights. In case you've forgotten, they outnumber us many to one and, however many of them we put down, they'll still overmatch us."

Aided by one of the foresters, they continued their search round the eastern edge of the forest and Hal studied the open slopes up towards Coverdale. It was hopeless. With barely a dozen men, he would not find Lady Eleanor. If she was still in the valley then others would find her first. All he could do was ensure that he found out about it as swiftly as possible.

"John and Walter," he said, "ride back up to the place where we came over the head from Coverdale. Find a safe place up there and keep a good watch on the open ground below you. Stay there and watch all day - unless you see Lady Eleanor. If she's alone, then you stay close to her and get her to the foresters' lodge - no matter what. If she's taken, one of you must return to the lodge whilst the other keeps a watch upon her."

The pair nodded and set off across the rough pasture that bordered the forest. Hal watched them start to climb up onto the scrub land where the becks glittered in the sunshine as they twisted and turned down the slopes. Then he selected two more men and sent them to watch the slopes above the forest at Buckden. Finally he nodded to the forester, who led the rest of them off through the forest to the west.

12

10th August 1469 late afternoon, in

Wharfedale

Eleanor was falling... through the darkness and cold of the river.

Upended and pounded by one mighty surge after another, striving to tear her apart. She was swallowed into holes, head scraping against columns of rock.

Beaten and concussed, feeling every blow... times beyond counting until she was tossed carelessly aside with only the roar of the water in her ears.

She found herself in a shallow stream with cool water lapping against her mouth and cheek. She spluttered and coughed up water. Dragging herself out of the stream, she lay beside it curled up and breathless.

She opened her eyes and screamed. The skull of a large animal lay a few inches from her face. She recoiled in shock and rolled backwards over a ledge. She fell only a foot or so but it winded her nevertheless.

The fall hurt, but at least she could see. It was a grey, imperfect light but light nevertheless. She explored her new world with frantic eyes. There was a low rock ceiling above and a series of ledges all around her. Water lay everywhere.

She eased her aching body onto her knees and lifted herself up to where the skull lay. Keep calm, she told herself. It was just a lump of bone, nothing more, and the poor animal must have died a very long time ago. It could certainly do her no harm now, she reasoned. She tried to get her bearings in the gloom and turned to face the dull glimmer of light. She must rein in all hope until it was certain there was a way out. And Mary… she must find Mary.

She crawled along the stream bed for a few yards and then it seemed to disappear. Casting about, she felt her way over the smooth, damp surface. Suddenly she lurched forward as her right hand met only empty space. She gasped and her face smacked down onto the rock. For a moment she lay still, shivering with fear. Before her there was a vast hole in the rock floor and she could feel water running down into it. She began to explore again, but this time more carefully. She found other, smaller holes - too small even for poor Mary to have fallen through.

"Mary!" she cried.

At once the word resounded around the cavern, echoing off every rock face until it wore itself out. It was unnerving but at least if Mary was anywhere near, she must have heard. Eleanor sat still, waiting for a response. None came.

It slowly dawned on her as she sat listening that she was taking only shallow breaths. The air smelt stale - would she be able to breathe for long underground? Was she breathing the air she had gulped in before she jumped? She didn't think that could be right, but she didn't know. Perhaps she should move on or she might stop breathing altogether.

"Lady…" It was a whisper, caressing the rock walls before it died, and it came from the darkness.

Reluctantly, Eleanor retreated from the source of light towards the sound. Unable to see, she cast about again with her hands. Every few feet she paused, calling out Mary's name and waiting for the echoes to subside. Every yard she crawled was a yard further away from the light… and the light was her escape.

She tried to take a deep breath but it made her cough and then her chest hurt. It was getting harder to breathe and the sound of rushing water was louder now. What if it suddenly burst out of one of the holes and washed her away? Yet, Mary had answered once.

"Where in the name of Christ are you?" bellowed Eleanor.

Her words rattled belligerently around the cave.

In the silence that eventually followed, a small voice said: "I'm just here…"

Eleanor felt a gentle touch on her face and stretched forward to find Mary's hand, gripping it tightly lest some wilful torrent should rip the girl from her grasp at the last moment.

"Are you hurt?" whispered Eleanor.

"My head's cut, I think," Mary sobbed. "Everything feels broken."

Eleanor took Mary's face in her hands and passed her fingers lightly over it. The temples and forehead were sticky to the touch. Then she ran her hands over the rest of the girl's body and since Mary did not scream with pain she decided there were no broken bones after all.

"Come, you'll be alright," said Eleanor. "We must crawl towards the light now. Can you move?"

Mary gave a groan and moved slowly to rest on her haunches beside Eleanor.

"Come, then," said Eleanor and they started forward together.

It was slow and painful. She had to stop several times to allow the girl to take a rest. Eleanor too was tiring and out of breath. She lost any sense of how much time was passing. The passage they were in suddenly opened out into a broader cavern but they were still obliged to bend double as they moved. Even so, Eleanor cracked her head on a low section and several thin shafts of rock snapped off to land by her feet. Her head felt as if it was split open and something trickled down her cheek - too warm to be water. She wiped it away and waited for the pain to pass. She picked up one of the broken pieces of rock. It felt like a little tube of stone, quite smooth, as if a craftsman had fashioned it.

"This is a strange place," she murmured.

"How do you fare, lady?" asked Mary.

"Now my head's cut too," said Eleanor.

The light was fading, of that Eleanor was certain. She turned around to check that they were still heading towards it. Then she realised that it must be getting dark above ground, probably close to sunset.

"It's too dark now," she said. "Too dark to move, too dangerous..."

"Time to rest," she said and lay down where she was, drawing Mary's slight body to her.

They lay together taking what little warmth they could from each other.

"I miss my father," said Mary.

Eleanor sighed. Mother, father, brother... she missed them all.

"What happened to him?" she asked.

"He was a forester, working in Langstroth Chase. He was gored on a hunt... by a boar. It was slow death, I think. I was younger then..."

"And your mother?"

"She died when I was very small - a fever my dad said. I never really knew her."

"My mother, Kate, died when I was very young," said Eleanor, her voice husky. "We have that in common at least."

"I'm so tired," murmured Mary, "I want to rest but... what if we don't wake up?"

"Then I shall be even more angry with God," whispered Eleanor.

§§§

They did wake up, though stiff and aching - but alive nonetheless. The light was quite bright again and, though it still seemed some way off, it gave them much encouragement.

"I told you, lady! I told you: God has watched over us!" Mary said with a smile.

Eleanor was pleased to see her smile again.

"The light is so strong…" said Mary.

"Aye, but just keep in mind what you told me: you've never seen a spring coming out of a hole big enough for us to pass through!"

Nevertheless, they set off and discovered the source of light sooner than Eleanor expected and it was not just a small fissure in the rock. It was a great shaft of sunlight, bathing the cavern with a golden sheen that glistened on the walls. They sat staring at it and hugged each other. Tears rolled down their cheeks, but they were not tears of joy.

The hole was certainly more than large enough for them to pass through but the opening was far, far above them. They said nothing. Even Eleanor had let herself hope a little and now the spectre of a slow death loomed over them once more. In the light Eleanor could see that Mary looked dreadful with blood over half her face and caked into her hair. The blood was mostly dry now except where tears traced streaks through it. The smile was gone.

Eleanor cupped some water to bathe the girl's face. Mary winced as the cold water exposed several deep cuts but she let Eleanor finish. Then Eleanor embraced her and held her close.

"What now?" asked Mary.

"We go on," said Eleanor.

"But the light was here…we'll be going into the dark

again…"

"There'll be more light, more shafts… further on."

"I can't go any further, my lady."

"Wait," said Eleanor.

"Wait for what?" breathed Mary.

"That!" said Eleanor as the child kicked them both.

"We are going on because you're going to help me save my son. He has only ever known darkness so surely we can crawl in the dark for a little while, can't we? He'll be born, this child, I swear it to you, Mary. And you'll be with me when he is."

Eleanor released her and stood up, stretching her limbs. "We can stand here, so make the most of it. Soon we'll be back on our knees again."

Water dripped down the vertical shaft and collected at its foot in a large pool. The pool was not deep, barely up to their calves so, once they had stretched out for a time, they walked through the water and found it overflowed to form a narrow stream out of the cavern. Eleanor went first, feeling the way with her hands. As the roof lowered she bent down until forced to crawl in the water on her hands and knees.

"Can you see any light ahead?" cried Mary.

"Just keep going," grumbled Eleanor, "and keep quiet."

There was not so much as a trace of light ahead but Eleanor was not going to tell Mary that. Wary of the long, hanging columns on which she had earlier struck her head, Eleanor felt both the ground ahead and above her. It took more time, but she did not care. She was going to crawl until she dropped, until the last ounce of sweat was wrung from her body.

"I'm tired," said Mary, who rarely complained.

"You'll get more tired," scolded Eleanor, "and don't lag behind. You were so eager to come with me - so keep moving. You can stop when you're dead…"

Then Eleanor herself stopped abruptly and felt Mary scramble into her heels. Eleanor stared ahead. Was she dreaming or was it now a little lighter in the distance?

"What is it?" gasped Mary.

"Nothing," replied Eleanor and set off again. It was far too early to embrace hope.

The passage began to narrow. At first she did not notice but then she realised she was having more difficulty squeezing through it, tearing her clothes a little. But the hint of a glow ahead drove her on.

"Is it getting lighter?" Mary asked in a trembling voice.

"It's getting narrower," replied Eleanor, "but keep following."

The passage turned sharply to the right and the light was suddenly much brighter. The sound of water roared above her head, yet only a trickle ran by her hands and knees. Eleanor crawled forward faster.

13

10th August 1469, in Langstroth Forest

It was well past noon. Hal thought they must have covered many miles deep into the western end of the forest. They explored every thicket and even two abandoned hunting lodges and only after all had been thoroughly searched did Hal call a halt. The patience of his men was wearing perilously thin and when the head forester, Tom, troubled to say anything at all, he only encouraged their discontent.

"I told you so," Tom grumbled, "not a sign of anyone. When folk set foot in a forest like this, they leave their mark - unless they're men of the forest themselves. We'd know if she was here, just as we knew when you came."

"Lady Eleanor's no stranger to the forest," said Hal, "but I had to see for myself. We'll head back now."

"I'll take you to the northern edge of the woods by Cray," said Tom, "then you can ride back across the scrub and grassland. It'll be quicker."

Hal nodded and they followed him as far as a small lodge near the forest's edge.

"This is Cray lodge," said the forester, "and if you ride out of the trees and on up the slope you'll come to a clear track. It's an easy ride south from there to the lodge at Buckden. I've work to do, so I'll see you back at the lodge. Be there before dark because after sunset I shan't be opening the gate for anyone."

He left them and Hal trotted his mount out of the forest. He had heard nothing from the men he had sent out as watchers, nor did he really expect to. Throughout the day he had come to believe that he was wrong about Lady Eleanor. He, of all people, should know how tough she was - it was not beyond her to steal a horse to make her escape.

It was the end of the day and he felt weary but it was the weariness of defeat. He found the track described by the forester and walked his horse onto it.

"We ride for home tomorrow," he announced and saw at once the mood of the men change. It was what they wanted to hear.

Bear drew alongside him. "Lady Eleanor?" he enquired.

"She must have made it out of the valley," replied Hal.

"Sure, Hal?"

"No, of course I'm not sure, but we can't stay here much longer. We've little coin, we're utterly outnumbered by the Nevilles - and I've seen nothing yet to convince me that she's here - or ever been here."

Bear gave him an inscrutable nod, but whether the Fleming was agreeing with him or merely showing him due respect he had no idea.

He continued along the track and studied the scarred slopes up to the ridge on his left. There were men scattered across the hillside, still searching.

"I'll ride up to fetch the scouts," said Hal.

Bear looked past him to the bands of men on the slopes. "Best we all go," he said.

Hal nodded and rode faster along the track which took them down the valley towards Kettlewell. Before the village he left the track to climb up to where he had posted his lookouts. The first pair looked all too pleased to see their comrades for they had nothing to report.

Hal had sent Walter and John further south where the broad slopes gave way to a maze of narrow ravines and becks. He was picking his way carefully towards their position when he heard shouts below them, carried on the wind. Drawing his mount to a halt, he looked southwards where his eye was drawn to four horsemen riding dangerously fast down a steep slope. Then, a little behind them, two more riders crested the brow of the ridge and Hal easily recognised the hunched form of Walter Close in the lead. It seemed they were all chasing someone but he could not yet see into the gully where their quarry must be.

He had been quite specific with Walter and John: the only reason they could be on the move was if they thought Lady Eleanor was there.

"Come on!" he ordered and rode after them. After fifty yards or so the whole slope was in his view and he realised he had made an error: his route would not take him to join Walter and John because another steep ravine lay in his path. Whoever was being chased down must be in the ravine. Now he would have to go further down the slope and then ride up the ravine from the bottom. His two men would overtake the four horsemen before he could reach any of them. He cursed under his breath and stabbed a heel into his horse's side.

He reached the lower end of the ravine where it flattened out into a shallow gully. The recent rainfall had swollen the beck and there were several gushing falls in the ravine. Riding up alongside the beck would not be easy. Bear gave a growl beside him and stretched his great arm out pointing further up the water course where the ravine was at its steepest. Hal could see now the figure they were all pursuing: a girl. Her hair was partly covered but she seemed far too slight to be Lady Eleanor Elder. But then, from a distance, neither Walter nor John would be certain of that. They must have seen her being pursued and realised it could be the lady.

He hesitated at the bottom of the gully, watching the girl

stumble down towards his men. She had not noticed them, her eyes no doubt fixed on where she was putting her feet. She was tiring though, and staggering more with each step. The first horsemen would catch her easily though they would have to dismount to negotiate the steep side of the ravine. She must be a hundred yards away still but Bear urged his mount up the gully. The others glanced at Hal and he nodded. He had not seen Lady Eleanor for months - perhaps she had grown thinner.

He watched the girl closely and the nearer he got the more convinced he became that it was some local lass and not Lady Eleanor. Even so, he could not risk being wrong and besides, it offended him that one girl was being hunted down by four men.

Suddenly the girl lost her footing and fell, rolling down into the turbulent waters of the beck. Her pursuers were almost upon her and whoever she was Hal could not bring himself to allow it. He pulled up and took out his bow to string. Then he snatched an arrow from his bag and took careful aim. For an archer of his skill, it was no distance but as soon as he loosed the arrow he would be stepping over a line. Whatever the girl had done, he was offering himself and Lord Elder's men in her defence.

The nearest rider had already clambered down the ravine into the beck. Now he stood over the girl as she tried to get up. Hal sighed and let his arrow fly. The man at arms was struck in the shoulder and spun around by the blow. He dropped to his knees and crawled towards his mount. For the first time the girl looked down the beck towards Hal. He waved her forward but she did not move. Walter and John had now stopped above the three remaining horsemen with their bows raised. The wounded man stumbled to his horse and another went to his aid, hauling him up and then leading him back to his fellows. All then fled down the slopes to the south but Hal knew they would not take long to find some of their numerous comrades. He might regret his mercy later on.

The girl was still crouched in the beck; she must be cold, he thought. She noticed Walter and John leaving their horses above the gully and moving down towards her. Suddenly she scrambled up out of the water and ran. Hal's men were coming at her now from all directions but she kept running, frantically searching for an escape route.

She's probably terrified, thought Hal. "Hold off!" he yelled. "Leave her!"

Walter and John stopped. Bear and the others looked at Hal.

"We're frightening her," he said. "Wait here and keep an eye open for any more of our Neville friends."

He left his horse with Bear and began walking up the beck, the water washing over his boots. The girl saw him coming and tried to climb out of the beck up onto the rocky ravine. Hal moved as swiftly as he dared, grateful for his nimble feet. The girl gave up climbing and slipped back down into the ravine, coming to rest against a large boulder. Hal approached her warily, close enough now to be certain it was not Lady Eleanor. He stopped a short distance away from her and sat down on a broad damp rock at the foot of the slope.

The girl was young and scared. She was shivering and her eyes darted hither and thither. She looked desperate - and why wouldn't she be? She was being hunted by several armed men. She would bolt if he moved any closer. He must try to put her more at ease.

"What's your name?" he asked gently.

She said nothing, still trembling.

"My name's Hal," he tried.

"Don't care who you are! Leave me be!" she cried.

"We mean you no harm."

"Doesn't look like it from here!" she spat at him.

She began to shake uncontrollably. Hal cursed his stupidity: she was not scared, she was cold.

He got up, took off his leather jerkin and held it out to her.

She ignored it. "Let me leave, I beg you," she said.

He moved to take the jerkin to her and she stood up, brandishing a knife.

"Leave me be! Please…"

Hal's mouth hung open for a moment, as he stared at the knife. Then he tossed the jerkin at her and sat down again.

"Tell me where you got that knife," he said quietly.

"I'll tell you nothing," said the girl.

"Well, you see," began Hal, "I was going to just let you go - wherever it is you were going -but then you pulled out the knife."

Her head dropped. "I didn't want it in the first place-"

Hal raised his hand to stop her. "It's not that you have a knife, it's that you have that knife."

"She made me take it!" said the girl. "It's not mine…"

"No, it's Lady Eleanor Elder's," said Hal. "Now, where is she?"

The girl held out the knife again. "You're looking for her…"

"I am."

"Well, you'll have to kill me before I'll tell you where she is!"

14

10th August 1469, at the head of Coverdale

Robert Radcliffe pressed his mount hard as he climbed the high moor above Coverdale so that Brace and the others struggled to keep pace.

"I just can't believe Ned Elder would come back to Yoredale," he said.

"We don't know for certain that he has, lord," said Brace.

"But yet… you say the one they call Bear has been seen and the archer, Hal - I shan't forget him in a hurry."

"Aye, lord, those two and about a dozen more," said Brace. "We met them in Langstroth Forest this morning-"

"Aye, met and mauled by them," complained Robert. "How many men have I given you? Yet you achieve nothing."

"I've ridden with all speed to tell you, lord!"

"Well I trust some of your men are a little more effective than you when it comes to a fight!"

He pulled up when he reached the high point between the two dales and gazed down upon Wharfedale.

"Where are they hiding?"

"The hunting lodge at Buckden," replied Brace.

"You've put men nearby?"

"As near as I dared - or the foresters will sniff them out."

"Brace, I care nought for a few Percy foresters. Their master, Henry Percy, lies far away in the Tower and long may he stay there! But if Ned Elder is there, we must have men close - men with bills, with bows."

"Aye, lord. I'll see to it."

"Where are the rest of your men?"

Brace stared at him in confusion. "Well, they've been scouring the valley for the lady... so... all over the valley..."

"Forget about the lady now," snapped Robert. "Go and gather all the men; then meet me south of Buckden, where the forest reaches to the riverbank."

Brace nodded and rode off.

Robert watched him go thoughtfully. Should he try to take Ned Elder? He had missed him at Edgecote and now... if the fool had dared to come back to Yoredale for his sister. There was a time when he would have struck down Ned Elder without any qualms, but if he harmed Ned here, then he would never be reconciled with Emma. If it happened in battle, then so be it, but not here. Having said that, he could hardly ignore Ned's presence and Ned would not take kindly if any harm came to Lady Eleanor. It was a colossal mess.

He sighed and nudged his mount forward onto the long slopes that would take him down to the river Wharfe and the forest at Buckden.

15

10th August 1469, near Cray in Wharfedale

The light had lost its midday brilliance and that meant that Mary had been gone for a long time, perhaps too long. Except the girl knew the land and knew where to go for help - but who could afford to help her?

Voices!

She got up from the floor and squeezed as far as she could through the opening, straining to hear. There were several voices but none of them was Mary's because they were all men. They were coming steadily nearer and she could already sense their excitement: they knew she was here.

There was no flare of torchlight so they would not be seeing too clearly but even so, if they found the passage, they must see her. Better to be cautious, she decided, and began to stretch her legs back along the passage and ease her head and shoulders into the shadows.

She could hear every step they took on the rock and pressed her body back hard against the wall. A few small pieces of rock were dislodged and she held her breath as they rattled down onto the floor.

"I heard something," said someone - someone who could only be a few feet away from her now. She screwed up her eyes.

A hand touched her shoulder and her eyes flew open.

She saw a face wearing a broad grin of triumph in the midst of a thick black beard. He pulled her towards him.

Eleanor gave a growl and clamped her teeth onto his wrist.

"You bitch!" he roared, snatching his arm away.

She retreated further along the passage. She could hear them talking - many voices all at once, still buoyed by their discovery.

Mary said there was a price on her head, so they were probably already discussing how they would spend it. Well they did not have her yet. She could stay where she was for now. Aye, stay where she was and slowly die.

"Lady Eleanor Elder!"

Perhaps this was her chance.

"You'd best come out Lady Eleanor. You know you're trapped. Better to come out now. You must be cold and hungry…"

Eleanor did not reply but edged forward again towards the narrower part of the passage. What, she wondered, might they offer her? She peered through the opening but against the light all she could see were dark shapes.

"Come, lady, we'll get you some food. You're lucky we found you - we wouldn't have but for the girl."

"Is Mary safe?" She bit her lip in anger - she hadn't intended to speak to them; the words just came out unbidden.

"Oh, she's long gone - chased by a few fools." There was laughter at that. "But we saw where she came from."

Eleanor felt sick.

"I can't…" she began but her mouth was dry and her voice cracked. "I can't get out," she said finally.

There was a pause and some muttering before she had a reply.

"Well, my lady, you'll do fine just where you are." The voice sounded so reasonable but the words did not seem right.

She peered at the ring of men more carefully. They were moving in and out of the light, all save one. One stood motionless. Suddenly she understood and drew her head back. The arrow grazed her cheek as it flew past her and clattered into the rock wall beyond. She cried out and scrambled back, much further than before. In a moment a second arrow struck the side of the passage and skittered across the stone. She went back to a wider section and flattened herself against the rock wall. A final arrow passed by harmlessly. She swallowed hard and then relaxed a little.

Crawling back on her knees into the darker caverns, her hand lighted upon one of the arrows and she clutched it gratefully. She sat down on the wet rock floor and waited.

Sooner or later, they would send someone in after her.

§§§

Eleanor jerked awake. It was the smell of him that alerted her. She opened her eyes and there he was, squatting opposite her. She fumed inwardly whilst she made a rapid assessment of him. He was young, thin - of course - more than a boy, less than a man. In his hand he held a long knife, but he looked terrified.

"Go home," she said in a hoarse whisper.

"Daren't go back," he murmured, "not without you. Have to show them you're dead, you see." He was sweating, despite the chill in the cavern.

"Go home," repeated Eleanor. "If you don't, I'll have to kill you… and I don't want to do that."

He moved onto his haunches. The hand that held the knife tightened its grip on the hilt.

Eleanor looked into his eyes. "Have you ever put that knife into a man - or woman?"

"Stop talking!" he said.

"Take your time," she breathed, "don't panic. Did you know I'm with child?"

"Stop it!" he cried.

"I've faced death before," she said, "have you? I won't let you kill my child, so go back and say you couldn't find me. Say I must be hiding further in."

"They said if I couldn't bring you, I shouldn't come back at all."

"What's your name?"

"Robin..."

"You know who I am, Robin?"

"Aye, aye, I do."

"Those men care nothing for you, Robin. Help me and I'll take you into my service."

"But... you'll never get out of here," he replied sadly. "There are scores of them out looking for you."

"They sent three men to kill me in Coverdale but I'm still here."

"Well, there's just too many this time, lady."

Eleanor smiled. "Aye, but they can only come through one at a time... and they're all going to be about your size and build, Robin."

The youth made no reply. She did not envy him but she wasn't going to sit there with him forever.

"Good Christ! If you're going to kill me, then do it - now!" She opened her arms and laid bare her breast. He did not move and cast his eyes down to the floor.

"Go back, as I said. Tell them you couldn't find me..."

He nodded and got up. She let him go and cursed her own weakness. She should have killed him and taken his knife. Now they would just send someone else... someone better.

It was not long before angry voices drifted along the passage. Robin's comrades were not pleased. She stood up and her legs almost folded under her. They were stiff and lifeless. She rubbed them and then stretched her arms out a few times. Though this part of the cavern was darker, at least she could move. Whoever they sent next, she would meet them here.

It seemed a long time before anyone came. She heard him moving long before she could see him. She braced herself against the wall at the point where the passage widened. There she would have most freedom to move and he would still be half bent over or crouching. She would be on his right hand making it harder for him to strike. She hardly dared breathe and her heart thumped so loudly she thought it must burst from her chest. He was taking his time; this one knew what he was doing.

There was a footfall close by - very close. She tensed, straining to catch a glimpse of him before he saw her. She heard the scrape of iron on rock: his knife would be ready in his hand. He emerged from the darkness, only a shadow. He must have seen her at the split second she saw him. He brought up the knife towards her stomach. She tried to grasp his hand and swept her right arm across him, the arrow clutched in her hand. She missed his knife hand and it sliced into her arm.

"Shit!" she cried out and plunged the arrow at his neck, but he seized her hand and tore the arrow from her grasp. He threw her onto the ground and she lay there on her back, winded and her arm running with blood.

He stood over her for a moment, this man she did not know. This was no callow youth and he was going to kill her.

16

10th August 1469, near Kettlewell in

Wharfedale

"We're not going to harm Lady Eleanor," said Hal, "we serve her brother, Lord Elder. We're here to take her home."

"So you say," said the girl, "but I don't know you… and I don't think I believe you either."

"But… we've just rescued you!"

The girl glanced up at Walter and John above her. "They were after me too."

"They were after the others, not you," said Hal.

The girl sat back down on the rock, shaking. "There are so many of you," she wailed. "And you'd do anything… say anything, to get that price on her head… and now… I don't know what to think…"

Hal said nothing.

"God curse you if you're lying to me," she said through her tears. She laid the knife down on the rock beside her and put her head in her hands.

"What are you called?" asked Hal, holding out his jerkin once more.

"Mary." She looked pale, exhausted.

"You can keep the knife, Mary, as long as you don't stab me with it. Now, put on the jerkin," he said gently, "and then tell me where Lady Eleanor is. We're her only hope and there are few enough of us."

She nodded and half rose from the rock.

"Come," he said, holding out his hand.

She gave him one more nervous look and then took the outstretched hand. He pulled her up to her feet and wrapped the jerkin around her. She staggered half a step and he caught her as she fell, lifting her up into his arms. She weighed almost nothing.

"She's in a cave by one of the becks..." she muttered, "but she can't get out..."

Hal carried her back to where Bear waited with his mount. He waved Walter and John down to join them.

"Show us, Mary," he said, "and quickly - I don't think we've long before the others come back with a few of their friends."

He swung her onto his horse and mounted up behind her. She guided them up the side of the gill and back along the top of the gully alongside the fast flowing beck. They tracked up through some low scrub beside the gully.

"It's not far," said Mary.

They climbed another fifty yards or so and saw a waterfall ahead. Mary gave a frightened gasp for several horses were already tethered in the bushes near the falls.

Hal dismounted and set Mary down beside him. He lowered his voice to a whisper. "Where's the cave?"

She hesitated and looked him in the eye.

"Mary, whoever owns those horses, they're no friends to Lady Eleanor."

She nodded and took his hand. "I'll show you."

"Bear, Walter, with me," ordered Hal. "The rest of you wait here and keep a good watch. Our enemies are damned close!"

Mary led them to the horses but still Hal could not see the way into the cave.

"You have to pass to the right of the falls," she

whispered. "There's a passage where the water gushes out and another, drier, beside it."

"You stay here, Mary," he warned.

She put her hand on his arm. "When you go in a bit there's a small cave and the passage swings to the right, at the back," she said, "but Lady Eleanor can't get through it, not with the child…"

Hal stopped mid-stride. "The child?"

"Aye, she's with child…"

"Christ's Blood!" breathed Hal. "What next? Very well, but stay out here. Walter, have your bow ready."

Bear had already taken out his pollaxe and now Hal carefully slid his sword from its scabbard. They stood at the mouth of the cave. They could now hear the muffled echo of voices from within. Hal entered as quietly as he could and the other two followed him in. When his eyes adjusted to the gloom, he made out a group of men with their backs to him clustered around what he assumed must be the narrow entrance to the passage.

He crept forward, sword in hand, but after several steps he tripped and fell over a body on the ground. He grunted in pain as he hit the rock floor. One of the men turned around. He probably did not see Hal on his knees, but he could not miss the giant figure framed in the cave entrance. Stories of the one called 'Bear' were all over the valley. He shouted a warning to the others but they hardly had their weapons out before one fell to an arrow from Walter. Hal leapt up and stabbed another in the thigh which left only two defending themselves against Bear. It was not enough and Hal winced as Bear's axe swiftly despatched both men. More blood! This was going badly wrong.

There had not been much noise but enough, he thought, to alert anyone in the passage. Lady Eleanor must have heard, yet when he peered into the opening there was no sign of her. The men had been gathered around the gap in the rock, so what were they doing? What were they waiting for?

Mary stumbled into the cave. "Where is she?" she whispered.

"I told you to wait outside," snapped Hal.

"I'll go in," said Mary. "I know the passage and I doubt any of you will fit through."

"No, wait," said Hal. "They may have sent someone in there…"

He reached out to stop her but was too late. Mary slipped through the gap and was gone.

Hal slapped his hand against the rock.

"Christ's Blood! Well? Which of us is the smallest?"

§§§

Eleanor looked up at him but could not see his face clearly. She expected no mercy. He had come this far, so he would not baulk at finishing her. Yet it was worth a final try.

"What will it take for you to spare me?" she asked.

He shook his head. "Nothing. Whatever you promised the lad, it did him no good. There's nothing you can do will stop me taking your life, my lady. I take no pleasure in it, but it must be done. The word is out: if I take you alive, I get nothing. So, if you have any words for God, say them now."

"I have only bitter words for God," snarled Eleanor. "Make it swift then, if you please - cut my throat."

He crouched down close beside her and put the knife to her neck. Now she could see his face, his expression, his eyes…

"I'm with child," she whispered.

He gave a shake of the head. "It makes no difference to me, lady…"

"Aye," said Eleanor, "but, by the Virgin's blood, it does to me."

Before he realised what she intended, she clamped both her hands around his hand that held the blade.

"You'll not kill my child!" she screamed and pushed the knife aside with all her strength. He was caught off balance and cursed her roundly as he struggled to wrest his hand free. She could only hang on and try to force him to drop the knife.

"Lady!" screamed a girl's voice.

Her opponent seemed more disconcerted by the scream than she was, but then he might be wondering how the girl had got past his comrades. She was wondering that too and she was still wondering when he threw her against the rock wall. She let his hand slip free and staggered away from him. He followed her and slapped her face so hard that she fell backwards and landed in one of the shallow pools.

"That was foolish, lady," he said, "and it gained you nothing."

He took a pace towards her and then stopped, as if hesitating.

"Get it done then!" she roared at him.

But he turned slowly away from her and there, behind him, stood Mary. As he turned Eleanor saw the hilt of a familiar knife protruding from his back.

"You little bitch!" he snarled and swung his blade towards Mary. She cowered back against the rock. Eleanor scrambled to her feet, dripping with water. He lurched back towards her and raised his knife again. Then he grunted and Eleanor saw the point of a long knife emerge from his chest. Blood welled from the wound and his weapon fell. A short figure emerged from behind her attacker and pushed him to the ground.

"John Long, my lady," announced the newcomer cheerfully, "oh, and Hal sends you his greetings."

"Hal? But… how is Hal here?"

"Come, my lady." He took her by the arm and helped

up Mary.

Eleanor looked at the dead man at her feet.

"Wait," she said and bent down to draw out the small blade that Mary had driven into his back.

John helped them along the passage but they stopped abruptly when a loud hammering made the whole passage shudder.

"By Christ, I hope Bear takes care!" said John, "or he'll have the whole hillside down upon us!"

Eleanor smiled. "Bear is here too?"

"Oh aye, my lady," grumbled John, "he's making the gap bigger… in the only way he knows…"

When the blows subsided, they continued along the passage and found that the gap into the cave had indeed been enlarged with the aid of Bear's war hammer. He stood examining the blunted blade with concern but the hole was now just large enough for Eleanor to squeeze through.

She threw her arms around Hal and kissed him on both cheeks. Then she hugged Mary to her. "How did you find these men, Mary? In all Christendom, how did you find these two?"

"You're bleeding, my lady," cried Hal. "Bear, bind up my lady's arm. John, find her a cloak - she looks like death."

Eleanor saw Hal's worried frown and felt tears in her eyes. She must look truly terrible this time for he had seen her in strife often enough before.

"You've worked a miracle to find me, Hal," she said.

"We're not safe yet, my lady," he replied softly. "We must go - and quickly. There are scores of-"

"I know Hal - we've seen them, Mary and I. How many men do you have?"

"A dozen - which isn't enough, I fear."

Eleanor gave him a tired grin. "Just as it always was then."

John hurried in with a cloak. "Here, my lady," he said

draping it over her shoulders. "Hal! They're coming…"

Hal led them outside and Eleanor blinked at the sudden glare of light, though the sun was already low in the western sky. The fresh air, though, cleared her head and, when she looked around, she needed no-one to point out the source of their troubles. Men were at them coming from all directions: some were riding up from the village by the river, others tramping on foot along the track that ran above the forest. A few were already quite close.

Hal bellowed commands and helped Eleanor to a horse. Before she could protest he hoisted her up onto the saddle.

"Hal!" she cried, "I can't ride as I would. I need to walk the horse… I'm with child!"

"Walk close by me then," said Hal. "I'll be here if you need me."

It was not so much the risk of a fall she was worried about but that her slow pace would put everyone else at greater risk.

They started the descent through the gully heading for the nearest band of trees. Their horses trod nervously on the rock strewn slope beside the beck. Eleanor clung to the horse, took deep breaths and hoped for the best. Her arm was sore and though Bear had hastily bound it she was opening up the wound whenever she gripped the reins with her right hand.

Bear took the lead with Hal and Eleanor just behind him. Then came Mary sharing a mount with John Long. The rest were spread out to protect their flanks and rear. As they descended further down the gill they lost sight of the track to the village.

"Where are we going?" gasped Eleanor, already breathless with the effort.

"The only place we can," said Hal, "the forest."

"But won't we be trapped in the forest?" she said.

"Better than being trapped out here, my lady," retorted

Hal.

They were almost at the foot of the gully. The track was close now. They would have to cross it to reach the forest and the trees were still a further hundred paces away. To Eleanor, already exhausted, it seemed a very long way indeed.

They headed straight across the track at a walk. Now Eleanor could see once more the men approaching on foot from the north. She glanced in the other direction and there were the horsemen, thundering up the slope from Kettlewell. She turned to the front again and felt slightly dizzy. She almost slid sideways but Hal somehow flung out an arm to seize her shoulder and keep her upright - just.

Ahead of her lay a hundred yards or so of low scrub and then the treeline. After that, well that was another problem. Hal released his grip on her left shoulder as their horses drifted apart seeking their own paths across towards the trees.

"Archers!" roared Bear.

Eleanor followed his raised arm. The men on the track had stopped for a reason: they were stringing their bows and taking aim. Instinctively she bent lower towards the horse's neck and hung on more tightly. Better a bleeding arm than an arrow through the chest - like Ragwulf. The sudden memory tore through her... like Ragwulf... All she could see was Ragwulf's bloodied breast and her hands let fall the reins.

It was an arrow that saved her. It flew across her eye line and startled her mount, jerking her back to the present. Eleanor had never lacked for agility and her natural balance came to her aid now as the mare lunged forward. Arrows seemed to fill the air and it seemed her horse was no longer willing to move at walking pace. She hoped the babe would be alright - whatever happened now, she must avoid falling. She saw Hal veer back to her side to put himself between her and the archers. Sweet Hal.

Thirty yards now and they would reach the trees. Every stride ate up another yard or two… only a score more now. The horse behind her shrieked and went down. Panic gripped some of the other mounts. She reached the first oak sapling when she heard Mary's cry and whirled around. At the same moment, her mount made a sudden turn in the opposite direction and she slid straight off. Hal was a yard away but his outstretched hand grasped only air.

She screamed and braced herself for the fall but Bear's great hand seized her cloak and cushioned the impact. She rolled into the bracken and got to her knees. Mary's horse was down, thrashing its forelegs in vain. "Mary!" she yelled.

Hal was beside her at once. He took her arm. "Come, lady!" he said and pulled her up.

She winced. "Other arm, Hal, please!" she gasped.

"Come then," he urged.

"Get Mary!" she cried.

He shook her roughly by the shoulders. "John's with her. You're all that matters, lady, now come!"

Arrows thudded into the ground all around them. Hal's eyes were pleading but she wrenched herself free of him. "She matters, Hal!" she cried. "She matters…"

"Go with Bear, my lady!" Hal told her. "I'll see Mary safe myself!"

"You swear?"

"Yes - take her, Bear."

She knew further delay was foolhardy so she let Bear sweep her up and carry her into the forest. The other men rode through the trees and she saw that one or two had not come through unscathed.

A flurry of arrows slapped into the trees. Bear retrieved her horse and helped her to remount. He urged her deeper into the forest but she would move no further until she saw Hal ride up with Mary on his lap and John Long limping beside his horse.

"Is she alright?" demanded Eleanor.

"Right enough," said Hal, "but you should be long gone by now!"

Eleanor looked beyond him onto the open ground, now filled with men and horses.

"What does it matter, Hal," she said. "We can't outrun them!".

"No we can't, my lady," he said.

131

PART TWO: A PLACE BY THE RIVER

DEREK BIRKS

17

10th August 1469, at Corve Manor near

Ludlow

It was mid-morning and the gates of Corve Manor stood wide open. The courtyard was crammed with men, horses and wagons. Bathed in warm sunshine, Ned stood on the rampart and observed the activity below. The steps nearby echoed with the sound of heavy feet. His steward, John Holton, paused briefly in the doorway and then came out to join him. His misshapen face looked utterly miserable.

Ned gave him a sympathetic smile. "Your good wife, I suppose, has given you more than a few harsh words," he said.

"Aye, lord, more than a few words and every one barbed."

"I share your misery, John. Lady Maighread loses no opportunity to upbraid me, but what can I do? Our king sends me south, so I must go south - and this time I really need you with me. I'll have a new castle to run - or rather, you will."

"I fear it's not me you need to persuade, my lord," murmured Holton.

"I know. How goes the loading?"

"We're near ready, my lord. That's why I've come up."

Ned noticed George Spearbold loitering by the tower

entrance.

"Then we'd best get the farewells over with, John, and get ourselves on the road."

Holton nodded and went off - no doubt to face the wrath of his wife, Mags. Spearbold eased past him to join Ned, who nodded a greeting.

"The game begins in earnest then, my lord?" said Spearbold.

"Aye, Master Spearbold, it does."

"I can't say I'm surprised. It's been some time boiling up, but I always knew Warwick wouldn't stomach being left out in the cold."

"Well, now… who knows?" breathed Ned. "As you say, the game begins…"

"You could always… hang back, wait out events… see whether the king survives before you act for him."

"Before I act for him? What was I doing at Edgecote then, Spearbold? No. Whatever I do now, Warwick will see me as his enemy - and he'll be right. If I can bring him down, I will. He's robbed good men of lives they should have lived - and for what? His wounded pride, Spearbold, that's all. Now he's a traitor - plain and simple."

"Ah, my lord, if only things were plain and simple but, alas, they rarely are."

"You're still with me though?" Ned endured a flutter of uncertainty, but Spearbold gave him a wry smile.

"I believe I made my choice at that God-forsaken fort in Northumberland," he said.

"Aye," said Ned. The fate of Crag Tower was a sobering thought for them all. "I'll need you to be my eyes and ears… here at Corve, at Quenhull, in the north, in London - in short, everywhere…"

"You don't ask much then, my lord," Spearbold replied with a chuckle. "Well, I still have men who'll tell me what they've seen - for a small sum…"

Ned handed him a pouch of coins and Spearbold hefted it in his hand before undoing the leather tie. He nodded with satisfaction at the contents. "That should keep us well enough informed for a goodly time, my lord."

"I hope so - else none of us will survive this. What's the latest news of the king?"

"The king's held at Warwick Castle, but I suspect the earl will move him soon enough."

"You think so? Why? Surely he's well placed where he is - and not too far from London."

"Aye, lord, exactly: he's not too far from London. Both the king and the earl were ever popular in London - but which one will the capital favour now? No, I think he'll move the king further north, to Middleham - just to be safe."

"What of the queen, or her father, Lord Rivers, and her brother, Lord Scales? And where are Gloucester and Hastings?"

"Patience, my lord. Reliable news of anyone is scarce," mused Spearbold, "but rumours suggest the queen may be back in London. I fear though that Lord Rivers might have been taken."

"And his son, our friend Lord Scales?"

"Nothing yet."

Ned felt a pang of guilt: he should be doing more to find Scales. Without his help he would have perished at Yoredale - indeed several of the men at arms Scales had loaned him then were still with him now. In return Ned had promised his support for the queen's family, the Woodvilles. Now they would be at risk from Warwick but so far Ned had done little to help.

"And... what about Lady Eleanor and Ragwulf?" he asked. "Or Hal and his men?"

Spearbold shook his head. "As soon as I hear anything, my lord, I'll bring word to you at Quenhull."

Ned clapped him on the shoulder and nodded.

Spearbold was turning to go when Ned said: "Your men, those who… supply you? Are they safe men? Trustworthy?"

Spearbold grimaced. "I rely on them, my lord, because I must, but trustworthy? What man would you trust who trades information for coin?"

He strode off along the rampart and Ned gave a sigh. Spearbold was just about the last. One by one, he had received the various waifs and strays who lived under his roof. To John Goldwell, the once influential goldsmith from Cheapside in London, he suggested that now might be a good time to return to the city. The false charges against him had been dropped and with all that was going on, his return would probably pass unnoticed. Goldwell, though, had seemed surprisingly cool about the prospect.

Ned also commiserated with his eight year old nephew, Will, who had not seen his mother, Eleanor, for many months. The lad bore it well enough, much helped by Eleanor's good servant, Becky, and of course by the presence of young Jack Goldwell, his half-brother. They were of an age and now seemed inseparable. That was another storm coming when Eleanor returned - and another reason the Goldwells should hasten to take their leave, but short of throwing them out on their arses…

He still had one more to see: the one he cared about most. Having cast a final eye over the men waiting in the yard, he left the rampart to seek her out. As he expected she was waiting for him in the solar, her favourite chamber. She looked up from her sewing when he walked in and it pained him to see the dark shadows under her eyes. Even the burn scars on her cheek seemed somehow redder and angrier.

He sat down beside her. "It's time now," he said.

"Aye," she said, "though you've hardly been back a week…"

She dropped her head, seeming to concentrate once again on the intricate piece of embroidery that lay in her lap... upon her belly, a little swollen now with the child.

"I'm leaving you in good hands," he said, "and if it's safe to bring you to Quenhull, I shall."

"Very good," she replied, "but I doubt I'll want to travel far after another month or so."

"It's not so far..."

She said nothing, but her nimble fingers had stopped work.

"I have to go now," he said. "The men will be waiting."

"Well, I shouldn't want to keep the men waiting," she said. "I know fine how hard waiting can be."

"Maighread, we've talked about this for days," said Ned. "I didn't bring this upon us..."

She turned her face towards him, showing her unscarred left cheek, a work of natural grace and beauty. He blinked.

"Ned, the kingdom is split asunder... and once you ride out of our gates you'll be taking sides. We'll all be caught up again in the chaos."

"I made my choice ten years ago and I'm not changing my mind now. The king has put his seal to my orders-"

"The king? Is the king even still alive, Ned? And if he's not, then every step you take is a step nearer the axe."

Ned stood up. "I won't desert his cause, Maighread!"

"No, but you'll desert ours." She shocked him then by throwing aside the embroidery and kneeling at his feet.

"When I heard the stories about Edgecote... days passed and I heard nothing from you. Then I saw the first of a few bloodied Welshmen making their way home... and I feared you were dead. I lit candles for you... and then a week later, you came home, safe and whole. And now as I thank God for his mercy, you tell me you will go to war again.

"I know you, Ned Elder! However much I entreat you,

you'll do whatever you can to aid this king. But if you lose… you'll die and all your family, friends and servants will be cast down - marked for traitors. And your precious men, who you say you care about so much? They'll die too, their families ruined for lack of menfolk. You know all this! You've seen it before and yet still you go."

"Aye, my love, I know it… and still I go, for whichever way I turn now, I could lose all. Do you think Warwick will pardon me now, even if I do nothing more against him? Tell that to the Herbert widows. He took their husbands' heads though their only guilt was to answer the call to arms of their lawful king! I'll not change allegiance to save my skin. No, the only way to keep you safe is to fight and win."

He lifted her up and she trembled against him.

"You've always known what I would do," he said.

"Aye," she whispered, "but I've never been with child before… and never thought to be. I want the father to see his child and, just now, I would lie, cheat, steal… kill to make that happen."

Ned wrapped his arms around her. "I will see the child… no matter what befalls us," he said.

"You can't make such a promise, Ned. Only God can keep you safe and for every man going with you, a mother, a wife or lover will be weeping and praying that God will be with their man."

He raised her face to kiss her and wiped the tears from her cheeks.

"God be with you, Ned," she whispered.

"I pray God is with thee, too, in the birth of our child," said Ned.

"Be sure you send me word," she pleaded. "To hear some tidings will ease the pain…"

"I shall wear my messengers out," he said, leading her to a seat, "but I'm not going to war, Maighread. I'm just going to my new castle - it will be a fine place to live, I think."

"Go then," she said briskly, "you're starting to weary me with your boyish hopes."

He rested a hand briefly on her shoulder and then went out.

In the yard outside, a groom held his horse ready for him. He surveyed the assembled men. Maighread was right: he could see it on their faces. Many had been chastened by the final exchange of words with their loved ones.

He had stayed at Corve as long as he dared, hoping that Hal would arrive with Ragwulf and Eleanor. How he could do with Ragwulf just now. Their lateness worried him - had he heaped too much upon Hal? If he could have waited, he would, but the journey down to the Severn valley would be slowed by the wagons and he could delay no longer. The sooner he established himself firmly at Quenhull, the sooner he could be back at Corve.

"Mount up!" he ordered.

§§§

Firm ground and fair weather allowed Ned's train of wagons to make good progress towards the Severn. He was nervous when they passed through the lands around Gloucester, where he knew Neville influence held sway. If these lands did not belong to Warwick or his many clients then they belonged to the king's brother, the Duke of Clarence - and since Clarence now appeared to be Warwick's son-in-law and ally, it amounted to the same thing. The king needed an ally of his own in the south west, someone with more stomach for a fight than the likes of Humphrey Stafford, Earl of Devon.

Ned shook his head. Maighread was right about that too: this was a poisoned cup if ever there was one.

Crossing the river at Gloucester, they arrived at Quenhull Castle at noon on the third day of travel and a most impressive fortification it turned out to be. Set upon a low hill a mile or so west of the Severn, it had a clear view of the river and the surrounding land for many miles around. Its walls were mostly old and battle-scarred but there was one tower which looked as if it had been recently finished. A deep, dry ditch surrounded the castle and a large, quite modern gatehouse jutted out from the east wall.

Several pennants flew from the ramparts but Ned recognised none of them. He was relieved not to see Warwick's or Clarence's banners there - at least he was spared that.

He nodded with satisfaction at what he saw and rode with Croft and Holton along the track which wound up to the castle gates whilst the oxen pulling his waggons toiled up behind them. He had somewhere in the region of eighty men with him, but only a score or so of harnessed men at arms. The rest were archers or billmen from his estates - a few from Corve Manor but most had come south with him from Yoredale months before.

The wooden drawbridge spanning the ditch was down and the castle gates were wide open but at his approach they were hurriedly slammed shut.

"Friendly," observed Croft.

"It looks a sturdy place, doesn't it?" said Ned. "Let's hope the steward doesn't force us to take it!"

"I can see why he's shut the gates," said Holton. "In his place, I think I would too."

"Well, since you'll shortly be in his place, so I should hope," replied Ned.

"State your name and your business," ordered a gruff voice from the gatehouse.

"This is Lord Elder," announced Holton, adopting a formal tone, "and he has business with the castle steward."

"Wait there," said the voice.

A long silence followed during the course of which all of the wagons and men reached the castle and formed a queue around the line of the ditch.

Ned dismounted and eyed the gatehouse rampart above them. There were few men visible but that might mean nothing.

"This is disrespectful," muttered Holton.

"Keep a close eye, Croft," Ned ordered. "After what's happened in the past few weeks, we'd better be ready for anything."

There was a shuddering from the gatehouse and for a moment Ned thought the drawbridge was about to be raised but then he relaxed as the gates ground slowly open.

He walked casually towards the entrance, flanked by Croft and Holton. They were met on the threshold by a single knight. He stood tall, but his grey hair was streaked with white. He looked old - old and weary.

"Lord Elder?" he said thoughtfully. "The same Lord Elder who fought in Mortimer country years ago?"

"Indeed," replied Ned. "I've not thought of that battle for years, yet… it all started there, I suppose. Were you there?"

"I was, my lord," said the knight.

"And you are?"

"Sir Ralph Teller."

"Which side were you on, Sir Ralph?" asked Ned.

"Same as you, my lord - and I shan't forget it as long as I live."

"It seems so long ago now," said Ned, "too long…" In truth he had no wish to be reminded of that battle or any other… "Well, Sir Ralph, I bring a letter for the steward - is that you?"

"Hah! Steward? No, my lord, that honour lies with Sir Roger Cullen," said Sir Ralph. "I'll take you to him - we've told him you're here."

Ned looked to Croft. "Wait here," he ordered.

What he expected Croft to understand by that was: wait here and nose about whilst Holton and I explore elsewhere.

Sir Ralph led them up a narrow spiral stair to the first floor chambers. Inside the castle seemed smaller for, though it was much larger than his manor at Corve, it was not on the same grand scale as Yoredale.

Sir Roger Cullen, the king's steward, received them in his privy chamber. Ned made brief introductions and then handed Sir Roger the king's letter.

Sir Roger broke the seal and read the letter in increasingly sullen silence. Ned suspected he was rereading it several times in disbelief. Then the steward made an elaborate show of inspecting the royal seal.

"Sealed with the king's ring," he murmured, as if to himself. He blew out his cheeks and paced around the room.

Ned said nothing, understanding that his letter would come as a considerable shock to a man who had probably expected to hold Quenhull for the rest of his days.

"So," said Sir Roger finally. "I must surrender Quenhull to you?"

"Aye," said Ned. "That's it I'm afraid, Sir Roger. I regret the suddenness, but we are all servants of the king… are we not?"

"The king is… how was the king when you left him?" asked Sir Roger. "The last news we had was that the king was defeated by northern rebels, perhaps even killed…"

Ned was suddenly very aware of his own thick Yorkshire accent. "Always best not to act upon rumours, eh, Sir Roger?" he said.

"But when there are only rumours, Lord Elder, what is a man to think?"

Ned looked him in the eye. "I saw the king two weeks ago and he was still very much alive then. You have his letter. You see his seal…"

"I see all that," said Sir Roger, "but-"

"There is no 'but', Sir Roger. I've no wish to harry you

out of here but since I'll be moving my men in at once, you'll need to begin moving out any men of your own personal retinue. Those who serve the king will, of course, remain."

Sir Roger regarded him coldly. "You are most generous, Lord Elder, but when my men are gone, I think you may find it a little lonely here." He paused for a moment, taking care to meet Ned's eyes.

Ned smiled. "I shall look forward then to the peace and quiet."

"I said lonely," said Sir Roger, "but I can't promise you much peace. Do you know who holds all the land around this tiny royal scrap?"

"Oh, aye," said Ned, with a grin. "I know it very well, Sir Roger. Why do you think the king sent me here?"

"I shall be close by," said Sir Roger, "in case you should have need of me…"

"If I do, you'll know it," said Ned. Then he left Sir Roger and stepped briskly from the room. "Come, John, let's get everyone inside."

Several of the wagons were brought in and unloaded but space in the yard was limited since Sir Roger's men were busy trying to leave at the same time. Ned frowned as he watched them start to load weapons, barrels of powder and sheaves of arrows into a wagon.

"Croft," he said quietly, "I want our archers atop the wall at once. John, make sure Sir Roger doesn't remove any goods from the castle other than personal items - and you can start by unloading that lot!"

"What if…?"

"This is a royal castle and everything in it belongs to the king - not the steward or his thieving men!"

As it turned out, Sir Roger's men were not prepared to question what Holton told them. He was a fearsome looking brute of a man, even without the ugly scar across his face. Ned guessed that no-one was likely to challenge a man who had survived such a wound - and so it proved. Holton's visage and the presence of Ned's men on the ramparts above were enough to ensure a peaceful, if tense, transfer of tenure.

After the last of Sir Roger's men left, the gates were firmly closed and Holton breathed an audible sigh of relief.

Ned clapped him on the back. "That, John, was the very easiest part of our task!"

"Indeed it was," said Sir Ralph Teller.

Ned smiled at him. "You're still with us then, Sir Ralph?"

"Indeed."

"You're not of Sir Roger's affinity then?"

The old knight shook his head. "No, my lord. I was sent here by the king before Sir Roger was appointed steward. Sir Roger is Clarence's man and, be in no doubt, you've made an enemy there."

"Well, I've made enemies in most places," replied Ned, "so Sir Roger will have to wait at the back of a very long line of men - many greater than he."

"Sir Roger is known for many qualities, my lord, but I fear patience isn't one of them," said Sir Ralph.

18

10th August 1469 sunset, at Buckden

Hunting Lodge

"Hurry!" cried Hal, but the others needed no more cajoling. They rode through the trees as fast as they could, ducking under branches and veering from side to side. Eleanor was with Bear and all she could think of was the burden on his poor mount. She glimpsed Hal and Mary from time to time, the latter clinging to him for all she was worth.

Eleanor could not judge whether they were being caught or not, for the light was fading fast, the red sun sunken beyond the western treetops. In the distance she caught sight of a wooden lodge. They weaved their way towards it through the trees, getting ever closer, but so were their pursuers. Arrows flew at them and only the trees saved them from further wounds.

"Swords!" bellowed Hal, fifty paces or so from the lodge, and she soon saw why: drawn up well before the lodge was a line of men at arms on foot.

Hal, encumbered by Mary, wheeled to one side and allowed several of the men following to punch a gap in the line to gain access to the gateway. Bear drew out his blunted pollaxe.

"Head down, lady!" he ordered. It was as well she

obeyed at once for the axe swung past her head and bludgeoned aside one of the men at arms. Tiny flecks of blood landed on her bare face and instinctively she blinked her eyes tight shut. The evening air was heavy then with the clamour of a skirmish: hammer blows and cries of pain.

Bear shouted angrily in what she imagined was Flemish, his native tongue. She feared he was wounded and opened her eyes to find that their situation had somehow got worse. The gate remained resolutely shut and they were trapped before it, hemmed in by a tight ring of billmen who pressed in on them, cutting their horses and slicing at their legs. All they could do was try to deflect the long-handled blades, but she could see that it was only a matter of time.

Hal was bellowing: "Open the gates, Tom!" and battering on the timbers with his sword. "For God's sake, open the gates!"

Eleanor knew the numbers against them were increasing by the moment, as more men arrived. She was more afraid now than she had ever been underground, for here she was powerless.

Then one of the gates opened a crack. At the same time the billmen began to fall back and at first she could not see why. Then in the half-light she glimpsed arrows from the rampart finding their targets in the crowd of men. The gate swung inwards and Bear followed Hal into the lodge. The deadly arrow storm continued until all were inside and the gates firmly shut again.

Bear set her down on her feet and she leant for a moment against the sweating flank of his horse.

Hal brought a forester to her. "The head forester, my lady," he said.

"Tom, this is Lady Eleanor Elder."

Tom favoured her with a diffident nod.

"Thank you," she said, "but you took your damned time!"

"Didn't open the gate for you, my lady," he retorted, "I opened it for her." He pointed to Mary. "I was here when her father was head forester and I've watched that girl grow against all that's been thrown at her. I wasn't going to let some Neville bill man cut her to pieces before my eyes."

"Whatever your reason, you've served Lady Eleanor well this evening," said Hal.

"Aye, but I wonder whether I've served my own master well. Lord Percy doesn't keep me here to rescue the Elders. Now I've scores of men trampling through the forest and no doubt they'll lay siege to this place! And I must answer to Lord Percy - not Lord Elder."

Hal brushed aside the older man's concerns and they found a chamber for Eleanor. Bear tended to her arm once more and this time was able to effect a better repair. By the time he had finished, Hal arrived.

"How are the men?" she asked.

"All still alive, my lady," replied Hal, "so far."

"What of those outside?"

"Gone off out of bowshot, I expect. The foresters are better archers than almost anyone."

"What, even better than you, Hal?" she said with a grin.

"Even better than me, my lady," he conceded.

"So, is my brother near?" she asked.

"No, my lady. He's not near at all. Terrible things have happened…"

"Aye, Hal," she replied distantly, "I've seen my share of terrible things…"

Hal fell silent for a while, then murmured: "We found Ragwulf's grave, lady, and covered it with larger stones… none but Bear could move away those stones now."

"Well, it's done, Hal. There's nothing to gain by dwelling upon it and we've other matters to think on. Having done so well to get me here, do you have a way out?"

Hal shook his head. "I've just been taking each part as it

comes, my lady. This morning I wasn't even sure you were still in the valley. I hardly expected to find you at all with so many folk already out looking."

"I still don't understand why those men came for me at all. Ragwulf and I had kept to ourselves…"

"As far as I can work out, my lady, it's all down to the Earl of Warwick - who else around here commands so many men?"

"But isn't the earl away? He left the shire months ago - I know because my sister, Lady Emma, came to see me before she left with the rest of the household."

She studied Hal's bleak face. "You'd better tell me all that's happened," she said wearily, but by the time he had finished, she felt a lot worse.

19

11th August 1469 early morning, in

Langstrothdale Forest

Robert Radcliffe stood amongst the trees, eyeing the Buckden hunting lodge. He had slept little in the past few days. This whole affair was dragging on far too long.

"Are you certain that Lady Eleanor is inside?" he enquired of the tall man at arms beside him. He had posed the question several times to other men but some had already proven to be remarkably poor witnesses.

"Upon my life, my lord, she's in there," the soldier replied.

"Your life?" Robert shrugged. "Hardly of great value to me. Who are you?"

"I'm Hooper - and I'm sure I could be of value to you, my lord - given a chance."

Hooper had a severe look about him, face scarred by a few blows over the years. Robert might find a use for Hooper, but could Hooper lead others or was he just blunt weapon?

"What about Lord Elder then?" he asked him.

"No-one's seen him, my lord. Some of these folk would say anything if you paid them enough, but I've not spoken to any man that's certain. The big man at arms is in there right enough, but not Lord Elder."

"Could Lord Elder have got inside the lodge before?" asked Robert.

"No, lord. I've been watching that gate for two days. Apart from those who went in last evening, there's only foresters in there."

A man who watched for two days was long on patience at least, mused Robert. Hooper was no hot-headed brute. He turned at the sound of a horseman approaching at speed. It was Brace - at last.

Brace pulled his horse to a halt and casually dismounted. Robert seized him by the arm and dragged him away from the other men.

"What have you done here?" demanded Robert. "I sent you to find and bring Lady Eleanor to me - unharmed! Instead you start a fucking war!"

Brace shrugged off Robert's hand. "Some of the men must have misunderstood…"

"They didn't misunderstand," retorted Robert, barely able to control his anger. "I've talked to some of them and every man has told me the same: the price for Lady Eleanor could only be claimed if she was dead! Explain that!"

Brace said nothing for a few moments then smiled.

"I bring urgent news, my lord," he said brightly. "The earl has returned to Middleham - and he commands you to return there at once."

Robert cursed silently. He had been expecting Warwick's return but had hoped for a few more days. He dared not ignore Warwick's summons, but to leave Lady Eleanor at the mercy of Brace…

"Very well, Brace. You and the men had better come with me."

"Your pardon, my lord," replied Brace, "but the earl wants all the Middleham men back with you… I'm to continue the search for Lady Eleanor with the rest."

Robert almost struck him across the face but managed to control his reaction and merely gave him a curt nod. He paused then to think and walked a few yards away from Brace into the trees. He considered carefully for a moment. Scores of the men were not from Middleham but were raised locally for the recent rebellion. Now that the rebel army was disbanded, such men - men like Hooper - had nothing. The only reason they had gathered in Wharfedale was the price he set on Eleanor Elder's pretty head. They were not Warwick's men - most likely some of them answered to Brace, but perhaps some might yet serve Robert Radcliffe.

He returned to the clearing where Brace waited.

"No harm is to come to Lady Eleanor," he told him. "Is that clear enough for you?"

When Brace left him, Robert quickly rooted out Hooper once more.

"You want to be of value to me, Hooper?" he said. "Find me a dozen or so men who can fight hard and follow orders - it would help if they had no love for Brace. Do you think you can find such men?"

Hooper fixed him with a stare - there was little deference in this fellow. Then he nodded.

"Aye, lord, there's still a few trusty men to be found who can't make a living."

"Good. I don't care how you do it, Hooper, but you are to make sure that Lady Eleanor Elder is kept safe."

"Safe? But why, my lord?" enquired Hooper. "You set a price for her... dead."

"No, Brace decided that," replied Robert, "but I'll reward those who see her safely away."

"Very well, my lord," agreed Hooper.

§§§

Middleham was heaving with men and horses to such an extent that the outer bailey was almost impassable. The recent heavy rain had formed vast puddles which numerous wagons and oxen had now churned into a sea of mud. The mud would soon dry out and leave deep ruts which folk would be tripping over for weeks. He left his horse to the stable lads and picked his way through to the east gate. How the earl expected more men to be absorbed into this chaos was beyond him. He was relieved to step onto the stone flags by the gatehouse and knock the worst of the mud from his boots.

Robert could admit, at least to himself, much apprehension as he ascended the long flight of steps up to Warwick's inner chamber. He had not seen the earl since the victory at Edgecote when he had been brusquely despatched north with the remains of the rebel army. How much did the earl know about what he had been up to since he had laid aside his 'Robin of Redesdale' disguise? How much had Brace told him?

He was most surprised therefore when Warwick welcomed him with much warmth. It was the Warwick of old, bursting with energy and enthusiasm.

"Well met, Thomas - alright, I know, you answer to the name Robert now! A simple jest."

"I take it your affairs proceed well, my lord," ventured Robert.

"Well, Robert? Better than well, I think. I have the king here at Middleham - safe and secure in the bosom of his Neville subjects. My enemies are scattered or destroyed: William Herbert is dead and the Woodvilles will soon be taken. To cap all that, my king is willing to sign any request I might happen to dream up. What could be better?"

"That's great news, my lord. I hope that I played some small part in bringing you such a triumph."

"Indeed, Robert, you did. Your leadership at Edgecote did you much credit. But you've been busy since your return, Brace tells me."

Robert's dismay must have been all too obvious, for Warwick went on: "Now Robert, don't blame Brace. He serves me before you, remember. You've been pursuing the Elder girl. Why?"

"Her husband was killed and I thought she was in danger, my lord."

"Why do you care what happens to Eleanor Elder, Robert? You're a Radcliffe - and she all but destroyed you at Yoredale."

"I thought Ned Elder might come north after Edgecote and it was best to keep an eye on her."

"Hmm, Ned Elder is unlikely to be in the north but if he is we'll deal with him later. Now, forget Eleanor Elder - you can leave her to Brace."

"Very well, my lord," agreed Robert, wondering whether Warwick knew what Brace intended.

"I owe you a debt, Robert, and here is the payment - for your service so far."

He passed a document across the table. Robert glanced down at it and then studied it more closely.

"The king has granted me the Yoredale estates..." Robert could hardly believe what he was reading. "But Ned Elder is one of his most loyal men."

"The king has confiscated Ned Elder's northern estates, which includes the former Radcliffe lands and his grandfather's Northumberland estates, and has handed them all to you. So, now you have what your father coveted but could never achieve... and you've a knighthood for your service at Edgecote."

"But... how? I fought against the king!"

"How, Robert? The king has become my friend once more. I've only to ask, only to lay a document before him and he approves it. So you see, amongst so many royal favours, yours is only a little one for him to bear. Now, put the Elders behind you. They are all disinherited so you can forget about them now."

"I never actually caught Lady Eleanor, my lord."

"Well, no matter then. You've had your reward so let's discuss your next task. I'll give you a week to address matters in Yoredale, appoint men to act for you and so on - then I want you down in London. Warner is there and several other of my agents, but they'll need someone to direct their efforts. I must root out opponents swiftly whilst I hold the advantage. Warner will tell you what needs to be done."

"Am I to follow the commands of a lawyer?" asked Robert.

Warwick smiled. "Warner is a shrewd fellow so be guided by him... but take care you don't trust him too far. He knows a great deal, so keep your eye on him. Oh, and be ready to receive the countess and my daughters. They should be taking ship from Calais in a few weeks. I'll want you to escort them to Warwick."

"Very well, my lord, I'll set out for London in a week," agreed Robert.

He left Warwick's inner chamber clutching the land grant tightly in his hand. He still could not quite believe what had happened. He returned to his chamber to collect a few items and then left Middleham at speed, glad to get the stench of the castle yard out of his lungs.

He rode up to Yoredale Castle, which should have been the centrepiece of his estates, only it was an empty shell now, just a pile of rubble. He could rebuild it, of course, make it even more grand than it once was, but that would take time and coin. He had little of either.

His thoughts turned to Eleanor Elder. The disaster in February at Yoredale had all come about because of her - Ned Elder might have come in any case but it was she who plotted his downfall. She had come very close to success but the Earl of Warwick rewarded his servants well and he had survived. Now he had the power to have her killed and what had he done? He'd hired Hooper to keep her alive - a man about whom he knew even less than he knew of Brace.

He decided to leave it in the hands of God. He would hear soon enough from Hooper how things turned out. Either way, he would follow the earl's advice for now and forget about the Elders - all save one.

20

11th August 1469, at Buckden Lodge in

Langstrothdale Forest

Eleanor joined Hal upon the wooden rampart. They had let her sleep late into the morning but she was grateful. She had not slept at ease since the attack on the cottage.

"I hope you're a little more rested, my lady," said Hal.

"Our situation hardly lends itself to untroubled rest, Hal, but aye, sleep was welcome beyond measure."

She scanned the forest below. "They keep themselves well hidden," she observed.

"No, not hidden, my lady… gone," he replied.

Eleanor gave him a blank look. "It must be some ruse," she said. "Why would they let me go now? They've killed Ragwulf and they've been after me all week - why would they just give up?"

"Perhaps they're scared of the Percies' anger?"

"Hah! I doubt that - a Neville take a backward step against a Percy? It makes no sense. Are you sure?"

"Tom's been out and he can find no trace of them in the forest - and he would know."

"Aye, but still they could be waiting to catch us in the open."

"Shall I send out a few of our men to scout down the

valley?" asked Hal.

"Aye, best do that. We can't stay here forever!"

Hours later, when Bear and several others returned without having seen any sign of trouble, Eleanor had a decision to make. As far as she could reckon, she had carried her child for about six months, so the sooner she reached Corve, the better. Not only that but she longed to see her son Will again. What must he think of her? And then there were all the others. Yet... she was safe at the lodge; if she left, the risk of ambush was high and she was not well placed to ride at speed. They all looked to her to command but it dawned on her that she did not even know how to get to Corve Manor.

In the afternoon she gave up. Ned had sent her Hal because he trusted his judgement and so must she too. "Tell me what to do, Hal," she said.

"Well, my lady, I've been giving it some thought," he said. His enthusiasm for the next task always made her smile.

"If the valley's clear we should head home at first light tomorrow. It's going to take us a week or two to ride to Corve - and... well you won't be riding fast. I'll be surprised if we can manage a score of miles each day."

"Aye, well I'm worried about riding fast, it's true," she replied.

"I think we might have the answer to that, lady," he said. "Tom's found an old lady's saddle in the stable - Lady Percy used it once or twice it seems."

"A saddle for an old lady?" Eleanor pulled a face.

"No, an old saddle for any lady! It should serve you for this one journey."

"A lady's saddle?" Eleanor cringed inwardly at the notion.

"At least you won't be falling off, my lady."

"No, but I might throw myself off from the

embarrassment," she said with a weary tone.

"Think of the babe, my lady."

"Aye, thank you, Hal," she snapped, "because I'd clean forgotten I was with child!"

Hal said no more. He knew her too well.

"Aye, very well," she said finally, "we'll go at dawn then."

In the evening Eleanor relaxed a little as the whole group partook of a modest feast provided by the foresters. She knew that, as much as anything, the local men were celebrating the fact that she and her troublesome escort would soon be leaving. Yet she reflected that without the foresters' help, they would likely all be dead by now.

After they had eaten, Bear brought her a closely wrapped bundle which she recognised at once.

"You need this, lady?" he asked.

There were tears in her smile: she had thought the sword lost.

"Not need, Bear, but want it, certainly. Now if only I had the strength to wield it," she said sadly.

She wallowed in the gentle warmth of the summer evening and sat back, watching the others. She smiled to see Hal attend to Mary's every need - at least, she thought, it might stop him from brooding over poor Agnes. Hal grieved for Agnes still, but he was not alone. Before she could stop herself, Eleanor had conjured up the whole bloody scene at Yoredale, at the end. She cursed silently for once the chilling thought entered her head she could not shake it free. She got up and left the others to their drinking and tale telling.

Her black moods were not something to be shared with anyone else, as Ragwulf had found to his cost more than a few times. She went to her chamber and threw the sword down upon the floor.

"Blood of the Virgin!" she moaned. Will, Agnes,

Ragwulf… Another death, another bitter memory.

She lay on her bed for a time letting the anger flow and then, when it subsided, she got up to retrieve the sword. It was her bridge to the past, to the days of her youth, to her first love, Will. She unsheathed the weapon and marvelled again at its gleaming blade, kept sharp by Ragwulf. She lifted it high; it did not feel so heavy. The urge to wield it overwhelmed her and she swung it around in a wide arc until she overbalanced and fell back onto the bed. The child kicked inside her.

"Hush boy," she muttered crossly, "your mother's a bad woman - you'll just have to put up with it... I did!"

She lay down on the bed, clutching the sword hilt to her as she wept.

§§§

It was dark when she awoke and felt the cold sword still beside her on the bed. She sat up and peered across the small chamber to the door where a dark shape lay upon the floor: Mary. The girl was determined to stay close - perhaps she feared she would be left behind. Eleanor listened to her soft, regular breathing and lay back down again. She'd had her fill of rest - folk were far too fond of it, she decided. She got up and frowned. She was still fully dressed but Mary must have loosened her bodice. Well, it would have to stay loose for she could not tighten it herself. She pulled a shawl around her shoulders for even in summer time the darkest hours could be cool. How long, she wondered, before dawn would come?

She stepped over Mary and out onto the threshold. The hunting lodge was not very large so she could not walk far, but it would serve. She took care to feel her way to the top of the wooden steps which would take her down into the hall. She rested her foot upon the top step and it creaked noisily. She stopped there, grinning. Most of the men would be in the hall and they would not be pleased if she woke them so early. She was about to take the next step, when there was a loud creak from the foot of the steps below her. It seemed someone else could not sleep. A pity, for the last thing she wanted was company.

She descended the next few steps, but the noise on the lower steps told her that someone was on their way up - perhaps it was Hal. She waited on the stairs until a figure appeared and paused a few steps below her. Her eyes opened wide as she saw the axe in his hand.

"Hal!" she screamed. "To arms! The lodge is breached!"

The axe swung at her legs. She turned to run back up the steps, and stumbled. The axe splintered the wooden stair rail and she crawled up to the top step. By now the men were stirring, but the intruder was not alone. He struggled to free his axe blade and she hurried along the landing, crying out as she ran. He came after her. Mary was wide awake now and standing in the chamber doorway. Eleanor thrust her aside and made for the sword on her bed.

Her assailant followed her in and raised his axe. She drew out the blade and whirled around to face him, putting all her rage into the slashing stroke. Her blade caught him across the midriff, almost cutting him in two. He dropped the axe in shock. Mary cried out as he fell down on top of her.

"Peace, girl!" barked Eleanor, for her blood was up now. "Do you still have my knife?"

"Aye!" said Mary. "Here, you have it."

"Christ's blood! Why would I want it, you silly bitch; I've got a sword! You keep it. Use it if you have to - if you can!"

Footsteps thundered along the passage and Hal appeared. "Lady! Are you hurt?"

"No. We're safe," she said, though the wound on her arm had opened again.

"Not for long!" said Hal. "They're inside the fence - and there's plenty of them. Some of the foresters are dead. It's hard to tell who's who in the dark - and they've set fires! I can't believe we've been taken so easily! Come, we'll make for the stable. I've sent Bear and John ahead."

They crossed the landing and started down the stairs. On the long wall of the Hall a large tapestry of a hunting scene was already ablaze. Tom joined them with two of his archers.

"Got in over the rampart!" he shouted. "Neville bastards!"

"We're making a run for it!" said Hal.

Tom nodded. "Aye, you need to get out into the forest."

They paused by the doorway that led out into the courtyard. Hal opened the heavy door a fraction but could see nothing.

"They'll be waiting in the shadows," Eleanor murmured, "waiting for us to move, with the flames at our backs, knowing we must get out or burn..."

"They've lit us up nicely," said Hal, "but Bear and John are already out there and we've still got time. The fires haven't taken hold yet. We'll wait a bit."

Somewhere behind them there was a splintering of wood.

"The postern door!" said Tom, nocking an arrow to his bow.

Two men burst into the rear of the hall from the kitchen. An arrow from Tom threw back the first in an instant and the other hastily retreated. At the same time someone thudded into the door, knocking Hal and Mary to the floor. Two men at arms strode across the threshold. Hal parried a sword thrust and stabbed up at an unprotected leg. The other attacker drove Eleanor back with his pollaxe. She tried to block the assault with her sword but the first two blows shuddered along her arms and the third knocked the weapon from her hands. She dropped down on to the stairs.

"This is the one!" he yelled, standing over her in triumph.

"Lady!" cried Hal in vain. He was back on his feet but locked in a struggle with his own opponent and could do nothing to aid her.

Eleanor reached for her knife, but of course Mary had it. She glanced across to the door where the girl still lay. Then she laughed up at the warrior.

"You rejoice to be sent to Hell, lady?" he asked, puzzled.

"I wouldn't waste that axe on me, if I were you," she said. "You might need it against him." She pointed behind him.

He nodded knowingly, thinking he would not be tricked so easily. Eleanor nodded too and Bear raked his pollaxe down the man's neck. His weapon dropped onto the wooden steps and embedded itself next to her thigh. She tried to wriggle aside but he fell stone dead on top of her.

Bear heaved the bleeding corpse off her and helped her up. He recovered her sword and handed it back to her.

"Got tired of waiting," said Bear.

She gave him a nod of thanks. Hal grinned at her, his face smeared with blood.

"Ready, Hal?" asked Bear. "There's more out there."

"Better take care then," he said.

Mary, still on the floor, gave a groan as she came to. Hal scooped her up in his arms and went out quickly. Tom and Bear followed with Eleanor. Bear, she noticed, hovered beside her all the way to the stable and when they arrived he unceremoniously hoisted her into her saddle.

"I never thought I should ever sit upon one of these," she grumbled.

"Go west first before you turn south," advised Tom.

"When you've gone, we'll break out to the north. In the dark that should be enough to confuse them. May God be with you."

"And with you, Tom," replied Hal, "and thank you."

"Aye, the Elders owe you a great debt," said Eleanor. "It will be repaid."

Tom gave her a doubtful look and shrugged. "Not if you don't get out of here…"

Other men were arriving at the stables. She knew that Hal was calling a roll in his head as he looked around at the men. He turned to Bear. "Ralph? Shortbutt?"

Bear shook his head.

"Come then," he said bitterly.

Eleanor followed Hal out and they set off through the trees to the west. At once a dozen or so bill men appeared to block their escape. Hal and Eleanor pulled up, fearing the long bills would cut at their mounts. More men, at least half a dozen archers, emerged on their left flank and Eleanor's spirits fell for there would be no escape now. To her astonishment, the archers let fly at the billmen who fled into the forest.

"Go!" one of the archers told them. "Go, while you can."

Hal did not hesitate. He seized her reins and dragged her mount after his, with Bear and the rest hard on their heels. After a terrible first hour or so wandering through the forest in the dark, they picked up a track to the south and out of the dales. They rode the horses for as long as they dared, though their pace being steady rather than fast, the animals did not tire too soon. Finally, when dawn had long ago come and gone, Hal led them off the track and into a small wood where he called a halt.

"We've lost them, I think," he announced. "Either that or they're so far behind it doesn't matter."

Eleanor breathed a sigh of relief.

"Who do you suppose those archers were?" she asked.

"I've no idea," said Hal, "but, without them, we wouldn't be here."

She nodded and Bear lifted her down gently, setting her against the trunk of an old oak. She ached all over from the ride, but she ached especially in all her most tender parts. Mary squatted down beside her, smiling.

"I can't think what you've got to grin about," groaned Eleanor.

"Being away from the dale is enough for me," said Mary, "the dale, the garth, aye and the folk I left there…"

"Christ's blood! That saddle rubs me everywhere," Eleanor confided. "And I mean everywhere!"

"My head is fine, my lady, thank you for thinking of me," replied Mary sweetly.

Eleanor grimaced. "I promised to take you with me - I most certainly didn't promise to be kind to you."

"I saved your life," protested Mary.

"And I yours, several times," replied Eleanor, "so that counts for nought."

It seemed they had rested for only a few moments when Hal stood over them. "My lady, it must be but a brief rest," he warned. "We daren't stay here long."

Eleanor gave a weary nod and closed her eyes. "Where will we go next?" she murmured.

"South to Derby and Lichfield, lady, on one of the old roads. Then if all goes well, we'll head west to Corve."

"You've taken these roads before," she said, surprise in her voice.

"I've followed your brother about quite a lot, my lady," laughed Hal. "I don't remember all, but I hope enough to get us home."

He held out a small leather pouch to her. "Lord Elder gave me some coin for food and lodgings - best you take the rest of it now."

"What would I do with it?" asked Eleanor, her eyes still firmly shut. "You keep it, Hal. You decide how to spend it... I'm not used to handling coin."

"Very well, my lady," said Hal.

By noon, Hal was ready to move them on. Eleanor found her limbs ached more after the rest than they had before. Mary gave her a shoulder to lean on as she struggled to her feet. She stared glumly at her mount with its loathsome saddle.

"That saddle could only have been fashioned by a man," she said, "for it's a weapon of torture for a woman!"

"Would you like me to rub the stiffness from your legs, my lady?" offered Mary.

"No, I'd like you to help me mount!" retorted Eleanor. But whilst Mary was still wondering how she might do so, Bear launched Eleanor straight up onto the horse. Then she noted that he checked the saddle straps in case they had worked loose. It was a small thing, but it reminded her that she was truly back amongst friends.

The journey was painful but unremarkable. They crossed a bridge at the river Don - at least that's what Hal called it - and then turned south west on the old Icknield road. The rest of the journey was a blur to Eleanor: they stopped at many an inn, ate ten different sorts of pottage, slept in an assortment of unpleasant beds and rode day after day. They seemed to ride forever each day, though Hal claimed they were managing less than 15 miles.

Eleanor hated the ride and the saddle sores that came with it. She had to admit that Mary's company kept her going, especially when, after Lichfield, their coin ran out. For the next two nights they were obliged to sleep in the woods. The men cut armfuls of fern and bracken for her bed which she decided to share with Mary. The babe, who had been still all the time she rode, seemed always to wake when she wanted to sleep - he was going to be a very active little boy.

The rains came the following day when they began to climb over the hills to the east of the Corve valley. They were soaked through almost immediately and the weather showed no sign of improvement as the day wore on. Eleanor had never been to Corve Manor, so for her there was no sense of arriving home, no hope brought on by familiar landmarks.

"How far away are we now?" she asked Hal, not for the first time.

"One more day, my lady," he replied, "another ten miles, I should think."

"Ten miles?" she brightened at the thought. "But we could do that today."

"Not at this pace, my lady. Best to take our time though, eh?"

"No," she said. She had had enough. "I can do ten more miles today!"

Hal looked doubtful and shook his head. "I want to get you there with no broken bones, my lady. And if we try to go too fast..."

"For once, Hal, I'll decide," she said and nudged her mount forward into a canter.

Hal followed and she grinned at the horrified expression on his face.

"Blood of Christ, my lady, you'll never stay on!" he cried.

"It's not my fault if you can't keep up," she yelled back at him.

"Let me lead then," he pleaded. "You don't even know where you're going!"

She let him draw alongside her and he kept close - no doubt in case she fell. She felt exhilarated by the pace, despite the pain in her backside. All she hoped was that her mount, so sure-footed up to now, was still concentrating as they sped across the wet, slippery ground.

By late afternoon, the heavy cloud had still not lifted and the rain persisted. Water ran off her as she rode. Her wet clothing was making the saddle itself slippery and a particularly stern kick from under her ribs nearly unseated her. It was a timely reminder that she was not riding alone. She sighed and under the darkening sky slowed to a walk.

She turned to Hal. "Can we still do it?" she asked.

He smiled and nodded to her. "Just about, my lady," he said, "the next valley is the Corve, but for the last part, it'll be near dark so, if you please, no more rushing headlong."

She nodded wearily and they rode on with twilight slowly turning to night and rain lashing at them even harder as they descended the slope down to the river Corve. She did not see Corve Manor until they were almost upon it and her first sight was a disappointment for the house seemed very small. Very small and very much closed up for the night, its gates drawn tight shut against visitors. Bear was obliged to pound on the timbers before they were finally opened. Then they hurried inside the courtyard and the household slowly began to come to life.

Torches flared and spat against the falling rain and in a short time, the yard was bustling with activity. A large buxom woman arrived and pressed Hal in a fond embrace. Bear lifted Eleanor down from her mount and she leant on him for moment, suddenly dizzy. She hardly listened whilst Hal introduced her to several people. The buxom one was John Holton's wife, Margaret, but beyond that she took in nothing more.

Then a young voice called to her across the yard and she came alive at once: Will. She abandoned Bear's support and staggered across to her son. When he ran to embrace her she thought her heart must break.

"Oh, Will," she cried, "I can't believe how much you've grown - there were times I thought I'd never see you again."

He stood back from her for a moment and looked at her bloated midriff.

"You've grown too," he said.

"Don't be so cheeky!" she reprimanded him with a smile. "But aye, you'll soon have a little brother!"

"It might be a lass," he said, "but I shan't mind if it is."

"That's very grown up of you, Will," she said, starting to sob.

"Well, I've already got a brother," replied Will. "Come here, Jack."

Another lad stepped forward from the shadows into the flickering torchlight. Another boy who was the size and build of her Will, his amber hair glistening in the rain… like Will's… and his face, his face was Will's too.

She felt her knees give way - aware only of the two young Wills rushing forward to catch her as she fell.

21

24th August 1469, at Warner's house in

London

Robert Radcliffe studied the house with grudging admiration. Warner seemed to have done well for himself since returning to London. How was it, he wondered, that a lawyer - even a prominent one such as Warner - could afford a large house in Cheap? It was a district more closely associated with wealthy merchants and the like... or goldsmiths. Had not the Elders' friend, the disgraced John Goldwell, lived in Cheapside? Robert could not resist a smile as it all became clear to him: Warner had engineered the attack on Goldwell not simply to weaken Ned Elder's allies but to add some fluffy feathers to his own little nest.

Robert had gone first to Warner's rented chambers in Holborn, but a bored clerk had directed him to Cheapside. It was not ideal since his men would attract rather more attention in this affluent area. He turned to Hooper and tossed him a small leather pouch.

"Find an inn nearby and stable the horses," he ordered.

"We're not staying here then?" asked Hooper, eyeing the large house.

"Ha!" laughed Robert. "By all the saints - of course not! Find an inn."

Hooper led the troop of men off in search of lodgings

and Robert stared after them thoughtfully. Hiring Hooper had turned out to be rather inspired for not only had he managed to aid Lady Eleanor's dawn escape from the lodge at Buckden but he had also recruited an impressive band of men. They looked like the worst of ruffians but so far he had found them a good deal more to his liking than Brace and his cronies. Nevertheless, having to provide for so many men was a new experience for him - new, and expensive. He would need to ensure that his income continued to meet such needs.

At that moment the great door of the house swung open and he was faced by a burly door keeper: Warner was taking no chances. Even so, the lawyer must have been expecting him for he had barely given his name before he was ushered inside.

Warner was in the large hall at the rear of the house.

"You took your time," he remarked, as he studied the papers before him on his desk.

Robert felt his hackles rise at once since he was still dusty from the ride south and had come to Warner with little regard for his own comfort.

"Does it look as if I've taken my time?" he replied testily.

Warner looked up and nodded. "Very good," he said.

"So, perhaps we can conduct any pressing business and then I can retire to my lodgings - unless you wish to invite me to lodge here."

Warner smiled - a sight Robert had rarely seen and the last occasion had been very much to his disadvantage as he recalled.

"That was not my intention," said the lawyer. "What news do you bring from the earl?"

"The earl is cancelling the Parliament due to meet in York in September," Robert announced.

Warner failed to hide his dismay and seemed to hesitate

before responding.

"That is… unfortunate. Matters do not go well in the north then?"

Robert was a little surprised by Warner's weary tone. A man who grew weary of serving the earl was a man who grew tired of good fortune. Nevertheless, he ignored it for the time being. There were other matters to attend to.

"Sir Humphrey Neville has risen in the north for old King Henry…"

"God save us! I thought Sir Humphrey was for the earl!"

"He was, but it seems… only for a time."

"But surely he can be easily crushed?" said Warner.

Robert shook his head. "Aye he can, but tell me Warner, do you ever step outside this house?" he asked.

"Of course! I walk the streets of the city every day."

"Well, perhaps you should walk a little further afield, Master Warner. The land is in uproar and… I fear the earl is losing control."

"But he has the king in his hands!"

"Aye, and at first that seemed to be enough, but now… well, folk don't seem to know how to act. They're not sure who rules and they don't know what to believe. On my way south I heard more rumours than even you could dream up - and all firmly fixed in the minds of the men who told me them. Even here you must have noticed some trouble."

"Well some perhaps, but I'd no idea that it was so widespread."

"Make no mistake, Warner, the kingdom is hanging by a thread."

"Is it possible that the earl has reached too far?" Warner said it in a whisper as if merely saying it might make it true.

"Well he still has the king, but I'm starting to wonder."

They remained silent for a moment and Robert imagined that Warner's thoughts were shadowing his own.

"Perhaps it is time for men of conscience to begin to

distance themselves," murmured Warner.

Men of conscience? Robert thought it might take some time to find a man of conscience in the city.

"The earl and Clarence between them are still a mighty force," he said, "but you're right, Warner: it may be time for us to consider… alternatives… should our star begin to fall."

Warner held his gaze. Robert's instinct told him that Warner was weighing up how far he could rely upon him and he could not resist a grin.

"Between us two, Warner," he said, "there'll never be trust - but there can be common interest. You have the knowledge; I have the men. I'm sure we can work together… just in case."

Warner gave him a curt nod as if he had made a decision there and then.

"We'll need a new and powerful lord… and to hook one, we'll need some influence - that does not come cheap…"

"But you have coin, Warner - don't pretend that you don't. This is Goldwell's house, isn't it?"

Warner frowned. "It is, but don't imagine I benefited much from his fall. The confiscation was bungled and the court officials got their grubby fingers on his goods before I could spirit a few things away."

Robert looked around him. "But you have this house?"

"Indeed, but if I hadn't found a small chest of silver in it I shouldn't even have the house!"

"Hmm, but considering that Goldwell was wrongly accused in any case…"

"Let us not dwell on the errors of the past, Robert. We must look out for our own futures now."

It dawned on Robert that this was no sudden move on Warner's part. He had been planning this for a while, in which case he already knew of Warwick's difficulties.

"Do you have some ideas?" asked Robert.

"I have many ideas," Warner replied, "but none that I'm yet ready to share with you. We'll talk of this again though - if it comes to it."

"Aye," said Robert.

"Now, what else are you here for?"

"The earl wants me to 'keep an eye' on you," said Robert, laughing. "Also the earl's womenfolk will be arriving shortly and I'm to escort them north."

"Very well. Last I heard they'd not left Calais, so you'll be hanging about here for a while. That will give us some time to consider, to plan…"

22

26th August 1469, at Quenhull Castle in

Gloucestershire

"None?" breathed Ned in disbelief. "None? I send you out with a bag of silver coin and the king's authority to raise men at arms - and you tell me no-one has joined us? Not one?"

None of his trusted men seemed eager to answer his fierce challenge and in their faces he saw only dismay. Holton, Croft, Sir Ralph Teller and the newly-arrived Spearbold - all of his small 'council' of advisers were clustered around him on the rampart above the south wall.

"You report bloodshed wherever you go. You tell me Humphrey Stafford has been cut to pieces by his own men. Spearbold brings news that the queen's father and brother are executed. The rule of law is absent everywhere - and yet not one man will serve our cause... the king's own cause?"

He stared at each man in turn, seeking answers or some clever words of counsel. Holton looked abject, Spearbold shook his head and Sir Ralph just gave a shrug. When his eyes met Croft's, he paused. He had got to know the man at arms quite well in the past six months and it seemed to him that Croft's stare was different, uneasy.

"What is it?" Ned asked him. "What aren't you telling me?"

Croft exchanged a glance with Sir Ralph. Spearbold and

Holton said nothing.

"Speak freely," said Ned quietly.

"The folk around here aren't willing to support our cause," said Croft, "because they don't know what our cause is, my lord."

"But did you not explain to them that we want to restore the king's peace?"

"Oh, yes, lord," replied Croft, "but which king? It just seems to them as if you want them to take up arms and risk all for a king who's most likely dead - or..."

He broke off and Ned finished his sentence. "... or is, at best, the prisoner of his brother, the Duke of Clarence - or else the Earl of Warwick?"

"And most of the landholders around Quenhull owe allegiance to the Duke of Clarence," added Sir Ralph, "or... Warwick."

Ned looked out over the manors to the south and beyond to the river. It was true: all the land he could see was Clarence land and if he turned west he would gaze only upon Neville lands. The king had made him lord of a small outpost - a royal island in a sea of enemies.

"I have letters under the king's own seal," he declared.

"Letters are but thoughts on a page, my lord," murmured Croft, "and they can't match steel."

"This is what happened before," said Ned softly. "Do you know it must be ten years ago now - less a month or so..."

"Lord?" Spearbold gave him a look of concern.

"The day I learned that the law meant nothing, if the king was not strong enough to enforce it. I lost everything that day - and I've no intention of losing it all over again. Neither Clarence nor Warwick is here - but I am!"

"You've a fearsome reputation in the field, Lord Elder," said Sir Ralph, "but that's all men know about you. Sir Roger Cullen is well known in these parts..."

"Aye, I know that," replied Ned.

"So…" mused Spearbold, "perhaps, my lord, we need to show them there's more to you than wielding a sword?"

"Go on," said Ned.

Spearbold looked to Sir Ralph. "Tell me: how is Sir Roger Cullen regarded?"

There was a glint in Sir Ralph's eye when he replied. "He's the most powerful landholder in these parts, but it's enough to say that he's robbed some and cheated others. He does all to his own advantage. There are some with grievances…"

"Then let's offer them an alternative," said Spearbold. "Get them all here, my lord, and hear their complaints. Let's see if you can win their trust. These men share only their allegiance to Clarence or Warwick - they have little regard for the king because the king's man here for the past ten years has been Sir Roger Cullen."

"Do you have such authority, my lord?" asked Sir Ralph.

For the first time Ned thought Sir Ralph looked worried.

"Aye," answered Spearbold, "he does. He has the king's letters which give him power of oyer and terminer."

Holton nodded enthusiastically. "So he can judge local disputes."

"But you'll divide the shire, my lord," warned Sir Ralph.

"Dividing the shire is our only hope," said Spearbold, "I'd sooner have half of them with us than none!"

"If we're to gather support for the king, then there will be divisions," said Ned. "God's blood! How can there not be division when the king himself wrestles with his own brother?"

"Without fighting men, this king will lose his throne," observed Croft.

"His grace knew that when he sent me here," said Ned. "The loss of the Herberts, Stafford and some of the queen's family has weakened the king fatally in the west. Our task is to find him allies. Whatever it takes, we must make some friends here. Spearbold, prepare letters!"

"Lord?"

"Every local landholder receives a letter, Spearbold. Sir Ralph, he'll need your help with that, your local knowledge."

"And what will these letters say?" asked Spearbold.

"The letters will tell all landowners to present their grievances to me before Michaelmas. On that Quarter day I'll dispense the king's justice to them. No doubt I'll make a few enemies. Let's just hope I make enough friends."

"What about the lawlessness?" asked Spearbold.

"Croft, I want regular patrols by your men. Any law breakers will be imprisoned here at Quenhull and sentenced - also at Michaelmas."

Croft nodded.

Sir Ralph gave Ned a rueful smile. "Well, Lord Elder, it certainly won't be dull serving you…"

"It's only five weeks," said Holton quietly, "until Michaelmas."

"Five weeks to build a following," said Croft.

"Five weeks to hold our nerve," said Ned, "and trust that our enemies will not."

He glanced at Spearbold. "I've not had time to ask you: how fares my Lady Maighread at Corve? Is there any news of Hal? Or Lady Eleanor and Ragwulf?"

"Your lady is well, my lord," replied Spearbold, "but there were no new arrivals before I left."

Ned sighed. "I need you here, with me; yet, I need you there too. We are spread too thinly, Spearbold…"

"Corve is in good hands, my lord."

"Aye, Maighread and Mags between them would be enough to frighten off any man with trouble in mind."

"And your good friend, Felix of Bordeaux, will visit to

ensure all's well. Here is where the struggle will be won or lost, my lord. All's quiet at Corve."

23

26th August 1469, at Corve Manor near

Ludlow

A sudden, wounded scream shattered the morning calm and brought to a standstill every man, woman and child at Corve Manor. Folk stopped as they were about to pass through the gate, the boys in the yard, Jack and Will amongst them, lowered their wooden swords. Workers in the bake house, grooms at the stable, guards on the rampart - all turned their heads towards the solar. Hardly any of them had ever met Lady Eleanor Elder - until now.

Maighread was sitting in the hall with Mags and in the echo of the scream they exchanged a look of despair. They had no need of words for this was a moment both had been dreading: Eleanor had at last met Sarah… and so the tirade began.

"You craven, treacherous bitch! Filthy slut! Could you not get a man of your own that you must take mine? You whore… you London whore, Cheapside whore! Did you buy him with your father's gold, you shit-faced coward? You think you can match my looks with your turd-shaped nose and your barn of a mouth! I'll cut your face to the bone! My poor Will must have been desperate to lie with you! Or did you trick him with witchcraft? I'll slice your innards for the dogs to feed on!"

Wave upon wave of cruel, venomous insults resounded around the stone walls. Together Maighread and Mags rushed for the staircase up to the solar. Mags reached it first and hurried up the steps. Maighread, heavy with child, was much slower, but all the while Eleanor's words clattered relentlessly down the stairwell.

"Will was my first love! He died upon a sword trying to save me! And you snared him with your evil wiles, like a serpent, drawing him to you... into you... You stole my sweet man... but you stole my memories too and for that I will kill you!"

Maighread staggered into the solar in time to see Eleanor throw a punch at Mags that sent her spinning onto the floor.

"Get out!" Eleanor bellowed at them, rage spitting from her like embers from a fire. She launched herself then at Sarah, scratching at her face. Sarah tried in vain to grasp her flailing wrists.

"He was the father of my child!" Eleanor cried.

"Lady," pleaded Maighread, "leave Sarah - think of your child to come."

Eleanor threw Sarah back against the wall and turned to glare at Maighread. "I told you to go!" she growled.

"Eleanor!" said Maighread. "I'm no milksop to be told what to do in my own house!"

"You knew!" Eleanor's stare cut her like a knife. "I trusted you... loved you, Maighread, but all along you knew."

"Not all along-"

"Get your ragged face out of my sight!" Eleanor shouted. She pointed a trembling finger at Mags sitting on the floor. "And take her with you!"

Sarah edged towards Maighread at the door.

"Not you!" rasped Eleanor, moving to block her path. "You're not leaving, you cunning bitch, because you're going to pay a high price for fucking my man!"

"But you were dead!" protested Sarah.

Eleanor slapped her hard across the cheek. "Do I seem dead to you now?"

"Eleanor," pleaded Maighread.

"I wasn't dead! I was fighting for my life," cried Eleanor, "not sitting on my arse draped in cloth of gold in some grand town house!"

Sarah put her hand to her bruised face. "Will said you were dead," she said softly, "he thought you were dead…"

"He was in shock! Hardly a few months had passed!" railed Eleanor. "But you didn't care. You couldn't wait to drag him into your bed and open your legs!"

"That's not how-"

"No? I'm sure you had many sisters scouring the city for a husband! But you stole my Will, my first, my sweet love…"

She seized Sarah's arms, driving her back against the wall. "… and I'm going to kill you for it." She wrapped her hands around Sarah's neck.

"Oh, Eleanor…" Maighread shook her head in helpless despair, for even an Eleanor weakened by her journey, would surely crush the life out of Sarah.

Maighread could see the desperation now in Sarah's eyes, as she lashed out wildly at Eleanor's breast and face.

"He thought you dead," insisted Sarah. "He thought you dead and then he fell in love with me - but that was not my doing!"

"Hah! Don't play the innocent maid! You drew him on!" She pressed her fingers harder into Sarah's neck.

Sarah snatched off Eleanor's coif, grabbed a handful of red hair and pulled at it.

Eleanor's face flushed with anger. "Go on! Tear out all of my hair, but you'll still die today in this chamber, just as a filthy whore should!"

Maighread leant against the door frame, powerless as Eleanor squeezed her fingers tighter around Sarah's throat. She could hear Sarah choking as she tried to speak.

Sarah released her hold on Eleanor's hair and tears streamed down her cheeks.

"False tears won't save you either," said Eleanor bitterly.

"He thought you were dead…" gasped Sarah, "so what did he do when he found you alive? What did he do when he saw you again? Tell me that!"

For the first time, Maighread saw doubt in Eleanor's face and she seemed to ease the pressure on Sarah's throat.

"He died," muttered Eleanor, "he died…"

"He died," breathed Sarah, "And God took him from us both."

"No." Eleanor ground out her words. "God looked on while Edmund Radcliffe's steel took Will from me…"

In a final burst of anger she raked her clenched fist across Sarah's face and knocked her to the floor.

§§§

Felix of Bordeaux approached the familiar walls of Corve Manor with apprehension. His customary pleasure at seeing his friends again was tinged with the deepest regret at the knowledge that Ragwulf would not be there to greet him. When Hal brought him the news early in the morning, it struck him hard - harder than he would ever have believed. He did not mourn just for Ragwulf but for all of Ned Elder's affinity. One by one they perished: men, women - even the children were not safe. Was there to be no end to the slaughter?

Only a few short months ago he reflected that they had all come a long way from the first days when they had met in war-torn Ludlow. There, where the streets ran with blood and wine, they had begun their long struggle. Yet, it seemed they had not come as far as he hoped.

He had made few visits to the manor in recent months

and seen little of Ned Elder since his return in February. Then, just as it seemed that the kingdom was at peace, rebellion had broken out and Ned was off again in the king's service. Over the years, John Holton had made himself a very effective steward on Ned's behalf and his wife, Mags, was a formidable hostess. Yet now, with Ned, Holton and most of the men gone south, he feared for the household at Corve. Since the rebellion, many worrying rumours were abroad.

"It's good to see the old place again," he said to his companions.

Hal grinned in reply - the poor lad looked exhausted. Ned asked a great deal of this young man.

John Goldwell looked at them both as if they were mad for he was a man of the town - born and raised in the city of London. There he had made his fortune and, though for the time being he was an exile, he would always be a Londoner. The wooded hills around Corve Manor were a foreign land to him and Felix knew he was happier in Ludlow than out here.

The gates lay open at their approach, which was normal enough, but the sound of raised voices was anything but normal. The three men entered the yard and looked upon it in dismay. It seemed as if the entire household was out there chattering. They dismounted and found Sarah Goldwell advancing towards them. Her kirtle was torn, her coif missing and her hair in wild disarray. Blood from her nose trickled down onto her chin and above a cut on her left cheek the eye was beginning to swell up.

John Goldwell took several faltering steps towards her.

"Daughter?" he murmured in confusion. "What has happened to you?"

"We're going back to London, father - now!" She spat the words at him; this was a Sarah none of them had ever seen before.

"But-" he protested.

"Now!" she repeated then turned to Jack who stood, open-mouthed, beside Will amongst the crowd of boys.

Jack stared at his mother and then at Will. "Your mother hit… my mother," he said, bewildered.

Will still seemed to be absorbing this appalling notion when Jack unleashed half a dozen punches at him.

"Jack!" screamed Sarah, but he paid her no mind as he wrestled Will down onto the cobbles.

She swung around to the others. "Father? Felix! Hal, for the love of God, part them please!"

Both Felix and Hal took a step towards the pair of lads, then paused and looked at each other. Felix knew he should intervene and pull the boys apart, yet some small part of him was weighing up what the outcome would be - and he knew that Hal was doing the same. Will was the stronger of the two, but Jack was agile and swift of movement.

"Felix!" Sarah implored him. "Don't just stand there!"

Felix sighed and stepped forward. The boys were rolling away across the courtyard, encouraged by the on-looking men at arms and stable lads. But before he could reach the pair, Eleanor's servant, Becky, strode out of the brew house. She kicked both boys in turn and when they yelped she bent down and seized each one by the ear. She dragged them, protesting, across the yard and then turned on the assembled crowd.

"Men! You're all just little boys!" she declared. Then, after favouring them all with a scorching glare, she marched the boys into the brew house and shut the door with an ominous slam.

Those in the courtyard held their breath and there was a collective wince as several more yelps followed. Then all was quiet again and slowly, a little reluctantly it appeared to Felix, folk returned to their work. He puffed out his cheeks and gave a loud sigh.

"You know, Hal," he said, "even if you hadn't already told me, I think I might have guessed that Lady Eleanor was here…"

Hal just gave a weary shake of the head.

John Goldwell had an arm around his daughter. "Please take us back to London," she sobbed. "We cannot stay here."

"Of course, I see that," he replied, "but we shouldn't make a hasty decision at such a… difficult time."

She pulled away from him. "Difficult? Do you call being thrown around the solar by a mad woman, difficult?"

"There's no reason not to go now, John," said Felix. "After all, the charges against you have been dropped."

"You didn't tell me that," said Sarah.

"But go back to what?" asked John. "I'm ruined - when we fled, I lost everything!"

"Well, not quite everything," said Felix, "I seem to recall a rather weighty chest you brought with you - and you still have many friends in the city."

Now that Felix thought about it, he was surprised that Goldwell was so reluctant to return.

Further thought on the matter was cast aside however when Mags bustled out into the courtyard and spied the two brothers emerging battered and bruised from the brew house.

"I don't want to see either of you again until supper - and only then if you're the best of pals again! Now get!"

The boys scampered away before she changed her mind. Felix gave a wry grin and left the others so that he could catch Mags on her own. He was astonished to see that she too bore a few facial scars from the day's excitement. It was a brave - or foolish - woman who tackled the indomitable Mags.

She greeted him with her usual warmth though her sadness was all too evident.

"You're hurt, mistress," he said gently.

"Only a little, Felix," she replied cheerfully. "Don't trouble yourself for me."

"Was anyone else in… the path of the storm?" he enquired.

She shrugged. "I'm sure young Sarah had the worst of it. I blame myself. We all foresaw it yet still it caught us out. I thought Lady Eleanor was still sleeping - it seems not…"

"How did she…?"

"… find out?" said Mags. "She stumbled across Jack last night. I thought she might have forgotten it, she was that exhausted… but the moment she set eyes on Sarah this morning, she just knew."

"Dare one ask what the… lady is doing now?"

"Honestly, Felix, I really don't care - as long as she's not fighting anyone."

"We must resolve this, Mags. I'll speak to Lady Maighread. I think it's time, in any event, for our friends, the Goldwells, to see rather less of us."

She sighed. "I just wish my John was here, or even Spearbold - a household of women is all very well but…"

"Well, I am here now," Felix reassured her.

"Let's hope you're feeling strong then," muttered Mags.

John Goldwell was making his way over to them and she took her leave.

"Felix, a quiet word, if you please," said Goldwell.

Felix led him across to a corner of the yard where no servants were working.

"What is it, my friend?"

"I can't go back to London, Felix."

"Why ever not? I told you: the charges have been dropped - you are no longer implicated in the treasons of last year - Lord Scales told Lord Elder himself."

"It's not the charges I'm worried about," said Goldwell.

"What then?" Felix felt his exasperation swell. It seemed

his debt to this friend could never be repaid.

"There is another matter - a very privy matter and… I don't want Sarah to know of it."

"John, I shall never know of it either if you don't spit out!" said Felix.

"This is too… public," said Goldwell.

"Oh very well," conceded Felix and they went into the hall where they found several servants busy scrubbing the long tables and trestle boards. Felix led Goldwell up the stairs into the north tower. They went into a small chamber below the rampart and Felix closed the door behind them.

"It's cold in here," complained Goldwell.

It was true the chamber was cool for no fire would be lit in August and despite the wooden screen across the hearth there was still a chill draught. He had to admit that Goldwell looked positively ill.

"Never mind the cold," said Felix. "What else ails you?"

Goldwell took a gulp of breath.

"Out with it, man, or we may as well go somewhere warmer!"

"When we fled from the house in Cheap, Felix, I left something behind," began Goldwell.

"Yes, I know - I dare say you left much behind."

"Yes, but one thing mattered above all others…"

"Something you were working on?" asked Felix.

"Exactly! I always reckoned you for a clever fellow, Felix. I left a piece I had just finished. It was due to be collected very soon and it was so valuable I hid it in one of several secret places I have in the house."

Felix noted that Goldwell was beginning to sweat profusely, despite the cold.

"Just how valuable was the piece?" he asked.

"It was worth more than any other work I've ever done," the goldsmith replied.

"For an important client, then - a wealthy client?"

"The most important client imaginable," said Goldwell, "the king."

Felix shook his head in disbelief. "And this piece of work…it was gold?"

Goldwell nodded. "And a sapphire…"

"A sapphire! Good God, man! And you left it behind?"

Goldwell had turned as pale as a shroud. "You rushed me out of the house, Felix - I didn't think of it until we arrived in Bristol. Then it was far too late and since I was charged with treason it hardly seemed to matter. But now…"

"Now the king just might remember it! Did you receive any payment?"

"Yes, for the materials… I bought the gemstone from an Italian merchant - that alone cost two hundred pounds…"

"Two hundred pounds! God save us… so the king is now without both his jewellery and his two hundred pounds?"

Goldwell nodded. "As long as I'd disappeared, there was a chance… but if I were to return…"

"Hold!" said Felix abruptly. "Is there aught else I should know?"

"What else could there be? Is that not enough? I told you: I'm ruined!"

"Let me think for a moment, please, John."

He sat down on a chest by the wall whilst Goldwell paced around the small chamber.

"Who else knows?" asked Felix. "Apart from you and his grace."

"No-one."

"Nonsense! You bought the sapphire from a merchant and I doubt the king came to see you in person, so some others must know."

Goldwell nodded sadly. "Now you see why I must stay

here."

"No, I don't," replied Felix. "True, your house and goods were sold, but I heard nothing at the time of such a jewelled piece. If it was secretly hidden then there's every chance that the owner of the house has not discovered it. Why would he?"

"So you think we might recover it? Even so, the king will still be angry that the commission was not delivered."

"Well, he might have been at the time, but I'm guessing he's worrying about a few other things just now. Let's assume he returns to London. If you were able to retrieve the jewel and give to him, explaining that you were wrongly accused and forced to flee the city, I think he might show clemency."

"But how could I get the jewel - I can hardly walk up to the door and ask to fetch it, can I?"

"Perhaps not, John, but I think you'll agree with me that only by returning to London can you restore your good name. You must go there, rent a small house and find out who now owns your house in Cheap. Do you have enough funds to buy it back?"

Goldwell looked horrified. "Perhaps, but then I should not have so much as an angel left!"

"You're a skilled man and, with your debt to the king resolved, you can rebuild your business. Clients will come flocking back to you, I'm certain."

"But what if the jewel is already gone?" asked Goldwell. "What then?"

"I'll say no more, John. But think on it today - going back is your best hope."

John Goldwell gave him a bleak look and went to the door. Felix followed him out and shut the chamber door behind him.

For a moment there was silence in the room save the whispering of the wind through the fireplace. Then the wooden screen was scraped aside and there was a long sigh.

The two boys crept out from behind the screen and grinned at each other, all rancorous thoughts forgotten.

"That was close!" said Jack.

"I thought I was going to cough!" said Will.

"I was trying not to sneeze with all the dust!" replied his brother with a laugh.

"What do you make of all that then?" asked Will.

"I don't know," said Jack thoughtfully, "but I think my grandfather's in trouble..."

24

7th September 1469 dawn, at Corve Manor

Eleanor loved to watch the sun come up, loved its measured, relentless radiance and loved the hope of a new day. This morning she could find no such hope. She stood in the lee of the tower rampart, staring blankly at the hills to the north, whilst dawn stole in unnoticed against the grey backcloth of drizzle.

Her mood matched the day's dreary awakening. Her son hated her. He had made that abundantly, brutally clear. She thought, after a day or so, he would relent but it was a few days now since the Goldwells left for London and his sullen anger showed no sign of abating. He avoided her, seemed unwilling even to catch sight of her… unwilling also to contemplate the child she carried. It was the first time she saw parts of herself in him - the worst parts, it appeared.

"Lady!" It was Becky, tramping up the tower steps, probably to nag her into talking to him again, for the rift caused her pain too.

Eleanor determined to meet her with a brave smile, but Becky's worried expression banished that thought. She had climbed the steps so fast she had to catch her breath before she could speak.

"What is it?" asked Eleanor.

"Will's gone!" choked Becky. "Gone…"

"Gone? But when? How? We have gates - and guards…"

"I think he's gone… after Jack," said Becky. "He was so unhappy…"

Eleanor slumped forward onto the wall. As she found so often, bad things got worse.

"Come," she said and took Becky's arm to descend the steps. The stair was too narrow for both of them at once and Becky squeezed past her.

"If you're going to fall, lady," she said, "I'd rather you fell on me!"

In the hall below, Maighread awaited them, but not just Maighread. Hal, Bear, Felix, Mags, even Mary - they were all there, bearing witness to her failure of motherhood. The men stood aloof and uncomprehending, but Maighread enveloped her in a warm embrace. For that gesture alone Eleanor knew she would love her forever.

Maighread should be scratching her eyes out after all the abuse she had hurled at her the week before but the woman's capacity for forgiveness seemed boundless. No matter that her kindness brought tears to Eleanor's eyes, for, if there was a time to weep helplessly, this was surely it.

"Take a deep breath," whispered Maighread as she unfolded her arms and released her.

Eleanor did so, tried to compose herself and then faced the others.

"What do we know?" she asked.

It was Hal, dependable Hal, who spoke first.

"Beck noticed he wasn't abed," he said. "She got me up and I woke a few others. We looked everywhere - couldn't find you either, my lady."

"I was… never mind. What then?"

"I spoke to those on the gates…"

"Don't make me drag each word out of you, Hal, I beg you," she groaned.

"We think Will went out the postern gate, my lady. It seems there was a short while when it might have been unguarded."

"A gate was left unguarded…" It was more of a growl than a question.

"You may be sure, my lady, that it'll never happen again…"

"Well, Hal, I'm sure that'll be a great comfort to me if my eight year old son turns up dead!"

She could feel the rage boiling up inside her but she fought it hard: losing control now would do Will no good at all.

"He took his favourite horse…" said Hal.

"And he took his knife…" added Becky.

"Some coin is missing…" murmured Mags.

"There are already men out searching for him, my dear," said Maighread. "They'll find him soon enough. How far could a boy have gone?"

Eleanor glanced at Hal. They knew each other too well and his look was not so reassuring.

"Tell me, Hal," she said softly.

"Will may only be eight, but he's big for his age, strong and a fine horseman. He knows the area well. He's ridden all over with… Jack. If he takes the shortest route to London, we should overtake him swiftly, but… he's a clever lad, my lady."

"He can't even know the way to London!" she protested, but saw a look pass between Hal and Becky. "What?" she asked.

"Lady, we don't think he needs to find London," said Becky, "he just needs to catch up with the Goldwells."

How Eleanor dreaded to hear that name. "The Goldwells?"

"Their wagon will travel slowly," explained Hal, "and… I wouldn't be surprised if he and Jack didn't have something worked out between them."

"That Goldwell bitch is not having my son!" she cried, glaring at each of them in turn. "She's not! Who's gone after Will?"

"Men I trust," replied Hal.

"Well, I don't!" she said. "I'll go myself."

Maighread took her hand. "You, my dear, are not going anywhere," she said, "for you have another child to care for…"

"But I must… must…" But even she knew she could not.

"It's already settled, lady," said Hal. "We'll go after him."

"We?"

"Beck and me - we've talked about it," said Hal.

"Aye," said Eleanor, feeling a little relieved. "Aye, he'll listen to you two for he loves you both better than anyone. Bring him back to me… safe."

Hal nodded. "We'll see him safe, my lady."

"We'll leave as soon as we can," said Becky and she hurried away to get ready.

The others drifted away too leaving only Maighread. Eleanor suddenly realised that she still held her by the hand.

"Sister," said Maighread, "let others help Will now. We must both look to our birthing. With two of us, the household will need to be made ready. Mags and the midwives will see to much of it, but we must prepare ourselves - and you, especially, must take more rest."

Eleanor had never felt less like resting.

§§§

Outside in the yard Hal stood with Felix whilst he waited for Becky.

"Do you know where you're going?" asked Felix.

"I ought to - it was you took me there!"

"That was a very long time ago, Hal."

"I've a good head for east and west," said Hal.

Felix smiled. "You've a good head for many things, Hal. See you come out of this storm with that wise head still attached!"

Hal grinned and wondered what was keeping Becky.

"Perhaps you should take others with you," suggested Felix.

"I don't see how I can," replied Hal. "As it is I'll have to send back those who are out looking this morning. Bear must go south to Lord Elder at Quenhull and take with him most of those I brought back from the north. A few of the older men are needed to swell the ranks here - you know how over-stretched we are. I've already sent two with the Goldwells - we shan't see them back for a month I shouldn't think - if at all!"

"Even so, the tales I've heard are worrying. Some of my merchant friends have been set upon and robbed. It's not safe even if you go in strength, but two of you? You'd be prey for any that chanced upon you."

"With luck two can avoid being noticed - and we don't look very wealthy, do we?"

"You'll have two sound mounts - that alone will get you noticed," said Felix.

Hal wanted to stop talking about it and get going. What a time Becky was taking!

Finally she emerged carrying a weighty looking cloth bag. She looked a little flustered - flustered yet still, he decided, rather splendid. She flashed him a nervous smile. He took the bag and helped her to mount.

"I thought we'd travel light," he said, passing the bag up to her.

"Well, I am!" she replied. "But a lass needs a few things with her…"

"You're sure you want to go?" Felix asked her. "It could be dangerous, my dear."

She shook her head. "Have you forgotten, Felix, that I've buried all my kin: father, mother, sisters, cousins - every last soul? What's this task alongside that? And my mistress has taught me a few things about staying alive... over the years."

He nodded and reached up to take her by the hand.

"Well, God be with the pair of you," he said, "and I'll expect you back in a day or two."

"Unless of course, Will won't come back," said Becky.

"Then you must tie him to his horse and bring him back!" said Felix.

"Er... right," said Hal.

They rode out of the gate at a canter. Hal was glad to be away, for though he was pleased to be home at Corve, he was also relieved to have a break from Lady Eleanor. It was raining but it was a gentle, forgiving rain. He kept up the pace until they began to climb the track winding eastwards out of the Corve valley.

"Did you imagine," asked Becky suddenly, "that you would ever see far beyond this valley?"

"Nope."

"For fifteen years I thought I'd spend all my days in Yorkshire..."

"It seems not," said Hal. He was studying several tracks as they talked, but they could have been anyone's tracks.

"Is that a smirk on your face, Hal?" she asked. "Are you making fun of me?"

He grinned. "Only a bit..."

She rode closer and punched his shoulder.

He put on an aggrieved look. "You're a hard woman, Rebecca Standlake."

"Oh, I am, Hal - I am." But she said it with a smile upon her lips.

They rode in companionable silence for most of the morning, skirting villages and keeping their distance from groups of travellers if they saw them soon enough. If not, they rode fast, looked to their front and offered up a silent prayer.

In the early afternoon Hal called a halt to give their mounts a rest and they sat in the shade of twin oaks.

"How do you know where you're heading?" asked Becky. "Have you been this way before?"

He nodded. "Strange enough, I was with Will's father - also Will-"

Becky nodded sadly. "Aye, I knew Will Coster very well, very well indeed…"

"Of course you did…of course… all those years ago. Well, Felix took us both to London."

"Aye. And you think the Goldwells came this way then?"

"I do."

"Why?"

"Because my men are taking them and I told them to come by this route."

"Shouldn't we be asking folk… if they've seen young Will?" she asked.

"Only if you never want to catch him - we need to gain time on him not give it away."

"So we just keep going… day and night?" She wore a trace of a smile.

"Will's going to stop at night," said Hal, "and so must we."

"Poor Will," she said. "He'll be spending the night under a hedge somewhere…"

Something in her tone made him look up and he saw to his surprise that she was weeping.

"Don't worry," he said, putting his hand upon hers. "He's a tough lad."

Somehow his touch released more tears. "I love that little boy," she said, "and I've always been with him…

whenever there's been any trouble."

He made to draw his hand away, fearing he had upset her, but she grasped it more tightly. He put an arm around her, feeling both awkward and yet comfortable at the same time. He held her close and she felt warm against his breast.

"This is doing no good," she murmured into his shoulder.

"Not for Will, perhaps," he replied softly.

She drew away from him as if appraising him for the first time.

"Do we sleep in a hedge somewhere too?" she asked.

He shrugged. "You can if you like; I'm going to an inn."

She regarded him doubtfully. "You can't afford an inn."

"Felix slipped me a few coins," he said.

A broad grin lit up her face. "Lady Maighread gave me a small purse too. We could travel quite well!"

"Let's hope they don't talk to each other about it," said Hal. "Anyway, the Goldwells will stop at inns, so we've a better chance of finding them if we do."

"Will might already be with them."

"He might and I hope he is - he'll be safer that way."

He found he still had hold of her hand, so he stood up and pulled her to her feet.

"We should be getting on," he said. "I hoped to make Hereford by nightfall. We should overtake them sometime on the morrow."

"And if we don't?"

"Then… we pray a little harder."

They rode on with purpose and though few words passed between them, they encouraged each other with a smile every so often.

Dusk was fast approaching when Hal estimated that Hereford lay about a mile ahead. He was keen to get through the gates before curfew.

"This is the hard part," he said, slowing a little.

"Towns."

"I've never even been in a town..." said Becky.

"Well, don't get too excited."

"What's so bad about a town?" she asked.

"All I've ever found was trouble: drunks, cutpurses, whores - nothing but trouble. And just outside a town can be worse - that's where the really bad folk make a living."

"How?"

"How? Well, here we are with our two sturdy palfreys - and horses, even stolen horses, will earn some coin. Then there's our purses and weapons... and then... there's you..."

"Ah..."

"Yes, after a time they'd be turning a profit from you too."

"Aye, I get it, Hal. Bad men, bad women... but if they jump out at us, we'll just ride on through!"

"Mmm, if we can," agreed Hal, but he was staring ahead at the line of trees that lay between them and Hereford. In the dusk light the trees were bathed in a hazy autumn glow.

She smiled. "Who needs towns when you can see a fine sunset like this?" she said.

Pretty enough, he thought, but more difficult to make out what lay among the trees. He cursed silently: he was starting to worry himself with his dire warnings to Becky.

They passed the first trees and rode along a track towards a gap between two large elms. It was a well-trodden path he noticed and felt a little relieved. Yet a well-used route could also have its dangers...

"Once we clear the trees," he told her, "we'll ride hard for the town gates - and don't you stop until we're inside - you understand?"

Becky rolled her eyes. "You just look after yourself, Hal."

He stopped for a moment and peered ahead but the tall

elms flanking them stole much of the remaining light. He saw no movement in the gloom so they set off again at a walk. Almost at once several men appeared from behind the trees and stood in their path

"Shit!" he muttered, weighing up how long it would take to string his bow. Too long and the men were too close. He was willing to wager that there would be one or two behind them as well. He should have been ready for this - God knew he had been rattling on about it long enough!

"Hal?" Becky was looking behind them. He glanced back: one man - but he looked big enough to take them both out on his own.

"Take out your knife," he whispered, trying to keep his voice calm. "Keep it hidden if you can…"

She lifted her bag slightly to reveal a glint of steel under it and met his surprised look with a shrug. "A lass never knows what's going to happen next…"

He nodded and continued at the same slow pace towards the men that blocked their way to the town.

"What are we going to do?" she hissed.

"Follow my lead," he murmured.

"Wouldn't it be a good idea to draw your sword?" she asked.

"Just follow my lead," he said. "And when I say 'go', ride as fast as you can."

"Is it going to be long before you say it," she breathed, "'cos I can already smell them."

"If you're quiet long enough, I'll say it!" he snapped, regretting it at once.

She glared at him for a moment and then without warning urged her horse forward.

"God's breath!" said Hal and set off after her. Bear had taught him well and his sword came out well before he reached the first man. His assailant raised the club he carried, but Hal's razor-sharp blade sliced open his neck and throat.

One of the men had seized Becky's rein and pulled her to a halt. She was swearing at him and stabbing down at his arms and chest. Hal looked about him: the last man standing ahead of him had a sword in his hand and his comrade from behind them was running up fast to join the fray. He had only moments to decide what to do.

He swept his mount around the far side of Becky's mare and slashed her attacker across the face. He raised his arm to protect himself and Becky, screaming abuse, plunged her blade into his exposed neck. Hal was still on the move, riding now at the swordsman, wondering how skilled he was. He made a pass and they parried each other's first strokes. Hal's hand stung with pain. Shit! Not such a good block - he was cut!

"Hal!" Becky screeched and he whirled around to see the burly man drag her from her horse.

The bleak truth struck him: he could not overcome these two with his sword.

"Be strong, Beck!" he shouted to her and then rode off towards the town with her screams echoing in his ears.

25

7th September 1469, aboard ship in the

English Channel

Emma Elder smiled at her young charge. They stood together at the ship's prow as it pounded into the waves. The timbers beneath their feet shuddered but Emma did not care for she could see the thin strip of coastline now. Anne Neville laughed as the wind buffeted her cloak, wrapping it tight around her small frame. Emma felt strangely proud of this thirteen year old who was braving the weather and riding the sea's power whilst her elder sister and mother sheltered below. She must have her father's strength for Emma had heard several times that the earl was most at ease on a ship.

After so many delays in leaving Calais, they were close now. It had been a rough crossing, so their captain, no doubt anxious that his valuable charges were kept safe, had diverted from London to Southampton to avoid a late summer storm blowing up off Dover. Southampton would do well enough since the earl often maintained ships there, so at least someone might be able to meet them.

This would be Anne's time, decided Emma, because with her sister Isabel married, Anne would now be the centre of attention. Her household - with Emma at its head

- would be enlarged and her marriage prospects would be a subject on everyone's lips. Emma envisaged her son, Richard, flourishing as a page in one of the great noble houses and training for knighthood.

Whoever Anne married would already have wealth and power - only the best for a daughter of Warwick. Isabel might have captured a royal duke, but there was another still available: Richard of Gloucester. But why not a foreign prince? This marriage adventure was Emma's chance to escape her past, her sister… her brother…

They were in the lee of the wind now as they neared the port and the fleeting exhilaration passed. Anne seemed to feel the change of mood too for she seized Emma's arm and squeezed it.

"I feel as if I'm about to leap from the highest tower!" she exclaimed.

"I hope not, my lady," said Emma, "but it will be an exciting time for you, I think."

Anne dragged her away across the deck and there was a mischievous look on her sweet face as Isabel's head and shoulders emerged from below deck. Her face was a grey shade of green and her eyes were sunk deep under her brow. Isabel apparently took after her mother in her ability to cope with sea travel.

"You'd best stay below for a little longer, your grace," advised Emma.

Isabel closed her eyes and swayed slightly before giving an almost imperceptible nod and retreating back down the steps. Anne followed her descent with an unsympathetic gaze.

"Mind your manners, my dear," murmured Emma. "Your sister's a duchess now and must be respected as such."

"She's still my big sister," said Anne, but her expression soon softened. "Come on then, Emma. Shall we go and see what sort of a state the "duchess" and my mother are in?"

Emma gave her a thin smile and followed after her. Anne would swiftly learn that her childhood was coming to an end. The game had changed and it was Emma's role to help her understand how the new game would be played. If she was to protect the young heiress, Emma would need all her wits.

26

7th September 1469 at dusk, outside

Hereford Town

Hal counted to ten as he rode away then stopped to look back: he had given himself about fifty yards. In the fading light he hoped to God he had judged it right. He leapt from the horse, almost falling over as he landed.

"Don't be too hasty, don't be too hasty," he told himself, as Becky struggled to fight off the two men. He wished he could stop his ears to her screams.

"Concentrate, you fool!" he said aloud, as his fingers worked to string the bow.

It seemed an age before he nocked the first arrow. Oh, good Christ! They had her down on her back. He let fly. The first one was easy. He watched it pluck the swordsman off his feet as he nocked the second. The larger man looked up at once, forewarned now. He knew he was a good-sized target and crouched down to pick Becky up and use her as a shield. She kicked and screamed at him but couldn't dislodge his strong arms. Hal loosed his second arrow and ran towards them, trying to put another to his bow as he moved.

"Shit, shit, shit!" he cried as he saw the arrow graze Becky's head and miss the man.

He was barely thirty feet away when the man tossed Becky aside and ran straight at him. Hal stopped, raised the bow and let fly. The arrow struck the oncoming man full in the chest and, from such close range, Hal knew it must kill him but, though it rocked the fellow back for an instant, he kept on coming. Before Hal could reach for another shaft, his victim cannoned into him and knocked him to the ground, pummelling him with his fists. Blow upon blow thudded into his head and body. Hal lay helplessly taking the beating, all the while wondering how the man could still be alive. Then the blows became less frequent and the man coughed and spat out blood over Hal's face. He was still alive, though, and stared down at Hal.

"I'll take you to Hell with me," he whispered, shifting his weight onto Hal's throat. "I can still snap your-"

The body on top of him went still. The man was dead, but not from his arrow. Hal could see the knife point sticking out below the jaw. Becky hovered over them, shaking.

"Holy Mother!" she cried, "Do you know how hard it is… to get a blade through that lot!"

Hal tried to shift the dead weight upon him but he was too weak. Becky crawled down alongside him and pushed with him until between them they rolled the corpse away. She laid her head on Hal's chest and he wrapped an arm around her.

"Are you alright?" he asked.

"Aye, just about. You?"

"Well, I can't see very well… or breathe right… and my ears are still ringing, but mostly just cuts and bruises - big bruises, I think."

She lifted herself up and offered him her hand. With her help, he staggered to his feet and took her in a trembling embrace.

"You fought like a she-wolf," he said proudly.

"As I told you, my mistress taught me a little," she murmured.

"That was a little too close, though," he said softly.

"I thought you were going to leave me," she said, starting to sob against him.

"Never…"

"Never?"

"Oh, I thought about it," he said, "but then I thought of all the grief I'd get from Felix if I lost a horse."

"I should give you a slap for that…" she breathed.

He winced as she laid her hand upon his bruised cheek, but her touch was gentle as she drew his lips to hers. It was a long kiss and after it they stood in silence for a moment, just leaning against each other.

"It's almost dark," he said, breaking the spell.

"Aye, we'd better hurry then, hadn't we?"

He picked up his bow and Becky retrieved her horse. Together they walked to where his horse grazed contentedly and then headed for the gates of Hereford.

"Hold!" yelled Hal, for the town gate was closing as they approached. You never knew with gatekeepers, but Hal was relieved that on this occasion he took pity on them and let them through before the city gates slammed shut. Once in the town they hurried to find an inn with some room. They avoided the grandest establishments as, given the way the pair of them now looked, they could hardly expect to be admitted.

They discovered a place just as the curfew bell stopped tolling. It was a building which had seen better times and Hal wondered if the ramshackle stable would survive the next strong gust of wind. They paid for a bed, expecting to be sharing a room with several others, but found they were lodged in the tiniest chamber at the top of the house. It was gloomy for there was no candle, only a single rush light. The innkeeper brought them a bowl of water, making it clear that it was not part of his usual provision for guests. Hal grinned until Becky started bathing his face.

"You look awful," she said. "Pity, I always thought you used to be quite handsome."

He winced as she moved on to clean the cut on his wrist.

"It's not very deep," she said. "Lady Eleanor's had far worse."

"Well, I suppose she's used to it."

"She doesn't go looking for… well, alright perhaps she does… but she doesn't deserve what happens to her."

"Why are we talking about her?" he asked.

"I don't know," she said. "I suppose, I'm still a bit nervous."

"We're safe now," he said.

"Well… It's a day of firsts for me," said Becky. "Never been to a town before, never been dragged from a horse and half-killed before, never been abandoned by one I'd have called a friend…"

He felt suddenly crushed. "I didn't abandon you!" he protested.

She ignored him. "And never slept in an inn before… with a man I could love and… do you know your mouth's wide open?"

The rush light smouldered out.

27

9th September, south of Gloucester

Will had ridden slowly for the first few miles and then, once the sun was fully up, he pushed his horse harder. He wanted to be well on the way to Hereford before anyone set off after him. He had left it too late to leave, really. Jack would be expecting him to arrive sooner. Will chuckled to himself: Jack was probably even now dreaming up a hundred ways of slowing down the Goldwell's wagon. It might not help though because Will had delayed for so long. In truth, he didn't really want to leave Corve at all - they had been good to him there - nor did he want to leave Becky, or John. Despite what had happened, he did not want to leave his mother either - even if she had become something of a stranger to him. So, he had put off the moment and now his task would be all the harder.

He rested his horse for a while and then pushed on. He had been told that it was safer to travel with others and there were other travellers on the rough tracks south of Corve, especially as he came closer to Hereford. But who amongst all these strangers could he trust? Mostly, the larger groups of travellers scared him to death and he hurtled past them at speed. What he needed was a small family group, perhaps travelling in a wagon - but then wagons moved too slowly.

He had arranged with Jack to meet him at Leominster.

Failing that, he would find him at Hereford, or Gloucester, and the brothers had agreed that if Will did not reach them by the time they stopped at Cirencester, then he would not be coming at all. It had been a terrible moment, he reflected, saying farewell to his brother.

He entered Leominster posing as a messenger, thinking folk might be less inclined to stop him if he would soon be missed - as the bearer of urgent news just might be. He had learned from Jack the names of the inns Felix had recommended to the Goldwells but he found no trace of the family in the town. He also missed them at Hereford and Gloucester too and, as he hurried along the road south to Cirencester, he knew that this was his last chance. Surely he must overtake them soon.

He saw dust in the distance ahead and his hopes soared. He sped up but it was not the wagon he sought - in fact it was not a wagon at all but a single rider on a mule with a pack mule following behind. He buried his disappointment and approached warily. One man on his own might be safer than three or four... or not. He followed the mules, trying to pluck up the courage to speak. After a while he thought better of it - it was too great a risk. It was slowly dawning on him what a dangerous folly he had embarked upon. He was lucky to have survived so far.

He was about to gallop on past when the rider called out to him.

"You going to be staying at my back all the way to Cirencester, boy?" he asked.

Will slowed his horse to a walk, uncertain how to answer.

"Best bring yourself in front of me where I can keep an eye on you!"

Will reasoned that he could probably escape if he had to, for the stranger could hardly chase after him with his mules. This gave him some confidence, so he trotted a little nearer to the rider. He expected to see a wool merchant perhaps but instead he found a scruffy-looking character. He stared at the man for several moments, transfixed: the fellow's left arm ended at the elbow.

"Don't look good, do it?" the rider said cheerfully.

"Does it hurt?" asked Will.

"Not any more, not for fifteen years," replied the stranger. "What's a young lad doing out here on his own, then?"

"A man's business is his own," declared Will, borrowing a phrase he had heard Felix use.

"That may be," replied his fellow traveller, "but a boy's business best be told!"

"I'm a messenger," said Will.

"Are you? Got an important message, have you?"

"Aye," said Will.

"Well then, you're the sorriest messenger I've ever met! What are you wasting time talking to me for?"

Will felt the flush of embarrassment on his cheeks.

"Let's start again then, shall we? You got a name?"

"Will."

"Well, God give you good day, Will. Folk call me Pinner."

"Good day to you, Master Pinner," replied Will, with a grin of relief.

"Now then, if you're not a messenger, what are you doing out here on your own?"

Will hesitated for a moment but the man seemed pleasant enough - and he only had one good arm.

"I'm looking for my brother," he said.

"Hah! And who let you out to look for this brother?"

"No-one…"

Pinner stared at Will for a short while as if making up his mind about something.

"You thirsty?" he asked.

Will nodded.

"And hungry, I should think," observed Pinner. He pulled up and rummaged into a leather bag slung from his saddle. Will was impressed with the way he moved despite his disability. He unearthed a large apple and tossed it to Will. Will caught it deftly and nodded his thanks.

"Want some ale?" asked Pinner.

"Aye!" said Will.

"Yeh, so do I - pity we don't have any!" Pinner cackled. Will grinned back at him.

"So, do you want me to help you find your brother?" asked Pinner.

"Would you?"

"I might - depends if it takes me out of my way. I'm a busy man."

Will could see that the second mule was heavily laden, so perhaps Pinner was more successful than he appeared.

"You can see I've a load to deliver - I'll lose out if I don't, so what's in it for me?"

"I could pay you," said Will, taking out the small purse he had acquired at Corve, "but I haven't got much…"

Pinner waved the purse away.

"Good Christ! Old Pinner take from a young lad? I don't want your coin, Will. But could someone else, your brother perhaps, pay me a little fee for my time - only if it could be spared, though."

"Jack - that's my brother - he's the same age as me but he's travelling with his grandfather and he's a goldsmith! I'm sure he'd pay you a great deal to keep me safe."

"Fair enough then, Will," he said. "Tell me all you know about where they might be. If I can't help, I'm certain I can find someone who'll have spotted them on the road."

Will silently thanked the Lord that he had chanced upon Pinner when there were so many ruffians he might have stumbled into.

THE LAST SHROUD

"I'm sure you'll be well rewarded if you can get me to Jack," he told Pinner.

"Well then Will, this old soldier will do his best to help."

28

9th September 1469, on the Ermine Way

to Cirencester

Hal and Becky spent another day and night in Hereford to make sure they had not somehow missed either Will or the Goldwells. Now it seemed like time wasted, yet he would not have missed that night for all the world. They rode out of Hereford like excited young children, setting off upon a new adventure. They could not stop grinning at each other and rode for a hundred yards or more with Hal still holding her by the hand. He only let go when it became clear that Becky would fall off her horse if he didn't.

"I'm not used to riding," she said. "We mere servants don't get much practice. I don't like it much - my arse is still sore from before!"

"I should have thought a sore arse is the least of your worries," said Hal. "You took a few blows from that great lout."

"And what's more," she said, leaning towards him once more, "a man came into my chamber and had his way with me… stole my virtue away… what other man will touch me now?"

"If any other man touches you, I'll kill him!" declared Hal.

"Well, you'd better make sure you've got your bow," she

scoffed, "because you fight like shit!"

"There were four of them!" laughed Hal.

Their good humour sustained them for several more miles but then worries began to crowd in upon them once more. What if Will had got lost and they were even now leaving him far behind them, or if he had been set upon as they were? As the morning wore on, they began to lose heart.

"We should rest the horses for a while," said Hal.

"And my poor arse…" said Becky.

They sat under a tree in the forest, just off the road which cut a swathe through it. It was an ancient road, they'd been told, but Hal didn't care how old the road was, as long as they found Will somewhere along it.

Becky dozed against him and the swell of her breasts made him want to touch her, kiss her - how could it be that they had shared a roof at Crag Tower for four long years and yet not found each other? Perhaps he was less of a man then… but, whatever the reason, she seemed to see him differently now. Perhaps reason didn't come into it at all…

"What are you thinking?" murmured Becky.

"Ah, you're awake."

"No, I talk in my sleep!"

"I was thinking about you…" said Hal, "thinking your bodice is half unlaced…"

"It was too tight," she said. "Anyway, you should be thinking about Will…"

He sighed. "I haven't forgotten him, Beck. It's a damned long way for a boy to travel without getting into some trouble."

"So what do we do?"

"Only thing we can - keep trying to find the Goldwells. I'm certain he'll be with them by now."

"You're better at fighting than lying, Hal…"

She slowly unwound herself from Hal's body and

stretched out. She stood up gingerly then smiled down at him and offered her hand. He took it and rose up to envelop her once more. She buried her face into his shoulder.

"Tell me we'll find him," she said.

"We'll find him," he said. "We'll find him today."

She gave a long sigh and broke their embrace. "Better get going then, hadn't we?"

She tugged at her bodice and hastily tied it up. Hal saddled the horses and they shared the remains of the oat bread they had bought in Gloucester. Now both their purses were empty; there would be no more nights at an inn. Nevertheless, their horses were fresh and they made good time, passing a number of covered wagons on the road. Hal could see why the road was so much used for the surface was dry and firm for wheels to run on and oxen to walk on.

He noticed that some travellers pulled off to rest up amongst the trees, sometimes well off the road. They were out of sight there and no doubt they hoped they were out of harm's way too. What if the Goldwells had also pulled their wagon off the road? They might ride past and never see it. So many possibilities, so many fears.

"You see that priest or friar ahead," said Becky. She pointed to a figure in black riding a mule. He was about fifty yards ahead of them on the road.

"What of him? He's just a travelling friar."

"He's just come out of the forest onto the road," she said.

"So? He's been having a rest - as we did."

"I'm sure I saw him earlier, just after we left Gloucester. I'd forgotten him until now."

"It's just a friar, Beck - he's the last man we're looking for."

"I'm sure he left the road earlier too…"

"Well, perhaps he just needs to piss a bit more often than most men! Don't trouble with him. Just keep those pretty eyes on the forest for something useful - like a wagon that's pulled over."

"I was only saying what I saw." Becky scowled at him and stuck out her tongue.

"Always the lady…" muttered Hal.

There was a sudden scream from the trees on their left hand and some birds took flight in alarm, black shapes against the blue September sky. Then all was quiet again. Becky and Will pulled up and exchanged a glance. A single cry, thought Hal, but sharp enough to pierce a heart. There were others on the road and some nearby also stopped in their tracks. But when the scream died, they continued on their way. Far ahead of them, the friar too brought his mule to a halt and stared back briefly before resuming his journey.

"It could have been Sarah," said Becky.

"It could have been any woman…"

"Aye, any woman in trouble…" said Becky. She nudged her mount off the road towards the forest. Hal followed and prepared to string his bow.

"You're right, I suppose," he said "we can't ignore it."

Becky drew out her knife.

"Stay close," he warned, "perhaps this isn't such a good idea."

He moved ahead of her and walked his horse with caution through the trees. If someone was in trouble, the worst thing they could do was to ride in blind. Then another scream came… and another… and this time the cries did not let up.

Becky set off past him at a canter.

"God's breath!" said Hal and set off after her. In no time he lost sight of her and just had to follow the cries - cries that grew fainter and then ceased with awful suddenness. He stopped to listen for a moment, cursing Becky's wilful rashness. After a moment he heard sounds of a struggle and then a wail of frustrated anger that he would know anywhere.

He set off once more and found them in a clearing. He took all in at a glance: a wagon pulled up under the trees - two men ransacking it; a woman leant back against it - bodice and kirtle torn apart, throat slashed; Becky's mare standing still - Becky rolling in the grass with a short, squat man; two other men lying on the ground - dead or wounded he couldn't tell which.

He brought his bow to bear but could not use it without risking hitting Becky. One of the men on the wagon saw him and drew his knife. Hal loosed the arrow at him instead and saw it find its target. Then he threw down the bow and vaulted from his horse to help Becky. He drew out his sword and ran at the pair.

"Beck! Move away!" he shouted. Her opponent though was quicker and made sure he held her in front of him. She put up a struggle, kicking behind her at his shins.

"Leave her!" ordered Hal, "or I'll kill you."

"Alright, there you are then," replied the man and pushed her towards him, slashing at her as he did so. She grunted and fell into Hal's arms.

"Can you get to your horse?" he said.

She nodded and he released her. Only then did he see the blood on her kirtle and glared at her attacker. Becky, her face pale, stumbled over to her horse and leant against it.

The surviving man on the wagon jumped to the ground, brandishing a long knife. Hal held his sword high, hoping he looked like a skilled swordsman. They had him between them. It was an impasse: they dared not get too close and he could not fight the pair of them at once.

Then Becky took a step towards them. "No!" he told her. "Stay back!"

But her movement was enough to distract one of his opponents and he took his chance. Crouching low he lunged forward at the other and cut his thigh. The man gasped and drew back whilst his comrade then hurled himself at Hal, who hastily brought his sword around. The man ran straight onto it, the blade carving through his shirt into his ribs. Neither had sustained a fatal blow, Hal suspected, but it was enough to send them off into the trees.

Becky staggered to him and he helped her to sit down against a broad oak. He quickly examined the deep gash just below her shoulder, where a little blood still seeped out.

"It's not so bad," he said gently.

"It's not your shoulder," she grumbled. "It fucking hurts, Hal!"

"You've only lost a bit of blood," he said.

"I'd sooner not have lost any!" But she forced a smile and patted his hand. "I know," she said, "it was my own fault… "

Hal heard a movement behind him and swung around to see one of those on the ground trying to get up. From his attire, Hal doubted he was one of the robbers.

"You alright?" Hal asked.

The man ignored him, his eyes fixed upon the dead woman at the wagon. He crawled across to her and began to sob at her feet.

"You should go to him," said Becky.

"You first," said Hal. "You're still alive."

He untied her bodice and his hand brushed her breast. She pulled a face.

"I need to bind up the wound," he explained.

"Men always find some excuse for a grope," she said.

They helped the survivor of the attack, tending to his wounds and lifting the two corpses - his son and wife it turned out - into the wagon. Instead of completing his journey to sell his wool in Gloucester he would return to his village and bury those he loved.

Thus it was after midday before they rejoined the road, much chastened by what had happened. Hal could tell by Becky's quiet manner that the wound was hurting her more than she let on.

"You've got a nasty one, love. It's just as well we're only going to Cirencester tonight."

"How far is it, do you think?" she asked.

"Can't be more than two or three hours' ride," he said, "but you're taking a rest every mile or so - I don't want you opening up that wound."

"That poor man," said Becky.

"You should worry about yourself," said Hal.

"But to lose… when I think of young Will on his own, Hal… and what may befall him?"

It was no good telling her not to worry, he knew that - for he was worried too. Will must surely be on this road somewhere for he didn't believe the Goldwells' oxen-drawn wagon could possibly have got any further than Cirencester.

"You go along at whatever pace is best for you," he said.

She smiled at his feeble attempt to change the subject. True to his word, he pulled off into the trees not long after and helped her to dismount.

"Sit and rest. At least for a little while," he ordered. He sat her down and paced through the trees.

"Come and sit with me," she said.

He came to her, but his reluctance must have shown.

She held up her hand. "Right then. Come on: help me up."

"You've only been sat there a moment!" he replied.

The hand remained where it was in mid-air and finally he took it.

"You should rest," he pleaded.

"What? When you're stalking about, too worried to sit?"

she retorted. "Don't you think I'm as terrified as you, Hal, that if we waste another moment, we'll be too late? This wound's not going to kill me - I'll have time to rest enough when we've caught up with Will. Now let's get on."

So once more they returned to the Ermine Way and he noticed that Becky rode a little faster than before. Christ's blood! Before, he had only Will to worry about!

They rode only a further mile or so before they came upon the black friar once again.

"I thought he'd be further ahead of us by now," Hal mused.

"He's off into the forest again!" grumbled Becky. "I think you're right - he keeps going for a quick piss!"

But Hal suddenly stopped and stared at the friar. He passed into the trees but this time he was not alone. "Can you see the one with him?" he asked her.

"No, but perhaps they're taking a piss together," she replied, then she noticed Hal was not smiling. "It's just another traveller, Hal, isn't it?"

But Hal's keen eyes had noticed that the mounted traveller with him was much smaller than most.

29

9th September 1469, on the Ermine Way

to Cirencester

Will was feeling weary. The road seemed endless with its thick forest on either side. They were moving slowly at the pace of Pinner's mules and all Will could think of was the time he was wasting. Pinner's 'help' had so far consisted only of a succession of stories about his exploits during the French wars. Will liked a good adventure story but he had long since had his fill. Now he was just impatient to move faster.

"You said you'd ask folk along the road," he said, "but you haven't asked anyone yet."

"Now you see, young Will," explained Pinner, "the secret in finding someone along any road is to know who to ask."

"And who's that?" asked Will.

"Well, take that friar up ahead with his mule."

"Aye."

"Well, that friar travels this road a lot and I've seen him many a time - talked to him as well. Believe me, if your brother's wagon is on this road, the friar will know it."

Will was puzzled because on the face of it, it seemed that Pinner had the answer to all his troubles, yet the look on Pinner's face did not seem quite right - he looked very serious.

"So," said Will, "we just have to ask this friar and he'll know?"

"Oh, he'll know," said Pinner, "but we aren't going to ask him."

"But he's just there," cried Will, "what could be easier?"

"No, we'll find others to ask…"

"I don't understand."

"I know you don't and that's what I'm saying: if you ask the wrong man, you can get into worse shit than you're in already."

But Will had stopped listening to Pinner. All he could see was that the friar would bring his troubles to a speedy end. He spurred his horse forward and, despite Pinner's shouts, he hurried to overtake the friar. It wouldn't take long since the friar was only riding a mule like Pinner.

The friar glanced back at him, his attention no doubt attracted by Pinner's continuing cries. Then the friar darted to the left towards the forest.

"Shit!" muttered Will, "Pinner's scared him off with his shouting!"

He pushed his mount to a gallop, anxious not to let the friar slip away into the trees. He caught up with him just before he could escape off the road. The friar stopped and regarded him sternly.

"What, boy?" he said. "Would you attack God's messenger on the road?"

"No Friar!" Will cried. "I need your help!"

"Help? What help?"

"I'm looking for… a wagon… with my brother in it… and his family!"

"Steady lad, you're spitting out up words like a mouthful of hot pottage!" complained the friar.

"A wagon," said Will trying to catch his breath, "have you seen one?"

The friar laughed. "A wagon? I've seen at least ten

wagons so far today, lad."

"There's a boy, and a woman, and a couple of riders…"

He paused for the friar's expression had changed.

"Anyone else looking for your wagon, boy?" he asked.

"Well, there's Pinner," he pointed back to where the old soldier was hurrying up behind them.

"Pinner? I know Pinner," said the friar with distaste. "You've fallen in with a bad sort there, lad. Come, I'll get you away from him and we'll see if we can find your wagon."

Will glanced back at Pinner. He might be a 'bad sort' but Pinner had done him no harm.

"Do you want my aid or not, boy?" demanded the friar, "I can't waste my time here - I've friar's work to do!"

He set off into the trees and Will followed with a final backward look at Pinner who was waving his good arm frantically. Will smiled. If the old man wasn't careful, he'd fall off his mule. He turned back to where the friar had disappeared into the forest, and hurried along until he came across the mule tethered to sapling. He was wondering where the friar had gone when a quarterstaff cracked him on the head.

§§§

"Do you think it could be Will?" asked Becky.

But the friar and his companion did not reappear.

"Shit!" said Hal. He was in two minds: he did not want to leave Becky but if it was Will then he should be going after him now or he might never find him again in the forest.

"Go!" she said. "Go! I've still got my knife - I'll follow at my pace. I'll be fine. You go find out if it's my Will."

He gave her a kiss and then rode off. He noticed another traveller on a mule leave the road where Will had gone. Hal's mount was fast if he pushed it hard and now he did, hurtling into the trees and quickly catching up with the mule rider. He pulled up sharply in front of him and drew his sword.

"You! You followed a boy off the road - what do you want with him?" he demanded.

"I could ask you that," was the stranger's surly response.

"You've a bold tongue for a man with only one arm," said Will. "I can see how you might have lost the other one!"

He moved in closer, his sword point raised. "What's the boy to you?" he asked.

"Will's my friend," replied the other.

"Will? You're lying. He's no friends on this road," declared Hal.

"We met on the road - he seemed a good lad - what's he to you then?"

"If it's the same Will, then he's my friend too," said Hal.

"I'm Pinner," said the stranger, "and if you're truly the boy's friend then you'll help me find him - the friar's got him."

"I saw him follow the friar," said Hal. "Why should I be more worried about a friar than you?"

"Why? Because he's not a friar!" said Pinner. "Now get after him. I'll leave my mules and follow you on foot."

Will hesitated, but then he recalled the friar's earlier behaviour - leaving the road but ignoring the screams for help… Pinner had already slid off the mule and donned a thick leather jerkin. Now he reached into one of the bags slung from his mule's back.

"Are you coming or not?" he said, "Because I'm going after that lad - now!"

Will turned his mount into the trees and set off on one of the forest trails. He heard Pinner padding along in his wake. Despite his concerns, he forced himself to take his time - if he rushed headlong after Will, he might make matters even worse. He needed to keep his wits sharp and his senses alert.

He was surprised to find that Pinner was almost keeping up with him, jogging just behind him. They entered a large forest glade and Hal pulled up: he had no idea which way to go.

"Christ's blood! Where are they?"

"Hush, man!" hissed Pinner. "Use your ears!"

Hal listened in silence. He could hear something, raised voices perhaps.

"Do you hear?" asked Pinner.

"That could be from the road…" said Hal.

"Well, it's not - but I feared as much. Can you use that sword?"

"Well enough."

"There's a place the friar uses - he has several along this road in the woods. It's far enough off the road to draw in foolish folk who have something worth stealing…"

"You know the place?"

"I know a few of them, but we'll have to be careful. You don't cross the friar twice."

"Careful," agreed Hal, "but swift!"

Pinner nodded. "Follow me, it's not far and you'd best leave your horse here."

A host of unwanted thoughts crossed Hal's mind as he now followed Pinner through the trees: by leaving his mount behind he was putting himself in a weaker position - and Pinner could be leading him straight into a trap. Who was the more trustworthy: an old cripple or a man of the cloth? All thoughts were suspended when Pinner slowed up and Hal began to hear the voices much more clearly.

They crept closer and Hal knew what to expect for he had seen it before. There would be a clearing, a wagon perhaps, men killed, wounded or perhaps still fighting. Was Will caught up in the middle of it all or was he safe with the friar? He inspected the contents of his arrow bag: four only…

Pinner came to an abrupt halt and crouched low in the cover of some clumps of tall grass and bracken. Hal squatted beside him and drank in the scene. His head dropped for they had come too late: whatever fighting there had been was over.

30

9th September 1469, on the Ermine Way

Hal cast a bleak eye over the scene: Sarah and Jack were being held, John Goldwell was on his knees on the ground whilst two of the men attempted to prise open his strongbox. Hal's expression hardened as he saw that his own two men were both down and Will lay motionless on the grass before the wagon.

"I've had enough of these thieves and murderers," he breathed. "Are you with me in this, or not?"

Beside him, kneeling in the bracken, Pinner gave a solemn nod. "Can you hit anything with that bow?" he whispered.

"I can hit everything with my bow," said Hal.

Pinner drew out a knife.

"Christ's blood! You'll need to get in damned close to use that!" said Hal.

Pinner grinned.

"I'll take three," said Hal, "the ones holding Sarah and Jack and the friar standing by his mule. Can you get to the fellows trying to open the chest?"

"I'll go in as soon as your first man falls," said Pinner.

Hal wiped the sweat from his hands and nocked an arrow. He had pressed three more into the earth close by. If he missed with those… well, he had no more. He watched Pinner creeping nimbly around the clearing. When Pinner stopped, Hal took aim.

The thieves attacking the box had stopped and one of them now seized Goldwell's arm to pull him up. Voices were raised louder. Sarah, who had seemed calm, now began to shout and kick out at her captor. The friar said something Hal couldn't make out and then everyone seemed to be on the move.

"Shit!" muttered Hal, struggling to choose a target.

Sarah was abruptly knocked to the ground and Hal saw his chance. He loosed his first arrow and the man who had struck Sarah was driven back against the wagon. At once Pinner was on his way towards the wagon, blade in hand.

Hal dared not rush his second arrow and was relieved to see it strike home: the man holding Jack released him and clutched at his breast. The thieves by the chest threw Goldwell aside and leapt off the wagon. Pinner had stopped - what was the old fool doing? Hal watched dumbfounded as Pinner threw his knife at one man and then in the blink of an eye produced a second knife which soon thudded into his second opponent.

In his surprise Hal lost sight of the friar, who had dragged his mule into the trees. Well, he might escape but most of the thieves were down. Hal ran into the clearing, a third arrow nocked ready. Sarah had gathered up Jack and together they were lifting Will up.

"You were supposed to get the friar!" said Pinner.

"Well, you distracted me," retorted Hal. "Why didn't you tell me what you were going to do?"

"I'm called Pinner - I thought you might have worked out why!"

"Well, can you go after him?"

"Not a chance! He knows these woods like he was born in them. I'd never find him. He's gone!"

John Goldwell sat against the wagon, head in hands. "It was terrible, Hal!" he wailed. "Thank God you came when you did - or we'd have been cut to pieces... cut to pieces."

Hal looked beyond the goldsmith and shook his head. He bent down to examine Walter Close and found that his throat had been cut. Walter... that was hard to take. He moved to the back of the wagon where John Long lay. He looked as if he had been beaten to death but he lifted his arm as Hal reached him.

"God's breath, John, you look as if the oxen trampled over you. Any broken bones? Can you move?"

Long stared down glumly at Walter Close then got gingerly to his feet and leant on the wagon. All his limbs seemed to be sound but he winced at every slight movement.

"Thank God they didn't get into the strongbox," observed Goldwell.

Hal gave him a bitter look and went to see if the others had any injuries.

"How in God's name did you find us here, Hal?" asked Sarah.

"You've Jack's brother to thank for that. If we hadn't been following him, we'd never have found you."

For the second time in the day, Hal found himself lifting a corpse into a wagon. He prayed it would be the last time. They took the wagon and horses back nearer to the edge of the road, keeping a watchful eye lest the friar should reappear.

Becky was waiting by Pinner's mules and squealed with relief when they came out of the forest. Hal hugged her close.

"Hey! Mind my shoulder, Hal," she grumbled. "I really thought I'd lost you this time!"

Will ran to her and she folded him into her arms, weeping at the sight of him. The wagon stopped at the edge of the trees and Goldwell got down.

Hal looked at them all in turn and then back at Will and

Becky.

"Well, what now?" asked Becky with a nervous smile.

Hal smiled back. She was such a quick wench, he thought.

"John Long's taking Walter's body back to Gloucester, and then maybe Quenhull - it's nearer than Corve…"

"I could take Will to Quenhull with them," she said.

"No," he said. "There's a reason that Lord Elder didn't take any of the women to Quenhull yet. He's in the heat of the fire there."

She gave him another smile. "Well, I've never been to London," she said softly.

"Excuse me," said Goldwell, "but I think such decisions are up to me, lad."

Hal wanted to ignore the pompous fool but he turned to look him in the eye. "Only if you want to die on your own, Master Goldwell."

31

11th September 1469, at Caversham in

Oxfordshire

Emma was weary from the ride and welcomed the sight of the bridge over the Thames that promised to carry them across to the manor. Their party was large with several wagons to carry their goods - one of which carried the Countess of Warwick and her elder daughter, the new Duchess of Clarence. Lady Anne, however, preferred to ride and so Emma rode with her but she cast more than one wistful glance at the covered wagon.

They were surrounded by men at arms and archers supplied by the Duke of Clarence, though there had been a day's wait at Southampton. Emma was relieved that someone at least had decided to meet them. The countess did not remark upon the absence of her husband's men, but her thunderous expression made it clear that she would be talking to the earl about it upon her arrival in Warwick. All of which assumed that the earl would actually be at Warwick to greet them.

The procession of wagons and horses came to a halt at the southern end of the bridge. After a few moments, the countess was handed down from the wagon, followed by her daughter, Isabel. Both looked pale and tired.

"Come," ordered the countess, "we shall all walk across

together."

Emma dismounted and followed Lady Anne who joined her mother and sister as they walked past the first chapel on the south bank and then across the stone bridge. On the north side of the bridge was a larger chapel dedicated to the Blessed Mary. Here the ladies prayed at the chapel for it was very dear to Lady Warwick. Emma had never seen it before and knelt in awe before the statue of the Holy Mother crowned with gold.

Whilst they worshipped, the guards led the wagons and horses across the bridge. They then resumed their journey, turning east from the bridge to follow a long lane beside the large open field stretching up the gentle slope away from the riverside meadow. Soon they passed a watermill and a scattering of stone buildings came into view.

Emma took an instant liking to the manor house at Esthorpe. It looked old but safe, raised up above the wetlands around it and heavily fortified against attack. It reminded her a little of her first home, Elder Hall, where she had once been mistress. The river lay close by, no more than a mile or so distant, and a stream fed the wide moat that surrounded the manor. She nodded to herself in quiet satisfaction: she would feel safe enough here.

As always, Lady Anne was keen to explore the manor and its gardens at once though Emma would rather have rested, or bathed. Her legs were stiff and she ached all over. She could still feel the salt in her hair, though she had kept her head covered throughout the journey. She wondered how the salt seemed to penetrate all her clothing.

"My lady," said Emma, "would you not prefer to change out of those dirty clothes?"

"Later, dear Emma," replied Lady Anne, continuing her progress unchecked across the yard.

Anne had taken to addressing her as 'dear Emma' for the past year or so - even before she had charge of the young girl's growing household. Now Anne used the term habitually but Emma was never entirely sure whether it was a term of endearment or ridicule.

Anne entered the building and at once disappeared into a warren of narrow passages. Emma, trying to absorb a flurry of instructions from the steward about who would sleep in which chamber, momentarily lost sight of her. She was obliged to explore some of the passages but she could not find the girl anywhere and her irritation increased.

She came to an open gate - a postern gate for the manor house. She passed through it already rehearsing the scolding words she would use when she eventually located her errant charge. It was just too much to be chasing around the estate at their journey's end - too much. Soon she was muttering angrily to herself for the girl was still nowhere to be seen. She would now have to confess to the countess that she had, at least for the time being, lost her daughter. Then she heard a footstep behind her.

She stopped abruptly and turned around. "There you are…" she began, but it was not Anne. She gasped then stuttered as she tried to say his name. She felt faint, her legs losing their strength as she looked him in the face. It was all she could do to remain standing.

He smiled at her and she felt the blood drain from her cheeks.

"Thomas… Thomas Gate," she murmured.

"My lady Emma," he said.

Her voice was a hoarse whisper. "You should be dead - on the word of the earl - you should be dead…"

He offered her his hand for support and without thinking she took it then dropped it as if it were a hot coal. She pushed past him and retreated to the nearest wall, pressing her back against it.

"How… Thomas?"

"Thomas Gate is truly dead," he said softly. "It was

never my own name…"

"But it was not your name that did such evil deeds," she breathed. "It was you."

"It was Joan who was to blame for what happened at the end at Yoredale! I tried to save the girl Agnes, tried to save your sister…"

"It was your men who killed and maimed."

He shocked her then by dropping to his knees on the stone flags before her.

"It was Joan, and her man, Weaver - you know better than most the evil that witch could do!"

Emma did not reply. He was right in that; she had witnessed the woman's cruelty herself - yet how easy it was for him to lay all the blame on his dead wife.

"I shan't rise until you forgive me my part in all that misery," said Thomas.

"Forgive you? Then you'll spent the rest of your days kneeling," she said, but her voice carried no fire; there was no venom in her words, only regret. "And what are you even doing here, in Oxfordshire?"

"I'm still Warwick's man," he said. "I command the escort to take the countess north. I came straight from London as soon as I had word that you'd already left Southampton."

He looked up at her, meeting her eyes and she recalled another moment when he had looked up at her, lifting her down from her horse at Yoredale Castle.

"If you're no longer Thomas," she said, "then who are you? What are you?"

For the first time, he seemed to hesitate.

"I bear the same name as you, my lady."

"You lie! You're not an Elder!"

"No, but neither are you, Lady Radcliffe."

His blunt reminder stung her… dismayed her somehow.

"You are not a Radcliffe either," she replied, but then

realised she would not know if he was or not.

"My name is Sir Robert Radcliffe."

The name alone sent a chill of fear through her - if he had known, he would have chosen another name.

"Robert Radcliffe," she breathed, "how I hated that man… His name only serves to revive the most terrible memories for me: he was the author of all our troubles."

"He was my father. I'm his bastard…"

Emma shook her head. "Well, well… but of course you are - that makes a deal of sense, I suppose."

"I may be his bastard but I'm the only man of Radcliffe blood left alive," he declared.

Emma was recovering now from the initial shock, gaining renewed confidence.

"No, you're not: my son Richard carries the Radcliffe name. He's the undisputed heir so, if you're hoping to get the Radcliffe lands, you're going to be disappointed."

He remained on his knees and smiled up at her.

"Well, my lady, that was true but… of late his grace, the king, has seen fit to disinherit your son and grant me all my father's lands."

Emma was speechless: he surely must be lying.

"And," he continued, "all your brother's lands in Yoredale."

Emma chewed at her lip in frustration. The Radcliffe and Elder lands, all in this man's hands; it was unthinkable yet he could not hope to sustain such a great lie.

"You're not making it easy for me to allow you off your knees," she said coldly.

"I understand," he said, "but I didn't come to bring you any further troubles. The feud between the Radcliffes and Elders is over - dead and finally buried in the ruins of Yoredale Castle. I want no more of it… I want no enmity between us."

"Between us? There is no 'us'! There has never been any

'us'!"

"My lady?" Lady Anne's light voice cut through her thoughts. The girl was framed in the postern gateway - she had been inside all along!

Emma pushed herself off the wall and hurried to her. Then she turned back to Robert who was still on his knees.

"Oh, get up!" she said and ushered a startled Lady Anne through the gateway.

DEREK BIRKS

239

PART THREE: THE RULE OF LAW

DEREK BIRKS

32

Michaelmas: 29th September 1469, at

Quenhull

All morning they had been arriving in their scores. It was not just the lords themselves but the retinues they brought with them - even though they knew that none of their armed men would be allowed into the castle. Yet, in all conscience, Ned could not blame them for travelling well-protected, such was the lawlessness any traveller faced. They all feared some sort of ruse or trap - and they were not alone in that. He had prepared everything with Spearbold and Holton so that nothing was left to chance and every possible problem foreseen, notably treachery. These were men he did not know and he had yet to find out how they would react to his judgements. He did not trust them any more than they trusted him.

He stared down from the old square tower which joined the south and west walls. Below him beside the dry moat, was a great throng of men, colours flying and badges prominent for all to see. He could hear their laughter and shouts of approval when one man took on another in some trifling trial of strength or wit. It amused him to see them all mingling together like old friends. Every landholder would want his men at arms to keep to themselves yet there they all were below, swapping new boasts and old stories.

If it came to it, each man would fight for his lord, but these men were cut from the same cloth. Many were probably born within 10 miles of Quenhull. Who was Ned Elder to them? Did he pay them, or supply them, or employ their daughters in his household? No, he did not. He was the outsider here, the alien - with his voice that jarred their southern ears and his men who mostly hailed from the far away dales of Yorkshire.

His attention was drawn then to a column of men who appeared out of the trees down by the river: Sir Roger Cullen's retinue. So, at last, the former royal steward had deigned to arrive. Ned was not surprised Cullen had brought a good number of men with him but it would gain him nothing for none of them would accompany him into the castle.

Croft joined him at the tower wall. "There's a lot of them," he observed.

"Aye," agreed Ned, "and your job is to make sure they don't get in."

"I know, my lord. I have archers on all the ramparts, men on the stairwells, and we have the mighty Bear below with a score of men at the gates."

"The postern?" asked Ned.

"Sir Ralph holds there with several of his men - all is shut up tight."

Ned sighed. He had rarely felt so nervous. He was not used to giving justice except to his own tenants or men at arms - and that was different. They knew him.

Spearbold clambered breathlessly to the top of the steps. "All is prepared, my lord," he announced. "Sir Roger's arrival completes the gathering."

"The bishop's representative?"

"Seated on the dais, as you asked. He'll be able to give

the bishop a first-hand report of what is done today."

"Good. And you have all the documents ready?"

Spearbold grinned. "Aye, lord - everything and everyone is ready - all we need now is the presence of our judge!"

Ned gave him a tired smile and went to the tower steps. At the top he paused and took Croft by the shoulder. "The hall doors are barred from the inside?"

"Yes, lord, all done - and all else that you required: men where they should be, doors closed if they should be…"

"Aye, I know, just…" He set off down the steps past the castle's small chapel and almost stopped there to offer yet another prayer but he had visited it twice already this morning. He carried on, arriving at the small gallery that overlooked the hall. There stood one of Croft's men at arms, alert and watchful. Ned clapped him on the back and walked on past, down the last flight of steps, broader than the rest, into the body of the hall.

Spearbold followed him down the steps and sat at a table nearby where a large sheaf of letters and other assorted scrolls lay ready. Elsewhere in the hall were servants with ale and the remains of the food offered as refreshment when men arrived. There were no armed men in the body of the hall for he had not wanted his tribunal to seem to rely upon force. So the lords had left their arms outside the gates and his own men were outside the doors or above in the gallery.

He smiled to see Holton on the dais, an imposing figure, as tall as any man there. Ned glanced at the bishop's man and was horrified to find that he had forgotten the cleric's name. Well, no matter, he was just an observer - and he looked the part: a well-fed observer, Ned noted, well-girthed and sweating heavily.

Ned stepped onto the raised platform and Holton stood aside with a slight bow to let him take charge. The whole room fell silent as he surveyed the assembly. The men before him held most of the land west of the Severn, from Gloucester in the south to Worcester in the north, and almost as far as Hereford in the west. True, some were hardly masters of what they held as clients of either Clarence or Warwick. Yet, they were here and he, in King Edward's name, was going to tell them what would happen now.

He was about to speak when Sir Roger Cullen rose from his prominent seat in the front rank.

"Sir Roger?" said Ned, feeling his hackles rise.

"I would address a word to these good men, Lord Elder - with your permission, of course."

"No, Sir Roger, not yet," Ned replied, not troubling to disguise his irritation at the interruption. "You'll have every chance to speak later."

Sir Roger's eyes swept around the room as if weighing up the strength of any likely support. Ned knew his game: he wanted to take control of the gathering - well he would not.

Sir Roger nodded to him and sat down with good grace, which surprised Ned a little. Whatever Sir Roger was doing, he was doing for a reason and submission was not Sir Roger's way. Ned suspected his purpose when he tried to remember what he had been about to say. Sir Roger knew he was unused to such situations and was trying to unsettle him - and he was succeeding.

"My lords," began Ned, "I've invited you here to see justice done and to show you that I act for the king, not for myself."

Sir Roger suddenly broke into a noisy laugh.

"Your pardon. Lord Elder," he said swiftly, "I couldn't help myself…"

He left the words hanging in the air for Ned to grapple with or ignore as he chose.

Ned made a point of ignoring him. "Many of you have

brought grievances to my attention in the past month - serious complaints against the previous king's steward here, Sir Roger Cullen."

Sir Roger stood up at once and raised his arms aloft as if acknowledging some great feat of arms. Then, chest thrust out like a proud cockerel, he grinned at the lords.

Ned glared at him and he sat down with a mock bow.

"The grievances," continued Ned, "will be read aloud so that no man can be in any doubt what's happening here."

"I assure you, Lord Elder, no-one will mistake what happens here," Sir Roger said in a whisper loud enough to carry all around the chamber.

"You need to be silent, Sir Roger, whilst the charges are read," said Ned crossly, yet even his curt reprimand sounded hollow.

"I shall be silent, my lord…your grace… your… whatever you please."

Ned gave Spearbold a sign to begin and he started on the list:

"Article 1: It is claimed that Sir Roger Cullen did order the confiscation of some estates previously held by Sir Thomas-"

"Tell me: is this a long list?" Sir Roger interrupted once more. "I do have other business today."

Ned observed a few chuckles at that and ground out a response. "You've no other business today, Sir Roger, save this."

"What? The false words of liars and thieves?" cried Sir Roger. He remained seated but at once several of the lords stood up to support him.

"This is not justice!" shouted one.

"Lord Elder has no authority here!" another called out.

It seemed to Ned that in the blink of an eye order turned to uproar in the hall. More men began arguing furiously as he attempted to regain control.

"My lords!" he bellowed but to no avail as angry voices echoed around the chamber.

Ned looked towards Sir Roger and found him sitting quietly at ease amid the chaos, smiling back at Ned. Then Holton was by Ned's side with a staff in his hand. He banged the length of ash down onto the dais once and men broke off their arguments. His formidable presence had the desired effect and Ned gave him a tight smile of gratitude. Some of those standing sat back down on their benches. They had gone to the brink of disorder - it had been close, Ned thought, but order had been restored. He nodded his thanks to Holton and waited for the assembly to return to silence.

Then, out of the corner of his eye, he saw Spearbold get up and throw himself to the floor. At first Ned thought he had imagined it, but there was also a sudden rumble of dismay from the benches in front of him. The servants beyond the assembly were running towards the barred doors. Holton was at Ned's elbow, trying to tell him something. There were renewed shouts from the lords in the hall and cries of "Traitor!"

Ned swivelled to his left where Spearbold lay on the floor yelling at him. Several men had come in through the kitchens: there were four of them, armed with crossbows. And there was Sir Roger Cullen, still sitting, still smiling.

Ned watched powerless as the four crossbows were levelled at him.

33

29th September 1469, at Warwick Castle

At Michaelmas, the entourage eventually arrived at Warwick where Emma threw herself into reorganising Lady Anne's household to match her elevated status. The young girl was now the wealthiest heiress in the land, so her household expanded to include several more chambers. More chambers meant more servants, for the lady must look and act the part. Emma immersed herself in the task, glad of the distraction from the other matter which had given her sleepless nights from the moment she had seen Sir Robert at Esthorpe. Unfortunately, he too was now at Warwick with his small band of rather intimidating men.

Mercifully, she had been too busy with her duties to dwell too much upon Robert during her waking hours and, for his part, he had left her alone, for which she was heartily grateful. Even so, that did not dispel her concerns if what he had told her was true. To lose her inheritance… what would become of her son - eight years old now and ready to be sent to one of the great houses? If King Edward could strip the Elders of all their lands then how far had Ned fallen from favour? She had hoped by putting clear distance between herself and her brother and sister that she would not fall if they were condemned. Yet, Robert Radcliffe's reappearance had somehow made her feel more an Elder than a Radcliffe.

It was several days after their return when Robert asked to see her. His request was polite, charming even - as she knew he could be - so she agreed to meet him just once so that she could banish him from her forever. The very sight of him overwhelmed her, conjuring up forgotten terrors. She burst into tears and he was at her side at once, supporting her by the arm, begging forgiveness.

"You're beyond forgiveness!" she cried.

He fell upon his knees again. "Lady, no-one is beyond forgiveness…"

"Oh, get up!" she said.

Robert rose awkwardly.

Emma turned her back on him. "I can't forgive you," she declared, "no matter if you beg me forever! Please… please, take this as my final answer."

Even then he seemed undaunted by her utter rejection, seemed almost to ignore it.

"One day," he said in a quiet voice, "you'll need a champion."

"I don't need a champion - and I don't need you."

"But one day, you will." He smiled - she wished he would stop doing that for it made her feel strange.

"What about your dear son, my lady? How old is he now?"

"He's almost eight."

"High time he was sent from your side then," said Sir Robert, "and of course, with no inheritance now…"

Emma gave a sigh of resignation. "Say what you want, Sir Robert, apart from forgiveness, and then you must go."

"I'm offering a way out of your troubles-"

"Troubles of your making!" she retorted.

"A way out for you and your children," he continued.

"I've no need of your charity in any case," said Emma. "I'm mistress of Lady Anne Neville's household; I neither need, nor want, anything from you!"

"But your children…"

The man was a killer, Emma reminded herself, with no scruples at all. He was all charm and no substance. She wrestled aside her strong desire to slap him across the face, but only for her son's sake, she told herself.

"You're a widow, my lady - you should marry again."

"Marriage? You're more of a fool than I took you for," she declared. "I can't think of anything in all Christendom that would persuade me to marry you."

"Well, perhaps not, my lady… but I can."

He was so infuriatingly confident. How in God's name could he imagine that she would even consider marrying him?

"You would be a wealthy lady once again," he said.

"I've an income to match my position - more than enough for my needs!" she replied.

"Aye, my lady, but what about your son's needs? As my wife, you could place him in a noble household-"

"I can do that now - I'm in Warwick's household! I'm valued, trusted. The countess suggests that there may be a place for Richard with Lord Thomas Stanley, or his brother William."

"The Stanleys? Well perhaps, but Warwick is playing a dangerous game with his king - what if he loses? Without him, there is no household. The Stanleys would not take your son and who would you look to then?"

"You speak of 'what if this, what if that'… but if Warwick falls, you fall too."

"I tell you this, my lady: I'll not be dragged down with any lord."

"No," she said, "because that would require loyalty and no-one could accuse you of that, Sir Robert."

He gave a slight shake of the head, still wearing that irritating smile.

"Take your time, my lady," he said as he left her, "but not too much time, eh?"

"Don't bother to ask me again!" she called after him.

She watched him go with a kind of fascination. Once she would have fallen for him, believed his boasts and promises, but not now. There had been too many disappointments, too many scars that only God could heal.

§§§

Robert had hardly left Emma before he was accosted by a man whose breathless manner and dusty clothes marked him out as a messenger. It was, he thought, one of the men Hooper had left at Middleham.

"Sir Robert, Sir Robert!" he cried.

"What, man? Calm yourself," said Robert, "let's not draw so much attention, shall we?"

He drew the man into a recess below the steps. "Now, what's so urgent?"

The messenger gulped down a breath. "The king, Sir Robert... The king is in York."

"Very well, he's in York - is the earl with him?"

"Aye, he is."

Robert relaxed a little hearing that. "What is the king doing at York?" he asked.

"I think he's seeing some rebels executed, lord."

Robert froze. "What rebels?"

"Lancastrians, my lord - the name Humphrey Neville was mentioned."

Robert breathed another sigh of relief - for a moment he thought that Warwick's ship had foundered, but no, just some fools rising on behalf of the old king - now, if there was a lost cause, that was surely it!

It took a few moments for Robert to grasp it, but then he saw that his hopes were lost - suddenly, brutally lost. For, if the king was no longer held at Middleham, how could Warwick ensure that he remained within his power?

The answer was all too simple: he couldn't. The king was free and if that was the case Robert could forget about keeping the Elder estates for long.

It was time to put other plans in motion. Sadly, Lady Emma Elder would have to wait for it seemed he must revisit Benjamin Warner.

"Find Hooper," he ordered the messenger. "I want all the men mounted and ready to leave here by noon."

34

Michaelmas: 29th September 1469, at

Quenhull

Croft was on the rampart above the main gates with half a dozen archers. All was calm: Bear was below in the courtyard with about a third of the castle garrison, the motley collection of retainers outside the gates were still gaming or talking. Occasionally a scuffle broke out but it always came to a swift end. Croft took a particular interest in Cullen's men for if any were likely to cause trouble it would be them. Yet they seemed as relaxed as the rest, soaking up the late September sunshine.

Croft took his new responsibilities in commanding the castle garrison very seriously - and he was determined that no man would fail him. He walked along the rampart towards the new round tower, its upper stone work so recently completed that he could still smell the lime. He nodded with satisfaction to see the man posted there was on the move and peering over the wall.

"Seen anything of interest out there?" asked Croft and the man gave a start.

"I'm sorry, Master Croft," he mumbled, "I didn't see you come along."

"Not to worry, man!"

"It's all quiet towards the forest," said the guard.

"Good," said Croft, "I'll be in the hall gallery, if you need me."

"Oh, it's fine down there too, Master Croft."

Croft nodded. "I'm sure, but I'll go down anyway and see how far they've got."

But at the top of the steps he paused. How did this man know that all was well below? He half-turned and saw the knife swinging down at him. He leant back against the wall and the blade rang against the stone. Seizing the arm that held it, he pulled hard and dragged the man down onto the steps. His assailant lost hold of the weapon and Croft butted him in the face with his helm. He heard the nose crack and a grunt of pain. The man sagged against the wall. Croft drew out his knife and drove it though the soldier's throat so hard the point scratched the wall. Then he drew out the blade, letting his victim tumble down the steps.

He ran to the rampart nearby and looked down into the yard. All seemed quiet still. Bear was staring up at him.

"Stay alert!" Croft called down and made his way back to the tower. He leant out over the outer wall but again saw nothing suspicious, so he hurried down the tower steps, working it through in his mind. The dead man lying at the bottom of the circular stair was one of Ralph Teller's men. There should have been another guard at the foot of the stair but he was nowhere to be seen - and he too was one of Teller's. Croft moved swiftly then down to the next floor - no man there either. Shit!

He headed across to the gallery above the hall where he had placed one of his most trusted men at arms. The fellow was still there but he was lying on the wooden floor boards. Croft examined him quickly - stabbed in the back.

Voices were raised in the hall below and he looked down to see men arguing. He decided he could safely leave that mess for Lord Elder and Holton to deal with and made for the steps down to the postern gate where most of Ralph Teller's men should be. As he approached he realised that the damage was already done: several men were hurrying up from the gate along the passage to the hall itself.

He shouted a warning, but the noise in the hall was so loud he doubted they could hear him. He started to move towards them but Sir Ralph mounted the steps from the gate and cut him off. More were coming up with him.

He faced Sir Ralph and barked at him angrily: "What have you done?"

"Surrender your sword, Croft," said Sir Ralph, "no-one else needs to die here today."

"None should have if you'd kept your oaths!" replied Croft, raising his sword. "I didn't think see you turning traitor."

"The king is dead or beyond help, Croft. Lord Elder won't believe it, but it's true. There's no need for more blood to be shed in his name."

Sudden cries from the hall distracted them both. Above the noise Croft recognised Ned Elder's cry of rage and he hacked at Sir Ralph, forcing him back.

"It'll all be over now," protested Sir Ralph, parrying his blow. "Ned Elder's dead - accept it and live!"

But the war cry of "An Elder, an Elder!" rang out from the hall.

"Doesn't sound as if it's over to me!" snapped Croft and drove the older man down the steps towards the gate. Sir Ralph tumbled backwards, taking another man with him.

Croft glanced behind him, wracked by indecision. There were no men in the hall to help Lord Elder, yet the postern gate stood wide open and he could not leave it thus.

§§§

Bear was leaning nonchalantly against the great oak door to the hall when it dawned on him that the noise coming from inside was more than just a few men arguing. He stepped away from it and stared at it for a moment. The door was barred from the inside and breaking it down with an axe would take some time. Yet there were other ways in. He seized one of the others by the shoulder and together they made for the steps up to the old north east tower. They were half way up the steps when Bear heard men running past below them into the courtyard. He hesitated but the shouts of alarm in the yard made up his mind.

"Come!" he said to his comrade and retraced his steps down to the yard.

A ring of men, Ralph Teller's men he noted, stood facing the main gates. Only two or three men at arms blocked their way.

"Lay down your arms," ordered Teller's men. But the guards at the gate were Yoredale men and they would not concede ground except on their lord's command.

Teller's men at arms glanced back to see Bear approaching and had little choice but to carry through their attack on the defenders at the gate. Bear thundered into the back of them and took the head of one in his bare hands to dash it against the wall. Then he snatched up the small pollaxe he carried at his belt and buried it into the man's chest.

"An Elder, an Elder!" he bellowed.

When he looked up though, he saw that the defenders at the gate were already being overpowered. Two of Teller's men were attempting to lift the great bar holding the gates shut. Since the drawbridge was down and the portcullis was up, only the gates were keeping Cullen's men outside. He could hear shouting outside now too. All around him his own men were being forced back. The archers above the gatehouse tried in vain to find targets in the melee but risked killing their comrades if they loosed their arrows.

Then the bar was raised and the gates opened a crack. Bear roared in disgust and returned his axe to its belt loop.

Instead he grabbed a longer handled weapon from the wall and swept a path before him to the gate.

"With me! With the Bear!" he bellowed and threw his colossal weight at the opening gates, slamming them shut. His men at arms formed up beside him.

"Get the bar on!" he ordered, but a surge from outside pushed the gates apart once more. One man came through the gap and Bear struck him with the butt of his weapon. He fell to his knees and Bear kicked his head for good measure.

"Stay down!" he growled.

An arm holding a pollaxe thrust through as Bear forced the gates closed. There was a crack and a scream as the arm was crushed between the two gates.

"Can't get it closed, Bear!" said one of his comrades as they struggled to hold the heavy bar aloft. Bear brandished his long weapon in one giant hand whilst with the other he took up one end of the bar and helped to drop it onto its supports.

Teller's men fell away then, hurrying out of the yard towards the postern.

Bear followed with others in his wake.

§§§

"No!" shouted Ned as Holton leapt in front of him. He heard several bolts striking the steward's great frame. Another bolt grazed Ned's shoulder and one flew wide. Ned was left trying to support Holton's weight. He gently laid him on the dais and found two bolts buried deep into the man's chest. Ned had never felt such loss.

The attackers threw aside their crossbows, knowing they would take too long to reload, and drew their swords. Two ran to the great door to stop the bar being lifted and the servants scattered before them. The pair stood with their backs to the door and their sword points aimed at the crowd of angry landholders.

The other two armed men made straight for Ned. Sir Roger Cullen was on his feet now too, urging them on. Ned had only a knife blade at his belt - he had expected to be spilling ink today, not blood. He looked for allies: Holton lay dead at his feet, Spearbold was quivering under the table, the fat priest sat whimpering in a spreading pool of his own blood - the wayward quarrel protruding from his belly. There was no-one else he could call upon.

"An Elder, an Elder!" he cried, but instead of taking out his knife he picked up Holton's ash staff and waited for the two men to come to him. They split up and came at him from two sides. Ned was poor at handling a quarterstaff but his opponents were no better at countering one. They darted at him but, despite Cullen's encouragement, they were wary of the swinging length of hardwood.

Ned seethed with anger at Holton's death and every blow he made was an expression of his growing wrath. Of all men, the gentle Holton did not deserve such a death. One of the men got too close and Ned cracked his head with a blow from the staff. The other called the two from the door to help him.

"Stay there!" Sir Roger ordered them and picked up his dead man's weapon. For a few moments he tried to get past the staff but then it was all he could do to defend himself as Ned unleashed a tide of rage. The staff punched and rattled against breastplates, shoulders and heads.

"Come on then!" Sir Roger told the three men guarding the door. "Leave it and take Ned Elder down!"

A blow to the head knocked Sir Roger back. "Hack that staff to pieces!" he snarled.

The three men ran at Ned. His arms were growing weary but he managed to disarm one man before the other swords snapped his staff in two. He still held one piece barely a yard long and all he could do was wave it as he retreated across the platform. His foot slid in the priest's blood and he crashed to the floor, losing his grip on the broken staff.

"Now finish him," ordered Sir Roger and raised his sword.

Ned was on his back when there was an almighty crash and the chamber was flooded with daylight. He was struggling to rise up from the bloody floor when both men standing over him just disappeared as if some unseen hand had plucked them away. He gave a grim nod and looked up to the gallery where two of his archers stood, each with another arrow nocked and aimed at Sir Roger.

Sir Roger bolted but an arrow caught him in the shoulder, spinning him to the floor. Ned staggered to his feet and other men came in from the yard with Bear.

"Lord, lord! Are you safe?" It was Croft running in from the kitchen passage. There was blood upon his chest and his face was cut. Sir Roger, bleeding from his wound, pushed Croft aside and staggered out into the passage.

Croft leant against the wall and grimaced with pain.

"Get after him!" ordered Ned and Bear took several others in pursuit.

It took some time to restore order. Croft's wound had to be dealt with but Holton was beyond any save God's help. Spearbold sat head in hands and wept.

Remarkably, most men in the hall had suffered no injuries at all, but then Ned supposed that Sir Roger had intended them to emerge unscathed from his little plot.

"Are the main gates secure?" asked Ned.

Several men shouted: "Aye."

"Not the postern," Croft said through gritted teeth, "but Bear will have it safe soon enough."

"How did they get in?" demanded Ned.

"Sir Ralph Teller," said Croft.

"Sir Ralph? But why?" asked Ned. Then he looked at Croft's pale visage. "You need some help, man - ignore me.

We'll talk later."

He swept the pile of legal documents off the table and they laid Croft upon it to tend his wounds. Then he turned to face the muttering crowd of landowners who fell silent under his stern gaze.

"Lords and gentlemen, I have read every complaint that you have submitted to me and I find that Sir Roger Cullen abused his trusted office as the king's steward at Quenhull. He fined men for no lawful reason, and when they refused or were unable to pay these fines, he confiscated land - rich farm land from loyal men."

Murmurs of assent greeted his pronouncement and he held up a hand to continue.

"By the authority of his grace, King Edward, all such confiscations are hereby reversed and the fines levied shall fall upon the estates of Sir Roger Cullen. Pending the payment of such fines, Sir Roger's estates will revert to the crown. Sir Roger, for his part in this bloody attack today on Quenhull, is declared an outlaw."

If Ned expected wild cheers to greet his decision, he was disappointed. Some men nodded their approval and one or two cried: "God save King Edward!" but the general response was muted. They made their way out of the hall, slowly and thoughtfully. Many cast a last look at the blood-soaked bodies that lay on the floor and the dais. By the time they reached the gates, which Bear had now opened, they had seen a few more lifeless bodies. They had seen justice done, but only by virtue of sword and arrow.

One of Ned's men at arms hurried in from the passage to the rear gate.

"Well?" asked Ned.

"Gone, my lord... they rode off into the trees down towards the river."

"How many of them were left?"

"Sir Roger, Sir Ralph, half a dozen more..."

"Aye and the rest of Cullen's retinue will join up with him there," said Ned. "We'll have to let him run for now - until we can get more men."

The last of the landholders filed out of the chamber and Ned surveyed the carnage. He was pleased to see that Croft was sitting up, his wound expertly bound up by one of his men with an obvious talent for such work. Spearbold was examining the corpse of the cleric.

Ned gave a weary sigh. "I suppose I'll have to explain to the Bishop of Worcester how his envoy was slaughtered whilst ensuring that my judgement was fair."

Spearbold frowned. "I think not, my lord, look."

Ned peered down at the body, the smell of blood almost overpowering.

"Mylord?" Spearbold held up the man's hands and removed the cowl from his head. "These are not the hands of a priest, nor the tonsured head of a monk. God knows he's fat enough to be a cleric, but I think he might be an imposter provided perhaps by Sir Roger."

"Aye, that makes some sense. I doubt Sir Roger would want a bishop's man witnessing what he intended here."

He sat down on the dais beside John Holton's body, which was still warm to the touch.

"You know, Holton still believed he had a debt to repay to me, though he had repaid it many times over." He turned to Spearbold. "What will I tell Mags?"

"That a brave husband died here today," murmured Spearbold.

"Aye, I'm sure that'll give her every comfort over the years as she raises her four children without a father."

"They're not the only fatherless children, my lord, and you did not put Holton in harm's way. He chose to do what he did."

Ned shook his head. "Aye... but I should have left him at Corve with his family and that's what Mags will say to me. It seems that even when I use the law rather than the sword, I still bring death to my friends."

"Perhaps, my lord, yet you must be doing something right for at least you still have some friends."

"Aye, but I've lost my oldest one today."

35

11th October 1469, at Cheapside in

London

Robert Radcliffe dismounted and let Hooper take his reins.

"Use the same stable as last time," he said, slapping the dust from his clothes.

Hooper grunted a response and went off with the rest of the men. Robert watched them go with a sense of relief. They were a tight group, reliable and skilled with their chosen weapons, but in Cheapside they stood out in the worst possible way. Having them beside him shouted to all who passed by that he was a ruffian, plain and simple.

He crossed the broad street to Warner's house, irked still by the lawyer's apparent good fortune - no doubt refined by a measure of sharp practice. Lawyers! He spat in the gutter as a couple of street urchins skittered past him. He despised them all: lawyers and merchants, they were all the same - not worth a bucket of shit when it really mattered.

At the side of the half-timbered house he hammered upon the main door. His journey had been long but it had not dulled the keen edge of disappointment that had greeted him at Warwick. Emma's refusal even to consider his suit was crushing enough but the prospect of losing his newly acquired lands was a disaster. His fears, first stirred at Warwick, were borne out by news that travelled south like a great north wind: the king was free of Warwick's control and royal authority was once again to be restored.

All that he had been granted under duress would most likely soon be taken away and he would be ruined - again. Marriage to Lady Emma Radcliffe suddenly acquired an importance beyond his own feelings towards her. Through her he could hold onto his lands or at least some of them. What he needed was a way out, an alternative to Warwick. If the Nevilles fell, then Emma too would need a friend.

The heavy door was drawn slowly open by a thin-faced, feeble-looking clerk or servant or… he cared not what. He pushed the man aside and found his way to the large hall on the ground floor where Warner sat surrounded by opulence: Burgundian tapestries covered the walls and heavy wooden furniture was crammed into every available space. Too good for a lawyer - and a crooked one at that!

"God give you an excellent day, Warner," he smiled at his host.

Warner dismissed his hovering servant with a gesture. "I'm a little surprised to see you back so soon, Robert," he said. His voice, always quiet, was almost a whisper.

Robert had to strain to hear him and realised he was stooping forward to do so - the devil would have him bowing! He straightened his back abruptly and sat down though he had not been invited to do so.

"You've heard the news from the north though?" said Robert.

"Indeed, such news is all too quickly delivered. Yet, surely… there's no cause for alarm just yet, is there?"

"I think there is," said Robert, "for Warwick could be finished and if he's a sinking vessel, he'll go down with all of us on board."

Warner was silent for a time, leaning his large head on

his clenched hands in front of him.

"You think it might already be time for us to… disembark then?" he asked.

Robert cast a glance around the room as if the earl might be lurking in an alcove nearby.

"If we don't act soon," he said, "then it may be too late."

"It's true the mood here is not in Warwick's favour," agreed Warner, "and few have a good word to say about the Duke of Clarence, yet… we shouldn't be too hasty. The earl has been thwarted before and come back even stronger."

"You really believe he might yet triumph?" Robert had not expected that.

"'Believe' might be putting it a little too boldly…" murmured Warner.

"This is not the time to hesitate!" urged Robert.

Warner regarded him carefully. "To act too late may seem hesitant, but to act too soon would certainly be rash…"

"Perhaps, but where do we stand on the matter we discussed in the summer?" asked Robert.

"Ah," said Warner, "well, as for that, plans have been laid, words have been spoken and letters have been written."

Robert stood up and paced around the room.

"Trust a lawyer to talk in riddles," he complained. "In God's name, speak plain, man!"

Warner nodded. "Very well, I've been developing my connection with the other prominent clients I have… the Stanley brothers. And I have done as you asked: I have written a letter of introduction for you to William Stanley - should you wish to use it. It details your various… skills and recommends you as a man who gets things done."

"Well then," said Robert, not a little relieved. "That's excellent! I'll take it with me now."

Warner smiled and Robert sat down again.

"Of course," he said with a wry smile. "What is it that you want of me in return?"

"My fee is in two parts, Robert. First, I want your service - and that of your men. I want them guarding the house, my legal offices and me."

"How long for?" demanded Robert.

"Until it's clear whether Warwick is finished or not. If he is… then you're going to need that letter."

Robert puffed out his cheeks, knowing that Warner would force him to pay more than he wanted for his little prize. "And the other half of the payment?"

"Three days ago, I had a visit from the fellow who used to live in this house - you'll recall that he was an accomplice of Ned Elder from time to time."

"Goldlock? Golding?" suggested Robert.

"Master John Goldwell - a very suitably named goldsmith - and here we sit amid the fruits of his considerable skill and labour."

"Get on with it, Warner - I've ridden thirty miles today!"

"Master Goldwell wanted his house back," chuckled Warner.

"And I doubt - since we're still here - that you gave it him. What of it?"

"You can be a tiresome fellow, Robert. Well, the man still has funds, I dare say, and I'd like to relieve him of the burden - with your help."

"You want to sell him back his house?"

"Certainly not," replied Warner.

"Well, what do you want me to do?"

"Anything that's required. Do you agree to my terms?"

"Do I have a choice?" asked Robert.

Warner smiled again.

"I told Goldwell he couldn't have his house and enquired why another large house wouldn't do just as well.

He replied that he had great personal attachment to this house. Now that set me thinking, Robert, because for a merchant, he's a very poor liar. If he has the funds to buy this house back, then he could buy any other house. This story of an attachment to the house has more to it - I can smell it. I think he might be a man we could press a little. If we're to survive in a Christendom that lacks the Earl of Warwick, then Goldwell's silver coin would be very useful to us - don't you think?"

"Very well," agreed Robert, "but do you expect me to do all this for just one letter?"

"An important letter that could secure your future, Robert - but I'm sure we can arrange for some of Goldwell's silver to come your way. So, even if Warwick doesn't fall, there'll be gain in it for you."

"Very well, where do we start?"

"I had him followed to his present lodgings - I want your men to watch him for the moment, but soon we'll get him back here for another little talk."

36

12th October 1469, at Corve Manor near

Ludlow

Maighread held Ned's letter in a trembling hand. When had she shed so many tears for a man she had known for so little time? She remembered their first meeting - who would not remember it? Holton, with the fearsome wound across his jaw, and she with her fire-ravaged face. They had laughed at each other and it took her no time at all to learn that the man beneath the ugly scar was among the best of men - the very best.

The dreaded knock came at her chamber door: Mags. It would not matter that Ned had troubled to write a separate letter to Mags for she would know in an instant. She would know by the urgent summons and Maighread's tears that a man was dead.

"Come in," called Maighread.

Mags wore a smile as she entered the room but it faded after a single step across the threshold. Maighread said nothing but held out the sealed letter to her. Mags shrank away from it, pressing her back against the door - stiff with fear.

"I'll not take it," she breathed. "If I don't read it, it mayn't be true."

Uncertain, Maighread still kept her hand outstretched and after another moment Mags leant forward and took the letter. She turned it over in her hands and then stuffed it into her kirtle.

"Thank you, my lady," she said briskly and turned to go.

"Mags, wait!"

Mags looked at her miserably. "If I stay, I'll be angry with you - and you of all folk don't deserve it, my lady. So it's best I go."

"Stay, please - angry or no," said Maighread. "I've known such anger too - such bitter all-consuming wrath that I thought it would destroy me as surely as the fire!"

"But my wrath strikes at your man…" said Mags.

"Aye, I know."

"So many have died for your man - and what has been won, my lady? Tell me, what has been worth the death of even one such a man as John Holton, let alone the countless others?"

"Here, sit on the bed. Read the letter, here with me," said Maighread. "Let your bitter tears wash over us both."

Mags hesitated, then gave a sigh and carefully retrieved the letter. She stared at it for a long while before breaking the seal.

"I'm a better woman for loving John," she said. "How else would the daughter of a soldier's whore be sitting in this fine chamber at all - let alone able to read?" She gave a hoarse laugh. "John taught me to read, he taught me not to throw things at people - taught me patience. If only I could have taught him that he owed no more to Lord Elder…"

She opened the letter and read it through in silence, then hurled it to the floor as her tears came.

"He died at Michaelmas and it's taken near two weeks for his lord to tell me!"

"It must have been a hard letter for Ned to write," said Maighread.

"Hard? Not so damned hard as reading such a letter! Nor so hard as dying neither!"

Whatever Maighread said, she knew it would sound wrong, so she said nothing.

"Christ's blood!" Mags railed at her. "He threw himself in front of your man! How like him, the fool! No thought for his young children, no thought for his loving wife - he just had to throw his life away for Ned Elder... He worshipped his lord, but I knew... sooner or later... I knew that Ned Elder would get him killed!"

"Ned always tried to keep him safe," said Maighread.

Mags stood up. "Aye, well he didn't do a very good job of it, did he?"

Maighread got to her feet too, feeling a sudden twinge in her belly.

"Did Ned ever take John into the field?" she cried. "No. Did he send him to Crag Tower where the flames roared and blistered us? No. Was he at Yoredale when it was blown asunder? No, he wasn't! He was here at Corve, with you... and his children."

Mags turned to face her. "But he's dead now! Dead! And when 'your Ned' is dangling his grandchildren on his knee, I hope you'll remember that!"

Maighread had no answer. She felt strange and looked blankly at Mags.

"There!" said Mags. "Now I'm angry with you - and I told you I didn't want to be! You should have just let me grieve alone."

Maighread was not listening. There was another pain in her belly, lower than her belly. She gulped as her knees gave way and she felt liquid flow from between her legs. She fell back onto the bed, suddenly terrified.

Mags stared at her. "Oh, blood and shit!" she cried. "It just had to be now, didn't it?" She took Maighread's arm. "You'll be fine," she said, helping her onto the bed. Then she rushed to the door, wrenching it open.

Mary stood on the landing.

"Mary! What in the name of Christ are you standing there for?"

Mary started to gabble excitedly but Mags cut her short.

"Never mind! We need the midwife - now!"

"I know, I know!" said Mary. "But... how did you know?"

"Did you leave your wits in the dales, girl? Lady Maighread is here with me and she needs the midwife!"

"Oh," said Mary, "I meant for Lady Eleanor..."

"What? Oh, no," screamed Mags. "Not both of them!"

"What?" said Mary.

"Never mind, just send someone to fetch the midwife. Then you'd better go back and stay with Lady Eleanor."

Mags turned back to Maighread and shook her head.

"I fucking hate the Elders," she muttered and hurried downstairs.

37

20th October 1469, at Quenhull Castle

Ned broke the seal on the letter and almost dropped it on the steps as he read it with a broad grin on his face.

"Two births!" he cried. "Maighread and my sister!"

"I'm very pleased for you, my lord," said Spearbold.

"I have another son, Spearbold, a new son. I must go to Corve at once."

"Best not go to Corve just now, my lord," advised Spearbold. "This land is still uneasy - and will be, until certain news reaches us of how the king fares."

"But I must go, Spearbold!"

"To what purpose, my lord?" asked Spearbold. "What service do you expect to perform for them? It's a woman's time isn't it? You'll only get a quick glimpse of the babe - which won't look pretty - and then you'll be swept out by the coven of ladies, midwives, wet nurses and mewling serving girls."

"I'm going, Spearbold," said Ned, "and there's nothing you can possibly say to dissuade me!"

They reached the courtyard and Ned called for a horse. "And where's Bear?" he demanded. "I'll take him with me."

"He's out with Croft at present, my lord, as are many others - patrolling the lands west of the Severn - as you promised at Michaelmas."

Ned gave a nod of assent. "Very well, but tell Bear to

get ready as soon as he returns!"

Spearbold left him and Ned mounted the steps by the gatehouse to go up onto the ramparts. Poor old Spearbold had never been a father - he didn't know how it felt. When John was born Ned had not even known it, had not experienced the joy he felt now. He felt reborn himself for it had been a dire autumn so far, but this - this was surely a sign of hope. He knew how excited Maighread would be and he wanted to share it with her. He should have been there for the birth, though Spearbold was no doubt right that it was no place for a man.

A shout came up from the lookout a few yards further along the rampart and instinctively he searched to see what had caught the man's attention. He frowned: a party of horsemen were heading for Quenhull. By their pennants they were his men but something in the ungainly manner of their progress gave cause enough to be concerned. It was clear that several bodies were tied onto some of the horses.

He descended the steps and passed through the gate, striding across the wooden boards of the drawbridge to await the horsemen.

Croft dismounted at once. "You've lost men?" asked Ned,

"No my lord, we've found some - but all are dead save one and that one looks nearer to death than life. Bear's tended his wounds but they are... they'll be enough, I fear."

Bear lifted the wounded man from one of the mounts and carried him inside.

"Lay him on one of the tables in the hall," ordered Ned. "See to the rest, Croft, and then come to me."

He followed Bear to the hall where a table was cleared at once to receive the wounded man.

"Can he speak?" asked Ned and Bear gave a nod.

The man tried to rise but Bear put a firm hand on his chest. "Lie still," he said, "or you die."

Spearbold tugged at Ned's arm.

"Aye, what is it?" Ned hissed at him.

"Do you notice his livery, my lord?" asked Spearbold.

Ned had not, but now he looked more closely and noticed the white boar badge which he had first encountered the previous year. "Blood of Christ…he's one of the Duke of Gloucester's men."

"Aye," agreed Spearbold.

"But what's he doing here?" asked Ned.

"An important question, my lord, but even more important is why would anyone attack some of Gloucester's men - Gloucester is hardly an enemy of Warwick or Clarence - not unless it's come to open war between the brothers?"

"A mistake, perhaps?"

"If it is, then someone's going to pay a heavy price for it."

The wounded knight gave a sudden gasp and reached sideways to seize Ned's hand.

"Lord Elder?" he breathed.

"Aye, I am."

"We were bringing news from his grace…"

"Who attacked you, man?"

"The black bulls…" The man spat out the words with a mouthful of blood. "We feared no attack - thought them friends…"

"Rest!" ordered Bear.

Ned suspected that only Bear's pressure on the knight's chest wound was stopping him bleeding to death, "Bind him up - if you can…"

"Wait," said the knight, "His grace bade us tell you…" He lifted himself up a little, despite Bear's grumbling. "The king is free and… riding for London,." said the knight and sank back down onto the table.

Ned touched man's shoulder and left Bear to minister to

him. He crossed the hall and went up the steps to his privy chamber. Spearbold padded up after him and Ned held up a hand before his adviser could even open his mouth.

"Don't bother to say it!" he snapped. "I know… I can't leave here now - or at least not before I find out who's been hacking Gloucester's men to pieces."

"He said 'black bulls," said Spearbold, "so…"

"Aye, the badge of the Duke of Clarence but I doubt he's close by - last we heard he was in Warwickshire. No, the culprit is much nearer - who do we happen to know that would wear the black bull of Clarence?"

"Sir Roger Cullen," said Spearbold with a heavy sigh.

"And who else would dare such an act? This was no chance attack. Cullen wants to blind us to what's happening in the north."

"Aye, to be sure, rumour helps him more than us but let's not forget he failed. The news is good: the king is free of Warwick - at least for now. That knowledge can only help our cause down here - that's why Cullen was so keen to stop it reaching us."

"But Cullen is still out there and he still has powerful friends," said Ned. "But we can't just sit here licking our wounds, because sooner or later young Gloucester will start to wonder what's become of the men at arms he sent here."

38

13th November 1469 in the evening, in

London

A door below slammed with such force that the whole house shook - not, Hal reflected, that it took much to make this particular building tremble.

Becky sat up in the gloom and cracked her head on a rafter. "Shit!"

He pulled her to him and gently stroked her hair. "Take care with that pretty head," he murmured.

They were squeezed together in a bed too small for one, in a space beneath the thatched roof but they made no complaint. Mostly they simply took pleasure in each other's company. It was a luxury neither could remember and, since their accommodation was free, lying abed was not so much of a hardship.

"Master Goldwell coming home?" asked Becky.

"Yes, that'll be Master Goldwell," he said, "and it's becoming a habit. If he stays like this he'll be ruined. He said he was going to start up his work again this week, but he's done nothing. Soon his coin will run out with the rent of the house, the food… and his drinking…"

"It's time we were leaving, Hal - long past time. Don't mistake me: I love being here with you… and Will. But we're not helping here and we have to take Will home to his mother…"

"At least we sent her word…"

"Aye, but that won't have pleased her much," said Becky. "She doesn't want Will here - and I don't blame her."

"I know, but… the boys are so close. I don't like to part them again."

"It's not up to us, Hal! We've already gone too far in this - we shouldn't be here at all! We said we'd stay for a day or two - it's already been weeks and weeks! We can't stay in London forever and the longer we wait, the harder it'll be for Will… for all of us."

He gave a great sigh. How easily his solemn oaths to Lord Elder were forgotten.

"You're right," he said. "We've got to go. Winter'll be coming on hard soon. We'll tell the boys tomorrow."

Becky shifted her position and he wrapped his arms around her.

"At least they'll have had a bit of time together, Hal," she said, "and so have we."

Her soft mouth found his and she gave him a long kiss, then she pulled away a little.

"When we get back to Corve," she said in a whisper, "are we still…will we still, I mean will you…"

"Will I still want to lie with you?" he asked.

"That's not quite what…" Her words hung between them for a long moment.

"I suppose it's all been a bit sudden," he said.

"How did it not happen before?" she asked. "We were at Crag together all those years and never…"

"Different people then, Beck…"

"Aye. So, then… what do you think?"

"I suppose Lord Elder will give us the nod," he said.

"If he won't then his sister will - I'll make sure of that!"

"Then… we should say some words," he said.

She laid her head on his chest and he felt the warmth of her smile against his skin. "Go on then…" she murmured.

"By God's Grace, I'll be your husband, Rebecca Standlake - if you'll have me…"

"And I'll be a good wife to you, Hal… By Christ, have you got another name? For I'm sure I've never heard it."

"Almost forgotten it myself," said Hal. "I think it's Ford…"

"You think? Well, Mistress Ford will do me well enough."

He was about to kiss her when he saw a glimmer of light coming up the narrow stair.

He got up to investigate, bending low to avoid the beams.

"Short wedding," observed Becky.

On the tiny landing in the wavering candlelight, stood Sarah Goldwell.

"Mistress Sarah, what is it?" asked Hal.

"It's the boys!" she cried. "They're not in their beds. They've gone!"

"Oh good Christ!" exclaimed Hal. "Not again! I swear I'll whip the pair of them this time!"

Sarah stood trembling on the threshold.

"Have you told your father?" asked Hal.

"No," she whispered. "But what can he do? He's a broken man, Hal."

"Alright," said Hal. "Go downstairs. We'll come down."

"God save you, Hal," she said, weeping.

Darkness filled the room again as Sarah padded back down the steps.

"You heard?" he said to Becky.

"Aye, husband," she said.

"We'd better make haste - though how I'm to find those lads, God knows."

"Wait," said Becky.

"What?"

"I think the search will go better if you've got your breeches on…" she said, holding them out to him.

39

13th November 1469, at Cheapside in

London

Will peered at the house across the street. He could just about make out its outline in the dark. "Are you sure that's the one?" he asked.

"Of course I'm sure - I lived there for years!" hissed Jack.

"But how will we get in?" asked Will.

"I can get us in," said Jack.

"What if someone wakes up?"

"We've got our knives…" said Jack.

"Have you ever used a knife on a man?"

"No… and I doubt you have either."

"Well, you'd be wrong because I have," declared Will, "and it isn't so easy…"

"We'll just have to be quiet then," insisted Jack.

When Jack's grandfather, the goldsmith, returned home that evening once again in such a poor state, Jack decided that they could delay no longer. They knew what ailed him - and they resolved to do what they could to help. Now that they were here though, Will was not so sure.

"Are you coming or not?" asked Jack.

"Aye, course I'm coming!" Will said, but he wished he had told Hal. Hal would have known what to do.

"Come on then." Jack led the way across the street. A

dog barked angrily nearby and Will jumped. Jack laid a hand on his arm. "There's a lot of dogs in the town, brother," he said.

Will nodded. They reached the house and stood beside it for a while.

"Right," whispered Jack. "We climb the fence and that gets us to the porch, but we're not going in there."

"No?"

"No. We're going round the back - over the next fence and into the back yard. The second fence is higher - grandfather put it there to keep out thieves."

"The likes of us then..."

"Don't worry. I used to go in and out all the time and he never even knew! I made a gap to crawl through and put a barrel in front of it. From the yard we can shin up to one of the windows - there's a shutter loose on the chamber I used to sleep in."

They soon found the fence - and to Will's surprise the barrel was still there. Will stared at the fence but only when he knelt down on the ground could he find the small hole at its base.

"You see?" said Jack. "It's there, isn't it?"

"Oh, aye, it's there," agreed Will. "But... how old were you when you used to crawl through it?"

"Well, we've been away for the best part of a year, I think, and I didn't use it much for a year or so before that. Why?"

Will sighed. "Because you've got bigger, you fool - and I'm broader than you anyway!"

"Let me look," said Jack, kneeling down by the hole. He examined it in silence whilst Will glanced nervously at the nearby houses.

"God's blood!" said Jack.

"Aye, God's blood it is. What now?"

"We can still get through, I think, but it'll be a bit tighter is all."

Will eyed the gap doubtfully. "You might, but not me."

"Well we can't stand here all night so let's give it a try!"

Jack put his head and arms through the hole, then wriggled his shoulders through and the rest of him soon disappeared.

"See? It's alright," said Jack from the other side of the fence.

Will sighed and started to follow. He squeezed his hands through and his head. That was easy enough but when it came to his broad shoulders he knew it was hopeless.

"It's no good, Jack. I can't get through," he cried.

"I'll pull you!" said Jack.

There was a clattering noise by Will's head.

"Shit!" said Jack.

"What was that?" cried Will.

"Knocked something over - it's so dark!"

Whilst Will was struggling to move himself one way or the other through the fence, he heard the bolts being drawn back on the house door a few yards away. His head dropped. "Keep quiet, Jack," he said softly.

There were suddenly raised voices behind him and a wavering light. His legs were seized and he was dragged roughly back through the hole, banging his head on the wood. Strong hands hauled him to his feet and an oil lamp was thrust at his face. There was one man holding him and another with the lamp. A third appeared in the doorway.

"Who is it?" asked the newcomer.

"Some little stray!" answered the one that held him. "Christ only knows how he thought he was going to break into this place." He gave Will a slap to the head. "Picked the wrong house, you little tosspot, didn't you? I'll give him a quick thrashing, Master Warner, and throw him back into the gutter, shall I?"

The one called Warner studied him for a moment. "I

suppose…but wait, take him inside. Let's just make sure there's no special reason he chose this house. You make more than a few enemies, Hooper, in my profession."

Will was thrown through the open door and it slammed shut behind him.

Warner looked at Will closely. "There, you see Hooper - already we have a mystery."

"A mystery?"

"Well, look at him, man! He's not dressed for the gutter, is he? Now I find that a puzzle, lad," Warner said, addressing Will for the first time. "Why don't you tell me what you're doing here?"

Will said nothing.

"Thieves often send a young boy to find a way in," said Hooper, "He looks a bit large for it but I'll have the lads do a quick search in case there's anyone else outside."

"Very well," agreed Warner, but his eyes never left Will's face.

This was a man to fear, Will decided. Silence was his only hope. With God's help, Jack would manage to get away and they would lose interest and throw him out.

"Answer me, boy. What are you here for?"

Will stared at the floor and made no answer.

"I can get Hooper here to beat it out of you," advised Warner.

Will remained quiet.

"A stubborn lad, it seems," said Warner. "Hooper?"

"What?" asked Hooper.

"Persuade him!"

"He's only a lad…"

"Do as you're told!" snapped Warner.

"I don't serve you, master lawyer," retorted Hooper.

"No, but your master has offered your service, so get on with it."

"Alright," agreed Hooper, "I'll take him down to the

cellar."

Hooper lifted him up by the ear and, despite himself, Will gave a squeal of pain as he was dragged across the hall and down a flight of stairs.

"I'm sure I've seen you somewhere," said Hooper, dropping Will down onto the cold, damp flags of the cellar floor.

Will sat still, steeling himself for a beating, but Hooper just smiled.

"I thought so," he said, "you're the goldsmith's boy."

"Are you going to beat me?" asked Will.

Hooper gave a chuckle. "Only if you're a lying, thieving little bastard, but you're not are you…"

Will made no reply.

"I've been watching you for a while," Hooper told him, "and I know who I'm talking to. Why don't you think about it? And in the morning you can tell me what you're doing here."

Hooper went out and slammed the door shut.

It was dark in the cellar, very dark.

§§§

Jack waited until the main house door closed then he moved swiftly, climbing up the corner of the timber-framed part of the house. He knew where every hand hold was, every protruding beam - even in the dead of night. He levered open a wooden shutter on the second floor and for a moment thought someone had troubled to mend it, then breathed a sigh of relief as it scraped open.

He reached in and clambered over the sill. A year ago his own bed would have broken his fall but it seemed that someone had moved it and he landed on the floor with a heavy thump. He lay still for a while, expecting someone to investigate the sound but no-one did. He rubbed his bruised shoulder and then crawled across the floorboards. The chamber seemed empty now, no furniture of any kind.

He found his way to the door by feeling along the wall.

Now what? What could he do to help Will? Perhaps he should go back to get Hal. Still, he was here now and he knew the house better than anyone. He should find Will, but he might as well see if the jewel was still hidden where his grandfather had left it. Then all he had to do was find his brother and they could both climb out of the window. Simple - except Will wouldn't fit through the fence... so perhaps they'd have to leave by the door.

He left the chamber and went out onto the landing, which he knew led to the two other bedchambers. The doors were closed so he listened but heard nothing from within. Voices drifted up from the landing below. He waited at the top of the stairs. Doors opened and closed until finally all was quiet.

There was no light at all on the stairs and he crept down, taking one tread at a time, pausing frequently but hardly daring to breathe. He crossed the first floor landing and passed on down the next flight of stairs to the ground floor. Halfway down a tread creaked alarmingly and he froze, holding his breath. No-one stirred, so he continued downstairs. Where might they have put Will? Most likely the cellars - a place he had never been very fond of because they always smelt of something unpleasant. He hesitated by the steps down to the cellars but decided he must find the missing jewel first.

He entered the large hall which ran to the back of the house. There were two places in the room that he knew his grandfather used as hiding places. One he had been shown but the other he had observed the goldsmith using almost by accident. He prayed the jewel would be in one or the other. He moved across the chamber and cursed the new owner as he rapped his knee. The man Warner must have moved all the furniture about. Jack frowned as he tried to picture in the darkness how it had been before.

THE LAST SHROUD

He went to the rear of the room and stood with his back to the shuttered window. He turned and felt along the oak beam which ran under the window. The wall between the beams was filled in with some sort of cob plaster but beneath one section of window Jack knew there was a cavity covered by a thin wooden board painted to look like the rest of the wall. He located it easily enough but when he tried to remove the board, it put up some stubborn resistance. He drew out his knife, slid the narrow blade in and then levered off the cover. Deftly, he caught it before it dropped to the floor and grinned to himself in the dark. He reached his hand in to explore the secret cavity: it was empty.

He was not truly surprised for it was in the other hiding place that he really expected to find the jewel. He crossed to the hearth, which boasted a fine stone surround that only the richest of households could afford. He was a little less sure of the exact place but he knew that behind one of the stones was a hidden recess. He was convinced the jewel would be there but it never occurred to him that he would not be able to find it. He tried every stone but to no avail. No part of the fireplace seemed to move at all. He tried scraping away here and there with his knife blade, but could not find the hiding place.

Perhaps he had missed out one of the stones in the dark. Wearily, he leant his shoulder against the wall and his disappointment overcame him. All his hopes of helping his grandfather were ruined. Worse still, he would have to go home empty-handed and explain where he had been and why. And Will, he had still to free Will! He took a deep breath and then leapt up only to crack his head on the stone lintel of the fireplace. He leant against it for a moment, dazed, waiting for his head to stop hurting. Then he felt his legs go and he dropped into the hearth.

§§§

Jack awoke to find thin fibres of light filtering through the rear shutters. He blinked open his eyes. Shit! It must be dawn! No! He must get down to Will - and quick! Only when he got onto his haunches did he remember hitting his head, which now began to throb.

He stood up gingerly and at once forgot about his head because there were three men in the room, staring at him. Two were tall and had the look of fighting men. The other was short and fat.

"Well, Hooper," said the fat one, shaking his head. "Either the boy's escaped from the cellar or we've found another just like him!"

The man, Hooper, looked him up and down. "This one's dressed different," he said.

"Indeed," said the fat one, rolling his eyes. "Bring up the other one," he ordered and Hooper went out.

The third man stepped forward. To Jack he seemed as tall as Ned Elder and he wore a sword at his belt. Jack edged away from him until his back was hard against the stone of the fire surround.

"Scared, boy?" the man said. "No need to be. Tell me your name and I'll tell you mine."

"Jack Goldwell." The words were out before he realised what he was doing.

"Ah," breathed the fat man, smiling. "I was right!"

"God give you a good morning, Jack," said the tall man, "I'm Robert, Robert Radcliffe…"

Jack had heard the Radcliffe name many a time from Will, heard the stories of the feud between the Elders and the Radcliffes and the role his own father had played in it all, long ago. Surely, this man could not be one of those Radcliffes? He prayed not for if he was, then Jack feared he had just made the biggest mistake of his short life.

40

13th November 1469, at Quenhull Castle

The whole castle was alive with men, horses and wagons - the courtyard was close to bursting with them. Outside the walls, tents had been hastily erected to house those who could not be accommodated inside. Within the castle the stone passages and oak floor boards echoed with the passing of scores of feet. It was as if a small army had descended upon them, rather than the modest retinue of a duke - but then this was no ordinary duke.

A fire had been lit in the privy chamber for the first time since Ned had taken up residence - he hadn't even realised the chamber had a fireplace. The Duke of Gloucester sat as if holding court, flanked by several lords. He was young - barely seventeen, Ned thought, but he looked the part of a royal duke. He had met Gloucester only once before and the duke lost no time in reminding him of it.

"I offered you my hand last year. Lord Elder," he said, "it's a brave man who rejects the friendship of the king's brother… but you chose to take the hand of another instead. Tell me, have you heard from Anthony Woodville of late?"

"Your pardon, your grace, I never rejected your friendship," said Ned, "but you seemed so…"

"Young?" suggested Gloucester, with a half smile.

"I thought you had burdens enough, your grace, without me adding mine."

"Yet, Anthony - Lord Rivers, now his father's dead - his shoulders are no broader than mine, are they? He's a fine man for a tourney, Ned, but if I came up against him in battle, he'd yield soon enough."

Ned waited for Gloucester to cease raking over last year's perceived insult and move on to the real reason for his visit, though Ned already knew very well what it was.

"So Ned, my royal brother seems to think you might be in need of some help and - in my new role as Constable of England - I've come to offer you my hand once more. In truth, I'm bound for Wales to take up new offices in the north - time someone took charge there, eh?"

"I would gladly accept your offer of aid, your grace, but all is quiet here now," Ned replied, hoping he did not cause any further offence.

"Well, that is good to hear, Ned - my half dozen knights were of some use, I trust?" said Gloucester.

Ned swallowed hard. "There was some trouble, your grace," said Ned, "a few weeks ago. The knights you sent to tell me of the king's return to London were ambushed. My men found them dead - or all but. One survived long enough to deliver your message - a brave man."

Gloucester frowned but said nothing for a moment or two, as if weighing up his response.

"You're telling me only now that six of my best men at arms were butchered near here - where you hold the king's authority?"

"It's awkward, your grace, they were killed by men wearing the badge of your brother, Clarence."

"His grace, the Duke of Clarence, my lord - give him title at least!" replied Gloucester.

Ned tried to read the young man: which way would he jump? He was young - would he lose his temper? The duke stared at him in silence and Ned felt his anger - not hot, but cool.

"The murderers have been taken, punished?" asked Gloucester finally.

"Not yet, your grace, but I have the matter in hand." Even Ned thought his answer sounded lame.

"Some might say," the duke said thoughtfully, "that you're no longer the man who fought so valiantly at St Albans, at Towton… You were routed in the summer at Edgecote - to your king's great cost… but still he gave you coin and authority by letters under his personal seal. Such is my brother's loyalty. So, you have the men and the power yet nothing has been done?"

"Much has been done to rebuild the king's peace, your grace," Ned protested. "I have restored the rule of law here west of the Severn."

"Hah!" Gloucester turned to his companions and laughed grimly. "Tell that to my dead knights but I doubt you'll convince them. I'm a man who believes in the rule of law, Ned. You say this butcher wears my brother's livery? It's true that the Duke of Clarence has yet to submit to his king, but… what we need, Ned, is someone's head - the head of the man that ordered the death of my men. You'll find that a severed head will do much to restore obedience in these parts. Now, can you bring me his head, or not?"

"I'll bring you his head, your grace," said Ned evenly, "or die trying."

"Well, that's good," said Gloucester with a smile, "that's sounds more like the Ned Elder of memory!"

§§§

Gloucester and his entourage stayed overnight at Quenhull, consuming much of the provisions Ned had begun to accumulate for winter. Despite what had passed earlier, the young duke was good company at the modest feast in his honour. The following morning, genuinely upset by the loss of his men at arms, he spent some time at prayer in Ned's private chapel, ordering masses to be sung and candles lit for the dead men in all the local churches.

All in all, Gloucester remained a mystery to Ned and by the time he left Quenhull around noon that day, Ned could not claim that he knew him any better than when he arrived. Nevertheless, when Gloucester's retinue departed Ned heaved a short-lived sigh of relief. Now he must make good his promise to deliver Cullen's head.

In the days that followed Ned was far from idle but Cullen proved elusive and, despite all their efforts, the fugitive was not found. Perhaps, Ned pondered, Gloucester was closer to the mark than he liked to admit. Perhaps his mind was too often elsewhere of late, dwelling upon Maighread, his new son... and the loss of John Holton.

There had been no news from Corve for several weeks. He longed to return to Maighread - and where in God's name was Hal? He should have been at Quenhull long ago. Ned missed Hal a great deal and he was plagued once more with headaches... and so tired, always tired. But tomorrow, he would go to Corve Manor - for there were matters he must settle there.

41

14th November 1469, at Cheapside in

London

It was quiet, a peaceful Sunday morning, but Will's heart was thudding in his chest like the clapper of a great bell. He ran as fast as his strong legs could carry him, racing along Cheapside, slipping here and there on cobbles shiny with morning dew. He was grateful the streets were still deserted, for he could hardly see for tears. A few folk were about and he startled one or two of the watch already on their way home. It would have been easy to grab one and tell him all - but he didn't. He just ran.

Run, they had told him - run to the goldsmith. Fetch Master Goldwell quickly and he might just find his grandson still breathing when he gets here. So Will ran on, cutting down through Bread Street. It was a long street and he was running fast, too fast he suddenly realised as he saw a church ahead of him that he didn't know. He came to a skidding halt - there were too many churches. Shit! He had gone too far and missed the lane. He tried to keep calm as he recovered his breath and looked about him.

He turned about and trotted back up Bread Street again, this time paying closer attention. All the side lanes looked the same so he slowed to a walk and looked more carefully.

Take a little time, he told himself, but not too much. Then he knew it: the entrance to Pissing Lane, where they were lodged. He darted down the lane and reached the house out of breath once more. He stood at the door, panting, and then it struck him.

'Tell no-one,' they had said. 'Fetch the goldsmith and tell no-one'.

But how could he do that - unless he and Jack had not been missed? Only then might he be able to sneak in without the others noticing. He tried the door and found it open. Thank God for that, at least! He stepped inside and was seized at once by Becky, who hugged him and screamed at him all at once. She held him so tightly that what little breath remained was crushed from his breast.

"Will! Will!" she cried, brushing away her tears and holding him close. "Oh, Will - how could you do that to me?" she chided him.

"Where's my Jack?" demanded Sarah.

"Where have you been?" cried Becky.

"Where's Jack?" screamed Sarah.

Will shied away from her and glanced up at Hal for help. Hal gently prised Will away from Becky.

"Let the lad speak," he urged, "all of you! Come now, Will. Where's your brother?"

Will hesitated. What should he say? What could he say?

"Leave the boy with me," said Hal. At once there was a chorus of complaint from the others but Hal shooed them aside. He offered his hand to Will who seized upon it gratefully. Hal led him into the solar and sat him down.

"Leave us alone," ordered Hal. "Beck, get him something warm to eat and drink, if you please, then fetch Pinner. Sarah, sober your father up in case we have need of him."

Will expected the two women would argue but he was surprised to find that they did as Hal bid them. Then Hal closed the door on them and Will breathed a good deal more easily.

"Now Will," said Hal, "I want you to tell me what's happened. Take your time and tell me all."

"But Hal, there's no time to tell anything - I must take Master Goldwell, now!"

"You know me very well, don't you Will?" said Hal.

"Aye, aye I do, Hal."

"Well then, that's why you'll know that you're not going anywhere until you've told me everything - I mean it."

"But it's a secret - I'm not even supposed to know... Jack'll get into trouble…"

Hal sighed. "I think we both know that Jack's already in trouble - isn't he? So just tell me."

So Will began to spill out the words and the more he said, the easier it was and the telling took far less time than he had imagined. When he stopped talking, he was met by silence. He willed Hal to say something.

The door opened and Becky brought Will some warm bread and potage - the latter was only slightly warm but he gulped it all down nonetheless.

In the doorway, John Goldwell and his daughter appeared, their faces scarred with worry.

"Has he said where Jack is?" asked Sarah, her voice breaking.

Hal made a gesture to dismiss them all. "Will's told me all," he said, "and now Master Goldwell and I need to talk to him a little longer."

"Why can I not hear too? Jack's my son!" protested Sarah.

"Master Goldwell?" said Hal.

John Goldwell came in and nodded to Sarah.

Hal closed the door and Will saw him press Becky's hand as he did so. She gave Hal a smile and guided Sarah away.

"Well," said Hal, "I know your secret now, Master Goldwell - and it would have saved a wagon load of shit if you'd told me it to start with, for now we must decide what can be done."

He held up his hand as the goldsmith began to protest.

"Will says we have little time, so let's not waste any of it arguing."

§§§

Warner stared down from the solar on the first floor into Cheapside. "We shan't see that boy again, Robert. He's gone. Still, I think the grandson knows more than he's saying."

"One of your clerks came early this morning," said Robert. "You work your servants hard, Warner - and on a Sunday…"

If Warner was annoyed that Robert had noticed the arrival, he did not show it.

"It wasn't a clerk," he replied. "It was a messenger from my man at court. He tells me that Warwick and Clarence have been summoned to London."

"Summoned? To be taken, you think?"

"Hardly. I'm sure they won't come at all without a few iron pledges."

"So perhaps they're to be reconciled," said Robert.

Warner shook his head. "There may be reconciliation, Robert, but there'll not be peace. The king knows it and so does the earl. Whatever words are said between them, they may as well break wind at each other."

"So?"

"The earl has one chance left: try to put his son-in-law, Clarence, on the throne."

"But who would want Clarence?" said Robert, aghast.

"No-one, but he's all the earl has left."

"What do you think the king will do?"

"He's already doing it: weakening Warwick in Wales,

and Clarence in the west, raising up Gloucester. He'll need others to bolster his power - men like the Stanleys, Robert. William Stanley is hoping for offices in Wales. He's a man of ambition and that's what we need. Time we were moving on, Robert. Time for well laid and profitable designs to bear fruit…"

"So, William Stanley for me then," said Robert, "armed with your letter of course - and some of Goldwell's coin!"

Robert had to acknowledge that Warner's instincts about the goldsmith had once again proved most reliable - the lawyer seemed to sniff out such opportunities with ease. On a whim Warner had kept eyes on John Goldwell - otherwise they might never have realised the lad's importance. Now they could exert a little pressure and he reckoned Goldwell would give up a good measure of whatever coin or silver he had left to get the boy back. The lad would be returned unharmed and the whole enterprise would yield a useful little windfall.

"If our little messenger doesn't come back with the goldsmith by noon, I'll pay Master Goldwell a visit with Hooper," said Robert.

Warner nodded his approval. "Hmm, it might be worth having another word with our young guest. It can only strengthen our hand with Goldwell. I know when someone's holding back - and that boy is definitely holding something back."

"He's just scared, Warner," said Robert, "Boys get themselves into trouble and they get scared - it's what happens." He grinned at the lawyer. "Perhaps you never were a little boy…"

Warner smiled back icily. "Perhaps I never got myself into trouble," he replied. "Come, let's see what the boy has to say - you can be the kind, reasonable one if you like - that should test you."

They went down to the hall where Hooper stood watch

over Jack Goldwell.

"Leave us," ordered Robert, and watched Hooper saunter out. "You too, Warner," he added.

Warner feigned surprise but then left. Robert hoped that Warner never needed to rely on his skills as a player. He squatted down on the floor beside the boy.

"Now Jack," he said, "I'm doing my best for you, but you need to help me. Warner - and the others - they're brutes… cutthroats. They want to kill you whatever happens - and I'm trying to persuade them not to. Do you understand?"

He felt Jack shiver beside him. "Yes, sir."

"Call me Robert. I'm your friend, Jack - and the only one you have in this house."

"Will you let me go then, Robert? If you're my friend…"

"They won't let me, Jack."

"But you've got a sword?"

"There are too many of them, lad. Aye, I could put down one or two of them but we'd both end up with our throats cut."

"So what can we do?"

"Master Warner thinks you have a secret, Jack and that's what he wants to get from you. If you tell him what you know, I think he'll be so grateful that he'll let you go free."

Jack bit his lip in silence and Robert waited.

"I couldn't do that, Robert," said Jack in a small voice and Robert smiled. Warner was right: the lad did know something.

He took the boy gently by the shoulders and looked him in the eye.

"Jack, I want you to think for a moment, just picture the scene when your friend brings your grandfather back into this house and Master Warner says to you: Jack Goldwell, tell me what you know or I shall kill your grandfather where he stands. What will you say then?"

The boy trembled in his grasp and Robert was tempted to shake the secret out of him, but he was interrupted by a loud banging at the door. He let the boy go.

"You hear that, Jack? I suggest you keep thinking about that question, because very soon you'll need to answer it."

§§§

Hal could hide his concern from the others, but not from Becky.

"I should go with you," she said.

"No," replied Hal flatly. "It won't help and it'll put you at risk too."

"That doesn't ease my fears much," she said. "If it's so dangerous, then why are you taking Will?"

"Because I need him - and so will his brother."

"What are we getting into, Hal?" she asked.

"I'm just trying to get us all out of it," he said, "unhurt… You stay with Mistress Sarah and we'll be back as soon as we can."

She pressed his hand in hers and kissed him long and hard.

"Bring those boys back safe, husband…"

Hal nodded and rejoined John Goldwell, Pinner and Will in the solar.

"Do you think they'll want coin? Silver?" asked Goldwell suddenly.

"We're not going to pay them, Master Goldwell - at least not yet. If Will's right, they know where you live - what's to stop them pressing you for more when they feel like it? But don't worry on that now."

The goldsmith turned his grey face away. "To be sure, Hal," he muttered, "I'll not worry on it now…but I'll worry about it soon enough."

They set off at a brisk pace along the lane and into Bread Street. Hal went through in his head what he planned to do. He knew the layout of the house well enough from years before, but the scheme he had agreed with Pinner was dangerous. Yet, whatever they did would have its dangers.

They walked into Cheapside. It was busy now - the churches would be doing great business, thought Hal. John Goldwell, despite his recent troubles, was well known and many nodded to the former alderman of the city as they passed. He seemed barely to notice though and Hal feared that he would not be up to the task.

When they were about fifty yards or so from Warner's house, Hal handed the small piece of wood to Will. "You know what you must do," he said to him.

"Aye," said Will.

"Good lad. But when you're in there, do only what I've told you - don't go taking silly risks!"

He turned to the goldsmith. "Are you set for this, Master Goldwell?"

Goldwell took a gulp of air and swallowed hard. "Yes, Hal, I believe so. I know what to do: I'll get you as much time as I may."

"Now, all of you: we must have them guessing," said Hal. "Our aim is not to spill blood, but blood might be spilled all the same - so be ready for that. All will hang upon our sharp wits."

He watched Will take Master Goldwell to the house while he lingered in the shadows nearby with Pinner. He was surprised at the sweat on his hands. He had survived many a bloody skirmish alongside Lord Elder - this surely could not be so bad. Master Goldwell arrived at the door and knocked loudly. Hal and Pinner remained by the corner of the house next door where they could not be seen.

The door opened and John Goldwell stepped across the threshold. Will followed and tripped to sprawl in the doorway. Someone hauled him up but Will then ran past him and there was a shout of annoyance from within. At once Hal and Pinner headed for the door just as someone was trying to close it. There was bitter cursing from the other side of the door. The wooden wedge Will had lodged there did its job and gave them just enough time to reach the door before it could be closed. Hal put his shoulder to it and the heavy door banged open. There was a gasp of pain and more oaths. He passed through the door and a body on the floor stretched out an arm. Hal felt a blade cut his shin.

"God's blood," he muttered and kicked hard at the prone figure's head. There was a crack of bone and the man went limp. They were in the gloomy entrance hall and ahead of him he saw Goldwell. The goldsmith glanced back at him and then disappeared into the main chamber. The door closed and Pinner stopped outside it.

"Anyone but a friend steps through that door," whispered Hal, "you put your knife to his throat."

"Through his throat?" whispered Pinner.

"No!" chided Hal. "If men start dying we'll not get out of here alive."

Will crouched by the stairwell waiting for him and Hal gave him a pat on the head.

"Well done, lad. Now, wait here while I see who's upstairs. You remember what to do? I'll be down once it's clear. If anyone comes up from the cellar, Pinner's close by. Alright?"

Will nodded and Hal began climbing the stairs. He would rather be fighting outside where he could move freely than stalking armed men from room to room. He reached the top of the first flight of steps and crossed the landing. The solar door lay open and there was no-one inside the room. He glanced up the next flight of steps. In his hand he held a small club, for he was reluctant to raise a sword against men who might be guilty of nothing worse than being employed by a lawyer.

He paused briefly, trying to clear his head, for memories

of his time as a young lad in the house were crowding in upon him. His memories almost got him killed as he dallied outside the door to the old apprentice sleeping quarters. It suddenly swung open but fortunately the figure on the threshold was even more surprised than he was. Hal struck him hard on the temple before he could cry out then caught the man as he fell forward. He dragged him into the room. It seemed smaller than he remembered, but it was all such a long time ago.

There was no-one else in the room, so he shut the door and continued up to the second floor. He remembered there being several smaller chambers upstairs - bedchambers in those days. For a moment he waited on the small landing, his mouth dry. Then he opened the first door and went in. No-one. He repeated the process for each door but only one chamber was occupied. It was dark; the shutters were still closed. In the gloom he saw a figure on the bed, fast asleep. Hal crept over to him. Still asleep. Good. Except, as the man lay there, Hal found he was reluctant to strike a sleeping, defenceless man.

He decided to let the fellow lie where he was and moved away a step. The floor creaked loudly under his feet and the sleeping man groaned. Hal took another step towards the door and caused a loose board to rattle.

"Who's there?" came from the bed.

"Shit," muttered Hal.

"Hooper? Is that you?" moaned the half-awake man.

Hal crossed swiftly to the bed and struck the man on the head as he was sitting up. He cried out as the club knocked him senseless. Hal hoped the blow sounded worse than it was for it sounded bloody. He moved fast now in case others in the house heard the cry. He only hoped he had not taken too long.

§§§

In the hall, Robert looked up when Goldwell stumbled

in and pushed the large door shut behind him.

The goldsmith stared at his grandson sadly. "Now Jack - there's no need to worry," he reassured him.

"Indeed, Jack," said Robert, "all will be well, now that Master Goldwell is here. All your grandfather must do is answer a simple question."

A tear or two dropped from the boy's eyes and he blinked them away.

"Master Goldwell," said Warner, "I'm a busy man so let's conduct this business swiftly. I want you to tell me what's so interesting to you about this house. But before you answer have a care, because I'll allow you but one answer before I have my friend here cut your grandson's throat. So it had better be the right answer."

Not very subtle, thought Robert, by Warner's standards; he must be consumed by this little matter.

"No!" cried Jack. "Don't tell him!"

Warner laughed. "Spirited boy, isn't he? But save your words, Jack, for I'm sure your grandfather will tell all to save you."

"Can't you let the boy go?" pleaded Goldwell.

"Don't delay, man!" snapped Warner. "You can both go when the matter's resolved!"

John Goldwell's head drooped and he moved towards the fireplace. His hand hesitated, brushing the stone face of the fire surround. Then he gave a small sigh and pushed at one of the smaller outer stones. With firm pressure it slid out to reveal a rectangular hole.

Goldwell paused and stared down at Jack for a moment. The boy tried to give him a reassuring smile.

He was a game lad, thought Robert.

"If you please, Master Goldwell," Warner reminded him.

The goldsmith reached into the recess and drew out a velvet pouch. He stared at it in his hand and Robert realised that he was weeping. For the first time, Robert's interest was awakened - he had expected a cache of coins but he doubted they would be wrapped in such cloth.

"Give it here, man," he ordered and took it from him.

He lifted the outer flap of the velvet pouch, feeling the eyes of all of them upon him. The cloth was soft to the touch, no doubt the finest quality velvet, but when he eased out the contents, even he was shocked. Warner's eyes lit up, Jack's mouth fell open wide and Goldwell gave a groan.

Robert was no great student of craftsmanship but he knew he was looking upon the finest gold work he had ever seen.

"Your work, Master Goldwell?" he said softly.

Goldwell nodded, tears tracing a path down his cheeks. He grimaced as if in pain.

"Wondrous workmanship," said Robert. "Christ on the cross… wondrous… and the stone, a sapphire of course, a sapphire..."

"Thank you, Robert, I'll take it now," said Warner, stretching out his hand.

Robert placed it back inside the cloth, handling it with something close to reverence. It was far beyond what he had expected - more valuable… much more valuable.

"My letter first, Warner," he said, "as agreed, and then I'll give you this."

Warner shrugged. "Very well, Robert, as agreed."

He reached into a wooden case and retrieved a small scroll from a bundle of several. It was unsealed.

"I'd like to read it," said Robert, "then you can put your seal upon it."

"Thought you might," Warner smirked and tossed the letter onto the table. "Perhaps I might examine the gold piece whilst you read the letter?"

"Wait," replied Robert, picking up the letter. He read it through and returned it to Warner. "Very good, Master

Warner - an excellent letter. Now sign and seal it - and we are done."

Warner frowned but signed the letter and, after only a moment's hesitation, applied a seal.

"Now Robert, perhaps I can have what is mine."

"Yours?" said Robert, placing the velvet wallet on the lawyer's table.

Warner smiled and leant forward to pick it up.

"What more can I do for you?" wheezed Goldwell. "I suppose you want the rest of my coin - well, there's a disappointment coming for you because there's nothing left! Not a single silver coin left."

His face had turned a shade of purple and he choked out his words. "Nothing!"

He made a sudden lunge for the jewel pouch. "Now run, Jack, run!" he cried.

Warner seized the pouch too and the two men grappled for it.

Jack did not move and Robert himself was astonished at the ferocity with which the two men fought for the jewel. Lawyers and merchants, he reminded himself, as the velvet cloth fell between the two men onto Warner's desk. Warner gained the upper hand and used his bulk to throw Goldwell back against the hearth. The goldsmith went over backwards and struck his head hard upon the stonework. Jack crawled over to him but Robert could tell at a glance that Goldwell was already dead.

Warner smoothed down his clothing and nonchalantly picked up the jewel pouch.

"Well done, Warner," mocked Robert. "You've killed the man."

"He was doomed from the moment he walked into this house," replied Warner, his eyes fixed upon the jewel. "Now, you'd better see to the boys - I don't want any witnesses but my own."

"I don't kill children," said Robert. "Jack, go and find your brother - or my man Hooper - tell him I said you can leave."

"I need you to help my grandfather," pleaded Jack.

"I'm afraid he's beyond any man's help now, Jack. And he told you to go, didn't he?"

"Robert!" said Warner. "We can't let them go… I won't leave it like that." He reached inside his robes and produced a small dagger.

"No," said Robert, "somehow, I didn't think you would."

He drew his sword. "Put up the knife, Warner and let them go - you've got what you wanted."

Jack stood, unmoving, beside his grandfather's body. Warner took a pace towards him.

Two men burst through the door but then stopped dead. Robert recognised one of them at once as Ned Elder's man, Hal.

Warner, knife in hand, made a sudden lunge at Jack. The man with Hal was the first to react: his right arm flexed and his knife pierced Warner's flabby chest as if it were a tub of fat.

The lawyer could not speak, but his anger was plain to them all as blood and air frothed about his mouth. He fell forward onto his desk and in no time, it seemed, he lay still.

Robert picked up the jewel pouch and turned to Hal.

They stared at each other in silence for what seemed an age.

"Thomas Gate…" breathed Hal.

"You're mistaken, sir," said Robert. "I am not this man, Thomas. I'm Sir Robert Radcliffe."

Hal, clearly wrestling with this revelation, did not move a muscle, but kept his gaze upon Robert.

"Gate? Radcliffe?" said Hal finally. "It makes no difference what you call yourself…"

"Listen to me," said Robert. "None of this was my doing. Warner did for Master Goldwell, as young Jack will tell you. But the lad's alright and I've no quarrel with you two."

Hal gave a bitter laugh. "No quarrel? I'd kill you for Agnes alone…"

Robert shook his head. "Of all the misdeeds I've done over the years - and I admit there have been some - you would kill me for the one sin I didn't commit?"

"She died because of you!" cried Hal, taking a step towards him.

Robert sighed. "Aye, I suppose she did, but I was the last man to wish for it. By the saints, I thought I had saved her!"

Robert knew that if they stood for much longer in that room there would be more blood. He moved swiftly, drawing out his sword and clubbing Hal with its hilt. Pinner raised his arm but Robert struck his hand aside and the knife flew across the room. Then he knocked Pinner down and both men lay groaning on the floor. They were at his mercy but he sheathed his sword, opened the door and turned back to Jack.

"You're my witness, Jack," he said. "I could have killed them both, but I didn't."

"Hooper!" he shouted and almost stumbled over Will who darted past him into the room.

Hooper appeared on the stairs and was helped down by another of his men.

"Come on," urged Robert. "I don't think we should linger here."

§§§

On a cold, damp November morning John Goldwell was buried. Felix of Bordeaux found it a sad spectacle, though many attended and no expense was spared in its provision. Some of the wealthiest merchants in the city contributed to the funeral costs else the former Alderman Goldwell might well have had a pauper's funeral. The goldsmith left nothing. Not a single coin remained of the vast fortune he once possessed. Sarah and Jack had only the clothes they wore and no income to pay for the lodgings in Pissing Lane, mean though they were.

It was only the arrival of Felix a few days after the events at Cheapside that prevented them all being thrown out into the streets to fend for themselves. He had been coming to London for trade every few months for years but such was the anxiety amongst the ladies at Corve Manor that he decided to make the journey once more before midwinter arrived. He also felt some responsibility for John Goldwell's unhappy return to London. Perhaps he should not have pressed his friend so hard, but he had thought it for the best.

Though he arrived too late to help the goldsmith, he could at least offer support to the now impoverished Sarah and Jack. Even Sarah put up little resistance to a return to Ludlow and, of course, Jack was overjoyed to return with his brother. Hal told him what he knew of the sorry story and Felix had no doubt that Jack had some knowledge which might shed a little more light on what had actually happened at the lawyer, Warner's house. But that was for the future - a more peaceful one, he prayed.

So, John Goldwell's affairs settled, they all took their leave of the city with Felix. He possessed coin enough to pay the expense of their journey and he felt it was the least he could do. The winter roads, though, were as bad as he feared and it was early December by the time their wagon arrived back at Corve Manor with its exhausted passengers. Felix promptly vowed that he would stay in his warm house in Broad Street, Ludlow until the spring. Yet despite the winter gloom, there was a faint glimmer of light: the two half-brothers were together and, with Jack in Ludlow and

Will at Corve, they would be close enough to see each other often. And then there were the two lovebirds: Becky and Hal. Felix smiled. He had not foreseen that, yet it seemed the Lord could still work some miracles.

42

Christmas: 25th December 1469, at Corve

Manor near Ludlow

Ned breathed in the heady mix of herbs, spices and smoke from the hearth in the centre of the hall at Corve Manor. He had not travelled to Corve in November and only in the past few days, as the December quarter day approached, did he finally prepare to leave Quenhull. Deep in winter, travel was not easy for there had been heavy rainfall across the Welsh marches.

Now, at least, that he was back at Corve, he felt at ease for the first time in months - though he told himself that his mood probably owed more to the spiced wine than to any feeling of peace. He laid his hand gently upon Maighread's and she smiled at him. She looked well and Eleanor said she was much stronger again now, after the trials of the birth. He had contrived to miss not only the birth of his second son but his wife's slow recovery and eventual churching. The boy was named Thomas after Ned's grandfather, of whom Maighread had been very fond. Young Thomas looked strong like his half-brother John.

As he stroked Maighread's hand, Ned caught the eye of his sister. She seemed content, as far as Eleanor was ever content - and how could he expect her to recover quickly from the loss of Ragwulf, though he thought perhaps the child helped. Her daughter had been born unexpectedly early but was robust and loud - very loud. Eleanor had called her Kate after her own mother. There was something there that he never quite understood. He had known his mother for only a short time but his few, dim memories of her spoke of a wild, untamed spirit... a fire that burned fiercely before it died. He feared for Eleanor, who seemed so like her... and now there was tiny little Kate... He prayed that perhaps she would take after her father.

The hall was crammed to the rafters with folk from all over the Corve estate but he was glad Maighread persuaded him to bring so many to their hearth. He grinned at the large pile of boots by the fire. It was going to be a very wet Christmas season with the Corve already swollen by the rains and the tracks along the valley clogged with mud. Yet it suited him that he could not travel far until the weather improved and for a while he could enjoy being with those he loved.

With them on the high table were the two lads, Will and John - Mags was there too though she would not speak to him.

Soon the table before him was littered with the debris of their feast - not a lavish one for he could not afford it, but there was more to be done this evening than eating and drinking. He decided he should do it before the wine took hold of him, so he stood up and around the hall quiet slowly prevailed. He realised he was right not to delay his speech any longer or many would not be capable of listening at all.

He felt Maighread's hand tense in his and he squeezed it gently. Then he moved around the table to where Mags sat and she glanced up at him, her face a mask of apprehension. Maighread and Eleanor spoke of Mags' steadfast support in their perilous journey to bring their babes into the world. He admired her all the more, knowing that her grieving heart must have split in two. He understood that she blamed him, understood that she did not want to hear that he was sorry for John Holton's death, yet he desperately needed to make his peace with her.

He knelt at her feet and a murmur went around the hall until once more silence fell.

"When folk gather, on days such as this," he began, "it is well to remember those who may not join us in our feasting, those who cannot share our ale or wine. There are many who have fallen this past year in my service... too many - some who have left widows and children. But it may stand for all if I mention one man by name: my steward, John Holton. I knew John since we were boys in Yorkshire and, as some of you will know, he died saving my life.

"No more loyal man ever lived, but how can I repay such a debt? I cannot. I can give thanks before God for John's loyal service but I cannot bring him back to his widow and children. We have the misfortune to live in a time of great strife where honest men and women are in fear of their lives. All I can do is pledge to you that I shall ever strive to shield you from the dangers that stalk our land."

He glanced up at Mags who inclined her head in solemn acknowledgement; it was acceptance, if not forgiveness. He got to his feet and there was a chorus of support for his words and folk banged their hands down hard on the tables, rattling the pewter ale pots and wooden platters. Cries of "An Elder, an Elder!" arose from some of the men at arms, no doubt already emboldened by the ale. He raised his arms aloft to quieten them and then continued.

"When I look about this hall I'm proud to behold such a great host, but... if truth be told, I am also worried. There are too many of us now at Corve for safety. This is but a small manor and we can't house or feed everyone in times of trouble."

This stirred the hall to a low murmur around him.

"I wish I could tell you all that our woes are over, that the kingdom is safe and that we shall have no more need of shrouds for fallen comrades... but I cannot. I fear the troubles of the past year will spill over into the next. So, after twelfth night, most of you… and those who live with you… will move south to my castle at Quenhull leaving only a small garrison here. You will all be safer behind Quenhull's strong walls and, with most of us gone from here, Corve will attract less attention from my enemies. So, enjoy each other's company during this Christmas season for very soon all will change."

He snatched up a pot of spiced wine from the table and raised it to his lips. There was a great cheer from them all and when he sat down the noise did not abate as every man and woman started to speak at once. Most knew nothing of Quenhull and would simply take his words on trust, but a few older heads would wonder more darkly what this great move would mean for them and their families. Ned glanced around the high table to judge his family's response but only Maighread gave him a reassuring smile and when he turned to Eleanor, he found a troubled look upon her face.

§§§

In the days that followed the Christmas feast, Ned did not immediately discover the reason for Eleanor's disquiet. He spent many hours planning the move to Quenhull but he dared not leave until the wagons could negotiate the boggy tracks from Corve to Ludlow. He was relieved to find that most of his men appeared content to be moving to Quenhull, especially when they heard from their comrades of its powerful defences. It was a castle that could withstand a long siege if necessary and, though Ned could not see a situation where it would need to, he was determined not to be taken by surprise as had happened before. The reduced garrison at Corve would mean that no-one could view it as any sort of threat which he reckoned was the best way to keep its inhabitants safe.

All seemed to be going well until New Year's Day. He had an inkling that something was wrong for Maighread was not her usual self in the morning, but he put it down to the troubles of motherhood. In the afternoon though, as all the family sat before a warming fire in the solar, Eleanor suddenly went to Ned and dropped down upon her knees before him. He was astonished for she had never done such a thing before.

"Ellie?"

"Brother," she said, "I ask you to grant me a new year's gift."

He smiled at that, but the smile faded as she continued.

"I want you to give me Corve Manor."

"Give it to you?" he said. "Why?"

"Because I don't want to go to Quenhull. I'm tired of moving on. I want a home for my children. Is it any wonder that my son ran away from me? He tells me that he wants to stay here... to be close to Jack - and I can't deny him that, Ned."

"No!" said Ned, standing up. "You are all coming to Quenhull where it's safer."

"We are simply women and children," replied Eleanor.

"But you'll be at risk - why do you think I want to move my family? My enemies will try to use you to weaken me - you could be taken hostage! I just can't allow it."

"You won't allow it?" said Eleanor, her cheeks flushed.

"No, I won't!" said Ned.

Maighread laid a hand on his shoulder. "Ned... perhaps..."

He shook off her hand. "No! All the family - and Mags' family - are going to Quenhull."

"Well Mags isn't going," said Eleanor, "and I don't see you bundling her into a wagon against her will."

"This place was Holton's place, I can see that," said Ned, "but neither she nor you can stay - it's too dangerous."

Eleanor got up off her knees and gave him a wry smile.

"Ned, just so you understand me: I'll stab the first one who tries to move me from here - even if it's you!"

He shook his head. Men he could deal with, persuade, or cajole if necessary; but women... they would remain a mystery to him forever.

"But what if... men come here!" he pleaded.

"Aye, what if they do?" asked Eleanor. "They will only be men..."

She took Will's hand and breezed out of the room, slamming the door shut behind her.

"Out of a clear sky..." mused Maighread.

"You knew that was going to happen, didn't you?" he accused her.

She smiled wearily at him. "I'll go with you Ned because I'm your obedient lady and I fear for your children. So we'll go: you, me, John and Thomas... but you won't move Eleanor, nor Mags, against their will. If there are two more determined women in all Christendom, I don't know who they are."

"But I fear for them here..." he sighed and studied her face. "I can't protect them here and there are men in this land who would... butcher children if it came to it... and I know some of them serve my enemies."

"You must leave Eleanor in God's hands," said Maighread.

"Forgive me, Maighread, but rarely has God seen fit to save those I love..."

"Except for me, of course," she replied.

"Aye, except for you - twice! And God knows I'm right

glad of that."

"She's lost, Ned. Eleanor is lost. Give her somewhere to cling to, somewhere to hold fast to, somewhere to raise her children - neither with a father. War will follow you, Ned - it always does. Let your sister be free of it."

THE LAST SHROUD

315

PART FOUR: REBELLION

DEREK BIRKS

43

13th March 1470, at Coventry

After Warner's sudden demise, Robert had intended to head north and make another attempt to win over Lady Emma. But before he could do so, Warwick himself arrived in the city to make his peace with King Edward. The earl, it seemed, was still plotting against the king with Clarence, and thus Robert spent the next two months riding across the land from one conspirator to another. He passed on secret assurances from Warwick to the Welles family in Lincolnshire, where a new rebellion was being nurtured. He conveyed privy messages urging support from the Earl of Shrewsbury and the Stanley brothers in the north-west - that was a rich irony if ever there was one.

By the start of March, Robert came to believe that Warwick's star, so obviously on the wane before Christmas, was once more in the ascendant. Warwick had left the capital and was now controlling events from Coventry. The Duke of Clarence was already on his way from London to join him in the rebellion.

Yet even before Robert himself left the city for the last time, several events sowed doubts once more in his mind. He was shocked to hear that Warwick's treason was already being proclaimed in the streets of the city - a city which, until now, had always held the earl in high regard. Added to that, King Edward himself had set off on a march to confront the Welles' rebels in the east. Commissions of array had been issued and it seemed likely that the king might gather a large army on his way.

Thus, as Robert rode into Coventry with Hooper and his men, he was desperate for some encouraging news. Here, at the heart of Warwick's new bid for power, he expected to find a host of Neville banners flying, and a few for Clarence, who it seemed was destined to replace his brother on the throne. Yet what he found was a town in denial: everywhere, the support for the earl and the duke seemed half-hearted. However busy the town appeared - and it did appear busy with horsemen cantering in all directions and restless knots of men at arms on every street corner - Robert judged that the underlying mood of the locals was a good deal closer to dismay than jubilation.

Warwick received Robert like a long lost friend, though that did not inspire much confidence either. Robert preferred the earl when he was bullish and aggressive; the figure that greeted him now looked drawn and tired.

"All rests upon Welles," said Warwick, "and they say he commands a large host."

Robert thought that was just as well since Warwick himself had by no means a large host.

"No sign yet of men from the Earl of Shrewsbury, my lord?" asked Robert. "Or Lord Stanley?"

"No, but the rising prospers in the north. It's all arranged: Welles will let the royal army pass him by and we'll combine our forces with his at Leicester - Welles may be there even now. Then we'll have the king trapped between us and our northern friends under my brother, John's command. And the best part, Robert, is that the king still believes that we are for him!"

Robert was with the earl when men from Welles' army began to arrive, but they were not the vanguard of a great rebel host. Instead their appearance announced the utter collapse of the rebel cause in Lincolnshire. They told of men fleeing at the first roar of the king's cannons before they had even drawn their swords in anger. It struck Robert that since these men were the first to arrive they were most likely the first to flee. Others had apparently thrown off Neville or Clarence livery in their haste to appear loyal to the king. The stories filled Robert with foreboding: this was not reminiscent of the heady success at Edgecote.

Worse still, a royal messenger turned up not long afterwards with letters from the king, ordering the earl and the duke to dismiss their men and go to him at once.

"What will you do, lord?" asked Robert.

"The king knows nothing for certain," replied Warwick. "All will be well if the north rises as it did last year and the Stanleys and Shrewsbury join us. Send out the word! I want every man ready to move today. We'll join the other lords at Derby and, with God's help, my brother's northern army will be close by then. Robert, you're to go to Lord Stanley at once for his support is vital. Do your best to convince him of our strength and then join us at Chesterfield."

Robert was tempted to mention that he had only been off his horse for a few hours but he thought better of it and instead sought out Hooper. The latter swore extensively when he learned that they must ride on yet again.

"The men will be in taverns and brothels all over the town!" he protested.

"I know and they deserve to be," said Robert, "but all the same, I need you - and them - with me."

How Hooper managed to persuade his men to leave, Robert had no idea but he managed to gather up all but one, who had already perished in a drunken brawl. The urgency of his mission enabled him to requisition fresh horses and they made good time to Burton and thence on to Stafford. The journey gave Robert ample time to consider what to do next though much would depend on the reception he got from the Stanleys. If they threw in their lot with Warwick and Clarence then there was still every chance of success. But at Stafford the news was catastrophic: everyone spoke of the king's victory and, worse still, there were rumours that Warwick's brother, John, Lord Montagu, far from leading the rebellion had in fact crushed the life out of it. John Neville, it was claimed, had decided to remain loyal to the king.

It took another two days for Robert to reach Lord Thomas Stanley's house in Cheshire and when he arrived, he found that Thomas Stanley was not there, though his younger brother, William, was. For Robert this was an opportunity too good to pass up. When he presented letters to William Stanley from both Clarence and Warwick, they were received coolly.

"My brother, Thomas, is away dealing with... some local matters," said William, "and thus he regrets that he is unable to offer the earl his support at this time."

This was the point at which his master, Warwick, would expect Robert to make the strongest possible case in his favour. But Robert knew that if there was a moment upon which his future hung, this was it. He did not hesitate but reached inside his cloak, took out the late Benjamin Warner's letter of introduction and held it out to William Stanley.

"Another plea for our help?" asked William with a weary tone. "I doubt you've a letter from anyone more persuasive than Warwick."

"It's not a plea for assistance for the Earl of Warwick..." said Robert.

William broke the seal and read the letter.

"Hmm. Warner's judgement has often been sound," he said, "up to a point. You seek a position with me?"

"Aye."

"Why with me and not my brother?" asked William

thoughtfully.

Robert hesitated, anxious not to overplay his hand. "I believe you're a man of ambition and I think a fellow with my skills could be of service to you."

"Well, Warner says you're a man who can see a task through… but your present task - are you're going to see that through?"

"I'll speak plainly. The Earl of Warwick's cause is lost - and I've expected this for months. The earl is finished."

"But is he?" asked William. "If you know the earl so well then you must know that his powers of recovery are legendary. He's been on the losing side many a time, cornered, apparently weak - and then… he appears as if reborn and all bow before his power."

"I won't deny it's possible," replied Robert, "but that doesn't change what I offer you."

"Warwick seems to trust you, but how many masters do you intend to serve, Sir Robert?"

"Only one."

"Let's say you stay with Warwick for the moment, see what unfolds. You might render me a service by being privy to his inner councils. Such intelligence would be valuable to King Edward…"

"So, if the earl succeeds," said Robert, "then I shall be your eyes and ears and I shall act in your interest; but if the earl falls, then you will grant me a position of prominence in your own household."

William took some time to consider. "Prominence? You don't ask much," he mused, "but very well. It seems that we have an arrangement, Sir Robert. We shall see where God places his faith in the coming days. I'll see to it that you're provided for tonight, that your men are fed and your horses stabled."

William gave a grim smile. "Then on the morrow you can take the earl your… disappointing news."

Robert could hardly disguise his elation as he left the hall and went to give Hooper his instructions. It was far too soon for his men to know his true position or they would surely betray their new loyalty when they returned to Warwick's camp. Already though, Robert was planning what to do next. If Warwick fell, he would go again to Lady Emma and press his suit with her. In the circumstances she was certain to accept him rather than abandon herself and her children to ruin.

He left the following day in good spirits and rode hard to the east. He expected to meet the earl at Chesterfield as agreed but almost missed him on the road. He would have done so had he not come across a small band of men wearing the ragged staff badge. When he asked them where the earl was, their horses barely broke stride as they uttered a terse response that he was on the road to Manchester. They were heading in the opposite direction to the south. Already then, it had begun and such desertions would soon bleed away all but Warwick's most loyal retainers.

It was late afternoon before Robert discovered the earl's small column of mounted men camped outside Manchester. He was not looking forward to bringing Warwick the news he carried. Yet, when it came to it and he delivered his dread tidings to the earl and the young duke, there was no railing or blustering by either man. They took the news in silence and it dawned upon Robert that they must have learned by now of the failure in the north. The Stanleys' desertion only confirmed what Warwick already knew: he had lost, and lost badly.

Robert remained whilst Warwick and Clarence discussed what paths were left to them, though their deliberations were brief. The choice was simple, Robert decided: throw themselves upon the king's mercy or flee. Neither alternative was very attractive.

"Are you fit to ride, Robert?" asked the earl.

Robert had been in the saddle a great deal in recent days but he had at least rested under the Stanleys' roof. "Aye, my lord," he replied.

"Then ride south, now, tonight," ordered the earl. "Go to the castle at Warwick. Tell the countess to be ready to leave by the time I get there - and I shan't be far behind you."

"Aye, my lord."

"And Robert, you understand the need for haste?"

"Of course, my lord..."

"While you're waiting for me, load up as many supplies and arms as you can - and Robert..."

"My lord?"

"Make sure your men load up a supply of black powder and the handguns..." said the earl.

Robert nodded and noticed that Clarence sat in abject silence throughout, showing little interest in their conversation. He looked a beaten man already, Robert thought.

His own men accepted the news that they must ride south again surprisingly well, he thought, probably because he pointed out to them the perilous situation of Warwick's main column. They evidently saw the advantage of putting some distance between themselves and the pursuing army of King Edward.

§§§

Robert did not enjoy the ride to Warwick. At every turn he expected the royal army to appear and cut them off - and his agreement with William Stanley would count for little if he was killed whilst in the service of Warwick. Nevertheless, his small party reached Warwick Castle without hindrance. Of course, his tidings threw the whole household into turmoil. The countess received the terrible news well, as he expected she would, but she pressed him with questions about the need for such an urgent departure. He had known her long enough to understand that she was not concerned for her own safety.

"And what of my daughter, the Duchess of Clarence?" she asked him.

"She will soon be on her way to safety in Exeter, I believe, my lady."

"But she is too heavy with child to travel."

"Indeed, my lady, but we shall go to her," replied Robert.

He knew that noble ladies did not travel on the eve of the birth of their first child - yet travel the duchess must. He left the countess and paused only to give Hooper his orders before seeking out Emma. Warwick would not be far behind him; the time for hesitation was over.

He found her in her chamber, already preparing her children for the journey. She looked up at him briefly and bade him a frosty good evening. Robert was caked in mud for the roads were difficult, mired by the spring rains. He was certain that his appearance did not present him at his best.

"You may see, Sir Robert, that I have much to do," said Emma, her words delivered like swift jabs with a short blade - deep enough to wound without killing.

"Yet, lady… I must speak with you," he insisted.

Not for the first time, he admired her even as he felt the chill of her stare. She was not beautiful and, if anything, her features gave her a naturally stern look. She maintained a steely self-control… yet beneath that armour, he believed, beat a fragile heart.

"Richard, take Alice outside," she told her son. The boy studied Robert for a moment and then took his sister's hand.

"What is it you want, Sir Robert?" asked Emma. "You must have known how busy I'd be - and I must go to Lady Anne presently. She'll need my help."

"Indeed," acknowledged Robert, "but still I had to see you."

"I can't see why," she retorted, "for surely we can have no more to say to each other."

Robert had rehearsed his next words many times in the past few months.

"I have a gift for you," he said. "Something I hope will prove to be… a wedding gift."

She frowned at him. "Sir Robert, must I keep answering that question every few months? I will not marry you - now, sir, is that clear enough?"

"But you've not heard me yet - nor seen my gift," he protested.

"A man will say anything to a woman - or give her anything - to bed her, marry her, or both," said Emma. "I may be a widow, Sir Robert, but I have a trusted position in the household of the most powerful nobleman in England. I don't need to marry."

"Then marry for love!" declared Robert.

"Love? You? Are you mad? What in all Christendom makes you believe that, of all men, I could ever love you?"

He stood in silence.

"You're serious," she breathed.

"Aye."

There was an awkward silence which he knew he must fill so he took out the velvet-wrapped object. "This is for you," he said.

"Whatever it is, Sir Robert, I don't want it."

"But you will, my lady. When you see it, you'll want it. You will!"

He took out the beautiful gold reliquary and, as he anticipated, she gasped to look upon it.

"Please, hold it," he said, taking her hand but she pulled abruptly away.

"Do you think my head will be turned by such a

trinket?" she said.

"Trinket?" he exclaimed. "Why, this was likely made for a queen! It's near priceless - certainly no trinket!"

He saw that her eyes were drawn to it, despite her words of rejection.

"And what would I do with it?" she asked. "How could I ever have such a piece? Aye, it's fit for a queen or at the least a duchess - but not for me. I could never have that. And we both know that you could never afford it either, so it's a stolen trinket. Now put it away!"

He fumbled the reliquary back into the folded cloth.

"For all you deny it," he persisted, "there is - and always has been - something between us."

"Aye, and that something is loathing," she snapped. "Now leave me, and don't come back to ask again!"

"There's something else," he said.

"No! There isn't - we're done. Now leave me!"

The flush of anger in her cheeks made her even more attractive, he thought.

"Listen," he said. "Why do you think this precious household of yours is in such a panic?"

"The countess and Lady Anne are to travel with the earl. There is no mystery there."

"With the duchess due to give birth in a matter of weeks?" he said. "You don't find that a little alarming?"

"What are you saying?" she asked.

"I'm saying that Warwick's house is falling... not in a few weeks or months - but now!" he blurted out.

She glared at him but did not reply.

"His house is falling as we speak," he repeated, "and I don't want you and your children to fall with it."

"You're wrong, plain wrong! The earl has survived the past year - and it doesn't get much worse than that. He's still in the king's affections and has regained his trust..."

"Is that what they tell you? Well, in London they name

him traitor - openly in the streets. I've seen a placard in Cheap that says exactly that! He's just made another attempt upon the king and I can assure you that King Edward will never, ever, trust him again. Warwick is doomed, my lady. Let me give you my help - even if you still refuse marriage. Let me help you to survive his fall, for I don't doubt it will be bloody..."

Emma shook her head. "You'll not win me with lies. He's not going to fall and all I want you to do is to leave me as swiftly as you can. I still have much to do this evening, even if you haven't!"

"My lady..."

"Peace, sir! I am not your lady and I never will be your lady! Now leave me, please... I beg you."

"Very well, my lady, but I will be nearby when you have need of me - and you will. I can wait until then..."

44

30th March 1470, at Quenhull Castle

Ned read the letter again. "Has anyone actually seen them?" he asked, looking first to Croft, then Spearbold.

"No, my lord," they replied in unison.

"But… this letter must have taken three days or more to reach us," said Spearbold, "and it's clear that the earl must have fled days ago - possibly a week or more."

"Not much is clear to me in this, Spearbold," said Ned, "because even I find it difficult to believe that Warwick has risen against the king yet again."

"Hmm, I'm less surprised, my lord," said Spearbold.

Ned turned to Croft. "You have men on watch?" he asked.

"Yes, lord. If the earl or the duke passes through the Severn valley, we'll know of it."

"Hah! Don't be so sure! Between them, Clarence and Warwick own half the Severn valley!" he said. "Still, we must be watchful. These men are no common outlaws and they will travel in as much force as they can muster."

"And don't forget the Courtenays raised their colours in Devon only a few weeks ago," added Spearbold. "We must be cautious, my lord - there are armed men everywhere and allegiances have become all too fragile…"

"Aye," acknowledged Ned. He looked at the two men thoughtfully. Their advice, as always, was sound.

"Very well, here's what we do. Croft, get all the men we can spare ready to ride the moment the earl's party is sighted - but don't weaken the garrison. We all have families here now and this time I want to know they're safe."

He watched Croft go and took Spearbold's arm to walk along the rampart.

"As to family, Spearbold," he said. "I still worry for my sister…"

"You need not, my lord. Lady Eleanor will be safe enough at Corve and Warwick certainly won't be running there!"

Ned shook his head. "You mistake me, Spearbold. I have another sister."

"Ah," said Spearbold. "You think she'll be with Warwick?"

"She'll be wherever his daughter Anne is. I know my sister better now than when I was younger. She's not Eleanor, but she'll defend that Neville child with all the fight she has."

"But what can we do?" said Spearbold. "Attempt a rescue?"

Ned gave him a wry smile. "I've learned that lesson too," he replied. "I fear that she trusts me less than Warwick. I'm just a man that kills people - she thinks the earl is rather better than that."

"So, your hands are tied…"

"She may have little love for me these days but I'll still seek to protect her - if she'll let me. If Warwick is caught, whether by me or any other of the king's men, there'll be blood. I've already seen often enough how innocents can suffer when that happens."

§§§

Overnight, Ned waited impatiently for news and in the morning it arrived from all directions: the Duke of Gloucester wrote that he had hurried north from Wales, given the Stanleys and the Earl of Shrewsbury a fright and was now moving south. The king too sent word that he was pursuing the rebels with all possible speed and urged Ned to cut off Warwick's escape until he could get there. The only news Ned did not yet have was the whereabouts of Warwick.

Not until the end of the day, as the castle gates were about to close at dusk, did another messenger arrive laden with the news he wanted: Warwick's column of fugitives had been sighted northeast of Tewkesbury.

"About twenty miles away," mused Croft.

"If we ride at first light," said Ned, "we can catch him!"

"It'll be close, lord," said Croft. "He'll outnumber us - and we still need to find him. Do we know where he's heading?"

"The south coast," said Spearbold, "where he has ample ships and more allies."

"We'll only get one chance to do this," said Ned. "The king isn't close enough yet. If Warwick and Clarence rebuff us and reach Devonshire, the Courtenays will see them to safety."

45

31st March 1470, south of Tewkesbury in

Gloucestershire

The earl had set Robert Radcliffe and his men to ride as a rearguard, knowing that the king and the many other dogs of York would be in hot pursuit. Robert was surprised that his masters were taking their families with them - sanctuary would have been a wiser alternative, especially given the condition of the duchess. Yet it enabled him to catch an occasional glimpse of Lady Emma when he rejoined the camp in the evening, having posted his sentries. He could stand there, in the shadows, looking on as she attended upon her charge, Lady Anne, or comforted her young daughter, Alice, for whom the journey must already seem interminable. As for the lady herself, if she noticed him at all, she did not show it.

The next day, a warm April day, they skirted Gloucester keeping about a hundred yards or so from the east bank of the river Severn. There were several wagons in their column which made progress slower than anyone would have liked but, since they carried all that the earl and the duke had left, no-one voiced their concerns. Robert knew that Warwick would abandon them if he had to, but he would not do so lightly. As was his habit, Robert allowed the riders and wagons to move off and held his men back. Since the bridge across the river at Gloucester was only a few miles away, it seemed prudent to take even more care than usual.

He led his men on a short sortie north towards the town. If anyone meant them harm they might cross the Severn at Gloucester - unless of course they were already on their side of the river. He had only a score of men and was forced to spread them thinly in a wide arc to the north and east of the column. They kept each other in sight as far as they could and managed to cover a broad front. They held this screen all morning until about midday when they unexpectedly caught up with one of the wagons.

Robert knew at a glance that it was the one in which Emma and her daughter travelled. Then he saw them sitting on a grassy bank whilst several men stared impotently at the wagon. A group of about thirty men at arms were also waiting with it, but no archers, he noted. Instinctively, Robert decided to draw his men closer in.

"What's the trouble?" he called as he rode up.

"Wheel's cracked," answered one of the carters. "We thought it would last; it didn't…"

"Can you repair it?" asked Robert.

"Oh, aye, it'll take all day though…"

"All day! You've not got time to fell a tree, man! And you most certainly haven't got all day!"

The man spread his arms in apology.

"Aye, well just do your best," said Robert.

He dismounted and went over to the passengers.

"My lady," he greeted Emma courteously. "There's no need for you to worry. The king is still far behind us."

She gave him withering look. "Why, Sir Robert, I wasn't worried - until I saw you…"

"My lady, I'm here to protect you - and little Alice," he replied, unable to keep the sadness from his voice.

"Don't let us keep you from your duties then, Sir Robert," she said.

He nodded and left her sitting stiff-backed and proud with her daughter picking wild flowers at her feet. He rode back to where he expected Hooper to be waiting, but Hooper had gone. He scanned the horizon and was relieved to see his mounted men at arms stretched across the route they had followed. Then he frowned, for beyond his screen of men was a broad thicket of trees from which a rider had just emerged, heading towards him at speed. He recognised Hooper's grey mare.

"Riders coming!" cried Hooper as he pulled up. "How far ahead is the main host?"

"Far enough," said Robert, "but we have some stragglers - and a wagon that won't move."

"Shit!" observed Hooper.

"How close are the riders?" asked Robert.

"The other side of the trees - a mile or two at most!"

"Good Christ! Call in all the men. Post a few scouts along the riverside and then send our archers to me!"

Robert hurried back to the wagon. He dismounted and carried out a swift examination of its load: powder and arms, mostly.

"How much longer?" he asked the carter.

"The wood's splintered," he explained, "we're having to replace it."

"Well, you've only a few moments - can you do it or not?" demanded Robert.

"Not a hope, Sir Robert."

Robert gave a sigh and looked at those around him.

The captain of the men at arms he knew well enough - he was a capable, trustworthy fellow.

He took him aside and swiftly explained their predicament.

"Escort Lady Emma and her child to the main column," he told him. "We'll try to slow down the pursuing group."

Lady Emma was disposed to argue when he informed

her, but she acquiesced as soon as she realised the danger her daughter might be in.

"Why are you not coming with us?" she asked.

"Because the king's men will overtake us unless something - or someone - delays them."

She nodded, he thought with a softer countenance - or perhaps he was imagining it. Before she could protest, he lifted her up onto one of the horses and then passed Alice up to her.

"Thank you, Sir Robert," she said stiffly.

"May God be with you, Lady Emma," he said.

She turned to go but then swung back to face him. "And may God protect you, Sir Robert."

He smiled at that for it was the nearest she had yet come to giving him a kind word. Then he watched her go, safely wrapped within the cluster of men at arms.

A little relieved, he set about organising his men. They had no choice but to make some sort of a stand at least until they could gauge how large a force faced them. If it was the king himself, Robert reflected, then it would be the last stand he ever made.

He was startled to see Hooper coming up from the direction of the river.

"I was wrong," announced Hooper, arriving breathless. "There's not one group; there's two!"

"By the saints! There are two parties following us?"

"One's following - the other... has outflanked us," said Hooper.

"But how?"

"Clever sods must have sneaked past us along the river's edge. Our scouts have just found their tracks."

"So, they're ahead of us now?" Robert struggled to come to terms with the sudden change in their position. "How far ahead?"

"Couldn't see them..." answered Hooper. "I've sent

two men to find them."

"They could be anywhere in our path!" cried Robert.

A sudden thought chilled him. "Could they be a threat to the men escorting Lady Emma?"

Hooper shrugged.

"Very well," said Robert. "There's nothing to be gained by making a stand here if we've already been passed by. Mount all the men, take all you can salvage from the wagon and then fire it," he ordered.

"There's something else," said Hooper.

"Well, spit it out, man! Can it be any worse? Don't tell me the king himself has come?"

"No, Sir Robert, not the king, but those coming through the trees yonder are wearing the same badges as Lady Eleanor Elder's men up in Wharfedale."

Robert puffed out his cheeks and gave a bitter laugh. "It just had to be him, didn't it?"

"It's Ned Elder then?"

"Aye, it's not so much of a surprise. Some of Clarence's men were complaining of Ned Elder. It seems the king sent him down here after Edgecote. All the same, since we have his sister up ahead, it may actually help us."

"Except, he won't know that, will he?" said Hooper. "And nor will the men who've outflanked us..." He stopped as Robert's attention was caught by movement on the treeline behind them.

"They're here! Make haste then, fire the wagon!" said Robert. "We'll try to catch the escort, but tell your archers to have their bows strung ready..."

With his men gathering around him, Robert set his horse off at a walk, waiting for Hooper. The carter was already hurrying the oxen away and as soon as a flame appeared on the cover of the wagon, Robert spurred his mount forward.

"Don't stop until we reach the escort with Lady

Emma!" Robert told his men, as he flew southwards away from the burning wagon. When he risked a glance back over his shoulder, he saw that Ned Elder's men had almost reached it.

46

1st April 1470, by the River Severn in

Gloucestershire

"They're not far ahead now!" announced Croft, returning to Ned's side as they picked their way forward through the trees.

"It's slow here," observed Ned, irritated.

"We're nearly there and they seem to have stopped in a shallow dell."

Ned halted his men on the edge of the trees. He could see the wagon down in a little depression but there was no-one with it.

"They've gone!" he shouted. "Come on!"

The men at arms beside him thundered out of the trees and down towards the wagon.

"They've fired it!" warned Croft.

In no time they were nearing the wagon and Ned could see a small knot of riders fleeing away to the south.

"Never mind the wagon!" he ordered. "Drive on after them!"

His last words were obliterated by a blast of flame and smoke that sent men and horses screaming in alarm. Ned, twenty yards ahead of the wagon, felt the blast of heat on his back and pulled up at once. Behind him he saw some knocked from their mounts but a few who were closer to the explosion fared worse. He dismounted from his nervous mare and ran back to the blackened carcass of the wagon. A brown palfrey was shrieking and thrashing her legs to get up but part of the wagon's wooden frame had speared through her flank. Her rider lay bloodied beside her, his head at an impossible angle.

"Look to the wounded!" he ordered and took out his dagger. He talked softly to the horse, laid his hand upon its trembling neck and then plunged the blade into it. The poor beast shuddered then, as the blood gushed from the wound, she succumbed. Her rider had been unlucky and the other casualties sustained only minor wounds - even so, it was another loss.

"We'll come back for our man later," he said. "We'd best hurry on."

He remounted and set off once again, worried that his archers, whom he had sent along the river bank, would now be far ahead of him. They would be awaiting his signal - but they would have a long wait.

§§§

Robert did not look back again, even when the wagon's black powder exploded. They must not hesitate now for even an instant, for danger lay ahead of them as well as behind.

"Hooper!" he shouted. "Take the archers down by the river. Get after those who outflanked us. If you find them, don't wait for me - attack at once. We'll try to keep ahead of Ned Elder!"

Hooper gave a brief wave in acknowledgement and veered across to his right towards the river, calling the archers with him. There were only about a dozen of them but Robert was glad to have them - there were all too few with the earl. He pressed his mount harder, knowing there would be a price to pay by the end of the day, but if he did not hurry then he would not see the end of the day.

The terrain ahead was crisscrossed by small valleys and gentle inclines and it was as he was climbing one of the steeper slopes that he heard voices. As he crested the rise he knew them to be the cries of wounded men and his heart sank.

"Hold!" he bellowed, pulling up to make a rapid assessment of the field ahead. The ground was flatter here and scattered across it were the men and horses of Lady Emma's escort… but where was the enemy? Then he gave a heavy sigh as all became clear to him. Amongst the dead and wounded, the grassy land was littered with spent arrows - the outflanking men were archers! A few moments ago the air was probably thick with arrows, now they were sporadic. He retreated a yard or two back down the slope.

"Do we not go to their aid, lord?" enquired one of his men at arms.

"Wait!" he snapped. The archers had launched their ambush from a gully by the river and they had probably not noticed Robert's men yet.

"We should wait for Hooper," he said, but all the time he was frantically scanning the field for a sight of Emma. Then he breathed more easily for he could not see her; perhaps she had ridden on beyond the archers.

"They're dying out there!" protested the man at arms, drawing out his sword.

"I know!" protested Robert. "Now, either go and die with them, or hold your tongue! We wait for Hooper."

The unhappy man stayed where he was and Robert nodded. The fellow was not such a fool then. Robert turned his eyes towards the hollow where he knew the archers must be. At times he could see the tops of their bows and one or two heads now and then as they searched for new targets. Several of the escort were certainly dead, some others were wounded and the rest were lying pressed close to the earth for safety. Some of the mounts were down and riderless horses still cantered across the field. They could tell from the pitiful cries of their fellow beasts that there was danger, but Robert thought they were just as likely to run towards death as away from it.

A shout from one of his men told him that Ned Elder was closing fast, but he did not bother to look. His gaze was fixed upon the archers and he prayed that any moment Hooper would launch an attack. His eyes flicked across to glance at the killing ground once more and he could not believe his eyes. Alice was standing still, looking about her. She looked utterly lost.

Before he could even think about it, or give a command, Robert urged his horse forward over the crest and made for the girl. His startled men responded slowly but followed him. He knew the archers would be licking their lips at the sight of him, knew he was putting himself and his men at arms in grave peril, but he could not stop himself. Sure enough, arrows soon began to fly around him and thudded into the turf close by. He tried to weave a ragged course towards the girl, who now bent forward.

"Oh, Good Christ," he breathed. There was a figure sprawled beside the girl and he knew beyond doubt that it was Emma. He was only a few yards away now and could see them clearly. He jinked his mount from side to side as he neared them. Alice looked up at him and screamed. His eyes were on Emma. Was she hit? He almost fell from the saddle in his haste to get to her. Alice yelped as he pushed her flat on the grass.

"Stay down, girl," he barked. She whimpered but stayed where she was.

He lay on the grass beside Emma. She was breathing. He searched for a wound and found no arrow, but her head was bleeding from a cut on the temple. She was moaning and he almost laughed with relief when she opened her eyes, but a scream from Alice reminded him where he was. One of his comrades had fallen wounded beside them and it dawned on him that they were milling about him, thinking he was hit.

He stood up and bellowed at them: "Those archers must be out of arrows by now! Have at them! Hooper will be with us soon!"

His men turned from him and cantered away towards the archers' hollow. If the archers still had arrows, they were all dead men. Where was Hooper? He looked to the north and his head dropped: a line of horsemen reached the top of the rise. He stared at them for a moment and then shook his head. He would know Ned Elder anywhere - and there he was in the centre of the battle line. He would be taking stock, as Robert had when he first saw the field.

He swept up Emma in his arms and lifted her onto his horse.

"Can you hold on?" he asked.

She looked down at him as if peering through a mist, then nodded.

"Sir Robert?" she asked.

"Aye," he said and lifted Alice up onto the horse in front of her mother. She squealed, though not in delight, he thought. Here was the price: his mount could not carry them all and he began to lead the animal away from Ned Elder and towards the gully where his men were even now engaging Ned's archers. He did not have any idea what he was trying to do but if nothing else it must have given Ned Elder pause for thought for he had not moved from the ridge.

He was halfway to the gully when he saw Hooper appear. Thank God! A few yards further on and he could see into the gully where there were several corpses. A combination of Hooper's archers and Robert's few men at arms had dislodged Ned Elder's outflanking force.

"Their archers are fled, lord," said Hooper.

"Well done!" said Robert.

A voice from the ridge cried: "Halt!"

Robert smiled grimly. It was a voice he knew passing well and Emma knew it even better.

She held her bruised head and looked down at Robert. "Is that my brother?" she asked.

He nodded. "Do you want to go to him? You may, of course, if you wish… It would be better for Alice…"

His voice caught as he uttered the words and she studied his face for a moment.

His archers took up positions on the edge of the hollow.

"Let no man loose an arrow except upon my order," announced Robert.

Emma stared towards her brother, a tiny trickle of blood still on her forehead. She brushed it away, smearing it down across her cheek.

"You'd better go," said Robert bitterly.

"I'm going to speak to my brother," said Emma, "but… please, don't leave yet."

"Lady…" he began, but could not think what he wanted to say.

"Wait," was all she said and then, clutching Alice to her, she walked the horse towards Ned's line of mounted men at arms.

"Find me a horse, Hooper," said Robert, "and get everyone else mounted and ready to ride." He fervently hoped that Ned Elder's mounts were as tired as his.

He watched Ned ride forward to meet his sister. Words were exchanged and though Robert could not hear what was being said, he could tell that the reunion was not a particularly warm one. She had told him to wait, but what was there to wait for - and how long dare he wait? Better to ride away now whilst Ned Elder's attention was elsewhere. Yet, she had told him to wait…

47

7th April 1470, in Dartmouth Harbour,

Devon

Emma stood at the ship's stern and contemplated the receding harbour for a long time. She watched it diminish in size until the dockside warehouses blurred into formless shapes of brown and grey. Then she stared down at the wake, pale blue and white, behind the ship. She had made the right decision, she was certain of it. Alice was too young for this: the journey by ship into exile, into a foreign land…

Ned would look after Alice. He had a wife and children too so she would grow up in a family. She might be miserable at first but she would be safe and in the end she would be happier with her uncle. It was the only sensible course to take and Emma was ever the sensible sister - except of course, that if she had always taken the safest route, then Alice would never have been born at all.

The ship gave a sudden lurch and swayed as it reached the mouth of the harbour and swung into rougher water. It shook her from all thoughts of the past: she must begin to look ahead. Warwick might never revive his fortunes and then she would have condemned herself to an exile where she might never see her daughter again. Perhaps looking ahead then was not such a good idea. She shivered in the chill sea breeze and pulled her cloak tighter.

Beside her, Richard put his arm around her - a gesture of filial love which was all too rare. He was a shy lad, inexperienced in the world. Nearly nine years of age, he should have been placed in a noble house but most likely that would not happen now. Yet she was glad to have him with her, glad still to be alive. And that she was still alive was due, at least in part, to Robert Radcliffe, who stood only a few short paces away from her - and of course because of Ned. She gave a great sigh - what a tangle her life had become…

"He let us go," she said, voicing her thoughts.

"His archers fled," murmured Sir Robert, "he knew we'd have seen him off…"

Emma gave him a grim smile. "You didn't see, did you? No, you couldn't: his archers had reformed below the ridge behind his men at arms…"

"But he had you and Alice there with him. He could have attacked - why didn't he attack?"

"Because I'm his sister. I'm his blood and I told him I must go back to Lady Anne. He asked me who you were."

"What did you tell him?"

"I told him who you once were and who you now are…"

"By the saints! What did he say?

"He asked me if I could trust you and if I felt safe with you…" She glanced at Robert. "… and I said 'aye' to both."

"You did?" he said.

She almost laughed at his surprise. "Aye, was I wrong?" she asked.

"No, no… but he just let us go."

"Aye, as you saw for yourself. He took Alice from me and turned away."

"How could he do that? The king will never forgive him for it…"

THE LAST SHROUD

"Then the king would be a fool…" said Emma.

§§§

The journey was wearisome, not for the motion of the sea for she did not mind that so much but more because of the uncertainty. She was relieved when the port of Calais came into view many days later. Calais would give them a breathing space and allow Duchess Isabel to deliver her child safely.

It would be good to feel dry land once more and inhabit a world that did not lurch and sway as you passed through it. She was on the deck, as usual, with Anne, as the small fleet edged closer to the harbour. She knew nothing about the sea, though she had learned enough to fear it. Yet, she would rather be staring its indifferent power in the face than cowering below trying to shut it out.

Suddenly one of the cannons on the walls of the port spat out a great plume of smoke and fire. An instant later a thunderous blast of sound forced Emma to cover her ears. She had never before seen a cannon fired, and watched, fascinated. Then there was a splash nearby and Lady Anne squealed beside her. The ship heaved and threw them both down onto the deck.

More cannon sounded and the two women clung to a wooden spar to peer out across the harbour. Smoke drifted towards them. Cannon shot plunged into the sea all around them and sprayed them with salt water. The ship veered perilously close to the vessel alongside - or so it seemed to Emma. The pair knelt down on the deck, the rough boards chafing their knees, as they muttered a frightened prayer. After a short while the bombardment ceased as abruptly as it had begun.

Emma realised their ship was pulling back, 'heaving to' if she interpreted the sailors' shouts correctly. She stood up and offered her hand to Lady Anne. The sea air reeked of smoke and they were still outside Calais. Apparently it was not the safe haven that the earl expected. She hardly cared now where they landed as long as it was soon. Anne took her arm and leaned gently into her.

"We shall endure, my lady," said Emma, raising her voice above the waves now crashing against their hull. "Never doubt that God will be with us, no matter how bleak it looks!"

"But Isabel!" cried Anne, "She's near her time… and now, we're so far from help."

"She is blessed with help!" replied Emma. "She is with ladies who know as much about birth as anyone in Christendom: your lady mother and I have helped many a babe into the light. All is as it should be."

But of course, as they both knew, all was not as it should be. Isabel was at the mercy of the sea, without all the herbs and potions her own midwife would have used and, worst of all, surrounded by angry, fretting men. Emma recalled the kindness of the countess when her Alice had been born and remembered feeling swaddled in the warmth of women who had lived through such trials and understood her fears.

"With God's help, we'll bring forth a new little nephew for you," she said, giving Anne's hand a gentle squeeze.

"I'll go down to her now," said Anne with a brave smile.

The girl went down the steps to the cabin and a few moments later Sir Robert emerged.

"You keep me close, Sir Robert," said Emma.

"I was worried about you when the cannons began," he said, "and when I couldn't find you below, I feared…"

"… that I'd been swept overboard?" Emma smiled grimly at him.

"I swore to protect you," he said.

A heavy wave suddenly rocked the ship sideways and threw her against him.

"Can you swim?" she asked.

"No."

She pushed him away. "You're not going to be much use if I'm drowning then, are you?"

"Then, my lady, I shall drown with you!" he replied.

"You men are such fools, Sir Robert - I was slow to learn it, but life has finally taught me that."

"The sea's getting rougher, my lady. You should come below for the ship's master fears a storm."

"Why won't they let us in to Calais?" she asked. "It would be so much better for the duchess…"

He shrugged. "Better for us all," he replied, "but I suspect the king's messengers have arrived before us and Lord Wenlock has orders not to let us in. "I'm afraid the duchess will have to take her chances."

"What does that mean?" His apparent indifference angered her. "What would you know about it? When did you last give birth? It's damned hard, Sir Robert - I can tell you that!"

"I meant no-"

"No harm? No offence?" She was just warming to her theme when she heard Lady Anne calling her name.

Anne's head appeared briefly above the stairway. "Lady Emma! Mother needs you! It's Isabel…"

"Oh no," muttered Emma, "not now, surely."

Robert took her hand. "What can I do to help?" he asked.

Emma shook off his hand. "Get someone to send out some wine to us at least - it may ease her pain…"

"Wine? Aye, of course - I'll do what I can."

"Thank you… though I fear it may take more than wine…"

She turned towards the stair and swayed as she tried to discover the rhythm of the waves, but just now there seemed to be no rhythm.

"Wait my lady," said Sir Robert, "do you remember the

gift I had for you?"

"Please, let's not go through that foolishness again," she protested. "Not now - of all times!"

"The piece I offered," he continued. "it's a reliquary… and I've had a priest inspect the inscriptions upon it - some of the words… well, I think it might help… in your prayers for the Duchess Isabel."

Emma's inclination was to refuse him out of hand but she hesitated. The power of such precious objects was well known and if such a thing could make a difference…

"First, tell me honestly if it's stolen - does it already have an owner?" she demanded.

"I swear to you that no other lady has ever owned it - it is but recently crafted by a goldsmith known to me."

He took out the small velvet purse and Emma wondered idly whether he carried it everywhere with him.

Another fierce wave struck and a gust of wind blew her back towards him. He drew even closer and she looked around to see that none of the crew was watching. He was close enough to kiss, she thought, then flushed and angrily banished the idle thought from her mind. What was she thinking! He began to unfold the velvet but she stayed his hand.

"Not out here in the salt wind and spray!" she said. "I know well enough what it looks like."

He nodded and released the small package into her hand, still keeping hold of her.

"Be careful," he said, "if anyone sees you with that jewel…"

"I know, they'll wonder how I could have come upon such a piece. But I shall pray with it against my heart and hope that God answers my prayers. I shall trust to God and strong women."

"And I shall be glad just to know that you have it near your heart," he said.

THE LAST SHROUD

She gave him a thin smile. "Men are such fools…"

Her cloak billowed in the wind and hid her face as he led her to the steps.

DEREK BIRKS

PART FIVE: KINGDOM LOST

DEREK BIRKS

48

5th June 1470, at Quenhull Castle

"This is on your head, my lord!" declared the Duke of Gloucester, quivering with rage. "You let the king's greatest enemies slip through your fingers! And now, a few months later, Warwick - the man you sent freely on his way - sits in France plotting to kill us all!"

There were only the two of them in Ned's privy chamber, but he thought it likely that Gloucester's words were echoing throughout Quenhull.

"Do you not know," continued Gloucester, "that even now, two months on, the king's anger burns as hot as ever? I've told my brother he should already have you in irons for what you did! And he will - he'll summon you to London… and take your head - for the traitor you are!"

The young duke paused for breath and Ned hoped that he was flagging in his tirade.

"Yet, your grace," he ventured, "the king has not yet summoned me to London, or anywhere else…"

Gloucester seemed not to notice his interruption. "I should have known when you let that murderer Cullen escape you that you no longer had either heart or stomach for the fight."

"But I wrote to the king and explained my reasons for not pursuing Warwick," said Ned.

"Reasons? Treasons more like, Lord Elder - treasons which nothing can excuse," replied the duke.

"The king is hot about this - hot, I tell you!" continued Gloucester, standing hands on hips. He was stocky and looked a little older than his eighteen years. Much heavy responsibility had been thrust upon him at a young age and Ned knew all about that... Small wonder the youth was so angry. Ned would have found his fervent loyalty to his brother quite admirable - if only it wasn't directed towards him.

He turned away from Gloucester and walked over to the narrow window embrasure to look out over the river Severn.

"I never had either Warwick or the duke, your brother, in my power," he said wearily, "so I could hardly have let them slip away… your grace."

"And don't think that past deeds will count for much!" retorted the duke. "The iron's no longer in your heart, my lord."

The last was said with bitter sadness rather than anger but it hurt Ned more than the barbs about treason.

"Your grace," he said, facing Gloucester once more, "I used to believe that all was possible with a blow of my sword or axe. And as long as I believed that, men died in my service - aye, and women and children too."

"Men are always dying," said Gloucester. "Blood will be shed; it can't always be avoided, Ned."

"Aye, your grace, but I've stopped looking for blood. I've had my fill of blood and broken bones and scattered brains - I've had my fill of it all. Aye, I could have cut down a few more of Warwick's rearguard - but to what purpose? The earl was too far ahead - I couldn't even reach him to slow him down - let alone capture him. So, I let my sister go with Warwick's escort to keep her safe."

"Your sister is of no account to the king," muttered Gloucester, but Ned could see that his storm of wrath had blown itself out.

He drew closer to the duke and looked him in the eye.

"But she is of great account to me, your grace. When I first met your brother, he was on his knees - as was I. Your father and your brother Edmund were freshly slain at Wakefield. We were of an age and we travelled the same road to Mortimer's Cross, spurred on by thoughts of revenge. I swore to help him then and never, since that time have I wavered from oath. My loyalty to the king has cost me - and those I love - very dear. But he knows my loyalty is not in doubt."

Young Gloucester looked away. "The past is-"

"The past is where we've been all these years!" snapped Ned. "So don't tell me it doesn't matter…your grace. When the king needs me, I shall be with him."

"Very well, I'll tell him that," said Gloucester.

He gave Ned a curt nod and left, calling for his companions as he descended the steps down to the hall. He was mounted in a few moments and gone from Quenhull, taking his large retinue of knights and men at arms with him.

Maighread hesitated on the threshold of the chamber and then came in. She wrapped her arms around Ned and leant against his chest.

"You did not deserve that," she murmured.

"There's no malice in him; he's but a young lad," said Ned, "puffed up with pride because he stands by King Edward's side and angry that his brother, Clarence, does not. I'm just a convenient target. His ire will pass, as mine has."

"Do you think the stories are true? That Warwick will return with an army?" she asked.

"There's a new story every day, my love," said Ned. "First they say Warwick will crown Clarence then they say he plans to make peace with Queen Margaret and bring back out of the tower her husband, poor Henry of

Lancaster. Who knows?"

"But… is the danger real or not?" asked Maighread.

"I would never underestimate the Earl of Warwick, my dear, but the king is ready this time and as well as that, I can't believe that Warwick and the old queen will make common cause. There's just too much hatred between them."

"All the same, I'm glad you brought me here, and the others," she said. "I feel safe here and you have your two sons with you."

"Aye," he said, pulling away from her. "But I wish Eleanor had come - I hadn't planned to leave her, or Hal, behind. I'd feel better if I had all the family here under my protection."

"But if Warwick doesn't come, what does it matter?"

"Aye, if he doesn't come…"

49

15th August 1470, King Louis XI's Palace

at Amboise in France

Emma sat in her chamber and stared down at the jewel in her hands. Did God hear her prayers without the aid of a priest? Did the reliquary make any difference? She had been praying for months, not for herself but for Lady Anne, whose world had been turned upon its head. The seemingly impossible had happened: the Earl of Warwick, the hero of York, had made a pact with his most ferocious enemy, the Lancastrian Queen Margaret. The pact was sealed by the betrothal of Lady Anne to the queen's son, Prince Edward of Lancaster. So now Anne was betrothed, though not yet married and thus, all their lives still hung in the balance: God's balance.

The prince, Edward of Westminster, was a well-favoured enough youth and would make an excellent match for Anne - if, of course, his father, King Harry, was returned to the throne. There were so many 'ifs'. Anne was excited by the prospect of her marriage, overly so in Emma's view, for though some solemn promises had been made, the deed was not yet done. Emma did not hold much with promises and she was afraid for the girl, more afraid than she had been at any time. Yet, at the very moment when she thought young Anne needed her most, her influence seemed to be diminishing fast. Even her chamber was far from Anne's, when once they would have shared adjacent rooms.

Now they all waited at the French king's palace at Amboise where Queen Margaret held court and all others deferred to her as if she was still the queen of England. They all waited, nerves a jangle, for the Pope to grant the dispensation required for the marriage to take place, but more than that, they waited for the Earl of Warwick and the Duke of Clarence to launch their invasion of England. For if Warwick did not capture England then Anne's marriage would be no more than a foolish dream.

Emma ran her fingers over the gold reliquary and thought of Anne's sister, Isabel. Poor Isabel, so nearly a queen, and now… just another duchess with the added humiliation that her younger sister might one day become queen herself. Perhaps it was as well for Isabel. The jewel did not relieve her terrible suffering on the ship outside Calais, nor did it bring forth a healthy infant for the young duchess. Did it though, with God's help, deliver Isabel from a pitiful death? Emma believed it did and was grateful for it, grateful to Robert for providing it.

Yet there was another cause of anxiety: Sir Robert Radcliffe. After they landed in France, he had been her constant shadow for months, her only ally in a world of strangers. He never mentioned marriage again but then he did not have to. She witnessed his desire in every glance, felt the heat of it when he brushed a hand against hers and heard the tremor of his heart through every word he spoke to her. He told her he would protect her with his life and she believed him - except now he was gone, off to remake a kingdom with the Earl of Warwick.

She smiled bitterly: could loathing turn to loving? She doubted it, doubted it very much. But then, did she ever really loathe Robert? Did she not just use the word to put him off? She glanced at the jewel once more and sighed.

THE LAST SHROUD

She should have thrown it away, cast it overboard at Calais; instead she had made herself his accomplice. She wrapped it up carefully again and hid it under her kirtle and underskirt as she always did. It was not exactly next to her heart but someone would have to explore her underclothing to find it and in that case she feared the discovery of the reliquary would be the least of her troubles.

She stood up and the velvet package slipped a little into a less comfortable position. She was still trying to reposition it when Lady Anne Neville ran in to her chamber. Emma had not seen Anne at all in recent days and only for a few brief moments in the past few weeks. She was always with her betrothed, or Queen Margaret, or her mother, or her sister. Emma felt as if she had been cast aside and it hurt when they had been so close. She knew the betrothal must bring change, but expected at least to be one of Anne's attendant ladies and perhaps even the chief amongst them. But no servants had been retained from Anne's former household and Emma knew that the queen was behind it: out with those tainted by Yorkist association and in with those fiercely loyal to Lancaster.

Now here was Anne rushing in as she used to do at Middleham when she wanted to share some exciting new discovery with Emma. Emma stopped adjusting her clothes and burst into tears. Anne came to a faltering stop. Emma could not stem the tears and felt the colour rising in her cheeks. Soon her face would be red and blotchy and her eyes would puff up. What must the girl be thinking at this sudden outpouring of emotion?

Anne came to her and wrapped her in a warm embrace.

"Dear Emma, what is it?" she asked.

"Nothing, my lady, perhaps I have a fever," replied Emma, keenly aware of the jewel packet that lay between them. "You shouldn't be so close," she warned and, without thinking, gently pushed the girl away.

Anne gave a gasp of surprise and Emma was horrified: such an act was unforgivable.

Anne said nothing for a moment but Emma saw the hurt in her eyes and also some confusion. She watched as Anne's expression slowly changed and Emma's heart began to thud against her breast.

"Emma," said Anne in a quiet voice, "you have something hidden… under your kirtle. Now, that's a mystery."

"There's no mystery, sweet girl."

"Is it some device to keep out men?" breathed Anne, warming to the role of conspirator. "Surely you're not afraid of all these handsome French courtiers?" she teased.

Emma tried to relax her face and smiled at her charge. "No. my lady, I think we both know that my chastity was lost long ago!"

But Anne's curiosity was aroused. "Then what is it that you have so close to your belly?"

Emma's mind was blank: she could think of no convincing invention or explanation which could prevent her revealing the jewel.

"It must be a gift then," Anne continued. "A lover's gift - oh, Emma, what have you been up to when I've not had my eyes upon you? Tell me!"

"Aye," Emma conceded, "you're right, my lady: it's a gift - just from a friend, that's all."

"A friend! What friend? Emma, you have no friends in the whole of France!" Anne was at least laughing now. "Come on then, show me!"

"It's nothing, my lady - a worthless trinket… I shall probably just throw it away."

"A gift from a secret friend? A 'worthless trinket' which yet you keep so close?" said Anne. "This really is a mystery now, Emma. You'll have to show me."

"It's not even worth looking at, my lady. I'm ashamed

how poor it is. And… you need to be preparing yourself for this evening's banquet."

"Lady Emma," declared Anne, "I'm not leaving until you show me. This is why I came: I miss our close times together…"

Emma nodded. To refuse any longer would bring problems of its own, so slowly she retrieved the velvet pouch.

"'Tis a pretty cloth for a cheap trinket, my lady," observed Anne.

Emma took out the reliquary and swiftly slid it back into the velvet. "There, as you see, nothing special."

"But I didn't see," said Anne firmly. "Now let me see it properly."

Emma had no choice: she took out the jewelled piece.

For a while they both stared at it in silence. Then Anne took it into her own hands and examined it, running a finger over the sapphire and trying to make out the words inscribed upon the gold. Emma watched, knowing that it was not only a jewel that Anne held in her small hands.

Finally Anne spoke, her voice low, cool. "Tell me again, dear Emma, how you came by this?"

"As I said, my lady, it was a gift. A secret gift…"

"From whom?" Anne's tone was sharper now. "You must know that this is not worthless, Emma! Do you think me so foolish?"

"I do not, my lady, but… can this not be our secret? We've shared so many in the past… Can you not just forget you ever saw it?"

Anne was pale now. "It's too much, Emma," she said sadly. "A little piece of jewellery? Aye, that could be our secret. But this… this could only be given you by… a duke, a prince… a king? Emma, what have you done to be worthy of such a gift? What have you done? Have you betrayed us to York?"

"No!" retorted Emma. "How could you think that?"

"Your brother is close to King Edward, I know - and ever the enemy of my father!"

"No, my lady, I've always been your loyal servant!"

"The queen warned me, you know. She told me that some would try to turn me from my betrothed but I didn't believe her."

"I have done nothing to warrant this, my lady!" cried Emma, "I swear it!"

"Nothing? Except you have a jewel worth a fortune. Who gave it to you, Emma?"

"Why not keep it for yourself, my lady," said Emma, "You'll be a princess and it would be a fitting piece for you to wear."

"No! Are you mad?" exclaimed Anne. "How could I explain such a priceless jewel to my mother, to my husband to be? Of course I can't keep it! But neither can you."

Anne snatched the velvet cloth and wrapped the reliquary in it.

"Stay here," she ordered and left without a glance back at Emma who sat down with her head buried in her hands, silently cursing Robert Radcliffe for bringing her yet more trouble.

It seemed only moments later that several guards in the royal livery arrived at her chamber. They opened the door without knocking. "You're to remain in your chamber, my lady," said one and slammed the door shut behind him.

She could hear them talking outside the door. Her sudden confinement would no doubt provide material for a few days' gossip in a palace which never seemed to tire of such diversions.

§§§

Emma expected something to happen swiftly - one way or the other. In fact, nothing happened for another week. She took that for a good sign but her optimism did not outlast the week. She was taken from her chamber and brought before Prince Edward. Save for two guards, he was alone.

He was still a young boy to her but he held himself well - very much the prince, she thought. She expected he would ask her questions about the jewel and she had already decided she must name Robert or risk being condemned. But it soon became clear that the audience with the prince was not to make inquiries, but to pass judgement.

"Lady Emma Radcliffe," said Prince Edward, "you have dishonoured the lady who will be my wife, my princess and in time… my queen."

"Your grace…" Emma began but he raised a hand.

"Put her on her knees," he said to one of the guards, "and if she dares to speak again, strike her down."

He sounded calm, composed. She must hear him out then she might speak. Obediently she dropped to her knees on the hard stone floor.

"By chance," the prince continued, "my betrothed has discovered your treason. You are found out, my lady."

"No, there's no treason!" she declared and cried out as the guard cracked her on the side of the head with his fist.

The young prince shrugged. "I did warn you. You have clearly been plotting for some time, holding secret meetings with agents of the usurper, York, even before you arrived here. Don't deny it. You met with your brother before you sailed for France and since then you have met with Sir Robert Radcliffe. You did not conceal your betrayal, nor your fellow conspirator, very well, lady."

Emma said nothing, for if they already suspected Robert then there was nothing more she could say. She herself had confided to Lady Anne how Ned had taken her daughter, Alice.

"Your wicked game is over, my lady, but you may yet save your life if you tell us all that you've done. You may speak now."

Emma took a deep breath and tried to compose herself, tried to put aside the pain in her head and think. It was hard to say what she had done when she had done nothing. The truth, and only the truth, could help her now.

"Your grace, you are right that Sir Robert gave me the jewel but he did so out of love - I did not share his feelings and I did nothing in return for the gift. I would never do anything against my mistress, Lady Anne - who I love dearly - or against you or any at this court."

The prince shook his head. "The Countess of Warwick tells me that this Robert Radcliffe is half-brother to your late husband and that he reclaimed his name only after he was outlawed. He has received lands from the usurper, Edward of York. Your own brother is loyal to Edward and will no doubt be fighting alongside him… against me! Do I need to go on?"

Emma had not realised how much the countess knew but she had no answer to what the prince said, for it was all true. She hung her head in silence - for it seemed that the truth could not save her after all.

"I would have hanged you like a common criminal," said the prince, "but my betrothed has begged me to be merciful."

Emma held her breath.

"One of my loyal Frenchmen from Anjou, the Comte de Bressuire, will take you to Valognes, where the English army waits. There you will find and identify this Robert Radcliffe to De Bressuire. If you do, you and your son may be freed to scratch out a poor living in France - that will rest with De Bressuire. But be sure that whatever you do, you will never see England again."

50

1st September 1470, at the port of Barfleur

in Normandy

Robert was glad to say farewell to Valognes. He had grown sick of waiting there, sick of rubbing shoulders with every vagabond posing as a soldier whilst drinking himself to oblivion. The townsfolk's resentment of their English guests could not have been more obvious. Not a day passed without an insult and not a night passed without injury, whether in a tavern brawl or a full scale melee through the filthy streets. He had lost two of his own men and, worse still, he had almost no coin left for his trouble.

He had been to the earl weeks ago and persuaded him that if his men weren't paid again - and soon - there would be nothing left standing in Valognes and no army with which to launch his invasion. Warwick's response was to order the men to Barfleur and Robert was far from surprised when they refused and instead attempted to dismantle half of Valognes.

Two days later Warwick found some silver from somewhere and distributed it amongst the men. For a while at least, they were satisfied. Yet Robert's own purse did not stay full for long. Ale and vittles for his men, fodder for their mounts and the price of another week's lodging in a flea-ridden, piss-soaked tavern soon swallowed his income.

When the army began to march grudgingly towards Barfleur, Robert made sure he was in the vanguard to secure the best lodgings he could. He knew only too well that they might be in the port for just as long as they had languished in Valognes. Weather was always fickle and there were rumours too of a Burgundian fleet off Barfleur. The Duke of Burgundy was no friend either to Warwick or the cause of Lancaster. If there was such a fleet, then Warwick's ships might have a long wait before they could leave for English shores. Robert was one of the first to reach Barfleur but the word in the port was depressing: there was indeed a Burgundian fleet off the coast and there would be no English ships leaving whilst it remained there.

§§§

Emma learned all she needed to know about the Comte de Bressuire the moment she met him. He was tall, fair-haired and utterly indifferent to her fate. He was waiting with his small escort outside the palace gates at Amboise when Emma was brought out to him just after dawn. Her son, Richard, was waiting with them and Emma wept to see the state of him. He sat on the ground, his hands bound in front of him as hers were. Gone was the fine black and red Neville livery he usually wore and in its stead was a dirty, ragged shirt. She bent down to him, saw the cuts and bruises on his face and rounded upon their captors.

"What have you done to him!" she cried, "he's just a boy…"

"He's the son of a traitorous whore - and he resisted," said De Bressuire.

She knew that a reply would only make matters worse, so she smiled down at Richard and whispered: "Have faith, my son, we shall endure. Be brave."

He gave her a nod but she knew he must still be in shock at the suddenness with which his little world had inexplicably come crashing down upon him.

De Bressuire indicated a single horse. "You share the mount. If it is tired, you get off and walk. Now, make haste. We have a very long journey."

Richard got to his feet and helped his mother to mount and then, though hampered by his tied hands, he managed to heave himself up to sit in front of her. Their comfort was not a consideration of importance to De Bressuire, Emma decided - a view that was reinforced many times on their journey. Nor was he given to exaggeration, for their journey seemed endless. Emma's thighs were sore from riding after only the first day and her condition did not improve in the many days that followed.

De Bressuire, though his manner was cold and his speech terse, did not mistreat them. He ensured that they were fed, and that their hands were untied for a few hours every evening. Though one or two of the men in the escort gave Emma an appraising look at times, De Bressuire permitted no rough or crude behaviour towards her. Thus, she came to believe that as long as she and her son did as they were told, they would not be harmed - at least until they reached their destination which, if the prince was to be believed, would be Valognes.

The ride seemed never ending. The sores on her legs and behind were rubbed raw and bled each day. Her son must be sore too, she realised, but he was uncomplaining and she was proud of him - how could she make any complaint when a nine year old boy made none?

Valognes, when they eventually reached it, was like a town in mourning. The English army had left it for dead and the local people were just beginning to restore its battered buildings and clear its narrow streets of debris.

"See," said De Bressuire bitterly, "see what your countrymen make of our towns. They are mad dogs."

"But if the English army has left," she murmured, "what do we do now?"

"We follow them to Barfleur," said De Bressuire.

"What if they've sailed already?" asked Emma.

"They won't have," said De Bressuire confidently. "Warwick must wait for me, since I am to go with him to England. I will be Queen Margaret's eyes."

"I thought we came to find Robert Radcliffe," she said.

"Hah! You fool! You think I'd ride across half of France to find one little traitor?" he laughed. "No, he's not that important. I was coming here already. The prince just gave me this task to do along the way."

"What will become of us at Barfleur?" she asked.

"If you show me this Radcliffe traitor, then I will leave you and the boy in the street, to make your way - if you can."

"What if I can't find him?" she said. "What then?"

"Can't? Won't? Don't? It's all the same to me," he replied. "I'll cut your boy's throat and give you to my men - God knows, they've had their tongues out long enough."

"But?"

"What? You think I've been… kind to you, keeping you safe from them? No, you deserve nothing, but I don't want the men fighting over you when there's still work to be done. So, give me Radcliffe or take what comes."

§§§

Another day passed slowly for Robert in Barfleur but he had to admit it was better than Valognes. The port was accustomed to the English - half the children probably had English fathers, or grandfathers. Yet, like every port he'd ever known, it was dirty and crowded with wretched souls trying to scrape a living. He was already weary of it. Like most of the others, he spent his evenings drinking cheap wine, cursing the men of Flanders and praying that the Burgundian ships would rot at anchor. Each morning, however, his prayers remained unanswered and he vowed to offer no more, though by the evening, he needed some hope and repeated his prayers.

Hooper had sniffed out a cheerful tavern near the docks and it became a near permanent refuge for Robert and his men. Additional hospitality, provided by several willing girls, could be purchased for a small price - it had to be small for everyone in Barfleur knew that the soldiers' dwindling resources would not last much longer.

So, they waited for an order to embark, knowing there might be no such order for weeks to come. Robert and his men always occupied the same long table in the tavern and he always sat where he could see the door. It was a habit that had served him well in the past. Thus he noticed Emma the moment she came in. He could feel the blood drain from his face at the sudden sight of her, ill-clothed and bedraggled. He was about to rise to go to her when Hooper's arm held him back.

"She's not alone," murmured Hooper.

"Warn the men," replied Robert. He watched Hooper go and then glanced again at Emma. She was scanning the crowded tables and the well-dressed swordsman beside her followed wherever she looked. She must have seen Robert at once but let her gaze light upon him for only for an instant, giving a slight shake of the head as their eyes met. Then she moved on to scrutinise others. Finally, she turned to her companion with a shrug. He did not look pleased and took her arm to lead her out.

Hooper sat back down at the table. "Snatch and Barker will follow them," he said.

"Find out how many men he has," ordered Robert. "I'm not leaving her with him."

Hooper nodded and went out.

Robert was seething but he was reluctant to show even Hooper how utterly devastated he felt. Emma should have been safe with the Neville women, but somehow she had fallen - and fallen hard. He had not been there when she needed him, but he was here now and it took all his resolve not to rush after her at once.

Hooper soon reappeared in the doorway and gave him a nod. Robert picked up his sword and strapped it on.

"Come, lads," he ordered the rest of them. "I have a task for you - a bloody task."

Hooper was waiting outside. "They've moved on to The Cross," he announced.

"Excellent!" replied Robert. "A brawl of any size will pass unnoticed there! How many of them?"

"Eight including the one with the flash sword - oh, and a boy."

"Does the boy run with them?" asked Robert.

"Only if he likes being tied up," said Hooper. "It's her son."

§§§

Emma was so weary she could have slept in the street, but De Bressuire pulled her along by the arm. Sleep, she reckoned, would be a very long way off yet. The Frenchman was already annoyed - sweet Christ, what would he be like when they had visited every alehouse and still not discovered Robert?

"If you can't find him," he reminded her crossly, "then you are no use to me. If you can't find him, then I'll have to go to the Earl and ask him to hand over the traitor - and I doubt he'll be very keen to give me one of his own."

"Perhaps Radcliffe's not in a tavern," said Emma.

"Where else would he be - except drunk in the street?" retorted De Bressuire. "Come, try this one."

He bundled her through the open door of The Cross and into the dimly lit and crowded interior. She made a show of peering at each of the clients in turn but of course she already knew that Robert was not there. There were men coming and going all the time, serving boys and girls pushing through with pots of wine and steaming plates of malodorous food. She could have just slipped away in the throng, but De Bressuire knew she would not, for outside they had her son at the point of a knife.

"Not here?" asked De Bressuire, interrupting her thoughts.

"No," she said briskly.

He glanced at her for a moment. "You seem very sure... and yet it is so crowded?"

"I haven't seen him," she said, swaying to avoid a burly stranger but he still caught her with a careless elbow and knocked her backwards. If it wasn't so busy she might have fallen but the press of the crowd held her up. Suddenly a knife hilt was pressed into her palm and she looked up into Robert Radcliffe's face.

Robert slurred an apology at her and then stumbled into De Bressuire, who tried to brush him aside.

Robert patted the Frenchman on the shoulder. "Your pardon, sir," he mumbled.

"Allez!" snapped De Bressuire.

"Ah, Frenchman...?" muttered Robert lurching back into him.

Several feet away a small knot of men began exchanging crude insults. One slapped another across the face and a scuffle broke out. In a few moments more voices were raised in anger and men started throwing punches. Emma's arm was grabbed and she was dragged into the melee. There, in the midst of it all, she found Hooper, Robert's man, and at once she knew what was afoot.

De Bressuire pushed Robert away and reached out for her. Robert swung a fist at him, knocking him backwards. De Bressuire was surrounded by faces she vaguely recognised, cutting him off from his own men. He cursed and struggled to free himself.

"Come!" said Robert, somehow beside her. He took her hand, pulling her close to him.

"But they have Richard!" she cried.

"No," he replied with a grin, "they don't."

In the crush, De Bressuire had his sword out and was carving a path towards her.

"It's him, isn't it? You English bitch!" he shouted at her.

"Go to the door with Hooper," Robert told her. "If anyone tries to stop you, use the knife."

He pushed her towards the entrance and turned back to face De Bressuire. She forced her way towards the door but it seemed that the whole tavern was erupting into a full scale brawl. De Bressuire's voice rose above the clamour, calling upon his French guards to block her path. Almost at once, one of them stood before her. She lunged with the knife but he grasped her wrist and easily turned the blade towards her. She gulped and closed her eyes.

But no blade pierced her breast or cut her arm and the pressure on her wrist soon eased. Her eyes flew open to see her assailant falling to the floor, blood pouring from his throat.

"Come on!" urged Hooper. He was a man she knew very little about, and had never wanted to learn more, but at that moment she would have followed him anywhere. Clubs were being wielded close by and knives flashed when they caught a glimmer of light, but Hooper guided her skilfully through the heaving mass of men. At the door several more of his men were waiting and they had Richard with them. She hugged the lad to her and then glanced back to seek Robert. She caught a sudden glimpse of him grappling with De Bressuire.

"Help him!" she cried to Hooper. "He needs help!"

"No, lady," Hooper laughed. "Your man doesn't!"

Her man… She soon lost sight of the pair in the crowd but then Robert emerged through the doorway and joined them in the street. He took her arm and led her away surrounded by the others. There was rain in the air and a stiff breeze was getting up.

Robert wrapped her cloak around her. "We'll find somewhere dry and safe, my lady," he told her, "and then you can tell me what has brought you to this."

They ran before the wind and rain, driven by the squall into a warren of dark, narrow lanes where the overhanging roofs sheltered them a little. Robert hurried them along an alley and bundled her and Richard through a door into a tiny courtyard.

"My poor lodgings," he explained. "Take young Richard and look after him well," he ordered Hooper.

"I'll wager there's a storm out to sea tonight," observed Hooper.

Robert looked at the lashing rain. "Perhaps," he replied, "and if the call goes out at first light, it could work in our favour. Make sure all are ready to embark!"

"Aye, Sir Robert," said Hooper and disappeared into the damp night, taking Emma's son with him.

She following Robert up the creaking steps to the small room he rented - all he could afford, she supposed. She entered the dark chamber and it occurred to her how much she was taking on trust.

"There's a candle somewhere," he said.

"No, don't bother," she replied. "I don't mind the darkness. It hides my appearance - and my shame."

"Lady, what have you to be ashamed of?" retorted Robert, taking her hand and squeezing it gently. She shivered but only partly from the cold for now she must tell him. He seemed to sense her dismay and drew her to him.

"I'm disgraced," she said in a whisper. "I'm utterly ruined! You may have released me, Robert, but I'm still disgraced and tomorrow I shall be just as ruined."

"My lady," he said, "come, tell me what has brought all this about."

"You!" she cried pounding her fist against his shoulder,

"you…"

"But… how?"

She said nothing but let him hold her as they stood together.

"The jewel…" he breathed.

"Aye, the jewel," she said, and as she spoke, a tremor swept through her. All the bitter resentment she felt burst out like a torrent sweeping over a weir. She sobbed against him as she tried to relate all that had happened to her.

"I thought I'd left such despair behind me," she said finally, "but the prince… he said I'd never see England again…"

"You will," he said softly, "I promise you. And the prince? Well, he's not quite a prince yet, is he?"

She eased herself free from his embrace and held him at arm's length in the darkness, with her hand pressed against his breast. Robert Radcliffe, enemy of her family, who had more than once tried to bring down destruction upon their heads, who had even plotted her brother's death, yet… his priceless reliquary was lost and he did not seem to care.

Here she stood, her cheeks wet with tears, her face still dirty from the journey, clothes stained and torn… but she knew beyond doubt at that moment that he loved her. What she was still not sure of was whether she could love him.

§§§

"Sir Robert!"

The shouts awoke her. It was Hooper and he was banging on the chamber door.

She saw that it was barely light, perhaps the first hint of dawn. She felt Robert stir beside her and shrank back against the wall. The bed was so narrow she could still feel him there. Had she lain with him? She remembered nothing of it, if she had.

"We're ordered to the ships!" bellowed Hooper through

the closed door.

Robert levered himself up off the bed and it occurred to her he was still dressed - and for that matter so was she. She sighed, unable to decide whether she was relieved or disappointed.

"The storm!" declared Robert. "I expect it's scattered the Burgundians out to sea. Come, my lady, we must hurry!"

He opened the door to Hooper. "Did you get what I asked for?"

"Did my best!" retorted Hooper, looking ill at ease. He tossed a bundle of clothes at Emma.

"What are those?" she asked.

"Quick, put them on!" urged Robert.

She examined the clothing - it looked and smelt foul. "What for?" she demanded.

"If you want to see England again, my lady, this is the only way," said Robert. "We'll have to smuggle you aboard our ship."

"No, not in those!"

"It's the only way - you can't just saunter on board as you are!"

"There must be some... other women?" she said.

He shook his head. "Do you think the Earl's invasion fleet has women on board?"

"Well, what about... you know... the sort of women who..."

"If there are any on board, my lady, you really don't want to be one of them," said Robert.

"But..."

"We'll be in the courtyard! Now hurry, my lady, please!" He slipped outside with Hooper.

She looked at the clothes; probably a young lad's, she thought. Well, it wasn't as if hers were much better now. She could see Robert's argument: embarking might be dangerous, especially if De Bressuire was watching. She quickly stripped off her outer garments and with a judicious rip here and there she managed to pull on the breeches, which were too small. The leather jerkin was already torn, which was as well for it was perilously tight across her breasts. She tied up her hair and put on the cap, thinking she must look ridiculous. Then she donned her cloak and hurried down the steps to the yard where Robert waited with Richard and some of the others. They stopped talking when she appeared and just stared at her.

Richard looked utterly bemused.

"She looked less of a lady before," muttered Hooper.

Emma gave him a stony stare.

"We'll take you aboard in our midst," said Robert, "but if you value your life, say nothing!"

They hurried down to the harbour where embarkation was in full swing and men jostled to get aboard their ships.

"Every man wants the best quarters, I suppose," said Emma. Her remark brought a chorus of grim laughter.

"Quarters?" said Hooper.

"I said say nothing," scolded Robert, "but imagine the worst conditions you can think of, my lady, and then imagine it twice as bad - but in truth it'll be beyond your imagining...."

"I've been on a ship - as you well know," she protested.

"Peace, my lady - or you'll kill us all," he snapped.

She noticed that Robert still seemed to have some influence for queues of men grudgingly ceded ground when he and his men approached.

"Can you see De Bressuire?" she whispered.

"I've men watching for him," replied Robert, "so don't worry and please, lady, keep silent."

Robert's comrades shielded her from view as they went aboard and hustled her down below the deck.

"My rank gives me a small cabin," said Robert, "but

you'll need to lie low. This ship's master won't want a woman on board."

"I understand," said Emma.

"I doubt it," he replied, "but just make sure you stay in my cabin and keep quiet."

"Of course."

He gave her a reassuring nod and a pat on the arm and then hustled her through the cabin door. The cabin was not what she expected. It was not small, it was tiny and she banged her head twice before slumping down with a heavy sigh onto a wooden chest. For the first time in many days, she was forced to confront what had happened and the utter destruction of the way of life she had built so diligently over several years at Middleham. Stark choices faced her now, assuming she made it back to England: run to her brother Ned and throw herself upon his good nature or make common cause with Robert Radcliffe... though she wasn't yet sure what that even meant. So many decisions - and that did not even take into account the fact that she was heading to England in a warfleet bent on rekindling the bloody war for the throne.

A soft but irritating scratching noise eventually distracted her. It did not sound like creaking timbers or salt-encrusted ropes under strain. It was coming from near the chest and suddenly something brushed by her left foot. She froze. She moved her foot aside and glanced down at the deck. A rat stared back up at her and she aimed a wild kick at it. The rat evaded it with an aggrieved look then carried on its way around the base of the chest.

Emma screamed and tried to stand up on the chest. She struck her head once more and fell onto the floor. She closed her eyes, expecting to feel the filthy rat crawling across her face and hands. She cried out and waved her arms about to discourage it. Then she squinted her eyes open a little, scouring the floor for the rat.

Richard rushed in. "Mother!" he cried. "What ails you?"

Sir Robert followed soon after and slammed the door behind him. She sat up and noticed the rat atop the chest. Robert glared at her and then at Richard, ignoring the rat.

Emma struggled to speak. "It's… it's…"

"A rat?" added Robert helpfully. "Aye, my lady, ships have rats - and if you didn't know that before, you do now."

"Well, kill it then!" she cried.

"It's not the only one," he said. His tone, she noticed, was weary. "If you value your life, my lady, you'll worry less about rats and more about people. The rats will do you less harm."

"It was a shock!" said Emma.

Sir Robert stared at her and shook his head. "It would help us all, my lady, if you could do one thing for me. Since you're playing the part of a young man, please… don't scream at the top of your voice ever again - or at least for the remainder of our journey - which, I should point out, has in fact yet to start. The ship's master, a curious man by nature, is now deeply suspicious of me, my men and what I keep in my cabin."

Emma sat on the floor and absorbed her scolding in silence, but she kept one eye on the rat as it hopped off the chest and disappeared, presumably in search of more interesting fare.

"And Richard," continued Sir Robert, "it might lend some weight to our little deception if you didn't call out the word "mother" for all of Christendom to hear!"

§§§

The first part of the channel crossing was foul. Emma spent all her time in the cramped cabin, breathing air that stank of all things putrid. She felt dirty, was dirty. Richard brought her water each day but it was brackish and tasted appalling. It was hot below deck and she dispensed almost at once with the uncomfortable leather jerkin and wore just the shirt Robert had given her. No-one ventured into the cabin but Robert had impressed upon her that the captain - who occupied the only other cabin - was nearby.

She saw only Richard and Robert and she did not know how to talk to either of them. Richard was hurting badly and hardly spoke to her. Yet she knew her boy was resilient and she told herself he would recover his spirits when they reached England.

Robert was a different matter altogether and she dreaded the first night alone with him in the cabin, alone with a man who loved her, a man who had saved her and who had lost a priceless jewel in doing so. What would he expect of her now?

As it turned out, he expected nothing. He gave her use of the narrow berth and then made a bed for himself on the floor. The berth proved an alarming experience from the moment she lay down upon it. She stayed rigid, hardly daring to move or even breathe heavily, as the movement of the ship threatened to roll her off it.

From below her came whispered words of advice: "Don't try so hard to lie still, my lady. Just try to relax and you'll sleep better."

Sleep? She could not sleep, though she did try to lie more easily. But how could she sleep with her head crammed full of so many terrible reminders. Yet she must have succumbed in the end because in the middle of the night she woke up to find herself falling through the air. It was a short fall and she landed on Robert with a grunt. A screamed formed deep in her breast but did not pass her lips for he quickly clamped his hand over her mouth.

"Softly, my lady," he breathed, "you're safe, I have you - best not let the whole ship's company know you're here…"

He took his hand from her lips and she let him hold her.

"I should go back to the berth," she whispered.

"Are you going to fall out again?" he asked.

"I expect I shall…"

"Then you should stay here."

"Should I?"

"Aye, but only if you want to…"

She told herself that she would stay because, if she didn't, she would fall. But then there were many ways to fall…

Robert began to talk to her. She was half expecting his invitation to be followed by some soft words of courtly love, but that was not what he wanted to tell her.

"I have not been a good man," he murmured. "Thomas Gate was a man driven by anger. I was angry with my father for not calling me his son; I was angry with your brother for killing him; angry with all of you Elders for taking what I thought was mine. I nearly killed your brother several times. I carried out tasks for the earl that other men, better men, baulked at. I have not been a good man…"

She stroked his face in the dark. "Thomas Gate is dead," she said.

She kissed him on the cheek then lightly on the chin - that was a misjudgement since she was aiming for his lips. When she found them she kissed him hard. She had not lain with a man for years and it shocked her how much she wanted to.

There were many ways to fall…

§§§

As the days at sea passed slowly by, she came to long for the nights, when Robert returned to her and they pretended for a few hours to live in a different world. He made love to her and she let him help her to forget for a while the harsh memories of France. But all too soon the sea crossing came to an end and she did not know what to do next. On their last night aboard the ship he proposed to her for the first time in many months. She refused him at once.

"But I still want to marry you," he protested, "and why would you lie with me night after night if you didn't intend to marry me?"

"Because I've come to like you, Robert, that's why. God knows how, but I have. But now… who knows what will happen when we land? I don't - do you?"

"Whatever happens, I want to marry you! I promise you-"

"No, make me no promises, I beg you," she replied. "I've heard men's promises before - and they are just so many words. Words mean nothing, Robert, and I can't trust anyone by their words. I need to trust what you do, what you are. Tell me no lies, give me no false promises. I can take the truth, however bleak…"

"Very well," he said. "The truth is that I don't serve Warwick any longer - though he still thinks I do. All the time I've been in France, I've been sending letters to England to my new lord, Sir William Stanley."

"Oh, no!" gasped Emma. "You really are a traitor!"

51

20th September 1470, at Quenhull Castle

Ned tossed the letter onto the table with the others but no-one seated there made any move to pick it up, not did anyone pass comment. He looked at them and saw only faces lined with anxiety, waiting for him to confirm their worst fears. Maighread laid her hand upon his in silent affirmation.

"It's as we thought," he said finally. "Warwick has landed…"

"In Kent?" asked Spearbold.

It could have been Kent, Ned supposed. The earl had found ready support there the previous year when he landed from Calais and went on to Edgecote.

"No," he said.

"In the north then?" Spearbold prompted.

Ned's head began to throb. "No, closer to home, I'm afraid… Dartmouth, Plymouth, one of those ports…"

"God save us," breathed Spearbold. "That's too damned close!"

"Do we know his strength, lord?" Croft spoke up for the first time.

Ned sighed. "No." He tapped the document he had just discarded. "But if folk believe this proclamation - and act upon it - he'll have thousands at his back."

"But the king… is he still in the north, do you think?" asked Spearbold.

"Aye, I've not heard different from Will Hastings, so I think he must be," said Ned, "and he has an army in the field, so this news will bring him south soon enough…"

"But, in the meantime?" asked Spearbold.

"We'll try to gain some intelligence for him. Croft, how many men could I have ready by the morrow?"

Croft paused to consider. "Fifty mounted men at arms at best, another fifty on foot and perhaps threescore archers. But if you wait a week, we can double that."

"If I wait a week, Warwick will be in London and he'll have the old King Harry dragged out of the Tower and put back upon the throne!" barked Ned. "Our first action must be swift or it'll be too late."

"You can't leave Quenhull undermanned," warned Croft.

"No - and I won't, not under any circumstances," said Ned. The pain in his head worsened but he knew that if he so much as rubbed his forehead those around him would fear the worst.

"How many men does Lady Eleanor have at Corve?" he asked.

"Men at arms and archers?" said Croft. "Thirty altogether - at most."

"We can't take any more from there then."

"Could you not wait here for the king to arrive?" asked Maighread.

"I could… but how long will that be? I need to know what Warwick and Clarence are doing…"

"My agents have always been reliable," Spearbold muttered, clearly aggrieved.

"Ned-" began Maighread, but he cut her short.

"Master Croft. Muster all the mounted men you can and have them ready at dawn."

"And the men on foot?" asked Croft.

"Keep them here with you - and start raising more. We'll

quarter as many as we can here."

"Yes, lord," said Croft and took his leave at once, his chair scraping on the stone flags. Ned winced, but hoped the others had not noticed.

"Spearbold - tell your agents we need news - any news at all of our enemies but especially what numbers they have. I think we must bring in more supplies."

"We've already enough to withstand a… siege, my lord," said Spearbold.

"Aye," said Ned, "but get more - there'll be more mouths to feed."

"Aye, lord," acknowledged Spearbold.

After Ned's informal council left, Maighread stood up and put her hands upon his head, gently massaging his temples.

"Do you think the others noticed?" he asked.

"Aye, I think so - Spearbold gave me a strange look," she replied.

A thin, tight smile crossed his lips. "He's a strange fellow," he murmured, "but you were supposed to say: no my love, no-one noticed." At least the ache was eased by her clever fingers. "Better," he told her and stood up.

He wrapped his arms around her, feeling her growing belly against him.

"How long?" he asked.

"The midwife says we'll have our second child in the new year, but I'm aiming for Christmas - if God wills it."

He kissed her hair and held her tighter.

"Don't go after Warwick tomorrow," she whispered suddenly. "Send others, Ned. Send scouts, messengers… send an army out there, but don't go."

He held her apart from him and studied her face.

"You mustn't do this again," he said. "Do you know what it felt like at Edgecote… when I looked into Hal's eyes and saw his concern? Do you know how it feels to be doubted by the men you lead? Do you understand the harm it does - for them to question themselves about my fitness to command?"

"I was worried about you - I've never had to worry about someone else before. I wasn't used to worrying… I'm still not used to being a wife!"

"I don't want to see fear in their eyes that you've put there," he said. "If you must worry about me, then worry alone."

Her eyes flashed at him. "Perhaps you'd rather I didn't worry at all!"

"Aye, I would…" he said. "I don't want to see fear in your eyes either. If I die, then I die."

"Hush!" she said. "Don't say that!"

He pulled her to him again and kissed her. The door flew open and Spearbold stood on the threshold, uncertain whether to come in or not.

Ned laughed and took Maighread's hand in his. "God's blood, Spearbold! I was embracing my wife, not someone else's! What is it?"

"Dark tidings, my lord… I've just heard that the rebel Welshman, Jasper Tudor, crossed the Severn at Gloucester yesterday and rode into Wales! He'll be raising men!"

"Your informant is sure it was him?" asked Ned.

"Aye, without doubt - flying his banners for all to see and calling upon men to rally to the old king."

"Then the rumours are true - and he passed right under our noses! This couldn't be any worse… I fear many will feel the tug of old loyalties and join the earl. We've never needed your agents as much as we do now, Spearbold, for without them we're blind…"

"Will you still go on the morrow?" asked Maighread. "With Jasper Tudor so close?"

"He won't be near us now. He'll be recruiting in south Wales and in the marches to the north. Let's hope he doesn't send men out as far as Ludlow."

"Eleanor…"

"Aye, but I must see how things lie in the south," he replied. "Rest easy though, I'll not be fighting anyone just yet - I've not enough men for that."

§§§

In the end, Ned's mounted column numbered almost sixty men. It was a healthy number and riding out with them he felt a surge of renewed confidence as they crossed the Severn and rode through Tewkesbury. His optimism lasted only two more days, however, for once they were well into Devon, Ned picked up the mood of the shire all too quickly. The banners most in evidence told their own tale: the swan banners of old king Harry. Alongside the royal banners flew the bright yellow colours of the Courtenay family, the most powerful family in the shire. Ned should have expected that for with Humphrey Stafford now dead, the Courtenays wanted their earldom back and the return of the old king was their best chance.

Less prominent, and Ned suspected less popular, were the ragged staff badges of Warwick. "If it were just Warwick," he told Bear, riding at his shoulder, "we could do it - we could throw him back into the Channel - but this… this is far worse than I ever imagined."

Every village Ned passed through greeted him either with outright hostility or, at best, truculence. It did not take a master of observation to gauge how the wind blew. It blew from France and soon Queen Margaret herself would come, with her young heir, to sit at the old king's right hand. The clever dog, Warwick, had held his nerve, swallowed his pride and turned the kingdom upside down.

"King Edward should be down here," muttered Spearbold. "He should be down here where the invaders have landed, not up in the north! I don't know much about soldiering, Ned, but I can see you haven't a prayer without him!"

"You're right, Spearbold; we can't hold them," agreed Ned. "Soon they'll have the numbers to sweep us aside like so much chaff. I'll be grateful if we can get back to Quenhull alive."

"But what are you saying?" asked Spearbold aghast. "Surely King Edward will overcome them! He'll come with his army and then they'll be the chaff, won't they?"

"Aye, Spearbold," said Ned, "that must be our hope…"

"The king's never lost a battle has he?" said Spearbold.

"No, but then he knows when not to fight…"

Ned had seen enough and he turned the column around, heading home and praying for better news from the north. That night they made a nervous camp in a broad forest still about a day's ride from Gloucester. Ned sent out scouts in all directions and during the evening they returned one by one with more dread news. From their observations he tried to piece together an impression of where their enemies lay now.

"So," he explained to Spearbold and Bear, "we're in the midst of them. To our south is Clarence, who seems to be lagging behind Warwick's main force to the east. Warwick is not our problem at present: he's heading away from us. But on our western flank and much closer are the Courtenays. Their force is growing by the day and they won't stand still. Like us, they're heading north and if they continue on that path, they'll meet us early tomorrow, about the time we'll be leaving this forest."

"Do you think they know we're here?" asked Spearbold.

"Oh, aye," said Ned, "we know where they are so, at the very least, they'll know we're in this forest somewhere."

"Well," said Spearbold, "why not simply wait here in this great wood for them to pass us by?"

"If we do that, my dear Spearbold, then we shall be completely surrounded by our foes," said Ned, "and there will be more levies coming up behind them. We'll be trapped here."

Spearbold's face was a grey mask. "Are you saying we can't escape?"

"No, I'm not."

"What do we do then… to get away?"

"First, we ride our poor horses into the ground and then, when that fails, we pray God sees our plight," replied Ned. "Bear, go build up some fires to the south of our camp."

Spearbold thought for a moment and then nodded. "We run then," he said.

"Well, we walk first," said Ned, "then we run."

It was a moonless night and the forest was dark with tall oak, beech and ash. They left their fiercely burning campfires and made their escape through the wood, keeping away from the more open coppiced areas, staying deep in the shadows and moving with as much stealth as they could muster.

Westward lay the Courtenay camp, illuminating the landscape with its own fires. Ned sent men on foot ahead to silence any of their prickers - or so he hoped. Even with all their care, there was always some noise: a harness jingling, a horse neighing.

Once they cleared the trees Ned took them off at a canter - fast enough he hoped to give them breathing space, but not so fast as to lose mounts. Even so, he knew such a ride was reckless before first light. They had only travelled a few miles when they lost the first horse. It fell on its side into a steep gully and rolled down over its hapless rider. The mare crushed the life from him and broke a foreleg. It was a sharp reminder to the others and they continued with a good deal more caution until, just before dawn, Ned called a halt to rest the horses. Many a nervous prayer was muttered when the sun rose and Ned led them off again at a faster pace.

"How much further?" asked Spearbold, breathing hard.

"I should say we're at least a day's ride from Quenhull," said Ned.

"So we'll do it!" declared Spearbold. "There's no-one in sight behind us - why, we'll be there by this evening!"

"On fresh horses perhaps, but not on these poor beasts," said Ned. "You'd best start praying a little harder, Master Spearbold."

By midday they reached the city of Gloucester and entered by the south gate. It seemed an achievement of some sort and Ned saw there were relieved looks all round. Even he began to believe that they had shaken off any possible pursuers.

"We'll stop in the town long enough to feed and water the horses," he ordered. "You can walk them through the town to the west gate."

"Still some miles to go yet, lord," observed Bear gloomily.

"We can do it, my lord!" asserted Spearbold, darting a look at Bear.

Ned chuckled to himself as he led them along the main street: Bear, the scarred warrior, always seeing disaster over the next hill and Spearbold, hoping and praying for the best.

Stallholders regarded the heavily armed men with suspicion and kept a close eye on their wares as the column tramped by. Ned purchased some fodder at the stables near the west gate. There they gave the horses a brief rest but Ned was anxious to move on and gathered his men around him.

"The last few miles now, lads," he said. "Once we're across the Severn we'll press on hard again - but stay watchful; we're not there yet."

As they left the city behind them, Ned kept glancing back but there was no sign of pursuit. After a few more hours they could see the towers of Quenhull in the distance and he began to think that Spearbold's hope was well founded after all. They were riding alongside a small wood, worthy of no more than a casual glance but, as they passed closer to the trees, a volley of arrows thudded into their left flank.

"God's blood!" Ned shouted and veered away from the wood. He glanced around him: several men had been unhorsed… or worse. Spearbold cried out for an arrow had pierced his arm. He grimaced with pain and Ned snatched up his reins to drag his mount away, calling the others with him. There was a shout from Bear just behind him. He looked back to see a party of mounted men at arms sweeping out from behind the woods.

He cursed, for the briefest glance told him there were too many. He tried to push his mount harder but the mare was feeling it, though every sinew in her was striving to keep going. She stumbled slightly but regained her footing and then continued gamely on. Ned knew it was no good: the animal, like all their mounts, could run no more. They could not outrun their enemies this time.

When the next flight of arrows landed harmlessly behind them, Ned pulled up and prayed to God that the men on the walls of Quenhull would see their plight. Yet, even if Croft could see them, there wasn't enough time for him to come to their aid on foot.

"Stand here!" he roared, turning his horse to face the oncoming riders. If he had to fight then he would fight on his own terms. He would not be routed and cut down like a coward.

"An Elder! An Elder!" Men bellowed out his battle cry in defiance as they gathered around him.

52

20th September 1470, at Corve Manor near

Ludlow

Eleanor was mourning. She had been mourning from the moment the arrow tore through Ragwulf's heart and nothing, it seemed, could make the anguish stop. It was a wound that never stopped bleeding.

The pain would not go away, Maighread told her, but it would ease with time. Becky said the same - and no-one had more cause to grieve than Becky - but the pain did not ease; it festered and grew, feeding her anger and outrage: the loss of Ragwulf was God's bitter vengeance upon her. She missed him more than she would ever have thought possible. She thought the child would help, but it didn't. She stared down at Kate now, lodged in Becky's comforting arms. The child blinked back at her and then started bawling again.

Eleanor's instinct was to shut her ears and walk out. "I should've drowned that girl at birth!" she cried.

"My lady!" protested Mary.

"Don't worry," soothed Becky, "she doesn't mean it."

"Mary doesn't need to be told!" snapped Eleanor. Then she saw that Becky's eyes were on the child.

"I wasn't telling Mary…" Becky said softly. "Was I Kate?"

"How can one so small, be so loud and troublesome?"

said Eleanor, pacing around the solar.

"Are we still talking about Mary?" asked Becky.

"Kate! Kate is loud and troublesome!"

"Aye," said Becky, "more like mother then, than father..."

"Mind your tongue!" said Eleanor, "and give Mary the child."

"She's happy with me," replied Becky.

Eleanor glared at her and Becky handed over the girl to Mary.

They all wanted to help her and it was suffocating. Only Becky stood up to her and, of course, she loved her for it.

The door of the solar was suddenly thrown open.

"My lady!" cried Hal, "There are men at the gate, asking for the 'lord' - and that would be you."

"How many?" she asked at once.

"There's only about half a dozen but they're well-armed and our gates were still open!" replied Hal.

"Make sure all the archers are up on the ramparts," Eleanor told him, "Then go to the guards at the gate - I want you close by."

She left the solar and hurried up to her chamber. Swiftly she looked out the sword, still in its old scabbard. She worked it in and out a few times then sheathed it and went down into the courtyard.

There were three horsemen in the yard, ringed by Hal and several of her men at arms. A glance up at the ramparts told her that the few archers she had were at least in place. She crossed the cobbles with a measured step, forcing herself to keep calm. She noticed another three strangers in the gateway. How was it that her gates were wide open anyway, she wondered? They had all become too casual.

One of the horsemen dismounted and she made straight for him. He was older than she and his face was scarred and discoloured; he was not a handsome man to behold.

"Who are you?" she demanded and her terse question seemed to wrong foot him.

"I am…"

"Well," cajoled Eleanor, "surely you know!"

"My lady, is it? I am Sir Walter Efford-"

"Fine. I'm Eleanor Elder, now why are you in my courtyard?" she asked.

"I serve the noble earl, Jasper Tudor…" began Sir Walter.

"Well, what's that to me?"

"Be careful, my lady, lest you insult Lord Jasper."

"Apart from telling me to be careful in my own manor, do you have anything else to say?" demanded Eleanor.

"The earl-"

"Is he still an earl? I thought Jasper Tudor was exiled," interrupted Eleanor, "I'm sure I heard that somewhere."

"My lady!" snarled Sir Walter. "Will you hear me willingly or must I insist?"

She smiled. "Insist? A bold word, Sir Walter, for a man who has half a dozen arrows pointed at his breast."

Sir Walter glanced up at the walls.

"Forgive my bluntness, my lady, but I've been on the road for a week, in the earl's service. I spoke rudely." He took her by the arm. "Let us walk and talk together."

Eleanor shook his hand off her elbow and called up to those on the rampart.

"If Sir Walter feels the need to touch me again, you have my permission to use him for an archery butt!"

Sir Walter took a step back towards his mount and eyed the battlements once more.

"Now, Sir Walter," said Eleanor, "you speak plainly - well, so do I. You may have noticed the sword in my right hand. This sword was wielded by a man I was very fond of against your lord at Mortimer's Cross. Have you heard of it?"

"I was there," declared Sir Walter, red blotches appearing on his face.

"Well then, it must be clear to you now that, unlike you, I don't serve Jasper Tudor - so please, be on your way."

"I came as a friend to raise men for the true king, Henry of Lancaster," he replied, "I shan't come as a friend next time."

"Even better, let there not be a next time. Now go!" ordered Eleanor.

Without another word, Sir Walter swung himself up onto his mount and rode out with his comrades.

"Hal," she called softly, "secure the castle. I think war has come to the Corve Valley."

53

20th September 1470, by the river Severn

near Quenhull

They had ridden together all the way from Exeter but, since Tewkesbury, Emma noticed that Robert had grown quiet.

"Have you any idea where we're going?" she asked. She was teasing him but he took her question seriously.

"I'm following the track I was told about," he replied.

"And you got this advice from..?"

"The inn at Tewkesbury. The landlord there was very helpful."

"That was not an inn," said Emma. "It was an alehouse with a few straw bunks... and rats... and lice - I'm still scratching! And the landlord was helpful because he was drunk - all of the time. Sweet Christ! Who is drunk all the time? For all you know he was telling you wrong just to amuse himself."

Robert grinned at her. "Hmm. I'm not sure he was ever sober enough to think that clearly."

She smiled back at him and looked nervously behind, where Richard rode.

"Thank you," she murmured. "This is dangerous for you, I know, so thank you. And I never thanked you for getting us out of France."

"Well, I was crossing the channel anyway…"

"You took so many risks for us," she said, "and now you're taking more. You should be on your way, not dallying here with me."

He reached across and took her hand. "There's nothing I wouldn't risk…"

"Do you think I'm right to go to Ned?" she asked. "Tell me honestly… because, from what I've seen, Warwick is sweeping across the land on a tide of support for the old king. Is it truly possible King Edward will be overthrown?"

"Nothing is certain, my lady, once weapons are raised in anger. I could ask you to stay with me, but my future is not certain either. I serve a new master and I must go where he leads. Whoever triumphs, your best hope now lies with your brother. He'll keep you safe - you and your children. Alice is already at Quenhull and without a mother. There's no choice to make here…"

Emma brushed her hand against his cheek. "You're a strange man. Where will you go next?"

"I'll ride to the Stanleys as Warwick has told me to. If Sir William Stanley supports Warwick then I, as his new client, shall do the same; if not, then I suppose I'll be at war with the earl and helping to prop up Edward of York."

Emma gave him a wry smile. "You would be in common cause with Ned and that would please me very much…"

He shook his head. "I don't know…"

"But God knows, Robert. He knows both you and my brother. He knows that at heart you are both good men. We must trust in God for He knows…"

"I wish I did!"

She smiled at him once more. "I've been thinking. I want you to know that, whatever you decide to do now, if it pleases God that we both shall live through this time, I'll say the words with you - if you still want me…"

He stared at her in surprise and then gave her a broad grin. "I swear, my lady, that whatever should befall us in the coming weeks, I shall still want to marry you."

She move closer to kiss him on the cheek, but he suddenly pulled up.

There was a narrow wood ahead and one of his scouts emerged from it riding back fast towards them.

"Ready your arms," Robert ordered the men, even before the breathless rider reached them.

"Quenhull Castle's only a mile or two away," the man told him.

"What else?" urged Robert. "You weren't riding that fast just to tell me you'd seen a castle - it's not going anywhere!"

"Riders - quite a lot of them, on the other side of the wood now. Looks like the Duke of Clarence's men. I watched them - they're attacking another column."

"Who?"

"I wasn't sure until I heard their battle cry... but it's Ned Elder."

Emma seized Robert's arm. "Will you help him?"

He laid his hand on hers. "I'll sound out my men," he replied. "This is starting to get very muddled, my lady. I think it may help if they know what they're fighting for..."

"I've seen them long enough," she replied. "They're fighting for you - nothing more. I believe they'll do whatever you ask."

"Well," he whispered, "let's see."

54

20th September 1470, near Quenhull Castle

"Spread out!" Ned bellowed. "Let's not make it too easy for them!"

He could see the approaching pennants now: not the yellow and blue of Courtenay, but the black and red of Clarence. Ned cursed, wondering how Clarence's men could possibly have overtaken them. They looked well-harnessed too and ready for a fight.

As he drew up his battle line to meet them, it dawned on Ned that these men were not from the pursuing army. They came from much closer by and it could be no accident. They must have been awaiting his return and only one local man could call upon such a force: Roger Cullen - God damn the man! He had stayed in hiding for months and now he chose this moment to exact his revenge.

Spearbold waited beside Ned with a trembling sword in one hand and the other arm limp by his side, the arrow still in it.

"Ride for the castle, Spearbold," Ned told him. "You're no use to me here. You'll do us better service getting Croft to make haste!"

Spearbold gave him a bleak look and then, sheathing his weapon, he set off at a canter towards Quenhull. Ned watched him go for a moment, then donned his helm and turned to face the oncoming riders. His men knew how to form the line he favoured - most could do it in their sleep.

They waited in a single line with Ned and Bear in the centre and the flanks ready to encircle the oncoming force. It was hardly an original tactic but most of the time it worked. It did rely, however, on the opposing commander behaving as expected and Cullen did not.

"God's blood, Bear!" cried Ned, "He's splitting his column!"

Cullen would strike the waiting line not in the centre but either side of centre, aiming to punch two breaks in Ned's line. Such a manoeuvre was not unfamiliar to Ned or his men at arms but with tired mounts they could not move rapidly enough to counter it.

Cullen's men, armed with lance and axe, smashed into Ned's defensive line with precision - and not one of them made for Bear or Ned.

"To the flanks!" shouted Ned to his comrade and fell back to drag his weary mount to the right. He did not look at Bear, knowing he would be peeling off to the left. Instead he focussed on the wedge of horsemen battering into his own.

"An Elder! An Elder!" he roared as he bore down upon the tight melee. The mace felt heavy in his hand but its power to shock and crush was unrivalled and, unlike a pollaxe, it had no long spike to become embedded in enemy armour. He struck down the first man he encountered but a lance speared towards him and grazed past his breastplate. He brushed it aside and swung his mace at his new opponent. There was a crack and his victim slumped forward in the saddle.

Another was already at him and ploughed his horse into the flank of Ned's mare. The impact shook him from head to toe and the animal shuddered beneath him. He was already falling when he swung angrily and caught his opponent a glancing blow on the thigh.

"Shit!" he cried out as the horse folded to its knees. He

leapt off, intending to roll to his feet in one smooth movement, but he was winded when he hit the ground and lay helpless for a moment on his back. His breaths came short and painful. He rolled off his back and onto his knees, straining to get up. A riderless horse veered towards him and he scrambled away to avoid its flailing hooves. He was surrounded by bellowing men and wild horses. He struggled warily to his feet and looked about him. His helm restricted what he could see and only at the last moment did he notice an axe arcing down at him. It caught him square on his chest, knocking him down again and gouging a great rent in his armour. He stared at the wound but there was no blood, just a dull ache. Holton's armour had done its work.

He staggered to his feet once more, tottering on legs like straw. He could hear Bear's thunderous voice - that at least was good - but he sounded so far off. Ned kept moving, making random strides to throw off any blows aimed at him. But he knew if he stayed on foot much longer, he would be struck down. His mace was still held at his wrist by its leather strap but it was a short weapon. Not good. Several horsemen came at him at once. All wielded axes but he was more worried about their mounts: he would likely be crushed to death before they dashed out his brains.

"An Elder!" he cried in vain, but his voice cracked and he decided to save his breath.

"Lord!" It was Bear, but he was at least a dozen feet away. Even the bold Flemish warrior would not be able to break through to him, but he roared again at Ned. "Lord!"

A weapon thudded into the turf at Ned's feet - Bear's long handled pollaxe. Even as he wrenched it from the earth, his assailants were upon him. He just brought up the axe head in time to parry the first blow, but the next rocked him backwards. He stumbled but managed to brace his feet firmly and swing the weapon around him. It struck one man's leg and sliced along the exposed flank of his mount.

Another charged at him but the reach of the borrowed weapon enabled Ned to keep him at arm's length. Still they gathered about him, trapping him in the melee, isolated from his men. He was already exhausted and every breath hurt his bruised chest. His arms ached from wielding the heavy weapon - how did Bear manage it?

Then he saw Cullen, pressing his horse through the others to get close to him. He had to break out. His opponents brought in longer weapons and blows began to rain down heavier upon him. He could not block them all - one lucky blow to his head and his skull would explode in agony. All he could think of then was that if he was killed Maighread would be angry with him, so angry...

§§§

Robert left two men with Emma and Richard and led the rest through the small wood towards the grassy slope upon which Ned Elder's men were slowly, but inevitably, being battered into submission. Robert's men were confused - he saw it written on every face. He was leading them against men who wore the colours of Clarence, Warwick's ally. Robert shook his head. If it made little sense to them, it did not make much more to him. It seemed that the Radcliffes and the Elders could not keep apart from each other. Yet, he had no intention of risking all of his men - and he possessed few enough of them - even to please Emma.

He intended instead to be careful, to be clever. There were Clarence archers ahead of them, trudging away from the woods towards the killing ground. They were collecting spent arrows and, their part done, were not keen to get to the melee too fast. Once the men at arms had almost finished that would be their time. Then they would slip in and find some easy kills.

Robert arrayed his own few archers amongst the trees where they had all the cover they needed.

"Wait until those archers are a threat to me - then you can give them something to ponder on. But if they run, let them go."

His men at arms, though unsure exactly what he was planning, rarely shied away from a fight and they followed him willingly, confident that the archers would watch their backs. As they crossed the few hundred yards to where Ned Elder's splintered column fought on, the toiling Clarence archers watched them. Robert was flying the Radcliffe colours which probably confused them for they made no attempt to launch their arrows at him.

He hurried across the grassland and a few of those in the melee suddenly noticed his approach. This was the awkward part. Ned Elder would know the Radcliffe banner and perhaps others would recognise it too. If he was not careful his men might end up being attacked by both sides! But he had schooled them well and, when he yelled a battle cry, his comrades took it up as if it were the dearest words they knew.

§§§

When the Elder battle cry echoed once more across the field, Cullen was only a few yards away from Ned. He looked bewildered and Ned himself was astonished that so many of his men not only still lived but had the breath to cry out at all.

For a moment Cullen held his mount still, as he stared at the oncoming riders. Then he shook his head.

"Your luck holds once more, Ned Elder - the devil's luck, I'd say," he called out as he turned away. "But it won't hold forever!"

Cullen withdrew his men leaving Ned to contemplate the remains of his small army. He peered then at his rescuers, riding towards them with the setting sun at their backs. It was not Croft, for Croft would not be coming from the west… and, of course, Croft had no mounts.

"Lord!" Bear shouted a warning but Ned had seen the banner too by then, the blood red Radcliffe banner. He had not seen it for years and thought never to see it again. He raised the axe in his tired arms but then it dawned on him that the new party of horsemen were not advancing to attack. They were taking their time. He ripped off his helm and stared at the man who led them. The latter also raised his helm and saluted him as he rode closer.

"Thomas Gate…" breathed Ned.

"Thomas Gate is dead and buried, Ned. As I think, Lady Emma told you. I'm Robert Radcliffe."

"A change of name only," replied Ned.

"You don't sound very pleased to be delivered from your enemies, Ned?" said Robert genially.

"That's because I see only another enemy before me," retorted Ned.

"I've brought your sister, Emma, back to be with her daughter."

"She's safe?"

"Aye, she's safe."

Ned observed with mixed feelings the group of riders heading up from the woods and smiled thinly. "So, now I am doubly in your debt," he muttered.

"Hardly," said Robert, "you let me go last time."

"I let my sister go."

Ned's men gave a cheer as a column of men at arms hurried out of Quenhull's distant gates.

Robert Radcliffe dismounted and walked across to Ned.

"A Radcliffe now?" remarked Ned.

"And a bastard Radcliffe…"

Ned gave a weary sigh. "All Radcliffes are bastards… but I believe I have you to thank for the safety of my niece, Alice and my sister. Now it seems I must thank you for seeing off these wolves too. God's blood, I'm already heartily sick of thanking you…"

"I want to end the bad blood between our families," said Robert abruptly.

"That would be a good trick."

"This seemed one way of doing so. We may well end up fighting each other in the next few weeks, Ned," said Robert, "but, for Lady Emma's sake, I will not see myself as your enemy."

"I promise you nothing," said Ned, "I can't forget, or forgive what happened at Yoredale…"

Robert nodded, turned on his heel and remounted. Emma rode up just then and went to him. Ned frowned to see her warmth towards him, watched her take his hand and kiss him on the cheek. Then Robert gathered his men about him and rode off, just as Croft arrived.

Ned greeted his sister and nephew whilst others tended to the wounded and retrieved the corpses of the dead. Croft brought him a mount and he led Emma away from the carnage. He wanted to ask her a thousand questions but they would have to wait. He was just too tired.

55

5th October 1470, at Quenhull Castle

Fear stalked the castle - a castle crammed with men, women and children who could see only a bleak, uncertain future. Ned had rarely felt so powerless. Reaching the safety of Quenhull somehow seemed like a defeat now. Not only had there been a cost in men and horses but he had only seen off Sir Roger Cullen with the unwelcome aid of Robert Radcliffe. Cullen had gone for now, but everyone knew that he would return unless help arrived soon from the king or the Duke of Gloucester.

Each day Ned expected to hear some news - a messenger from the king, a letter from his friends Hastings or Lord Scales, but no news came - just rumours. There were plenty of those: the king was dead, Warwick was dead, both were dead; old King Harry had been restored, old King Harry had been murdered in his bed… And so it went on, hearsay and gossip - who knew where they all started, except in hearts brimming with fear?

Everyday Spearbold assured him that a messenger would come, a victory… or a defeat would be declared and all would become clear. Ned knew that sooner or later Spearbold would be right; he just hoped it would be sooner. He was not good at sitting still and there were only so many times he could inspect his defences or check the castle stores. After only a week of that, he had taken to riding out beyond the walls with a troop of men at arms. Only God knew what purpose it served, other than to exercise the men and horses.

The rest of his time he spent with Maighread, who was heavy again with child, and his two boys. To have two healthy young sons made him a lucky man. For the first time he got to know his son John, so long a stranger, and found that he liked him immensely. The lad was an example to them all: he seemed to take every setback in his stride. Maighread had told him many times: your son is the bravest six-year old I know. It would soon be time to consider the lad's future - always assuming the Elders had a future.

A sudden shout from the gatehouse gave him a start. He ran so fast down the steps to the gate that he tripped and fell the last half dozen. He got gingerly to feet but no-one was laughing. They were just anxious to know what the hammering on the gates would mean for each of them.

It was a lone horseman and it was clear from the look of him that he had ridden long and hard. Bear helped him down from his trembling mount and then led the animal off to the stable whilst Ned took the rider into the hall. It quickly became crowded as many pushed their way in to see who had come and hear what news he brought.

A jug of ale was brought for the man who could hardly speak. When he had taken a healthy draught or two of ale, he glanced at Ned and then looked around the room at the host of faces watching him intently.

"Lord Elder?" he whispered and at once a sombre silence descended upon the hall. "I bring news but… it should be delivered to you alone and… privily, I think."

Ned shivered at that for news of a victory could be roared to the heavens.

"Come," he said, "and bring your ale. We'll go to my privy chamber and hot food will be brought there for you."

He turned to those crowded around him. "Go about your work," he ordered gruffly, though he knew that his men at arms had none. "You'll hear this man's tidings soon enough."

Now they would be resentful as well as afraid, he thought, as he led the messenger up the steps. He sat the man down and then ushered in Spearbold, Croft, Emma and Maighread. The messenger took a letter from a leather pouch and handed it to him. Ned recognised the king's seal.

"Do you need to return at once?" he asked.

The man shook his head.

"Ah," said Ned, "of course, you'll carry an answer for the king?"

"No, my lord, there'll be no need for an answer."

"Read the letter, Ned," said Maighread in a quiet voice.

He nodded and examined the letter written, he noted, in the king's own hand. He had found in the past that the prospect of bad news was often worse than the news itself, but this time the tidings were more dreadful than he could possibly have imagined. After the first few words he felt a chill pass through him and, with every line he read, the chill tightened its icy grip on his heart.

His face must have said it all, but he told them anyway.

"Warwick's brother, John Neville, has betrayed his king," he began. "King Edward's support has collapsed. He has taken ship to Flanders… with Gloucester, Hastings, Scales and a few other lords… Warwick and Clarence have triumphed."

"What does it mean for us?" asked Maighread.

Ned took her hand in his. "It means we're on our own."

"What of Eleanor and the others - will they be safe at Corve?"

"I don't know…" said Ned.

DEREK BIRKS

PART SIX: KINGDOM FOUND

DEREK BIRKS

56

17th March 1471, at Corve Manor near

Ludlow

"In truth, Felix," protested Eleanor, "I think I've done rather well these past few months!"

"You may think so, my lady, but you are besieged and you just don't know it. You should have gone to Quenhull with Ned."

"Felix, you are a valued friend, but don't tell me what I should or shouldn't have done."

"You must keep calm, my lady," urged Felix.

"I am calm, Felix!" she barked. "Who would not be calm with a small child in the household?"

"Ah, and how is little Kate?" asked Felix.

Eleanor could think of any number of answers to that but said only: "Little Kate is very... well."

"Then I'm glad and I know Ragwulf would be proud of you," he said.

Her smile faded, only for a moment, but Felix noticed and continued swiftly.

"And Becky and Hal are now pledged to each other and their marriage blessed by the village priest? Who would have thought it?" he said.

"They deserve to be happy... for, between them, they have kept me sane, Felix."

"And young Will grows taller by the day!" he said.

"Aye. You've brought him news of his… of Jack?" She could hardly say the words but she was trying, for Will's sake.

"Indeed, to everyone's surprise Jack's learning the wine trade," laughed Felix, "but perhaps only one drop at a time!"

"And his mother, the London whore?" asked Eleanor.

Felix sighed. "All are well, my lady," he said.

"And you've been to London too, so what news do you bring?" she asked.

"Well, in London at least, Warwick rules and, on the surface, all's well, all is… smiles," he said, "but…"

"But?" asked Eleanor.

"If you put a bear and a she-wolf in the same cage together, they'll soon stop smiling," replied Felix. "This alliance of enemies can't last, my lady. Already the cracks are showing: the Duke of Somerset has returned to the south west and the Courtenays scarcely ever left there. Now they just wait for Queen Margaret and her young prince to come. Warwick has few friends he can rely on, except the Duke of Clarence - but what is there in this new regime for Clarence? He'll not be king hereafter. The Stanley brothers support Warwick now because he's the power in the land, but how long will that last? No-one's loyalty is certain for all men ask the same question: what will happen when Queen Margaret arrives with her young prince?"

"What do you hear of Jasper Tudor, the newly restored Earl of Pembroke?" asked Eleanor. "His man paid me a visit at the start of all this and I can't say I wished him well."

"Jasper Tudor is Queen Margaret's man - he's for Lancaster, not Warwick. You must be careful, my lady. Many gossip about how you slighted his man, Walter Efford."

"Does anyone speak of King Edward?" she asked.

"Rumours, my lady, only rumours..."

"And do these rumours give any hope?"

"Some say he plans to return... but only a fool believes rumours..." said Felix.

"And your friends in the city of London: the vintners, the mercers and drapers - what do they say?"

Felix shrugged. "They would like to get back the money they've loaned to King Edward in the past ten years..."

"I had a letter from Ned last week," she said. "He begs me to go to Quenhull, for safety's sake. But it's safe enough here, Felix, isn't it? Surely if there was going to be trouble here then it would have happened after Warwick landed, when Walter Efford came."

"I fear not, my lady. Warwick has issued more commissions of array to some lords, including Jasper Tudor, which means-"

"I know what it means," sighed Eleanor.

"Sir Walter Efford returned to Ludlow only yesterday. I want you to understand the dangers you face, my lady, if you stay here... and I came to offer a refuge to Mags and her children with me at Ludlow... if you decide to go."

"I swear your place in Broad Street must already house a dozen of Ned's friends," said Eleanor.

"There's always room for another friend of Ned's," said Felix. "Without your brother, I'd have been dead long ago."

"Well, I'm not leaving," she said. "There's no-one for Jasper Tudor to recruit here - just women, children and old men. So, I shan't be going to Quenhull, but if Mags wants to leave then of course she may."

Felix frowned and shook his head. "You know she won't leave whilst you're still here... but I'll come again on Lady Day. You all know where to find me if you need me before then."

"Aye, and thank you, Felix."

She walked with him down to the gate and watched him leave with a sad heart. Then she turned on her heel and went to find Hal. Felix seemed to believe that she was an empty-headed fool but she took her stewardship of Corve Manor very seriously. Every day she walked around the fortified manor house with Hal, seeing for herself that Corve remained secure. She decided that a watchful leader must find some fault or other each day and, to Hal's constant irritation, she usually did. This morning she was struggling to catch him out until, as if for the first time, her eye lighted upon Pinner taking his ease in the yard.

"That man leaning against the brew house wall?" she said.

"That's Pinner, my lady."

"I know his name but he looks very old and he's only got one arm," she observed, "he can't be very much use with only one arm. What does he actually do?"

"He's… well, he's like a man at… arms…" said Hal.

"But he's only got one!" persisted Eleanor.

"Perhaps you should have a word with him yourself, my lady," replied Hal.

She rewarded him with a grim smile. "Very well, I shall."

In a few long strides she crossed the yard towards the brew house but stopped a dozen feet short of Pinner.

He looked up and raised his lone arm to give her what she imagined was some sort of mock salute. Then he scratched his groin and leant back against the wall again.

"You're name is Pinner?" she said.

"No, my lady, my name is George… but folk call me Pinner."

He gave a little smirk and Eleanor glared at him. "Can you do anything useful with that arm apart from scratch yourself?"

"I can throw a knife, my lady," said Pinner and Eleanor noted the slight edge in his voice.

"I could find a dozen men here who can throw a knife," she scoffed, "but can you hit anything?"

Pinner's hand flashed and a blade brushed by her hair. Eleanor blinked but did not move.

"Good enough for you, my lady?" enquired Pinner with a grin.

By way of response Eleanor retrieved the knife, still quivering in the post behind her, and walked over to him. She slammed it hard into a beam by his head.

"Ay, good enough, Master Pinner," she said, "as long as you weren't trying to hit me, because if I thought you were, I'd take your other arm."

He grinned back at her and she walked away.

Beside her, Hal winced. "I'm sorry for his rudeness, my lady," he muttered.

"Oh, don't be, Hal," she said with a smile. "I quite like him…"

All at once there was a chorus of shouts from the walls and the gatehouse. The gates were hurriedly slammed shut. Eleanor hurried up the steps to the rampart with Hal in her wake. What she saw outside the gates destroyed her good mood at a single stroke. Sir Walter Efford was back already and this time he had a score of men with him. She took a deep breath and swallowed hard.

"Open the gates!" Sir Walter bellowed at her from the ranks of his men outside. She looked at Hal and saw the apprehension in his face.

"Open your gates!" repeated Sir Walter, "or I'll break them open!"

The blunt warning echoed around Corve Manor.

"Stand fast!" cried Eleanor.

"Every man stay at his post!" ordered Hal.

Eleanor suddenly seized Hal's hand and led him swiftly down to the hall.

"Mags!" she cried.

Mags was already on her way into the hall from the kitchens with a small gaggle of children in her wake. Now Eleanor faced her with Hal.

"If I let them in…" she said, "there are few men worth recruiting here and mostly women and children."

"Aye," said Mags, "I'd not trust them once they got in."

"But can we keep them out, Hal?" she asked, almost whispering the question lest Sir Walter might hear the answer.

"Not for long, my lady. We're not strong enough. Lord Elder made some improvements last year but our walls are too old and too low - I fear they might be scaled quite easily. We have few men at arms, just some archers - ill-equipped to face trained men at arms."

"So, you think I should surrender, Hal?" asked Eleanor.

Outside Sir Walter's voice boomed once more: "I shall not wait long, my lady! Open your gates now!"

"No, I don't think you should surrender," replied Hal. "We all know what'll happen once they're in…"

"But you said we couldn't match them, we don't have the men at arms! What are you saying?"

"I'm not saying fight… and I'm not saying don't fight…"

Eleanor punched him hard on the shoulder. "Well, that's no help to me is it?" she cried. "Mags, what do you think?"

"I think I should have taken my children to Ludlow, to Master Felix," she breathed, "but I don't have an answer, my lady."

Eleanor groaned in anger, her head crammed with images of crumbling towers, burning stables, fleeing women and terrified children - amongst them her own.

Once again Sir Walter's voice reverberated around the manor house.

"This is no castle, my lady! It's nothing - give it up. Why

make yourself an enemy?"

"That man is starting to annoy me," she said.

She had never felt better, never felt fitter. She had been exercising with her sword for the best part of a year since Kate's birth and she no longer felt like a great lump of goose fat. Hal had been reluctant at first to spar with her - most likely because he feared she would accidentally wound him - but in the end he accepted it. She was as ready to fight now as she had ever been and all her instincts roared: fight! But there were so many others to consider.

If God were her friend she might have sought his guidance but after all the abuse she had hurled in his direction, she would not dare. She looked once more from Hal to Mags and saw that they expected her to decide. To resist might mean many deaths… but to open the gates might mean worse. She sighed, for she knew only one way to act… her mother's way.

"Mags, take all the women and children down into the cellar - if there's room… Hal, I want every archer we have on the ramparts - but not all in plain sight."

"You're going to fight, my lady?" he said.

"No, I'm going to open the gate."

"But if you're opening the gate, why the archers…"

"Just make sure they're ready, Hal," she said, "and I want you up there to command them. The gates will be opened but only to let me out to speak to Sir Walter."

"My lady, that's the worst thing you could do!" declared Hal, a look of horror on his face. "You'll be in the open… at their mercy! You'll be their hostage!"

She ignored his protest and stabbed her finger at his chest. "Just make sure that those archers are ready to loose every shaft they have when you see my signal."

"What signal?" asked Hal, bewildered.

"You'll find it clear enough when you see it," she snapped. "Now go!"

She tried to walk with a calm, measured step out of the hall and into the yard, though she trembled with fear. Not fear for herself but fear of getting it badly wrong and putting her whole household in peril. She stopped by the gates to talk to the men there for a few moments then tried to compose herself, taking long, deep breaths. She felt the comforting hilt of the small knife hidden in her palm, its point pricking the skin above her wrist. Amelie's blade had ever been her friend.

"My lady!" shouted Sir Walter. "I want your answer now! You have only to look out to see my men arrayed before you. Surrender your manor - you have no choice."

She nodded to the gatekeepers and one of the tall gates swung open a few inches to allow her through. The sound of it banging shut behind her almost broke her nerve as she stood before Sir Walter's small army. Some, including the knight himself, were mounted, but many were on foot as she was.

"What's this?" Sir Walter scolded her.

"I wanted to speak with you, Sir Walter," she replied.

"We can speak in more comfort in your hall, my lady," he retorted crossly, "now, for the last time, open the gates."

"You'll speak to me here, or you'll be the first knight to ride into the manor over a lady's body," she replied. She felt suddenly light-headed for this was the moment when it could all go so horribly wrong.

"Oh, very well," he said grudgingly and dismounted. In a few steps he crossed the ground between them.

"What is it that you insist upon saying to me?" he demanded.

She knelt down before him - and if he knew her better he would understand what a concession she was making to him.

"Sir Walter, I beg you to leave my household in peace. I have few fighting men - only those too young or too old to go to war. But I have women and children here who are afraid of you and what your men might do to them. I need you to leave us be."

"Get up, my lady, for your entreaties fall upon deaf ears. This is no game I play for my own amusement. My lord has charged me to raise an army and I intend to press what men you have into it. Now, though it is against all reason on my part, I'll allow your men to come out to me and leave the household undisturbed. That is all I will offer. Now, for the love of God, please submit to these terms!"

Eleanor sighed and stood up. "Very well, Sir Walter, then that is your last word."

"Yes, it is!" he retorted.

"It wasn't a question, Sir Walter," she said, with genuine sadness, and plunged her knife deep into his throat.

He pushed her angrily away and staggered towards his mount, clutching at his neck. Blood spurted between his fingers as he tried to speak but couldn't. Some of his men rushed towards him.

"Help him!" cried one.

"The bitch has a dagger!" shouted another.

She leant back against the gates with the bloodied knife still in her hand.

Some men tried to hold up their lord whilst others took a pace towards her. They never got near her, for above her on the rampart she heard Hal's cry of "Loose!" and arrows rained down upon the soldiers.

Sir Walter had arrayed his men in the open to frighten the inhabitants of the manor house, but in doing so he exposed them all to Hal's archers. Men fell in a great writhing swathe before her. It took only a few moments and then her archers ceased for the survivors, robbed of their commander, fled in disarray.

Behind her the gates opened and Hal emerged with his few men at arms.

"Are you hurt, my lady?" he asked.

"No," she murmured, but her legs could barely hold her up. She walked unsteadily over to where Sir Walter lay in his own blood, his eyes staring up blankly up at her.

"I did not want this," she said to him softly. "Even God knows that. I wanted you to leave for I grow tired of this bloodletting."

She was aware of Hal gently taking her arm. "Aye, Hal, even I grow weary of it…"

§§§

Hal escorted his mistress inside and then set about the grisly task of dealing with the dead. They found one man still alive. He lived on for several more hours and only in the late afternoon when the priest came up from the village to give him comfort did the poor fellow die.

At dusk they were still finishing their work of burying the dead. A cry went out from the southern rampart: a small column of horsemen had appeared. Hal hastily summoned the archers to the walls once more and the gates were slammed shut. But the cries of warning soon turned to cheers for it was not more of Jasper Tudor's men returning, but Master Croft under Ned Elder's banner.

At once the gates were thrown open and the riders came in. Croft dismounted at once to embrace his comrade, Hal.

"I thought you'd be long dead, Hal," he said.

"Very nearly, Croft, very nearly!" replied Hal.

"We ran into some of Tudor's men on the road. They seemed in a hurry and… now we see a row of freshly dug graves. What happened here?"

"I think you might say that Lady Eleanor 'happened'," said Hal.

"You had losses?"

"No," said Hal, "not one."

"Sweet Jesus!"

"I'm afraid their commander really annoyed her," said

Hal, unable to suppress a wry smile.

"What did she do?"

"She… sort of… ripped his throat out…"

"Sweet Jesus!" repeated Croft. "And I've to tell her that Lord Elder insists she goes down to Quenhull."

"Ah… I'm not sure I'd use the word 'insists'," said Hal.

"Do you think she'll go?" asked Croft.

Hal shrugged. "You might as well ask which way the wind blows!" he said with a grin.

Oh, shit!" breathed Croft. "Hal…"

"Come, I'll take you up to her." He led Croft into the hall. "Don't worry, the crazy bitch is sometimes quite fair…"

His voice failed him as he turned to find Lady Eleanor standing close by in the hall doorway.

She looked quite shocked, thought Hal, hurt almost… in a stony-faced, livid sort of way. He stared down at his feet and offered a silent prayer.

"Crazy… bitch," murmured Lady Eleanor, as if savouring the phrase to remember it for later. He was in no doubt that she would never let him forget it, if he lived…

"I crave your pardon, my lady," he whispered.

"Is that how you call me now? You, of all folk, Hal? I thought you knew me better…"

She turned to Croft. "You'd better come with me since it seems from what I've overheard that you're not here just to admire the 'crazy bitch'."

Hal watched them go. He felt like a whipped dog. She was right: he did know her better. He was showing off to Croft and he bitterly regretted it. She did not deserve the term he had so carelessly laid upon her. She was better than that, and now she would only think less of him.

§§§

Hours later he lay in the cold, dark chamber that he shared with his new wife. She was not there yet, which was unusual, but he had a fair idea where she was. In the small hours he still lay awake when she finally joined him in their narrow bed. She was cold and quiet, very quiet.

"Beck?" he said softly.

"She's just a woman, Hal…"

"Aye love, but she's a woman with our lives in her hands."

"You shouldn't have called her that."

"She told you then…"

"Of course she told me - I've been with her half the night!"

He put an arm around her, half-expecting it to be thrust aside, but it was not.

"Go to sleep," she said. "You'll be busy on the morrow, because we're leaving."

"What?"

"Go to sleep…"

In the darkness, Hal embraced his wife, but sleep did not come easily.

57

20th March 1471, at Quenhull Castle

Ned looked out upon the frosted ground north of Quenhull towards the Malvern Hills, just visible above the icy mist. It had been hard at Quenhull these past few months, when the winter was at its worst and food was scarce. It had been hard. Foraging parties trudged out each day but what was left to be foraged? Then there was Roger Cullen, whose men made regular raids on the local families who still supported Ned Elder. He was forcing Ned to take more and more folk into Quenhull. Cullen would know better than anyone exactly what reserves the castle could hold. Now he simply waited for weakness or desperation to bring an error on Ned's part so that he could strike at Quenhull.

Maighread joined him silently at the wall, slipping her arm through his and drawing him close.

"Little Margaret is sleeping?" murmured Ned.

"Aye, she's good babe, your new daughter," replied Maighread, "and the winter cold doesn't seem to worry her."

He hugged her more tightly. "Aye, she's tough like her mother, raised in the borders."

He wanted to tell her that spring was coming and all would be well, but he suspected that in the spring even more men would flock to Clarence's banners. He had heard that commissions of array had been issued for Hereford to the north and South Wales to the west. Cullen, like the rest of Clarence's captains, would be recruiting fast.

If King Edward did not return, then holding Quenhull would prove to be a colossal mistake - an act of treason against the restored King Harry. In the end Ned would have to surrender and he did not see the Earl of Warwick letting him off lightly. Death, attainder and the ruin of his family would all surely follow.

As if reading his thoughts, Maighread squeezed his arm. "Do you still believe in King Edward?" she asked.

"I believed in him once and, as I recall, we were both in a pretty bleak mood then. With his confidence, with his damned belief that he could prevail, against all the odds, I believed in him then."

"And now?" prompted Maighread.

"I ask myself whether the man who had such belief could possibly give up a throne he won with so much blood and steel… and I don't believe he could."

He took her by the shoulders. "That's why we're still here, my love. That's why I've put you, our young children and the rest of our affinity through all this. Because, in my heart, I believe he'll come back."

She smiled that half-twisted smile he had come to love. "Then we must keep believing and pray for his return - but soon, Ned, soon."

"Aye," he said, "but I fear the worst is yet to come and our prayers now must be for Eleanor and those who travel with her."

"Master Croft is with her - and Hal - they'll look after her," said Maighread.

"Aye, they'll do their best but Cullen will be close and he'll know she's coming. He'll be tracking her."

"You think he'll attack her?"

"No, not her, but he knows that when she gets here, I must open my gates, and you can be sure he'll be ready for that moment. Every day our scouts report greater numbers of Clarence's men in the area. For the moment they do nothing but wait."

"Do you think Clarence will try to take Quenhull?"

"Clarence? I don't know, but his client, Cullen, will try. I'm certain of that."

§§§

Hal exchanged a look with Croft. They had both seen the movement on their flank: several riders.

"I warned you," said Croft, "Cullen's scouts - letting him know where we are."

"But Lord Elder will send out men to see us in, won't he?" said Hal.

"Yes, he will, but I doubt he can spare enough."

Hal looked back at the straggling column behind them: the wagon, with a score or more of women and children trailing behind it and after them another score or so of archers, the youngest of which was barely fourteen and the oldest over seventy. Lady Eleanor walked at the rear, shepherding her charges onwards. Hal smiled to see Will walking beside her, leading her horse. The lad and his mother seemed to have overcome their differences. Pinner followed a respectful few paces behind and the whole company was flanked by Croft's dozen mounted men at arms.

Their progress was painfully slow, for the poor oxen struggled to pull the wagon, which was weighed down with all that Lady Eleanor could pack into it. Those on foot had walked for two days already and slept out in the open, exposed to the March winds and overnight frosts. The first day Hal reckoned they must have managed nearly twenty miles, but the second, barely a dozen. Now on the third day they were getting close, but all were weary and footsore. Some had once made the long journey south from Yoredale, but others were unaccustomed to walking so far.

He studied their faces and in some he found hope, but mostly all he saw was fear.

"We should send a man on," said Hal, "to let them know we're nearly there."

"They'll know," replied Croft, "besides, our man would be taken before he'd travelled a mile. Lord Elder will be ready, but it'll be tight."

As the morning passed and a few more miles were covered, Hal began to feel more confident. They passed folk at work in the fields and some early spring sunshine began to cheer the party a little. There was some bright banter amongst the women for a while until Quenhull came into sight in the distance. It was Hal's first sight of it and he could see it was an impressive enough fortress - as long as you were on the inside…

Croft called a halt and they waited for Lady Eleanor to make her way to the head of the column.

"Surely it can only be a few more miles now," she said cheerfully.

"Yes, my lady," replied Hal.

"The last mile or so… we may have to run for the gate," said Croft.

"I don't think those oxen will be running anywhere," observed Hal.

"There's certain to be an attempt to cut us off," said Croft. "If it comes to it, we'll have to abandon the wagon."

"They want to capture me?" asked Lady Eleanor.

"Well yes, but no," answered Croft. "Sir Roger Cullen will see you as a valuable prize, my lady, but Quenhull itself is the prize he really wants. Quenhull, and your brother."

"Tell us what we need to do," said Lady Eleanor.

§§§

"I see them, lord!" cried one of the archers on Quenhull's north tower.

Ned followed the line of the man's outstretched arm

and smiled to catch his first glimpse of them. Croft had them well organised, he thought: it was a compact column with the mounted men free to defend its flanks. He went over in his mind what he had agreed with Croft: if all went well, then there would be no need to take any action at all, but if Cullen attacked...

He left the ramparts and descended to the courtyard, giving words of encouragement to every man he passed. In the yard, Bear had assembled close to fifty of the men at arms. They wore such variety of livery and badges it was hard to tell who they fought for. Yet they were heavily armed and some, who had watched Cullen's men pull down their cottages, were spoiling for revenge.

Ned was about to summon a page when several converged upon him at once carrying his armour, helm and half a dozen other items they thought he might need. He grinned at their enthusiasm as they fussed about him, nervously strapping on his breastplate and other armour pieces. When they were quite satisfied, he took his helmet and walked to the gates. There he paused and turned to the wedge of men behind him. They ceased their anxious chattering.

"You know what your task is today," he said. "Do only what you've been told to do - and, above all, stand firm - no matter what happens, you must stand firm! We shall be out there, exposed outside the gate, until my sister's party is safely inside. If I have to go to fetch her, then Bear will have told some of you to go with me, but the rest must stay to hold the gatehouse."

He donned his helmet, but kept the visor raised. "Open the gates!" he ordered.

At once the tall gates began to draw apart, allowing a swathe of watery sunshine to light up the yard. Ned walked straight out across the drawbridge with Bear beside him and fifty men at his back. The men deployed swiftly for they had planned this often enough in the past few days. Ned turned out of the east gate and saw Eleanor's column still approaching slowly from the north.

For a moment, Ned's men were on their own, scanning in all directions for any possible threat. Then there was a sudden roar of men shouting which seemed to come from all around them. The first to show themselves were the horsemen, streaming out of the small wood near the river below. Then men at arms appeared on foot and began an assault on the southern slope. Behind them, archers formed up in ranks and prepared to let fly.

Before Ned could utter a word, Bear shouted: "Pavise!" and then the arrows began to fall.

Bear had suggested making some pavises during the winter when the men were largely idle. Ned, unfamiliar with the screens used by crossbowmen, had only agreed to keep them busy. Now the men furthest out from the gate hurried to prop up the flimsy screens and took shelter behind them. Even so, the arrows took some toll.

As always, Ned decided it was safer to be on the move.

"On me!" he cried and a score of men detached from the rest to follow him along the edge of the dry ditch towards Eleanor's company.

The horsemen from the woods were already thundering up the shallow slope towards the labouring column. Ned, still a hundred yards off, watched Hal's archers loose a volley of arrows as the wagon lumbered on. Another volley followed and then the archers atop the north wall added a host of their own arrows.

Ned was still too far away when Croft charged down to meet the knights with his own mounted men. It was a brave attempt but he was heavily outnumbered. All too soon Croft's men were pressed back towards the wagon and the rest of the group. They were almost at the castle ditch but still some fifty yards from the cluster of Ned's men at arms heading towards them.

"God's blood!" Ned cursed, worried that Croft would be overrun before he could reach him.

His men, hand-picked by Bear, were armed with long-handled pollaxes and did not fear mounted opponents. Even so, the weight of their armour and weapons slowed their progress towards Croft. Ned was already out of breath though he was moving at scarcely a trot. He was still twenty yards from the wagon when one of the oxen fell. He could not tell whether it was hit or not - but it mattered little. What mattered was that, whatever the cause, the wagon was now stationary and the refugees from Corve cowered behind it.

Croft's men were savagely forced back until their horses stood hard against the wagon. The sight of the children diving under the wagon to avoid the horses spurred Ned on over the last few yards. The enemy horsemen swung around to face him and at once Ned saw Cullen. Thank the Lord - Roger Cullen himself! Now the debt to John Holton would be repaid in full and Cullen would fall before the walls of Quenhull.

Ned's men did not hesitate but hacked and slashed into the mounted knights without mercy. Horses shrieked and shied away as their flanks were raked with steel. Their riders tried to fend off the long weapons but they were at a standstill. They would need pace and power to dislodge his men - and they didn't have either. Ned bludgeoned a path towards Cullen, but before he could reach him, his attention was drawn back to the gates. Cullen's men at arms had climbed the slope and were now crashing through the flimsy pavises into Bear's men defending by the gatehouse.

Cullen withdrew the shattered remnants of his cavalry and ordered them to dismount. They were well trained, Ned observed, as they reformed. But he also saw more men climbing up on foot to join them. Everywhere, his men were under pressure: he glanced at Eleanor by the wagon and then back to the gate where his men were being brutally pushed back.

Cullen cried exultantly: "What's it to be, Lord Elder: your castle or your sister?"

Ned hurried to Eleanor and Hal. "Leave the wagon!" he ordered. "Eleanor, see the women and children to the gates!"

"No!" she cried. "You need the supplies on this wagon! We'll starve without them!"

"And you'll die here if you stay!" he retorted, "Get to the gate and don't argue! Hal, make a screen around them with your archers! Croft, your men with me!"

Cullen was coming at them, his numbers swelled by the fresh men coming up behind, all wearing Clarence's livery. All Ned could do was abandon the wagon and retreat in the best order he could manage. So he fell back with his men stretched out in a thin steel line with the castle ditch at their backs. Cullen's men pushed and prodded at them, pressing them closer together, forcing them in on each other so that not all could bring their arms to bear. Some slipped backwards into the ditch and had to scramble up to rejoin the rest.

The gates were still thirty paces away when he heard a great, triumphant roar behind him. Bear's men were being driven back to the gates. Some of Clarence's men were already streaming in Ned's direction. He could only watch helplessly as they blocked his path to the gatehouse and joined Cullen's men at arms. They were surrounded. Women screamed, clutched their children to them and rolled down into the ditch as Ned's line buckled.

He stared in disbelief down the slope to the south where another entire column of men was advancing towards them. The Clarence banners fluttered at its head and he picked out several richly dressed knights in the vanguard. He had no doubt that the Duke of Clarence himself would be one of them. His men looked to him now, some willing him to surrender. He might have coped with Cullen alone, but not the Duke of Clarence himself with what looked like half an army.

Cullen now pulled his men back a yard or two, awaiting Ned's capitulation, for it was over.

58

20th March 1471, in Cheshire

Whilst he awaited the pleasure of his new lord, William Stanley, Robert Radcliffe sat thinking about Emma. She was never far from his thoughts, even though he had not seen her for six months, for so much had passed between them in France and during the sea crossing back to England. He was wishing now that he had not left her with Ned Elder, left her walled up at Quenhull. Only God knew what the conditions were like there.

Ned Elder was always such a stubborn fool. Why did he not just give up like everyone else? Surely some agreement could be brokered - for the women and children at least. He had no doubt that Quenhull was well stocked with supplies in October and perhaps they managed to replenish a little in November - but now? They must be down to eating the weevils and it made him angry. He left Emma and her children there so that they were safe not so that Ned Elder could slowly have them starved to death.

What in God's name was the fool waiting for? It was all over: the old king, Harry, was restored and the Earl of Warwick ruled - at least until Queen Margaret and her son arrived - that would be interesting. But King Edward had fled. He was gone and Ned could not wait behind Quenhull's walls forever on the off chance he might try to come back.

Robert could not see how King Edward could regain his

throne. With John Neville holding the north and with the Stanley brothers, the Earl of Oxford, Jasper Tudor of Pembroke and a host of other lords all now professing their undying loyalty to the old king, there was surely no hope of a return to the rule of York. In any case he supposed that Edward was comfortable enough in Flanders.

The chamber door was abruptly flung open and a messenger hurried through it.

"Come in, Robert!" called William Stanley through the open door.

Robert watched the messenger go, noting that the man was actually running to get to his horse. He entered William's privy chamber.

"Close the door," ordered William. "Events are moving with more speed that any of us imagined."

Robert did not ask what events. Years of serving Warwick had taught him that powerful men disliked being interrupted, especially when they have something of import on their minds.

"You came into my service, Robert, by offering to act as my agent in the Earl of Warwick's camp. You claimed to have no lingering trace of loyalty to your former master."

"My lord, I serve none but you," affirmed Robert solemnly, wondering where this was going. Did William doubt his loyalty? But surely they were all on the same side now?

"Unto death, Robert?" William pressed him.

"Unto death," repeated Robert, though he thought the words sounded over dramatic and possessed a certain finality which troubled him.

"Do you swear?"

"Aye, I swear it, my lord."

William nodded. "Very well, I want every man I have armed and ready to leave at dawn the day after tomorrow. Every man I have."

Robert gave a nod of assent. "Every man," he breathed. "Aye, every last one."

"My lord, may I know where we're going?"

William studied him carefully. "I trust you, Robert - and more than most - but no, you may not know. Now, get moving!"

§§§

Robert was surprised just how many men at arms William Stanley could muster when all methods of persuasion were used. They were arrayed in their hundreds in the early morning sunshine and yet, wasn't Lord Thomas Stanley, his elder brother, was still thrashing out his quarrel with the Harringtons? Even the sizable resources of the Stanley family would be stretched by the demands of deploying so many men at once.

Were the brothers acting together, or alone? They gave little away, these brothers. In fact Robert did not learn of his destination until after they set out when William called him up to ride with him near the front of the column.

"Well, Robert, what do you make of our little army?" asked William.

"You have a good number of men, many mounted, my lord, but…"

William stared at him and then laughed. "You're wondering what we're about with this fine body of men, eh?"

"Aye, my lord. I can only judge a force by its fitness to carry out its purpose."

William was still smiling. "We're going to Leicester, Robert, but this is just a small part of our army, as you'll see."

Well before Leicester, they were joined on their march by countless more men, many of whom wore a livery Robert instantly recognised, that of William, Lord Hastings but Hastings had fled to Flanders with King Edward. From that moment on his lord had no need to explain their purpose for it was all too clear to Robert: they were marching, it seemed, to restore another king.

At Leicester they met King Edward himself and Robert was astonished at how few men he had at his command. The exiled lords were there: Gloucester, Hastings, Scales and others, but the king's army was numbered only in the hundreds. He realised then the importance of Stanley's contribution, for he had brought Edward several thousand men.

"I trust you're a man who likes a gamble, Robert," said William.

"I see that you are, my lord," replied Robert.

"Yet, we are hardly alone - and there will be more. Still, I want scouts in all directions. The king needs to know where his enemies lie and what strength they have and…he needs to know that as soon possible, if you please."

As the hours passed and Robert's scouts came and went, a picture slowly emerged - not yet clear but he felt confident that his men had provided the most accurate information they could. What surprised him most was the sheer number of different armed groups all around them. He suspected too that many of them had not even decided yet which king to support.

He sought out William Stanley and found him with the king and several other lords. Robert had never been in such exalted company before but William waved him in and told him to report to the king what he had discovered. He was rarely overawed but he took a deep breath before he began to outline their situation.

"Your grace, Warwick is south of us at Coventry and the Earl of Oxford has just joined him with the Duke of Exeter and several hundred men raised from the eastern counties. Your brother, the Duke of Clarence, comes up fast from the west."

"Where is Clarence now?" interrupted Gloucester.

"Near Burford, we believe, your grace," replied Robert. At that, he noticed an exchange of looks between the royal brothers.

"Continue," ordered the king. "Where's Warwick's brother, John?"

"Lord Montagu's still to the north, your grace, but he'll be here in a few days."

"So, what you're telling me is that I'm surrounded," said the king with a smile.

"Aye, your grace, but there are other groups, as yet uncommitted…"

Edward dismissed him with gesture and Robert retired gratefully from the royal presence. Well, he had craved influence, a place with someone who mattered. Now it appeared that he had it, so he had better make the most of it.

59

20th March 1471, at Quenhull Castle

A single horseman detached himself from Clarence's host and rode up the slope towards the castle. Ned realised at once he was some sort of herald and waited for the rider to pull up and say his piece. But the herald ignored him and spoke to Cullen.

"His grace asks you to retire, Sir Roger," announced the herald.

Roger Cullen stared at him in confusion. "Pull back?" said Cullen. He tore off his helm and threw it to the ground. "What do you mean 'retire'?" he barked. "We've just spilled a deal of blood getting this far - and it's done. Lord Elder can do no other but surrender. Go back to the duke for he cannot understand our position."

"He understands, Sir Roger," said the herald impassively standing his ground. "You must fall back."

Cullen could scarcely speak but merely spluttered out protest after protest.

The herald turned towards Ned's men at arms crammed tightly around the knot of women and children, his eyes seeking their commander. Ned, still trying to work out what was happening, eased himself forward out of the line.

"Lord Elder?" asked the herald.

"Aye," said Ned. "And what would his grace like me to do?"

"His grace allows you to withdraw inside your castle

with certain conditions."

"This is madness!" raged Cullen. "I shall speak to the duke myself. No man fall back yet!" he ordered and stalked down the slope.

"What are the conditions?" Ned asked the herald.

"First, that both sides be permitted to retrieve their dead and wounded comrades without hindrance and second, that you agree to meet the duke to discuss terms. You may do so inside the castle as long as you give his grace surety of his safety within your walls."

Ned was incredulous. Whatever tales he had heard of Clarence had not prepared him for this.

"So, let us be clear," he said, "the duke allows all of my affinity to withdraw into Quenhull as long as I agree to meet him."

"Indeed, Lord Elder. I assume those terms are acceptable?"

Ned gave him a nod of assent.

"Shall we say a meeting at noon, then?" said the herald.

"Agreed," said Ned.

He looked to the foot of the hill where Cullen appeared to be remonstrating in the most vigorous manner with the duke. The herald addressed everyone now.

"Your commanders have agreed terms," he cried. "Let all men withdraw now with no further violence!"

And to Ned's surprise, Clarence's army turned and walked back down the slope, carrying their wounded with them. His own men stood perplexed at their sudden deliverance and wondered what it could mean. Ned wondered too, as he accompanied Eleanor and the others to the gatehouse.

§§§

When the sun was high and the moment came, George, Duke of Clarence, entered the castle alone. Ned was impressed. It appeared that the duke, like his brothers, did not lack for courage. Ned met him in the courtyard. The duke came unarmed and Ned led him up to the privy chamber where Maighread, Emma and Eleanor awaited them.

Clarence looked surprised to see the women there - and not best pleased.

"I must speak to you alone," he told Ned.

"No, your grace," replied Ned, "with respect - and gratitude for your generous terms - I will have my lady and my sisters here whilst we talk. Whatever you have to say will affect their lives as well as mine."

Clarence chewed his lip and remained silent for a few moments, considering.

"Very well, Lord Elder, I will allow that," he said finally, "but I must have the word of all that what is spoken of here will remain most privy."

"You have my word," said Ned. Each of the others in turn gave theirs and Clarence sat down. Maighread poured him some wine. He took a deep draught of it and she refilled the vessel.

Still he hesitated, looking to each of them in turn.

"I doubt you expected to be outnumbered at this meeting," said Ned, "but we know that we are in your hands. Speak freely."

Clarence gave a sigh and then began to speak.

"You won't know this yet, but a few days ago my brothers landed on the north coast."

Ned could not help grinning at the news but his joy was much tempered by the fact that it was his enemy delivering it.

"I have received letters from several of my sisters and, God defend me, from my mother. All were written to the same end: they want me to rejoin my brother Edward's cause."

"Have you decided to do so then?" asked Ned.

"No, not yet," replied Clarence. "It may be difficult to bring it about… there will be mistrust on both sides."

Aye mistrust, thought Ned, most definitely. The treason of his brother would have hurt Edward deeply - hurt his pride too. Mistrust, there would be in abundance.

"If it can be managed safely," continued Clarence, "then I want at least to meet with my brothers - and that's why I came to you."

"And why, no doubt, you wanted me heavily in your debt," said Ned.

"Perhaps," agreed Clarence. "I need a man that Edward will trust to make the arrangements - and he will trust you, of that I'm certain."

"He may do so," said Ned, "but why should I trust you when you freely admit that your own brother might not?"

"You have an obligation - a debt as you put it - but you don't have to trust me. I'll leave the conditions of the meeting up to you. All I ask is that you get Edward to agree to meet me somewhere safe for both of us."

"What if your brother doesn't want to meet you?" asked Ned.

"Oh, he will," Clarence said. "I've been assured by my sister Margaret that he will."

"If I were to agree, when would we go?"

"As soon as possible - the day after tomorrow at the latest."

"There would be conditions," said Ned softly.

Clarence nodded.

"If I go with you, I'll go in force," said Ned.

"Of course - and the king will need every man you have."

"I will not ride with Sir Roger Cullen. He is a murderer and I intend to hang him."

"Sir Roger is one of my captains," retorted Clarence, "and has been loyal in my service, but for now I'll send him south - well away from here. Is that all?"

"I shall consult with these ladies before deciding," said Ned.

"Do not find obstacles to put in my way, Lord Elder," warned Clarence. "This is a matter of the gravest importance for the kingdom."

"I know that, your grace. I know that. You will have my answer by nightfall."

"Very well, my lord," said Clarence, swallowing the last of his wine. "Then I suppose I must leave you to deliberate."

He rose and the others rose with him. Emma moved to the door.

"I'll take you down to the gate," said Ned.

"No, Ned," said Emma, "I'll do that."

Ned gave her a puzzled look. "Very well, sister, if you will…"

§§§

Emma led the duke from the chamber and walked slowly along the stone passage. She would have little time.

"Your grace," she whispered, "may I ask you about the lady Anne, your wife's sister?"

"Ah, of course," chuckled Clarence, "how could I forget: you left her in deep disgrace, Lady Emma - though I was surprised, I must admit."

"I never, ever betrayed her," said Emma with sudden vehemence, "it was a misunderstanding and I was the victim not the villain. I've been in her service for some years, your grace; I would never hurt her."

"Well, if it is any consolation, my lady, I believe that she'll be missing you - and even more so now that she is married to Prince Edward. She'll have no friends at the court of Queen Margaret, that's certain. All of her ladies were appointed by her mother in law so yes, she could have done with you by her side. And now, if I desert Warwick, she'll be even more alone. Queen Margaret will enjoy raging to her about false Clarence and Isabel."

They reached the foot of the steps and walked out into the sunlit yard.

"You may be sure, your grace, that if ever I have the chance to help her, I shall not fail her again."

"May God give you - and your brother - guidance, my lady," said Clarence, leaving her and strolling towards the gate as if he carried no burden at all.

§§§

When Emma returned to the privy chamber, raised voices greeted her.

"You can't trust him!" said Eleanor. "His treason has already cost this family and those they love very dearly."

"Yet," replied Ned, "he saved all our lives today."

"Only because he wants your favour!" Eleanor snapped back at him. "Am I the only one here who mistrusts him?"

"No," said Maighread. "You are not. You're just making more noise than the rest of us... My concern is what will happen on the way to meet the king: what if Clarence is persuaded to change his mind again? What if Warwick offers him a greater share of power? Would he not throw off his new cloak of loyalty to his brother? What price your head then, Ned?"

"Yet," said Emma, "he has saved us, as Ned says. That must be worth something."

"You would argue for him," said Eleanor, "you served his sister - you're a Neville, not an Elder."

"I've never betrayed either family!" argued Emma crossly.

Silence fell upon them all then as each held to their own thoughts.

"We should go to the chapel, pray upon it for a time..." said Emma.

Ned shook his head. "I think the Lord might wonder

why I've left it so long to seek his advice. If you wish to pray, then do so, but I've listened to all that's been said and I know my mind already.

"If the king really is back, then this is the best service I can do for his cause. If I bring him Clarence, with all his men, then I weaken Warwick greatly. I have no choice but to trust Clarence."

§§§

When the Duke of Clarence returned to his camp he found that Cullen was still raging. Clarence sighed. He would have to silence Cullen before he spread disaffection throughout his entire host, so he summoned Sir Roger to his tent later that afternoon.

The knight entered stiffly and bowed.

"Your pride is getting in the way," said Clarence. "I can't have you storming through our camp unsettling my other captains."

"Your grace-" Cullen began to protest but the duke cut him off.

"Listen, Sir Roger, don't speak," he said coldly. "If you are indeed my loyal servant then you will listen and then you'll do as you're told."

Cullen said nothing.

"You are confused by my actions today - I understand that, but you must learn to quell your temper. I will pursue whatever design helps the kingdom most - and therefore helps my clients too. It's not really in your interest that my head is put upon a spike on London gate, is it?"

"No, your grace," mumbled Cullen.

"So, you will take your men and go to my lands south of Tewkesbury. You will wait there until I tell you to do otherwise. You will ensure the safety of my lady, the Duchess of Clarence, and you will look always for news of the arrival of Queen Margaret. Once she has landed make sure you know where she is at all times - that is your task."

"Very well, your grace… and Ned Elder?"

"Forget Ned Elder and bide your time. I'll give him to you, but only when I no longer have need of him. Be patient, Sir Roger, be patient."

60

2nd April 1471, near the town of Warwick

Ned had never witnessed such confusion as he encountered on his journey north with Clarence. He found armed bands in almost every village but most of them did not seem to know what they had taken up arms to fight for. Near Banbury, an attack from a group proclaiming their loyalty to old King Harry, faltered when the men saw Clarence's banners appear behind Ned's.

Ned met with the duke only briefly on the road to Burford, before taking his own column on towards the town of Warwick where he hoped to find the king's army. He approached the town with all banners flying. The last thing he wanted was to be taken as hostile. He was soon confronted by ranks of archers on the outskirts of the town so there he identified himself and left his force, about 100 strong, outside the walls. He took only Bear with him to see the king.

As he passed through the straggling royal army, he was struck by the irregular nature of the force and the range of livery and badges that men wore. A few came to greet him, two or three knights who remembered him from Towton and others who had seen Bear before - not a sight one would forget easily.

Before he reached the king, he was taken to Will Hastings, who embraced him with a broad grin.

"Hah!" he exclaimed. "We watched you ride away when the king was captured, and Gloucester said to me: 'I think that's the last we'll see of Ned Elder.' But I told him: 'You don't know Ned very well yet, your grace!'"

"I'm still here, Will, but only by the grace of God."

"Well, all the same, Ned, it's good to see you. Though I should warn you that the king will want to know why you're here and not still in the west where he wanted you."

Ned grimaced. "I thought he might…"

"Come then," said Hastings, "I'll take you in. You'd better leave this tower of flesh outside!"

"He knows," replied Ned, with a nod to Bear. The latter gave Hastings a brief scowl and then leant against the wall outside the house which the king had commandeered as his headquarters.

King Edward and the Duke of Gloucester were both in the chamber when Hastings led Ned in. The king's greeting was warm, but a little guarded most likely for the reasons that Hastings had already told him.

"Your grace," said Ned, "I'm pleased to see you back in England where you belong and you may be sure that Quenhull is still held for you."

"My brother is wondering," said Gloucester, "why you and your men are not still in it."

"A greater purpose brought me here, your grace," replied Ned.

Gloucester seemed about to comment further but Edward laid a gentle hand upon his arm.

"This is my good comrade Ned," he told him. "I'm listening, Ned. Why have you come?"

There was something in the king's expression that brought a wry smile to Ned's face.

"You know, don't you, your grace?" he said.

"I hope I do," said the king.

"I'm here to arrange for you to meet with your brother,

the Duke of Clarence, your grace."

The king punched his brother's arm excitedly. "I told you he'd come back to me, Dickon. I knew he would!"

"He's had enough of the family urging him to do so," said Gloucester drily.

"Do you trust his intent, Ned?" asked the king. "What feeling do you have in your gut about it?"

"I think your brother sees no future with his father-in-law, Warwick, and certainly not with Queen Margaret."

"The lady, Margaret of Anjou, who claimed to be queen," said Gloucester pointedly.

"Indeed, your grace."

"So you think he's serious about changing to his old allegiance?" said the king. "If he were your brother, would you trust him?"

Ned considered carefully before replying. "Your grace, I'd trust his intent to make his peace with me… but I would ever after keep him near me - in case trust was not enough…"

"Well stated," said the king. "So, let us make it happen - if nothing else it might please my mother - never an easy thing to accomplish." He glanced up suddenly at Ned. "I hope I speak amongst friends…"

"You do, your grace," said Ned.

"Well then, Dickon and I best meet him alone at first."

"He has a thousand men with him coming up from Burford," said Ned, "and thousands more trailing in his wake, your grace. You'd best make sure you're accompanied by a goodly force."

"You still fear a trap?" Gloucester asked him.

"No, your grace, but I think that some at least of both armies need to see the accord, rather than just… hear about it."

"That sounds like sense," said the king. "Make the arrangements with Will Hastings - and as soon as you can for Warwick must already know that Clarence is close by."

§§§

The following day the three brothers met and Ned thought he had never seen so much royal livery. There was a long conversation between the three at the end of which it seemed that an agreement was reached. Ned had to smile at how the king used his charm to woo Clarence - though in this case the duke showed no little willingness to be wooed. The king milked the scene of reconciliation for all it was worth - and it had a telling effect on the watching soldiers. They stood in the fields either side of the Banbury road and cheered - well most of them did. There must have been some on Clarence's side though who were confused by his sudden reversal of loyalty. After all, had they not been recruited to defend an altogether different king? Yet, they could see for themselves the unity of the brothers and it made a powerful impression.

The remainder of the day was spent in organising the expanded royal host, though Clarence's army still kept apart from the rest. Ned wondered how easily the coat of loyalty could be turned inside out noting that where he had previously seen the colours of Lancaster, he now found only the badges of York and Clarence. Perhaps some of these men were still wearing their old livery underneath? How deep was their loyalty?

The king at once sent Clarence as a go-between to Warwick who was still sheltering behind the town walls of Coventry. When Clarence returned, King Edward met his brothers and other lords in council.

"I've offered the earl safe conduct to the Tower and quarter for all his men," announced the king, "but he's refused."

"Will he seek to give battle now, do you think?" asked Gloucester.

"Not yet," replied Clarence, "he's waiting."

"Indeed," agreed Will Hastings, "and his allies are getting closer: his brother, Montagu, from the north and the Earl of Oxford too."

"He's not just waiting for them, is he George?" said the king.

"No. He's hoping Queen Margaret and the prince will land in time to join him," said Clarence.

"Former queen, George," corrected Gloucester, with a glare at his brother.

"There is also news that Lord Fauconberg is recruiting in Kent," said Lord Scales.

Gloucester glared at him too. "Aye," he said, "and he's not coming to our aid, that's certain!"

"Your grace," said Ned, "Courtenay has a power in the south west already - if Margaret lands there… and if Jasper Tudor crosses from Wales…"

"If, Ned… if," said the king with a wry smile. "And whilst Warwick waits, we quietly starve here. He can afford to wait, we can't. We'll make all speed to London. Then let's see whether my cousin, Warwick, is still able to hold his nerve!"

Shortly, the king dismissed them to their camps. It was one of the things Ned liked about him: he trusted his commanders to do what they were supposed to do. As a result, the royal army was on the move within hours - and moving fast towards London.

On Palm Sunday they broke their march briefly at Daventry and Ned was glad of the rest. It was short-lived though and they pressed on to the capital, reaching it a few days later. Ned half expected the gates to be closed to them but they were not and he led his tired column of horsemen through into the city near the head of the army, behind the king and some handgunners from Burgundy. Bear grinned with pride to see his countrymen entering the city first.

There was no rest for anyone from that moment on. In

the next two days more supporters crammed into the city, though many of the soldiers were now camped in the fields to the north. Ned hoped to find better equipment and mounts for his men, but within a day both were scarce and prices for everything leapt skywards. His meagre resources were exhausted in finding food for his men and fodder for their mounts.

Despite his poverty he was desperate for new recruits to swell his ranks and any volunteer who brought his own horse was welcomed warmly. It was Good Friday and Ned assumed that nothing now would happen until after the Easter ceremonies, which would give him a little time to train any new men. That afternoon though, the king sent him an urgent summons.

"Warwick is hard on our heels, Ned. There are tales that his army has already reached St. Albans. You know it well enough?"

Ned knew its streets very well for he had fought in them, wading through bodies and blood, to drag the savaged remains of an army out of the wretched place. How long ago was it now? Ten years - but he remembered it all too well... and Bagot, Stephen, both dead now and many others besides... he remembered them too.

"Ned?" the king interrupted his reverie.

"I know it well enough, your grace," he replied.

"Take your mounted men at arms - and leave the city at once. I want you there today. I'll follow you on the morrow and you can tell us then how things lie."

"Aye, your grace," said Ned and left.

It was as if he had never been away. King Edward seemed to have the same energy and will that he possessed when he first won the throne. The king was the same age as he - how did the man keep going? For Ned was not the same... and for him it felt like twenty years had passed, not ten. Now he must get his tired men moving again and find the will to drive them forward. He had learned a few things though about handling men. He summoned Bear and told him to rouse the men - if you want to give soldiers bad news, then get a very large man to deliver it.

It was not a long ride to St. Albans, but Ned did not get there. At dusk he decided to call a halt at Barnet which lay a few miles south of St Albans. He decided they would camp north of the town and set off again the following morning. As he led his horsemen along the north road which ran through the town, he tried to recall if he had stopped there before - perhaps on the ride to Towton years ago. He was looking out for familiar inn signs when it dawned on him that the streets were uncommonly crowded. More than that, he suddenly realised that the town was awash with fighting men and many of them wore the bear and ragged staff of Warwick.

At first, amongst so many others, his company passed unnoticed, but soon one or two began to study more carefully the badges that his own men wore. A glance at Croft and Bear told him that they too were aware of their predicament: they had stumbled into the Earl of Warwick's vanguard.

There were a good many archers spilling out of the taverns or milling about by the roadside and he did not give much hope for his chances if they started to let fly. He dared not stop lest his column came under closer scrutiny. Though he was only part-harnessed, he could feel the sweat seeping into his gambeson. He took a deep breath and guided his horse off the north road and down a narrow side alley, trying to move without haste in case he startled the enemy into action. After a moment he looked back to check that the whole column had followed him and noted that Bear was drifting back towards the rear. Soon enough, someone would draw the right conclusion and then they would be in trouble.

The lane broadened out into the fields and he headed back south again, picking up a little speed. Moments later, Bear thundered up alongside him.

"They come, lord!" he bellowed.

Ned knew there was plenty of woodland ahead since he had just passed through it. If he could evade Warwick's men till nightfall, they would be forced to give up. Yet it occurred to him that he might do rather better than that. He took his riders into the cover of the first copse he found and pulled up, turning to face Barnet. He needed to discourage his pursuers but, without archers, there was only one course of action. Croft and Bear joined him at the treeline to watch the enemy's approach.

"How many, do you think?" Ned asked.

"Four - five score," came Bear's terse reply.

"We could try to lose them in the trees," suggested Croft.

"Not enough trees!" retorted Bear.

"We can't hide from so many," said Ned, "so let's convince them that we're stronger than we are. We must hit them swift and hard. Croft, take half the men, I'll take the others. Bear, with me. And remember, Croft - swift and hard - then fall back to the next snatch of forest! We'll meet you there."

"Lord!" acknowledged Croft.

The oncoming horsemen slowed a little as they neared the woods. Ned made a swift and final assessment: their opponents must have taken to horse with reckless haste and some were thus poorly harnessed.

He gave no signal but just darted forward, in the certainty that Bear and the others would follow. He bludgeoned his way into the horsemen, cracking heads with his mace and in the gloom they barely saw him in time to react. The ferocious attack threw the men of Warwick's vanguard into disarray. It was hard and fast, as Ned ordered, and it was also bloody in the dying light. The enemy force splintered: some veered away into the trees, where they were pursued and killed; others turned and raced back to Barnet, whilst the remainder scattered south and where they turned up only God knew. Those who returned to Warwick no doubt reported their abrupt encounter in the most vivid detail. Ned smiled at the thought for it would do no harm for Warwick to believe there was a strong force nearby.

As darkness descended, Ned's horsemen regrouped in the next band of forest. They were only a few miles south of Barnet but Ned reckoned he could settle there for the night. It was a cool April evening but he allowed no fires in the camp. When the men's fighting anger subsided they began to grumble - and not just because of the lack of fires. The brief skirmish had reminded them - reminded Ned too - of a brutal truth: they were there to fight and when the king arrived on the morrow they would fight.

Ned sent some prickers out during the night and with the dawn they brought back news: Warwick, perhaps chastened by the sudden arrival of royal troops, had withdrawn his men from Barnet and was preparing his battle lines on the northern outskirts of the town. So at last Ned knew where the reckoning with Warwick would take place - now all he had to do was await the king.

61

13th April 1471, at Barnet, north of

London

Ned had to wait all day for the royal army to appear and by then the sun was once more low in the west. Even so, King Edward pressed on without a pause.

"Get us in close, Ned," he ordered as they approached Warwick's lines in the dark. "I want us close enough that they can smell us."

Ned advanced as far as he dared, unable to tell exactly where Warwick's front ranks were positioned.

Croft returned ashen-faced from a final scouting mission. "Lord, if we get any closer we'll be sharing their whores!" he hissed.

"Very well, then," whispered Ned. The king laughed when Ned reported Croft's words later.

"This was always the first step Ned. Warwick knows we're here well enough, but he doesn't know quite how close we are. His ordnance will outmatch ours but here we can watch the worst of it pass over our heads. Mind you, Ned, we'll need to keep our men damned quiet."

It took hours to array the whole army but, considering their numbers and the darkness, they managed it very well. Ned passed along the battle lines with the other captains relaying the king's strict instructions. By the time he finished he thought he must have said the words a thousand times: "No fires, no loud chattering and no return of enemy fire!"

His instructions were greeted with an assortment of muffled responses in the darkness. Some murmured: 'aye, my lord,' but just as many ground out oaths about his birth, his parentage or some gross defect of his character. He grinned at their spirit and prayed it would stand them well in the morning.

During the night the king called him to his tent with the other lords and explained his plans. When the others left, he told Ned to stay.

"You've heard that I've given my brother, Dickon, command of the left battle tomorrow."

"Aye, your grace - you must be very confident of his prowess."

"Hopeful yes, confident no. That's why I want you with Dickon. The men will look upon him and see a brave, though untried, youth. In you, they'll see a battle-hardened warrior, the hero of St Albans…"

Ned gave a rueful grimace. "If I recall, your grace, we lost at St Albans…"

"Aye, but you got men out who should have perished. At Mortimer's Cross and Towton - you played your part in bringing victory and that gave you a name, Ned - a name that many soldiers know. The men will follow Gloucester more willingly if you're with him."

"I'm content to serve wherever your grace wishes," said Ned, though if he had been given a free choice, he would have chosen to fight beside his old friend Will Hastings as he had done several times before.

"I want your mounted men at arms to flank Gloucester. Don't get involved too soon - unless my brother is in peril. How many men do you have?"

"Less than a hundred, your grace."

"Very well, I'll send you another hundred. When victory

is won - and pray God it is - make sure your mounts are ready for the rout. This time I can't risk them escaping."

"Warwick?"

"Warwick, Montagu, Oxford, and my foolish brother in law, the Duke of Exeter. I doubt any will leave the field early - I'll give them that: none of them are cowards. Yet they must not escape to fight us again, Ned, but especially not the Earl of Warwick."

"Do you want him taken alive, your grace?"

The king hesitated for the briefest of moments. "If we can, Ned, but it may only be a short reprieve for while he lives, my throne will not be safe - nor my family, I fear."

"Aye, nor mine, your grace."

There was a moment of silence between the two men and then the king asked him: "Do you remember Towton, Ned?"

"How in the name of God could I forget it, your grace?" said Ned bitterly.

"I was thinking this evening of the night before Towton…"

"I remember men saying their prayers," murmured Ned, "young lads whispering for their mothers or pissing themselves, older hands honing their weapons. That's what I recall, your grace… and I recall reminding myself who my friends were. "

"Aye, friends, Ned. My cousin Warwick fought so well at Towton; we couldn't have endured their onslaught without him… It saddens me to think how we have come to this."

"Aye, Towton was bloody, your grace," breathed Ned.

"So many men… on both sides… and whoever won the day would have the throne. I thought it would be an end to the war, Ned, yet here we sit in harness once again."

"An end to war, your grace? There's no end to war… it just keeps coming back."

"Yet I shall put an end to it, Ned, I promise you. I shall finish it and this time I'll leave no loose ends..."

"There'll be no end to war until we're all dead."

"Do you know, Ned, you used to be a lot more cheerful..." said the king.

Ned shrugged. "Aye, I'm a poor companion now, your grace."

The king clapped him on the shoulder. "I already have a fool at court, Ned and I don't need another - assuming I still have a court after all this. There's a powerful host before us and I need a warrior. There's no man I'd rather have here beside me - or at least beside my young brother - than you. He's a young lion, Ned, but ... it will be his first time."

"I remember my first time, your grace... I was terrified."

"Only a fool wouldn't be, Ned. After all, where's the sense in it? Grown men pounding and shredding each other from dawn till dusk - we should be spending our time with women and wine instead!"

Bombards roared suddenly nearby and they looked at each other.

"Warwick's bombardment begins already," said the king.

"Aye, let's pray he hasn't enough powder to keep it up all night, your grace!" replied Ned.

King Edward clasped his hand. "Go back to your men... and God speed, Ned!"

Ned found his men cowering close to the ground as cannon shot flew over their heads. Soon they were all lost in the relentless, pounding thunder and the choking smoke that filled the air. There would no peace for these men tonight...

§§§

It looked like dawn, for there was light in the heavens but God had shrouded the field in grey. Ned could barely see a dozen yards in the gloomy mist. Warwick's cannon had fired all night and now every man's face was grimed with powder smoke. Men coughed and spat as they prepared themselves for battle. Even the Duke of Gloucester's resplendent armour was besmirched. Yet the youth exuded only confidence, as Ned had been warned.

Ned took care to move his men between Gloucester and the king. There he was well placed to go to the aid of either. He also made sure that their mounts, though at the rear, could be brought up swiftly. The mist worried him. If Gloucester was pressed back then he would need to be ready either to support him or aid his retreat. It was difficult enough to do so in the brutal heat of any battle, let alone when no-one could see more than a few yards. King Edward could fall and Ned would not even know it, Gloucester would not know it, nor Hastings commanding on the far right flank. To fight any battle was dangerous; to fight one like this was madness.

He sought out Gloucester to reassure him of his support, though given his previous dealings with the duke, he did not expect a cordial reception.

"I bring two hundred horsemen to your battle, your grace," said Ned.

"So my brother told me," replied Gloucester. "Horsed are you? Well, I shall be afoot - fighting with my men - as a good commander does."

"Your grace," replied Ned, "when battle begins I shall be on foot with my men too - the mounts will be ready though, when we need them."

"What, for flight perhaps?" suggested the duke.

Ned bit back his anger. "For the rout, of course, your grace..."

"All I ask is that you keep out of my way," said Gloucester. "I don't want your clumsy men at arms causing confusion in my lines."

"If I find confusion, your grace," said Ned icily, "then

I'll attempt to bring order…"

He was relieved when further discussion was cut short by a sudden blast as Warwick's bombards started belching fire once more and this time the king's gunners replied in kind.

"Ready archers!" shouted Gloucester but Ned wondered how many heard the duke's voice above the deafening cannons.

After a long exchange of shot, there was an uneasy silence. Then arrows seared out of the mist at them to strike or pass overhead as God decreed. Since no man on the field could see their enemies, they could not possibly be aiming at them.

A cry of "Loose, loose!" went out from Gloucester and other captains echoed the command along the lines. The arrow duel was short-lived though for, as both sides had to concede, their arrows might be peppering a barn for all that they could see.

The duke gave a shout for those around him, a cluster of heavily armed knights, to advance and Ned had to admire the way they moved with him, like a well-fitting harness of armour. Cries broke out for King Edward, for Duke Richard, and for the white boar - his badge. Others proclaimed their lords' names as Ned's men roared: "An Elder! An Elder!"

The whole battle shifted forward one pace at a time - even the young Gloucester, it seemed, would not charge headlong when he could see barely a few yards in front of him. Through the dense fog came the rallying cries of their opponents, close by - damned close by. Ned held his men to the duke's rear and waited for the shuddering impact of Gloucester's assault on the opposing line, but it did not come, which troubled him. Surely the Lancastrians must only be yards away by now. Then out of the mist to their left a horde of men tore into Gloucester's flank. The duke himself, in the vanguard, was so far forward he was unaware of the catastrophe unfolding on his flank.

Cries of: "An Oxford! An Oxford!" filled the morning air as Gloucester's men at arms were pressed back and driven sideways upon their hapless comrades. Before Ned could respond, the entire left wing was swept away before the men advancing with the star banner of the Earl of Oxford. Gloucester's men at arms fell back, broken and bleeding before the onslaught.

"God's blood! Where is he?" declared Ned, seeking out Gloucester's banners in the fog.

Gloucester could not be very far ahead but Ned must defend the flank or the king's centre battle would be exposed to Oxford's attack. Ahead he glimpsed dim shapes writhing in the mist and caught sight at last of Gloucester's white boar and royal banners. They were retreating towards him.

He rallied his own men and prepared to meet Oxford's men on the flank. Bear ghosted out of the mist to stand at his shoulder. There was a raucous cheer from Oxford's ranks and Ned glanced around, gripped by sudden fear when he could not see Gloucester himself in the cluster of men retreating towards him.

"Where's he's gone, Bear? Where in the name of Christ has he gone?" He hurled the words through his visor. So much for keeping an eye on the king's little brother, he thought.

When Gloucester's men reached him he must somehow part his lines to let them through without giving Oxford an opening. Gloucester's billmen and men at arms were almost there when they suddenly broke and ran, bursting though Ned's ranks.

"We're lost," they cried, "The duke's dead! Flee for your lives!"

"Hold!" bellowed Ned at the fleeing men, but to no

avail. Their panic shuddered along his lines and gave Oxford's advance renewed vigour. He peered in vain through his visor for a glimpse of Gloucester's armour or pennants, but all those coming at him now wore Oxford's badges.

He stood ready with a pollaxe in one hand and a mace in the other and he roared at the men around him to stand firm. Then he caught another glimpse of the duke. He was in the midst of his household knights - the most loyal and determined of his retinue.

"There!" Ned stabbed a finger at them. But he soon saw that the retreating group was isolated and being attacked from all sides by Oxford's men.

"An Elder!" cried Ned and surged forward towards the duke.

His shout was taken up by Bear beside him and a host of others nearby. But they would have to cut their way through Oxford's men at arms to get there. A spiked mace struck Ned's chest a glancing blow and rocked him back onto his heels. With breath-taking suddenness, he was in a melee - a tortuous, shifting melee of men, thrusting and hacking with steel upon steel. The noise was terrifying, the cries bitter.

In one instinctive, angry swing he took off the offending arm of his assailant with the axe and fell upon him with the mace. He abandoned finesse and delivered several ringing blows to the man's head. An axe blade swung at him out of the mist and he ducked, ramming the spike of his pollaxe under the shoulder joint of his new opponent. The man cried out and melted away into the mist. It was like that: weapons flailed at him for an instant only to disappear at once; sharp sounds quickly became muffled and distant.

He had a sense that the line was somehow out of kilter, but he had no idea why. All he knew was that the left flank was being heavily mauled. Men were falling all around him -

some cut down from behind as they fled. Oxford's men trampled over them in their haste to crush the lingering resistance.

A tangle of brawling soldiers appeared like wraiths only a few yards ahead. In the centre of the heaving mass of men and steel, Ned saw the duke again. He was in the press of the fighting with enemies all around thrusting in their bills and pikes. Gloucester's personal knights defended their duke with savage courage but they were falling, one by one, even as Ned pressed forward towards them. He saw the duke fall and cursed aloud. For all their valour his body guards had fought themselves to a standstill and were being slowly battered to death. Despite Ned's efforts, the king's brother had fallen and the army of York was disintegrating around him.

62

Easter Sunday: 14th April 1471 in the

evening, at Quenhull

The three women talked long into the night, letting the candles burn down low as they supped pot after pot of wine, or in Eleanor's case, ale. They had spent the afternoon with their children. Aye, they had their children and they had loyal servants, yet they were still alone and, just then, they felt as if they might always be alone. So they were drowning themselves, dulling their minds, their senses, to banish their fears.

"Oh, Eleanor," groaned Maighread, rubbing her head. "Once more you've led us along the devil's path. I've drunk far more than I should..."

"No you haven't, sister," replied Eleanor. "Trust me, if you can still remember who I am then you haven't drunk anywhere near enough yet! Becky!" she yelled. "Bring more wine!"

Becky was not in the solar with them but Eleanor knew she would be close enough to hear. Soon Becky dutifully arrived with an assortment of pots of ale and spiced wine.

Eleanor smiled at her and stroked her arm. "Thank you, my dear," she said.

Becky sighed. "I should be abed..."

"Oh, will poor Hal be getting impatient?" giggled

Eleanor.

"Have you no shame, Eleanor?" Maighread scolded her.

Eleanor grinned.

"No, she hasn't," said Emma.

"Go to bed, Becky," said Maighread wearily, "we'll all be retiring soon."

"Then I'll leave you ladies in the care of each other," said Becky, smiling as she closed the door behind her.

"But it's still hours until dawn!" declared Eleanor.

"Dawn is when you wake up," Maighread murmured. "My head wants to lie on a soft pillow."

"Mine too…" said Emma.

"Come then," said Eleanor, "let's sup these last few pots."

"I can't have any more," said Emma, "my belly already complains."

"Oh, Emma! Do you always have be a good little peascod? Good Christ! Let yourself go! You must have done so once or twice - with your new lover, Sir Robert, perhaps?"

"Don't speak of him, I beg you," said Emma. "Here. I'll drink it all down if I must - if it'll keep you quiet!"

She emptied the contents of the pot into her mouth, ignoring the wine that ran down her chin and dripped onto her kirtle. She drained it then threw it down onto the floor.

"Aye, that's more like it!" said Eleanor. "Now you, Maighread!"

"No, I crave sleep. My eyes are already closing," she said.

But Eleanor held out the pot of wine to her until she gulped it all down as Emma had done. Then Eleanor matched them with her pot of ale and together they swallowed the last drops from each of the vessels.

"Now, we're done then," said Maighread. "To bed with us all!"

"No, it's far too early for bed," said Eleanor, "especially a bed with no man in it. But, don't worry, sisters, for I've another idea…"

"No," Maighread replied sternly. "Whatever it is, it's a bad idea. So please, nothing more…"

"Aye, something more," Eleanor whispered, almost breathless at the thought of it.

"What now?" asked Emma. "I'm not drinking another drop!"

"No, neither am I," said Eleanor. "We're going to see the prisoner!"

"Prisoner?" murmured Emma.

"At this hour, Eleanor? No… no - it would be foolish!" retorted Maighread, but Eleanor was already at the door.

"He's been stewing down there since this morning," she said and left the solar, with the others clucking and fussing behind her.

"No, wait!" protested Maighread.

"Are you women or mice?" demanded Eleanor as she descended the spiral stair to the floor below.

"Eleanor!" hissed Maighread, but they were not going to stop her.

"I shall make him regret his careless capture!" she said.

"Leave him to Ned!" cried Maighread. "What have we to say to the wretch?"

"Enough!" said Eleanor as they headed down below the courtyard to the cells.

"It smells foul down here," complained Emma. "I feel ill…"

"Of course it smells foul," said Eleanor. "It's the shit and the sweat and the… God knows what else…"

"We shouldn't be down here at all," said Maighread.

"I'm going to be sick…" muttered Emma.

Eleanor ignored their protests and soon found the lone guard sitting beside the door to the cells, snoring happily.

She thrust out a boot and kicked him. He awoke with a yelp, clutching at his groin.

"Oh… your pardon," she said, as he rolled onto the floor. "I didn't mean it to be quite so hard… nor so badly aimed…"

"By Christ, lady! What was that for?" He stared up at the three of them in bewilderment.

"I want you to open the cell," ordered Eleanor.

He regarded her as if she had utterly lost her wits. "Open the cell? By Christ, lady, why would you want me to do that?"

"Stop calling upon Christ or I'll kick you again! Now open the door!"

The hapless gaoler looked to Maighread and Emma for support.

"Oh, just open it," said Maighread. "I'm too weary to argue with her anymore."

Still gently massaging his private parts, the gaoler fetched his keys and unlocked the cell.

If the prisoner had been asleep, Eleanor could see that he was wide awake now and no doubt wondering what his visitors had in mind.

"Leave us!" Eleanor ordered the gaoler.

"But, it's still open…"

"Aye, take the keys and wait out in the passage."

"I'll be in bother for this in the morning," complained the gaoler.

"You'll be in bother now if you don't get out!" barked Eleanor.

The gaoler trudged out and half-closed the cell door.

Ralph Teller was sitting on the floor. "What do you want?" he asked.

Eleanor took a step towards him and kicked his leg.

"We've come to see what a traitor looks like," she said. "Ralph Teller: the man who betrayed us to Roger Cullen and caused John Holton, among others, to be killed…"

"Aye," said Maighread, "it was a good day's work our men did when they brought you in…"

"Did you think you could hide from us forever?" said Eleanor.

"I wasn't hiding," said Sir Ralph. He leant back against the wall, a trace of a smile lingering upon his lips.

Eleanor thrust her face inches away from his, her fierce eyes boring into his soul.

"Good men died, when you betrayed my brother!" she declared, her eyes never leaving his.

Ralph met her stare without flinching. "I was Sir Roger Cullen's man long before I met Ned Elder. I acted out of loyalty to my lord, not treachery to yours."

He seemed so confident, but what had she expected? Had she thought he might beg for forgiveness, or show some regret?

"We shall make you pay dearly for what you did!" she cried.

"Whatever I've done, my lady, I'll be judged by God for my sins, not you," he said.

"Aye, God will judge you - I'm certain of it," whispered Maighread, stooping closer to him. "But you'll be judged by my husband too, when he returns."

"When, my lady?" replied Sir Ralph. "I think you mean if he returns. He's fighting a war and in war, men have a habit of dying."

Eleanor took Maighread's arm and lifted her to her feet. For a moment all three women were lost for words. Even Eleanor could feel her anger ebbing away. Though her wits were dulled by ale, she could see how powerless they all were. She could bluster as much as she liked, but nothing would happen to Ralph Teller until her brother came back.

"We should go," said Maighread finally.

Eleanor nodded and led them out of the cell.

"Please lock the door again," Maighread instructed the gaoler as they went out and made their way up to the courtyard.

"Can you believe that man's boldness?" complained Eleanor, as they ascended the stair.

"I don't know what to think, Eleanor," said Maighread, "but I need my bed - and so do we all. We'll talk about this with Hal and Spearbold in the morning, when our heads are clearer...."

"If our heads are clearer," grumbled Emma.

Eleanor let them go to their chambers and then made her way to the room where her son slept. He shared a small chamber with Ned's lad, John. Both boys were sleeping and she gave each of them a light kiss on the head. For all the dangers that faced them now, at least such a simple act of love was not denied her.

She moved on to the nursery where Mary slept with the young babes. All was quiet, which was a rarity, so she dared not enter lest she broke the spell of calm. She smiled to herself and went to her own chamber. She slept alone now that Becky was with Hal and Mary was fully occupied with the children but she was used to it now.

She closed the door and felt the chill of a cold steel blade against her throat.

"Your gaoler is a little slow," said Ralph Teller. Then he slammed her head against the door frame.

63

Easter Sunday: 14th April 1471, at Barnet

Ned watched, appalled, as Gloucester's diminishing group was consumed once more by the swirling fog. The king's brother was about to die and he knew he could not allow that to happen. Yet he was torn, for Oxford's men were still pressing them back. If Ned's men gave ground the whole Yorkist host might be rolled back upon itself.

"Croft!" he roared above the clamour. "Hold this line - no matter what!"

Then he punched Bear on the shoulder to get his attention. "Bring a dozen men!" he bellowed and broke out of the line heading for the beleaguered duke.

It was an act of folly and he knew it for the two sides were already becoming enmeshed and confused. He picked up his feet and tried to move faster; not easy in his armour. He thanked God that the mist that blinded them was at least a cooling mist. Bear crashed forward to join him followed by the dozen or so he requested.

"Look to your colours and badges!" he warned them. Some hope, he thought grimly, when a man was difficult enough to see - let alone his badges. Men screamed behind him and he prayed it was not Croft's men in such distress.

Bear carved a swathe through Oxford's ranks and many more sheered away just at the sight of him. Ned and the others followed in his bloody wake. Soon the duke's escort was only a few yards away and the wall of enemies around them was breached.

"Your grace!" Ned cried. "Fall back towards us!"

Richard of Gloucester, nursing a wound, darted a glance at him - and nodded. Ned's men hurried forward to swell the ranks of Gloucester's sore-pressed men at arms.

"Are you hurt?" asked Ned.

"A small wound!" retorted Gloucester, indicating the buckled armour on his leg. "I can still fight, my lord!"

"Aye, your grace, but your flank has been gutted by Oxford's men - we must reform our lines!"

"Very well!" agreed Gloucester testily. "If we must, then we shall!"

Together, Ned and the duke made a slow retreat and a score of yards brought them back to Croft and the remnant of the Gloucester's wing of the army.

Ned sensed at once that somehow the pressure on the line had eased.

"What's happened, Croft?" he demanded.

Croft laughed. "The stupid bastards charged past us - after those who were fleeing. I reckon Oxford's men must be off into Barnet now!"

Ned clapped him on the shoulder "Well fought, Croft! Well fought!"

Then he realised that he had no idea what was happening elsewhere on the field. Oxford's confusion was only a slight reprieve for the Lancastrian centre would discover soon enough - if they had not already - that there was little stopping them from outflanking King Edward's main force.

"See if you can get to the king, Croft. Tell him what's happened and ask him to send us some of his reserves."

Croft was gone at once into the mist, dragging a couple more men at arms with him.

Gloucester was taken to the rear for his wound to be tended and Ned knew that it was up to him now.

"Bear," he said, "put all the archers on our left flank and some behind us in case Oxford rallies his men and they attack our rear."

Bear nodded. Then Ned reformed his battle line and began to move forward again. He dare not delay in case the other commanders were also hard pressed. But he had only advanced a few yards when he stopped as a host of men at arms appeared through the mist ahead of them. He was about to launch an assault upon the newcomers when shouts of "An Elder, an Elder!" echoed across the field. It was Croft, returning with scores of men, but how could they be coming from ahead of him?

"Croft?" he demanded. "What in God's name are you doing there?"

"The whole battle line has somehow swung around, my lord," replied Croft, breathless. "The king is hard pressed but Lord Hastings has fared better I think on the far flank."

Ned struggled to make sense of their position but in the end just nodded and urged his men forward once more. Strengthened by the reserves, they hurried across the ridge where the Lancastrian line had once been. As had been the case all morning, figures came at them suddenly, breaking out of the mist, and probably just as surprised as they were, Ned reflected. Further reflection ended with the crash of a bill against his shoulder and battle was joined once more: bone-cracking, limb-aching battle.

Some took up his battle cry but he soon lacked the breath to utter the words himself as he sucked in lungfuls of the choking mist. Men wheezed as they fought, their movement gradually slowing as weariness told hold and mistakes were made… fatal mistakes. There was no time for thought, no space to rest one's arms, no respite from the crushing, soul-rending carnage.

He saw some of the banners against him now and recognised with sadness those of an old comrade, John

Neville, Lord Montagu - Warwick's own brother. By God, Montagu was a fearsome warrior to have against you. Ned felt rather than knew that they were still heavily outnumbered for the press of the enemy seemed to gain strength even as their own waned. Oxford may have left the field but his opening manoeuvre had taken more than enough toll on the Yorkist army.

An archer caught his arm and Ned almost took his head off but stopped mid-strike as he saw the dirty blue badge of the Elders.

"Lord!" the man shouted. "There are men coming up behind us!"

"Whose men?" demanded Ned. "They could be our reserve - the field is muddled!"

"Star banners again, my lord!"

"God's blood! It's Oxford, come to finish us off."

They were already buckling under the weight of Montagu's attack. If Oxford struck at their rear or left flank he would annihilate them. Now they really were lost.

"Take your comrades to the horses and hold there," he ordered the archer, then cried: "Archers to the rear!"

He wanted to warn his two captains, Croft and Bear, but had no chance of reaching them in time. All they could do when Oxford struck was to try to withdraw in good order… he must save as many as he could. It was St Albans all over again.

There was a roar from his left as the Earl of Oxford's men attacked. Any moment now they would join with Montagu's men. Then a strange thing happened: Montagu's men broke off from the line and turned to face Oxford, their ally. Ned could see Oxford's banners even in the swirling mist, surely so could Montagu's men. Perhaps they did, perhaps they were confused, like Ned himself. Whatever the reason, Montagu's archers let fly into the midst of Oxford's ranks and at once the air was filled with cries of "Treason!" and "Traitors!"

Ned looked on in astonishment as Oxford's men fell back in disarray. The confusion caused Montagu's men at arms to hesitate, so Ned pressed home the attack. His men took heart from what seemed like divine deliverance and advanced with more spirit. Montagu's ranks took a brutal battering from Ned's men, while the king in the Yorkist centre was also driving them backwards.

Ned never saw Montagu fall but he knew the moment it happened for the resistance of his men crumbled and they fled. Surprisingly quickly, the retreat became a rout.

"Call up the horses!" ordered Ned, impatient to seek out the Earl of Warwick.

The earl would have fought until there was no longer any hope but he would no doubt have had a horse ready - just in case.

As soon as their mounts were led up by the pages and a few of the archers, Ned set off in pursuit and discovered almost at once that, away from the field, the mist was much thinner and under the morning sun was beginning to disappear. Warwick's army was in full flight and being pursued with great vigour by the time Ned's horsemen caught up with them. His men, like all the rest, would be looking for trophies from the dead or soon to be dead: a sword, a dagger perhaps, or a finer bow than their own. Perhaps a few might tease out a purse or a ring, or pick up pieces of armour to be worn or sold.

Ned sought none of those things: he wanted the earl - the man who had sheltered his enemies and brought destruction down upon his family. No matter that he also tried to bring down King Edward - this was personal, a debt that must be paid once and for all.

He questioned some of the wounded Lancastrians and swiftly learned that the earl had fled north towards a swathe of woodland and that was where Ned went with as many of his men as Croft and Bear could cajole into following him.

They scoured the fringes of the woodland to no avail before Ned ordered them into the forest. They advanced in a long line on as broad a front as they could sustain. If the earl was there, Ned did not want to miss him. They searched until many of the men became restless. Ned could hardly blame them: they were exhausted and they wanted to gain the spoils which they believed were rightfully theirs. One by one they melted away, knowing they would have to face his wrath later - but that would be later…

When Ned actually found Warwick it was not as he expected. The earl had been tracked down by others and his personal retainers were attempting to defend his wounded body against a crowd that, from their livery, Ned knew to be Hastings' men. He removed his helm and called them off but they were angry and resentful at his interference.

"This is the Earl of Warwick," said Ned, "and the king has decreed that his life may be spared if he is taken."

One or two of Hastings' men knew Ned Elder of old and they drew their disgruntled comrades away.

Ned addressed Warwick, who lay against an oak, badly wounded.

"Tell your retainers to put down their arms and leave," ordered Ned, "unless you wish them to be taken or killed too."

Warwick removed his helm. "Ned Elder," he said wearily. "The day gets better and better."

But he motioned his men to yield and they did.

"Save yourselves," he told them, "your oaths to me are fulfilled… Whatever you do now, I am a dead man… so go…"

The men still hesitated and Ned admired their show of reluctance.

"I will arrest as a traitor any man who stays," said Ned. "Expect no clemency…"

THE LAST SHROUD

Warwick's men looked at each other for a brief moment and then hurried away into the woods.

"What now?" asked the earl. "I can tell you I'll be dead within the hour, Ned."

Ned dismounted and went to him. There was a broken spear protruding from his belly and blood seeped slowly out.

"When I reached the horses," muttered the earl, "I thought I'd make it. One of them got me with a lucky thrust - though unlucky for me."

"Do you want a priest?" asked Ned.

Warwick laughed. "They'll be a little busy, I think, just now. Besides, I confessed my sins this morning and I've committed few since then. But... if it's in your mind to grant me something, then you could swear to take an interest in the fate of my wife and daughters..."

"That's easily enough done," agreed Ned, "I would not wish harm upon them - as I did not wish harm upon my own..."

Warwick nodded. "I'm grateful for that... there's one other request..."

"What?" asked Ned.

"Give me a quicker death than I'll get if you leave me here to bleed."

"You may live..." said Ned.

"We know different, Ned, don't we? I'll die - either here, or on the scaffold."

"Why should I give you an easy death?" asked Ned.

"For the same reason that I would have done so for you."

Ned gave him a nod and turned to Croft. "Take the men back to Barnet," he said. "Bear, stay if you will."

He knelt down beside the earl and drew out his dagger. Then he removed the gorget from around Warwick's neck and tossed it aside.

"Italian armour, Ned," murmured the earl, "worth a bit... When I'm ready, I'll raise my-"

"Peace!" said Ned and plunged his dagger through Warwick's throat. The earl's body shook for moment and then lay still as his blood ran freely onto the grass. Ned looked at the corpse for a while, then stood up and faced Bear.

"Toss him onto his horse and bring him with us," he said.

64

15th April, at Bussheley, south of Quenhull

Eleanor woke up to a bright dawn after her first night in captivity. She found herself in a room that might once have been the hall of a manor house. The house must have been abandoned long ago, for the large chamber was now just a shell furnished only with debris. The floor was littered with broken beams and shattered tiles where part of the roof had fallen in.

She shifted her weight to ease her discomfort. She must have been lying there for hours and the stone-flagged floor was murderously hard on her back. Her head throbbed a little and she gingerly explored a tender lump on her forehead. Teller - the bastard! She could recall nothing of her abduction. How had Ralph Teller got free? And how had he got her out - and why? She was still alive though and she must take some heart from that.

She tried to get to her feet and at once found that her ankles were loosely tied together. Hobbled, she thought, like some troublesome mare - well, she could be a most troublesome mare when she put her mind to it. She shuffled closer into the corner and eased her back up the wall until she was upright. At the first sound of movement two men ambled into the hall from behind a partition. At once she recognised one of her captors from the Quenhull garrison. She did not know the other but he might have been there too. So, one question was answered: Ralph

Teller had found some allies.

"I need to piss," she announced abruptly.

"You've a pot there in your little corner, my lady," said the guard she knew.

"Turn away then," she said.

He grinned at his comrade. "We'll look at the wall…"

She dropped back to the floor and crawled towards the pot, her hands sweeping aside some fragments of tile in her path. The guards did not move to help her and she smiled to herself. Reaching the pot, she crouched over it, supporting herself with the wall at her back. She did not look at them though she knew they would be watching her, so she rewarded their attention by lifting her kirtle just a little higher than she really needed to. Whilst their eyes were elsewhere she stuffed under the back of her kirtle a sharp piece of tile she had picked up.

When she finished, she sat down in the corner and began to talk.

"You're from Quenhull," she said. "I need your help."

"Sorry, my lady, but we've made our choice." It was the other one who answered this time, his voice hard and flat.

He was not going to be very malleable she decided. But the first one… she had definitely seen him at Quenhull… She did not recall his name - it was always good to know a name, so what might it be?

She smiled at him. "It's Walter, isn't?" she announced.

"Thomas," he replied, then glanced at his comrade and turned away from her without a word.

"Thomas, of course," she said, with quiet satisfaction. "I remember you very well, Thomas."

"Keep quiet, if you please, my lady," the other man ordered sharply.

She gave him a nod of submission, but she was content. A connection had been made and every time she saw that one man she would refer to him fondly by name. A word here, a phrase there, until the chance came, because sooner or later she would be alone with him.

The door was abruptly thrown open and Ralph Teller came in.

"Bring her!" he ordered and the two men at arms lifted her up and followed Sir Ralph to the door.

"Wait!" cried Eleanor. "Where are you taking me?"

"Hah! Where are we taking you, lady?" retorted Ralph. "Out of the way, that's where. Whatever happens now, you'll play no part in it."

"I'll not let you!" she shrieked at him, kicking out at her startled guards. She shrugged off Thomas, managed to free one hand and punched Sir Ralph in the eye.

"You bitch!" he roared. "You'll be punished hard for that!"

He seized her fist and flung her against the wall where she struck her head. As she slid down the wall Ralph's features became blurred and then she saw no more.

DEREK BIRKS

THE LAST SHROUD

481

PART SEVEN: REBELS AND

BROTHERS

DEREK BIRKS

65

3rd May 1471, in the solar at Quenhull

Castle

Maighread and Emma sat alone, as if in mourning. It was agony waiting for Hal, who had been out scouring the area every day since Eleanor had been taken.

"It's been weeks… weeks!" said Emma.

"I know that," soothed Maighread, "but Hal will find her."

"No, he won't!" said Emma. "I feel it, I just feel it."

"Sister, listen to me. If Ralph Teller wanted to kill Eleanor then he would have done it here - as he did the gaoler… and the poor men at the postern. Aye, she's taken, but that doesn't mean she's dead."

Below they heard shouted voices and the sound of the gates being opened. They hurried from the solar down the steps to the hall, wondering what Hal would have to report. But it was not Hal, it was Robert Radcliffe.

Emma rushed across to embrace him, oblivious of Maighread and others looking on.

"I'm so pleased to see you!" she sobbed.

"I see, my lady, I see," said Robert, holding her close to him whilst attempting a polite bow to Maighread.

Maighread studied him coldly. This was the man she remembered as a mortal enemy, the man who wrought disaster at Yoredale, the man who tried to kill her Ned. She knew well enough what he had recently done for Ned, yet she did not find it easy to be in the same room with the man. The way Emma fell upon him so fondly astonished her and she struggled to make sense of this sudden reversal.

"You don't know how glad I am you've come," Emma told him once more.

"I've some idea, my lady," he said, laughing. "And it warms my heart to see it."

Emma wept against his chest. "I didn't know how much I needed you. It took the loss of my sister to make it clear. And now she's gone… and Hal has tried to find her… and I need you, Robert, I need you!"

Robert glanced at Maighread. She gave him a formal nod and then took Emma's arm to lead her back to the solar with Robert following.

"Tell me then," said Robert, "how is your sister… lost?"

Emma could only shake her head and weep, so it was Maighread who reluctantly laid before him what little they knew and answered all his questions whilst Emma dried her tears and leant her head upon his shoulder.

"I've never come across this Ralph Teller," he said.

"We thought you were Hal returning with news," said Emma.

"I don't quite understand how Teller could escape so easily," said Robert. "Did Hal question anyone before he set off? Did he discover how Teller got away?

"Who could he question?" asked Maighread. "The gaoler was dead and so were the guards on the gate."

"You said Sir Ralph was part of the old garrison here. Some of your men at arms probably served under him."

"I suppose a few did," said Maighread, "but Ned never doubted their loyalty."

"Perhaps he should have," replied Robert. "I should question them, but…"

"What? What is it?" asked Emma.

"I came here for another reason - aside from seeing the woman I love, that is…"

"You bring other news, Sir Robert?" asked Maighread.

"Aye, I came to warn you that the war now crawls closer towards you."

"But Warwick is dead, isn't he?" said Emma. "We heard he was dead."

"Aye, the earl is dead, my dear, but the old queen, Margaret, and her son landed in Dorset and they are moving ever westwards. They've stopped at Bristol but we think they now mean to meet up with Jasper Tudor's Welshmen. We don't know which route they'll take, but I've just passed through Gloucester where the gates will be closed to them. So they must cross the river further north and the next bridge is at Tewkesbury which would bring their host perilously close to Quenhull."

"How long do we have?" asked Maighread.

"Not long. They may reach Tewkesbury tonight but getting an army across the old bridge and the causeway at Tewkesbury will be difficult… and slow. I can't see them starting to cross so late in the day, but if they halt there, I think the king may bring them to battle tomorrow. He's not a man to hesitate with his quarry in sight. They might be forced to make a stand at Tewkesbury and, if that happens, then your fate will lie with the king's army."

"So, you have no time to look for Eleanor," said Maighread.

Robert looked at her sadly and gave Emma's hand a gentle squeeze.

"No, my lady," he said. "I shouldn't be here at all. I only came because of Emma. My orders were to find out how far Jasper Tudor has advanced and return with all speed to tell my lord, William Stanley. If the king takes to the field on the morrow, he needs to know how far off Tudor is. So, I've scarcely time even to carry out my own task, let alone search for Lady Eleanor."

"But you'll try," pleaded Emma.

"I'll see what I can do, but I can't delay. I fear there's much more at stake here, ladies, than the life of your sister - dear though that is to you both."

"We understand, Sir Robert," said Maighread, grim-faced.

"As soon as I've firm news of Jasper's position, I'll have to return to the king, but perhaps Hal will have some good fortune in his search."

Emma suddenly clutched his arm. "Robert, do you have any news of the Lady Anne - Princess Anne now, I suppose - is she with the prince?"

"I don't know, my lady, but I suppose that since the queen is there she will have the other ladies with her. It would be strange if they left Warwick's daughter in France - after all, they wouldn't have expected his death."

Emma gave a sigh. "Her father dead, her sister's husband, Clarence, deserted from their cause… She's only her mother with her now…"

Robert frowned.

"What?" said Emma, gripping his arm more tightly.

"We've heard that her mother, the Countess of Warwick… Well, it seems she was on a different ship and landed further east. Hearing of her husband's death, she has taken to a nunnery."

Emma gasped. "So Anne's alone with them now, without an ally. How swiftly things change…"

"Don't concern yourself about her," warned Robert. "She abandoned you, my lady, tossed you aside - despite your years of loyal service. I know you care for Lady Anne but you must worry about yourself now."

"But she's so young… and she was always a sweet girl to me."

"Not always, my dear," Robert reminded her, "but she's

a princess now and her husband is our king's mortal enemy. As you say, how swiftly things change - and how swiftly I must take my leave. I'm sorry Emma - your pardon, Lady Maighread."

Maighread stood up. "Aye, you must go, Sir Robert." She glanced at Emma. "You'll want to say your farewells. Join me in the hall, sister, when you have seen Sir Robert away."

She paused at the door and looked back at the two of them. "God be with you, Sir Robert," she said softly and left them.

§§§

Emma walked with Robert to the gate. There in Quenhull's courtyard his men waited, already mounted, their horses snorting and stamping in the midday sunshine. She had no idea what to say to him: beg him to stay, plead with him to stay alive, to come back and make love to her, or perhaps ask him to take her with him. But when it came to the moment and they reached the gate, she said nothing: no declarations of love, no weeping farewell words, just the light touch of her palm on his breast and the look in her eyes that told him all.

Then he rode out of the gate and was gone. She did not linger in the yard but went to the hall where Maighread awaited her.

"I know, you're shocked," she said.

"Aye, just a little," admitted Maighread, "but who am I to protest? Love came late to me too."

Emma gave her a bleak look. "Do you think Ellie's still alive?" she asked.

"Aye, I do. I think Cullen intends to use her to trap Ned…"

"But for a trap to work, Ned would have to be drawn into it before he returns here," said Emma.

Maighread was silent for a while then her eyes met

Emma's. "Aye, of course. Cullen would have to lure Ned there before we could warn him."

"But how would he do that?" asked Emma. "How would he get to Ned?"

"Come now, he's Clarence's man - he could move freely now in the royal army. All he'd need to do is point Ned in the right direction and Ned would fly to your sister's aid…"

They sat in silence then, each lost in their own thoughts, contemplating what could be done.

"Somehow, we must get word to Ned," said Maighread. "We must. I'll take it myself if I have to!"

"No," said Emma, "I'll go."

"You?"

"Aye, I'll take Pinner with me. We'll get word to Ned that Eleanor's taken and… at the same time… well, I want to go to Lady Anne."

"No!" cried Maighread. "Why would you do that? Her husband's a traitor, a rebel. She disowned you, betrayed you!"

"Aye, I know. But she's a young girl I once loved like a daughter… and she's alone - no doubt frightened and confused by what has happened. She's cut off from her mother and sister. Queen Margaret has no fondness for her new daughter - that, I do know! Anne's marriage brought the queen Warwick and all his power, but now he's gone and the marriage with Anne Neville brings nothing to the Lancastrians! I fear for her, Maighread, I truly do."

"But what can you do? How can you possibly help her? Even in her eyes, you're a traitor!"

"Well, I must persuade her otherwise! I can at least be with her… and, if she's in trouble, perhaps I can help her."

"She's wedded to their cause now - as close as I'm wedded to Ned Elder's! You'll be an enemy in their eyes! This is madness. I forbid you to go!"

Emma smiled and hugged Maighread. "No, you don't,

because someone must warn Ned…"

Maighread gave a great sigh. "Holy Mother! I swear that where the devil's fire failed, this family will be the death of me!"

$$\S\S\S$$

The first person Hal saw as he rode into the yard was Pinner, leaning against the inner gatehouse wall. Pinner moved from the wall the moment he saw him: he was waiting for him and his expression alone told Hal that nothing good had happened. He dismounted and at once Pinner told him of Lady Emma's intention to go to Tewkesbury.

"Christ's blood, Pinner! Why won't these Elder women stay where we fucking put them?"

Pinner gave a sympathetic nod. "Shall I get you another horse?" he asked.

Hal sighed. "I'm supposed to be here. I'm supposed to be looking after Lord Elder's wife and sisters, but how can I when they won't be told!"

Pinner gave a loud cough and Hal looked around to find Lady Maighread behind him.

"Your pardon, my lady," he mumbled.

"What for, Hal? Your loyalty?" said Maighread. "We aren't easy to keep safe, are we? I take it you've found no trace of Lady Eleanor."

"It's knowing where to look, my lady. I tracked them the first day, south across the brook and as far as the forest. But it's impossible to track where they went after that. They could have been right next to me and I'd not have seen them. I suppose Lady Emma won't be persuaded to stay here?"

"No, Hal, but it's her choice… If Ned was here or Robert Radcliffe, I think she might defer to them but not to me - or you. Her mind is set."

"I'd better go with her then - I dare say Pinner, left to

himself, will get her killed."

"Hah!" said Pinner, leaving them. "I'll find you a mount…"

"My lady, you'll not be on your own; you've got a dozen or so men here - and my Beck, she can be damned dangerous! These walls will keep an army out for weeks and I'll not be more than a day or two."

"We'll survive, Hal. As you said, we have our walls. I'd much rather you were with Lady Emma. She'll need you because from what Sir Robert told us there'll be a reckoning at Tewkesbury soon. Lord Elder should be with the king's army - you, or Pinner, must find him and warn him of Sir Roger Cullen's trap. Then perhaps together you can track down Lady Eleanor."

66

4th May 1471, south of Tewkesbury

There was a time, Ned thought, when he would have been affronted to be given the role of observer, isolated on the margins of the battlefield. Yet this morning, as he watched the three great battles of King Edward's army toil along the road from Tredington, he was content not to be among them. It was long after dawn when Gloucester's vanguard arrived, with much display and noise, then the king came with most of the ordnance and then finally Will Hastings brought up the rearguard and took his place on Edward's right flank. The king's army was aligned facing Tewkesbury but a labyrinth of lanes, closes, hedges and ditches lay between his army and his Lancastrian enemies.

If he was to attack then the king would have to find ways through that labyrinth. As for Ned and his two hundred or so mounted men, they were to be held in reserve. The king had asked him to take up a position in a wooded deer park overlooking the field, in case of a Lancastrian ambush though the trees there. So, here he was, sending his prickers out to watch for any incursion by the enemy. All they reported so far was a large number of startled deer, but then the battle was yet to start.

Had the king lost faith in him, his warrior lord? Only a few weeks before he had honoured Ned by giving him charge of his young brother, Gloucester, at Barnet. Had

Ned not rallied the left flank there after Gloucester's injury? Perhaps the king blamed him for the initial break Oxford made in their lines... but, whatever the king's reasons, Ned did not dwell upon it.

He was tired of fighting and only too glad to let the younger men, such as Gloucester, take the lead. Ned just wanted to go home to Maighread, to his children and to all those in his household who had served him so well. It was time to start rebuilding his family, his estates... his life.

From his vantage point Ned had an excellent view of the whole field. He could even pick out a few of the more obvious banners and colours in the Lancastrian host: the royal standard, of course, and the Beaufort banners - he had seen more than enough of those over the years.

His own command, scattered amongst the trees, included those he had brought from Quenhull over a month before. Like him, most were tired of war, though he observed that some stared wistfully at their comrades below forming up in the king's main army. No doubt they feared that if the king won they might play little part in the rout that followed and thus by the time they arrived, the pickings amongst the dead and wounded might be rather slim.

The king had promised him reinforcements and shortly after dawn a column of riders wound its way up from the south, far from prying Lancastrian eyes. He watched their approach closely and when he saw their banners, he shook his head in disbelief. Truly King Edward intended to punish him for some transgression for, of all the men he could choose, he had sent this one to help Ned: Robert Radcliffe. Though he fought now under the banner of William Stanley, he was also flying the red banner of the Radcliffes - the mere sight of which had once been enough to sting Ned into a rage.

Robert was a mystery to him. Was he really to be trusted after all he had done? True, he had come to Ned's aid once… and he had protected Emma, but Ned doubted that he could ever truly forgive him.

He was still fretting about it when the king's ordnance commenced a thunderous barrage. Once again Ned was forced to contemplate the smoke and chaos of battle with the memory of the utter confusion at Barnet all too fresh in his mind. There would be no repeat of that, for this time Ned had eyes everywhere.

After the exchange of cannon fire, the customary arrow storm began and, from the start, Ned could see that the Duke of Gloucester was hurling all he had at the opposing commander, who by his colours, Ned took to be Edmund Beaufort, Duke of Somerset. Somerset's men could not go on taking such losses; he would have to do something - and very soon he did. Ned watched the flurry of activity across Somerset's lines.

He suspected some planned manoeuvre but could not tell what it was so he sent more scouts down the hill to the lane that passed below the park. He dared not commit his force until he was certain that there was no Lancastrian force concealed as he was in the park or down by the river. He was still waiting for the return of some of the prickers he sent out at dawn. Until he knew for certain, he must assume the worst. Then he caught sight, just for a few moments, of a column of mounted men charging along the lane below before they quickly passed out of sight behind the hedges on the boundary of the deer park.

Their purpose was clear enough: Somerset was launching an attack either on Gloucester's left flank or perhaps even into the rear of King Edward's main force. It was a bold stroke for if Somerset could kill the king he would not only win the battle for the house of Lancaster but almost certainly the kingdom itself. But though Ned might guess what was about to happen, his hands were tied: he could not yet leave his post.

"It looks like Sir Robert's finally arrived, my lord," announced Croft, pointing out the column of men winding their way up from the south.

"About time," said Ned. "Somerset's moving to outflank the king. Go to Sir Robert and tell him to take his men to the northern edge of the park and wait there. He's not to show himself or do anything without my specific order."

Croft rode off to deliver his message.

"Bear!" called Ned. The warrior was hovering only a few yards away and came at once.

"Mount the men," Ned ordered.

Now he must wait a little longer and it would not be easy. Shouts of alarm from Gloucester's lines told him that Somerset's men had arrived. He could see some of them now as they moved into the open ground and crashed into Gloucester's rear. The shock of their attack scattered some of Gloucester's men and they pressed home their advantage, aiming for the king's standard in the centre of York's lines.

Ned could feel the eyes of his men upon him, willing him to act and act fast, but still he waited. King Edward would not thank him if he abandoned the high ground of the park only to find Lancastrian cavalry sweeping down behind him to shatter the entire army. His task was to hold his nerve and it suddenly dawned upon him why the king had given him the command in the first place - it was not a slight, it was a compliment. Very well then, he would repay his king's faith, by waiting.

Croft came back. "Sir Robert wasn't best pleased with his orders," he said with a wry smile.

"Hmm. Pity," replied Ned.

One by one, his scouts were returning and each reported no evidence of a Lancastrian reserve, either in the park or by the river.

"Send a trusty man to Sir Robert," he told Croft. "He's to move down onto the lane to support Gloucester's left flank, while we go after Somerset."

Slowly, Ned led the column of horsemen through the trees and down the hill to the east. Once they descended the slope, the battlefield would be out of sight so he fixed his eye on Somerset's position and hoped to God he could find it. At the foot of the slope the column fanned out, for the hedges were too thick and tall to charge through. To get to the lane beyond they had to pick their way over ground that was uneven and waterlogged. It seemed to take forever, with their horses stumbling and slipping with every nervous step.

Finally they entered the lane and the clamour of battle assaulted their ears. Ned heaved a sigh of relief when he saw that Somerset's men at arms were barely twenty yards away on a small hillock behind the Yorkist lines.

Ned urged his mount forward and roared his men to the charge.

"An Elder!" bellowed Bear, and others shouted Ned's battle cry as they hurtled towards the rear of Somerset's men.

Ned marked out the duke, their commander, who stared in horror at the horsemen descending upon his rearguard. Ned's spearmen swept into them and the force of their attack crushed several ranks of Somerset's men. At the first impact many were spitted on the point of a lance, others fell to those such as Ned and Bear who wielded pollaxes or ugly, sharp-toothed maces. Somerset's brave force was almost encircled as attacks came too from both Gloucester and the king. In a few brutal moments, Somerset's desperate gamble to win all at one stroke was over. Ned's charge took him clean through the Lancastrians and up to King Edward himself. The king raised an arm in salute and then, with hardly a pause, continued to batter his opponents.

Ned circled around to ride at Somerset once more but the duke was already fleeing with those of his shattered company who still lived.

"Get after him, Ned!" cried the king and then he was gone, turning his attention back to the main battle up the slope where the rest of the Lancastrian army awaited him.

Ned's horsemen, having finished off the remnants of Somerset's men, reformed and followed Ned back into the lane for that was the only escape route left to Somerset. Indeed had the duke been on foot, he could not have got away at all.

Ned harried them along the lane, driving them straight into Robert Radcliffe's men. The trap was sprung with brutal effect and hardly a man escaped yet, somehow, the Duke of Somerset did, for when the fighting stopped, Ned could find no trace of him.

"What now?" Robert asked him.

"We support the main attack," said Ned, though he could not bring himself to sound very enthusiastic.

Robert stared at him. "I know, Ned," he said. "I've been fighting since I was fourteen years old. I never expected to live beyond twenty, but here I am - as are you. And like you, I'll be glad when it stops."

Ned gave him a thoughtful look and set about reforming his men, noting with relief that the losses were light. The next part, though, would be much worse for now they must advance uphill through the tortuous lanes and hedged closes and that was no place for their horses.

"Dismount and leave your horses here!" he ordered.

To their right they heard the roar which signalled the Yorkist attack and Ned gave the order to move. At once his men at arms strode forward and hacked at the first hedge with their axes. It was slow, hot work but they forced several pathways into the close beyond. Ned was first through one of the gaps. He tried to leap across a flooded ditch and instead slid back into it, knee deep in water. Bear hauled him out and together they trudged through the mire and on up the slope. Behind him he heard the curses of his comrades as they slithered after him. Another knot of hedgerows faced them and the men spread out to find the weakest places to attack. Ned was running with sweat and beginning to feel the weight of his heavy armour and weapons.

Every now and then, as their enemies caught a glimpse of them, a flurry of arrows would send them all scattering for cover. Then they would climb to their feet and stumble onwards. The prospect of a savage fight at the end of such an assault terrified Ned but he kept going, knowing that his men must see him forging ahead.

At last they emerged into an open meadow and suddenly the Lancastrian host lay before them. To his right, the army of King Edward was spread across the slope and nearby Gloucester's men at arms were launching their attack with the duke at their head.

"God save King Edward!" bellowed Ned and took a pace forward.

At once his ears were filled with battle cries and the tramp of hundreds of heavy feet upon the ground. After a few yards he was aware that men were falling about him, but very soon the arrows dwindled to nothing and he quickened his pace as the slope began to level out.

Now he must do the hard part. He sucked air into his lungs as he strode forward with axe and mace raised. His face was set, all thoughts of mercy cast aside and he hurled abuse at the nameless men of Lancaster who were now barely thirty paces away. He would do as he had always done: stand toe to toe with another man and try to crack his skull, punch mortal gaps in his plate armour and rend his flesh.

He was ready to do it but in the event the whole Lancastrian right flank disintegrated in the face of the Yorkist assault, splintering into scores of isolated pockets of resistance. The Duke of Gloucester drove forward like a man possessed. Ned hurried to keep pace with him, flanked by Bear and Croft with Robert Radcliffe and his retainers close by.

In the blink of an eye, the retreat became a rout. It reminded Ned of the last hours at Towton, where mindless, numbing carnage followed victory. Yet he knew that hesitation now could still cost them dear. The king knew it too and Ned could hear his voice roaring encouragement to the men around him as they pursued the fleeing enemy.

Before him Ned could see the great abbey of Tewkesbury and many of the enemy were fleeing towards it, no doubt hoping for sanctuary. But there was a river between the field and the abbey and only one small bridge. Thus some of the Lancastrian men at arms were trapped with their backs to the river. Ned called upon them to yield but they refused. As long as their prince still fought on, they were not going to give up and they made a brave stand. By the time they realised the overwhelming numbers against them, it was too late for surrender. Most were slaughtered on the grassy riverbank and the abbot's nearby fishponds soon ran with blood.

A few made it across the narrow bridge and headed towards the abbey. Gloucester followed and got to the bridge first with Ned still struggling to keep up with him. The young duke snarled to left and right, a band of loyal comrades with him every step of the way.

Ned was tiring fast and others began to overtake him including the Duke of Clarence and a tight clutch of his men at arms. Ned cast a wary eye over them but could not see Roger Cullen's livery amongst them.

He glanced back to find that the king himself was only a

score of yards to his right with a mass of men at his back.

"Go on, Ned!" he roared. "Get me Edward of Lancaster, Ned. We must take the prince!"

Ned's helm felt heavier with every step and he struggled even to hold his head up as he trotted forward. Ahead, Gloucester and Clarence had been halted by some unexpectedly stubborn resistance. With the battle all but lost, these men could have only one reason for fighting on: they must be defending their prince.

Ned and Robert brought their men up beside Gloucester's and struck the melee from the left flank. Their opponents were fighting doggedly but they were doomed and Ned reasoned that the sooner it finished, the sooner most of them might yield.

"Bear!" he yelled, launching himself into the midst of the enemy - and Bear was with him, wielding his heavy mace so that every thunderous blow scattered those before him. All around Ned was the clash of steel upon steel and the stench of death. He struggled to breathe in a mist of blood, wondering how he had lost his mace but hacking with his axe until his blows became weaker and his arm hardly moved.

The Lancastrians fell back once more and Ned caught a glimpse through his visor of a slightly built warrior with a coronet on his helm: it could only be the young prince upon whom rested the last hopes of the House of Lancaster. Others had seen him too: Clarence and Gloucester seemed almost frantic to get to the youth - each royal brother no doubt desperate to outdo the other.

A sword thrust grated along Ned's breastplate and reminded him where he was. He lashed out at the arm that held the weapon and his savage strike drove it aside. Bear was ahead of them all now, wreaking havoc, though men struck at him from all sides. He seemed just to shrug them off as he battered each into bloody submission. Ned fought his way nearer to him, and a glance to his right told him that the two dukes were closing in on the prince.

The king's order was to take Prince Edward, not kill him. He looked little more than a young lad - about the age Ned himself was when he fought his first horrifying battle.

"Bear!" he shouted but the din around them was too great for Bear to hear him. Angrily he tore off his helm and shouted again. "Bear, if he yields, take him prisoner!"

Bear raised an arm in brief acknowledgement as his mace swept another man aside. The prince was only a few yards from him now but Clarence had almost fought his way there too. Ned was exhausted and tossed aside his helm - the one dear Holton had crafted so skilfully.

Clarence reached the prince first and began a merciless onslaught, hacking repeatedly at the prince's head. The last two men at arms remaining with the prince rushed to his aid. Gloucester swiftly struck down one and Bear almost decapitated the other.

Ned reached them as the prince fell on his knees under the weight of Clarence's pollaxe.

"Do you yield?" demanded Ned.

"I yield, I yield!" cried Edward of Lancaster, throwing down his sword.

Clarence turned to look at Ned and gave a shake of the head. Then he raised his pollaxe to finish the prince.

Ned grasped Clarence's arm. "He yields!" he roared at the duke.

There were cries of dismay all around them.

Clarence shook his arm free. "You dare lay hands upon me!" he blazed. "I'll have your head for that!"

"He yielded," insisted Ned, suddenly aware that Bear was the only one of his men with him. The rest were with Croft and still yards further away.

Clarence took off his helm. "Well, Lord Elder, I didn't hear him yield."

With that he delivered another crushing blow at the prince and the youth lay still, blood trickling from beneath his helm.

"No!" cried Ned. "You butcher!"

He felt a blow in the small of his back and crumpled to the ground beside the prince. He looked up to find Sir Roger Cullen standing over him.

"Lay rough hands upon a royal duke, eh? Is there no limit to your arrogance, Lord Elder?"

Ned staggered to his feet and moved close to him. "I didn't think you'd show yourself to me again, Sir Roger. That mistake will cost you dear!"

Sir Roger grinned back at him and lowered his voice. "Perhaps not, Ned, for I have your sister, Eleanor, though I'd gladly take you in exchange."

"Hold that man!" Clarence shouted and Cullen seized Ned's arm.

"The old manor by the mill in Bussheley," breathed Cullen, "I'd tell you to come alone but we both know that won't happen…"

Ned stared at him in disbelief.

Bear pushed Cullen roughly aside and hauled Ned away.

"Arrest them both!" Clarence bellowed, standing astride the dead prince. "I'll have Ned Elder's head!"

"You shall have it now, your grace!" said Cullen, raising his sword.

Bear glared at him. "You'll die trying," he growled and even Cullen took a pace back.

By then Croft and the others were there to form a protective ring around their lord.

At that point, King Edward arrived. "Why have you stopped?" he cried. "There are still men to hunt down. I want Somerset's head!"

Gloucester looked at Clarence and Ned for a moment and then, with a shake of the head, he set off in pursuit of the fugitives. King Edward, never slow to grasp the essence of a situation, removed his helm and looked from Clarence to Ned and back. Then he noticed for the first time the coroneted helm amongst the bodies. He gave a solemn nod and eased his brother aside to kneel down by Edward of Lancaster.

"Young," said the king, "too young, but... of an age with our brother Edmund, butchered at Wakefield..."

"I want Lord Elder held as a traitor!" declared Clarence.

"Your grace, the prince yielded before the duke finished him," said Ned.

King Edward looked up in surprise and then nodded. "Continue the rout, brother," the king ordered Clarence.

The duke stood his ground for a moment but then King Edward stood up to his full height, a fearsome sight in his blood-stained armour. Clarence darted a parting look at Ned which left him in no doubt that he had made a mortal enemy.

"The lad did yield, your grace," persisted Ned.

"Aye, Ned, but we both know he would have faced execution, had he survived. Better for all, perhaps, for him to die on the field."

"Another death, another shroud, your grace," murmured Ned.

"Aye, Ned," said the king, "but I pray there'll be no more shrouds after today."

"Amen to that, your grace, but I fear I've offended your brother..." Ned could not help a bitter smile as he said it.

The king grinned back at him. "Well, you're very good at that, Ned... but George was ever swift to take offence. Best you avoid him for a time."

He clapped Ned on the back. "Let my brothers track down Somerset and the last of the rebels, Ned, whilst you find me Margaret of Anjou - now there's a firebrand of a woman..."

THE LAST SHROUD

He set off after the others with his retinue of knights gathered around him, though all too soon, Ned observed, most were trailing in his wake.

Ned clasped arms with Bear and Croft and many of the others who congratulated themselves on surviving the battle. Some would be less pleased, Ned thought, when they realised that they would take no part in the plundering of Tewkesbury.

Robert Radcliffe stopped beside him and grinned sheepishly.

"Who'd have foreseen this?" he said. "A Radcliffe and an Elder as brothers in arms…"

"For my part," said Ned, "I want no more bad blood between our families. It was an old feud when I first learned of it, born of our parents and their petty squabbles. At least now we two can put an end to it."

"Aye," said Robert, "but there are other matters we must speak of…"

Bear's voice sounded across the field like a roll of thunder. "Hal? Hal? Is that Hal?"

Ned followed his outstretched arm and saw a lone horseman picking his way through the corpse-littered field from the west.

"Hal!" he shouted.

The rider quickened his pace and came across to them at a canter.

Ned was not altogether pleased to see Hal for he expected him to be at Quenhull with the ladies. Thus he greeted him anxiously. "There is bad news from Quenhull?" he said.

"Lord, I hardly know where to begin," said Hal bitterly.

"Then let me ease your burden a little, Hal. I've seen Cullen. I know he has Eleanor."

"Yes lord, Lady Eleanor has been taken, but there's more: Lady Emma is with the old Queen and Princess

Anne in Tewkesbury."

Ned was so confounded that he could not reply. He simply looked blankly at Hal, as he took in the fact that both his sisters were in grave peril.

"Are you saying that Lady Emma is here, in Tewkesbury?" barked Robert.

"Yes, Sir Robert, she is," said Hal. "She came to help her mistress, Lady Anne…"

"Her former mistress, Princess Anne," snapped Robert, "though I suppose she's a former princess now too. Dear God! Emma, you foolish woman! You sweet, kind, foolish woman…"

Ned, slowly recovering himself, glanced at Robert. "Why has Emma gone to the Lancastrian queen?" he whispered.

"I didn't know she had until now," replied Robert.

"God's blood, Hal," murmured Ned. "Why did you let her go?"

"She wanted to help Lady Anne. She feared for her… She would have gone alone, my lord."

"Then you should have bound her feet and hands until I got back!" cried Ned. "Where is she now?"

"I left her this morning in the town with Pinner. She insisted I come to warn you about Eleanor, but I couldn't get through to your lines till now."

"You've left my sister in Lancastrian Tewkesbury at the mercy of a woman who has just lost her only son…"

"My lord, I didn't know which way to turn," said Hal.

"Never mind," said Ned, "When Cullen told me he had Eleanor, I thought it was an idle taunt and scarce believed him."

Hal shrugged. "He's been busy against you, my lord. It was Ralph Teller who took Lady Eleanor."

"Teller? I owe him a reckoning too. Cullen told me to meet him at Bussheley but, if he's committed to the rout, perhaps we can reach her before he gets there."

"We must hurry if we're to find the queen's party," said Hal.

"You know where they are then?" asked Ned.

"I know where they were," Hal replied, "and I know Lady Emma was going to try to get Lady Anne away by the ford at Lower Lode - if she'll take your sister's advice..."

"You'd better pray she does, Hal! Croft, fetch up the horses," said Ned. "We must get to the river!"

"The pages have already gone to fetch them, my lord," said Croft.

"Robert, the king has told me to capture the renegade queen - are you with me?" asked Ned.

"If your sister Emma is with her, I'll track that woman across all Christendom!" replied Robert.

"Let's hope we find her before then," said Ned. "God's blood! Where are those mounts, Croft?"

"Coming, lord!"

"Very well, but let's walk back down to meet them. I can smell nothing but blood up here."

All his limbs ached and his temples pounded, but he forced himself to breathe more evenly and then set off at a steady walk across the bloody meadow that had cost so many lives. Bear handed him his battered helm and he took it with a show of gratitude, though he did not welcome the extra weight.

Hal began to tell him what had happened at Quenhull... and at Tewkesbury, but after a short time he just stopped listening. He already knew all that mattered: Maighread and the children were safe, Eleanor was taken, Emma was lost - that was more than enough for now.

67

4th May 1471, by the river Severn near

Tewkesbury

Emma was almost at the rear of the single line of riders with only De Bressuire behind her. She felt his piercing gaze on her back, watching every move she made. He was willing her to make a mistake, to reveal her treacherous heart - as he saw it. Anne was just ahead of her, with the queen nearer the front following close behind their guide, a local monk. In between were two clerics and several other ladies of the court… probably other widows now, she supposed. Somewhere, she hoped, Pinner was keeping a watch over her. She had not seen him since they separated in Tewkesbury, but he swore he would follow her.

It was not difficult to find Anne Neville - she simply asked for her and was taken there at once. She was fortunate to be admitted to see Princess Anne before the others were aware of her presence. The anxious look on the girl's face told Emma that she had been right to come. On her knees, she begged Anne's forgiveness and it was freely given for, as she expected, Anne Neville was desperately short of allies.

When De Bressuire learned of Emma's presence, he was livid and was all for hanging her there and then but her faith in Anne bore fruit and the princess would not hear of it. Emma expected more trouble from the queen but before the battle she was preoccupied in discussing strategy with her son and her captains. Hours later, with her cause in ruins and her son dead, she seemed not to care about anything at all and Emma could not blame her. How would she feel if her son Richard was brutally killed and her hopes for his future were ripped asunder? She would be empty… she would be broken… and thus was the queen and those of her ladies who lost husbands or sons on the field of battle.

Even before the fighting ended, De Bressuire persuaded them to prepare to leave. Emma realised she must work with him if she was to get Anne safely away. He was better prepared than she would have expected. He had rooted out the monk the night before and thus he had a way out. She too would have taken them to the river shallows at Lower Lode.

As the battered Lancastrian army disintegrated in Tewkesbury, news of the prince's death forced the queen to leave. The monk would lead them across the Severn and De Bressuire would take Margaret to Jasper Tudor. But there was the flaw in De Bressuire's plan: how could he find Tudor in a land he did not know?

Emma knew that De Bressuire would never trust her very far but she could claim to know the Gloucestershire country at least a little better than he. So here she was, following the other ladies across the Severn, the water lapping against her mare's thighs and washing over her legs as they crossed the ford. When they reached the far bank, it would be up to her, but she knew where she was going and what she must do. She prayed that Pinner had seen her go for, if not, then Hal, Robert or Ned would not know where to follow.

§§§

"You're certain they crossed the river here?" asked Ned.

"I am, my lord. I watched them cross myself," replied

Pinner, "then they headed away from the river and turned north."

"It's what we agreed when we parted on the road," said Hal.

"Aye," said Ned, "but she'll not fool them for long if she keeps heading north. Margaret will know that Jasper Tudor must lie to the west. It's weak, Hal - damned weak. Good Christ! What were you thinking?"

"Well, where in God's name did you want me to send them… my lord?"

"They'll pass within a mile of Bussheley where Cullen holds Eleanor-"

"Lady Emma understands," insisted Hal. "She knows that Lady Eleanor - and Cullen - may be close, my lord."

"Aye, but she doesn't know where! She could simply stumble across Cullen! And there'll be riders chasing down the fleeing men of Lancaster - don't you think some will venture across the river?"

Croft joined them on the river bank with a few of Ned's men and Ned could tell that the news was not good.

"Sir Roger Cullen's taken the road across the bridge and causeway to Bussheley, my lord," reported Croft.

"God's teeth!" declared Robert. "He must surely get there before us now."

Ned surveyed the few riders Croft had brought. "Where are the rest of the men?" he asked.

"Scattered all over Tewkesbury, my lord... I'm sorry…"

"Ah well, who can blame them, Master Croft? It will have to be enough. Pinner!"

"My lord?"

"You observed their passage? You know where the shallows lie?"

"I think so, my lord," said Pinner.

"Then for God's sake let's waste no more time," Ned told him, "but you can go first!"

They crossed the river as swiftly as they dared, almost losing several riders in the process. On the other bank it took only seconds to pick up the fresh tracks.

"They can't be far ahead," said Robert.

"No," said Ned.

Robert took his arm. "Ned, we shan't catch both our little birds with only one basket…"

"No, I know. You must go after Emma and, as it happens, the queen; I'll to Bussheley to find Eleanor and finish Cullen."

"Aye, but the king's charged you to find Margaret of Anjou…" said Robert.

"I know, so before we part, let us agree: Margaret of Anjou can't be allowed to escape - above all else…"

"Aye," agreed Robert, "above all else - except Ned, I'll not give up Emma to keep hold of Margaret. The old queen is nothing to me; Emma is everything."

Ned gave him a farewell pat on the shoulder. "Take care, Robert. Pray God we'll meet at Quenhull - with both my sisters."

They set off and their paths diverged almost at once: Robert taking his men to track the queen's party northwards and Ned leading his to seek Eleanor at Bussheley.

§§§

De Bressuire was now leading the group with Emma beside him and the ladies following. They had barely covered half a mile from the river when De Bressuire leant across her and seized her reins to call an abrupt halt. He stabbed a finger towards the river to the east.

"My lady, why are we still here by the river?" he demanded. "Our last report of Tudor was that he was at Chepstow - that is surely to the west, Lady Emma, not the north east?"

Emma was expecting such a challenge though not quite

so soon.

"Aye, Chepstow is to the west," she said, "but this land we're on is held by the Duke of Clarence - and I believed that her grace would not wish to be taken by the duke's men. If we ride further north we can skirt Clarence's lands, but if you wish to take the risk, then we can head west."

De Bressuire held her eyes for a moment, uncertain, until one of the clerics spoke to him.

"Why do we stop, De Bressuire?" he asked. "What's wrong?"

The Frenchman turned slowly aside from Emma. "Nothing, Dr Morton," he replied. "We just make sure of our course."

Dr Morton nodded and they set off again, still heading north across the flat swathe of land through which the Severn bulged towards Tewkesbury.

"There will be many in pursuit," Emma told De Bressuire as they rode. "All of them very keen to take the queen and to kill any Frenchmen they find. You are just one Monsieur le Comte, and you'll need my help if you're to get out of this shire alive. So remember that next time you think about taking my rein."

He said nothing but his eyes flitted nervously between the river to the east and a band of woodland to the west.

"Once we've crossed the road from Tewkesbury," she said, "there's less chance of discovery."

"It seems I must trust you, my lady, but if you betray us, I'll cut your throat without a thought."

They passed the woods without incident but she knew that very soon they would reach the road from Tewkesbury which followed the higher ground towards Bussheley. In the wake of a battle involving thousands of men it was inevitable that there would many upon the road. She glanced back at the others. The two churchmen kept their own counsel, though she noticed that Dr Morton offered

Margaret frequent words of comfort. As for Lady Anne, the queen and the other ladies, she sighed in sudden despair: well-dressed ladies, with grave faces, fleeing from a battlefield. It would not need the sharpest observer, she thought, to work out that such a group might be worth stopping.

In no time, it seemed, they reached the road, just an ill-made track etched into the land by ages of use. In the distance towards Tewkesbury they saw a straggling column of men with banners they could not quite make out trying to fight its way westwards. It crawled away from the road like a wounded animal, as its pursuers hacked it apart without mercy. Emma slowed, both revolted and fascinated by the savage spectacle of an army in its death throes.

"Make haste, Lady!" De Bressuire told her and she dragged her glistening eyes away. There were others on the road and she was still several miles from the safety of Quenhull.

They crossed the road and hurried on north though Emma then veered back towards the river. De Bressuire darted a look of suspicion at her but did not argue. She was relieved to see the forest ahead for they would be far less exposed there - half a mile more and they would be safe.

There were shouts from the road behind them and when Emma risked a quick look back, her heart sank. Some of the large party pursuing the Lancastrian stragglers had broken away and were coming after them.

"The trees," said De Bressuire, "That's our only hope, your grace."

"Ride!" urged Emma. "Ride as fast as you can!"

The ladies needed no encouragement for Emma could see that they were terrified. This was not the life they had anticipated at the court of Queen Margaret. Well, as Emma had learned, life at court could be dangerous. She wanted to look back to see if there was anyone else following them...

in the distance perhaps, but she dared not waste the time.

"Find me, Robert," she breathed, "or Ned... one of you, find me..."

68

4th May 1471, in the forest near Bussheley

Ned's men covered the two miles or so from Lower Lode in quick time and soon entered the great hunting chase which stretched as far as the Malvern Hills. Once in the forest, the going was much slower.

"An old manor house by the mill, you say, my lord?" said Croft.

"Aye," said Ned, "do you know it?"

"I think so, my lord," replied Croft, "I've ridden past it a few times. There's a windmill on a rise to the north. The house is falling into ruin, as I recall. There are some cottages strung out further to the east towards the church, a few larger houses beyond that and a few farms of course. The Abbot of Tewkesbury holds a lot of the farmland and several small holdings on the fringes of the village. The manor house isn't the easiest place to get to without being seen. We can use the forest cover as far as the mill, but after that…"

"Well, Cullen will be expecting me in any case and he knows I won't be alone."

"Good," said Hal, "because no matter what you order me to do, my lord, you're not going in without me!"

"Or me!" echoed Croft.

Ned looked at Bear and forced a grim smile. "Bear?"

"It will be a trap," announced Bear simply.

"Aye," said Ned, "and knowing our friend, Cullen, crossbows I should think…"

Bear nodded.

"So there's no point in all of us riding in like fools," said Ned.

"Aye, my lord," agreed Hal, "but that doesn't mean one fool has to go in on his own!"

Ned stared at him for a moment. "You're getting far too cocky with age," he said, "must be   Becky's influence rubbing off on you."

Hal merely shrugged in reply.

"But, because I want you to carry on rubbing shoulders… or whatever else you choose to rub with her," continued Ned, "I don't want anyone throwing their lives away here. God knows there's been enough senseless sacrifice."

"Come on," said Croft, "Let's find the place first, shall we, my lord?"

"Aye," agreed Ned, "but keep your wits sharp and your eyes sharper."

They headed up through the woods, spread out in a great wedge as they sought one of the foresters' paths to follow, to make it easier than wrestling through the undergrowth. There were eleven of them in all and so many men and horses could never move quietly. Still, they must move.

The moment Ned caught sight of the outline of the mill ahead, he called a halt.

"We mustn't get too close," he said.

"We're already damned close," said Croft, "and we have to reckon that Cullen's already here, my lord."

"Unless he stopped to take a few Lancastrian heads along the way," said Hal.

"Look for their horses," said Ned. "If Cullen's here in force, his mounts will be too - and hard by."

Croft nodded and despatched men in several directions to conduct a careful search.

"So, we wait?" asked Hal.

"Not for long," said Ned. "We've only a few hours of daylight left."

Nevertheless, he did wait at least until his scouts reported back to Croft.

"You look confused," said Ned.

"I am, my lord," said Croft. "They can only find half a dozen horses…"

"Perhaps Cullen really has been delayed," said Ned. "If so, this could give us the chance we need."

"But there are still men here, lord," pointed out Hal.

For the first time in a while, Ned smiled. "Aye, lad - just about the number you might leave to guard an awkward lady like my sister, but not enough to ambush so many of us!"

"Croft, send two men to get their horses and bring them back here - we don't want any escaping. Hal, you stay here with another two men. That'll leave half a dozen of you in reserve - just in case Cullen arrives. The rest of us will examine this ruined house and Hal, I promise you, we'll be most careful."

"There's a wall that encloses the manor house, Hal," said Croft. "Wait for us there with all the horses."

Ned could see that given enough time, Hal would be inclined to argue so he did not delay. "Croft, Bear, Pinner, William, Tom - with me," he ordered. "Take care, Hal."

Croft led the way past the mill to the long wall he had mentioned.

"There's a breach in the wall that'll get us into the courtyard, my lord," explained Croft. "Right across the yard is the doorway into the hall."

Ned gave the yard and the buildings in it close scrutiny. There were several timber-built stores against the outer wall in places where it must have been ten feet tall. The house looked derelict and part of the roof had fallen in. The main door was ajar so it was hard to believe anyone was being held in there. To the left of the hall were several smaller stone buildings and beyond those, he thought, a dovecote. There was no sign of life either in the yard or any of the buildings.

"Come," he said softly, "let's explore a little, shall we?"

Croft found the gap in the wall and they hurried through, treading carefully over the fallen masonry. Ned signalled Tom and Croft to inspect the stores whilst he went to the hall door and carefully pushed it further open. It gave a reluctant creak as it moved. He froze on the threshold but there was no sound from within. The floor was littered with debris from the damaged roof and they picked over it for any evidence of occupation.

Bear sniffed the air and glanced around the large chamber; then he gave a satisfied nod and pointed to the far corner. "Pisspot!" he announced.

A swift examination revealed that Bear's nostrils had not let him down. It was indeed a pot of piss, but whose?

They moved to the far end of the hall where cobwebbed partitions screened off doors to a kitchen and buttery but neither room provided any helpful evidence that Eleanor had been there.

"Croft?" said Ned, pointing to a small door in the kitchen wall.

"Must go out into the servants' yard at the back," said Croft.

Ned moved to the door and lifted the latch to open it but as he did so he heard voices on the other side. So did the others and each man drew out a weapon at once.

"Steady," whispered Ned and carefully opened the door. Facing him was a man who looked even more surprised than he was. His jaw dropped and for an instant he did not move, then his hand flew to the hilt of his sword and he cried out: "Sir Ralph!"

He never drew the sword for Ned clubbed him down with a blow from his own sword hilt. He stepped out of the door and then pulled back as an arrow thudded into the frame by his head. Dashing back inside, he slammed the door shut.

"We've found Sir Ralph Teller, at least," he said. "Tom, quick! Go and bar the hall doors!"

Tom ran back into the hall and the others followed. There was a muted cry and they found Tom pinned to the door by an arrow. Before they could reach him, a crossbow bolt struck his chest and punched clean through his leather jack. He hung twitching against the door.

"Shit!" said Croft, "He was a good man!"

Through the still open door they could hear the unmistakable clicking of crossbows being reloaded.

"How many men?" asked Ned. "Three? Four?"

"The one outside the kitchen door called out to Sir Ralph," answered Croft, "so that's two and at least two more in the yard out front - and at least one of them with a crossbow."

"More than one crossbow," declared Bear unhappily.

"Do you think Hal heard the shout?" asked Ned.

"Perhaps…" said Croft, "the breeze would take it towards him, I think. But what will he do if he did hear?"

"Aye," said Ned, "I don't want him rushing blindly in…"

"No more sound from outside," observed Croft. "Could they have gone?"

"No reason why they should," said Ned, "since they have us trapped in here and we all expect Roger Cullen to arrive at any moment. No, it's us that need to go… but we need some help to do that and the only man with a bow is Hal…"

"I'll go," said Croft. "You get their attention at the hall

door. I'll go out through the kitchen - I can run faster than the rest of you."

"Very well, Croft - we'll all die if we stay here." He clasped his arm. "Let us know when you're ready to go."

Croft went past the partitions into the kitchens whilst Pinner lingered where he could see both Croft and Ned.

"They reload by now," said Bear.

"I know!" retorted Ned.

Pinner waved his lone arm and Ned dashed across the open doorway. He shouted out into the yard: "Sir Ralph! We should parley!"

An arrow brushed past him and struck the far stone wall. Laughter echoed around the yard outside. "Nothing to parley about, Lord Elder - not yet at least, perhaps later…"

Ned moved out to stand exposed in the doorway.

"Lord!" warned Bear.

"I don't think Sir Roger intends you to kill me just yet, Ralph," he shouted.

Ralph laughed loudly once more. "Oh, he won't mind," he replied, "as long as you really are dead!"

A bolt struck Ned square in the chest. He gasped with shock and dropped to his knees. Bear stepped across to drag Ned back from the threshold and grunted as a bolt caught him under the arm on his left side.

"My lord…" Bear was distraught.

Ned looked down at the missile protruding from his breastplate.

"I'll have words with Holton about this armour…" he mumbled.

69

4th May 1471 in the afternoon, south of

Quenhull

Emma risked another glance behind her and saw at once that they could not reach the forest. Their horses were no match for those of the mounted men at arms in pursuit. She could see only one hope - a faint one. She pulled up abruptly, causing the others to falter so that the whole party came to a halt.

"What do you do?" yelled De Bressuire. "I should never have trusted you! This is a trap, isn't it?"

"Not of my making!" snapped Emma, staring back beyond the score or so of riders that were hunting them down. "We'll never reach those trees," she said.

"The forest will help us," insisted De Bressuire.

"We shan't reach the forest! "There!" she said, pointing southwards. "There is our salvation!"

De Bressuire followed her hand. "Pah! Those are just more men hunting us, and now you've doomed us all!"

"No, look!" she said "The chasing pack has slowed."

"Of course they've slowed becuase they know we can't escape them now!"

"But the second column hasn't slowed," said Emma. "See how fast they come to us…"

"But what does it matter, you fool - the others will still

get here first!"

Emma looked at them all: the fear in their hearts was plain on their faces. Only the queen showed no fear, but she was lost forever in her own private turmoil.

"If you want to live," said Emma, "then do as I do. Ride back towards our pursuers, wave to them if you can, put them at their ease and then… when I cry out, ride with me as if the devil himself is after you. De Bressuire, make sure you have the queen with you."

He shook his head but Emma ignored him and set off at a slow walk to meet the oncoming riders. She feared it might be Cullen since they were very much in his domain and, as she got closer, she recognised the banners that had laid siege to Quenhull: they were Cullen's banners. For a moment she doubted herself, fearing that De Bressuire was right: that she had condemned them all. Then she heard Robert Radcliffe's voice, loud and strong, shouting a warning to the men who were now blocking her path. Some of them turned towards Robert in confusion.

"Now, ride! Ride!" she screamed. "Ride for your lives!"

She veered her horse away from the waiting line of horsemen. De Bressuire led the queen after her and all the others followed. She could see that Robert understood her manoeuvre at once and he carried on his charge to intercept Cullen's men before they could catch her. Robert's men had all the momentum and they crashed heavily into Cullen's force but Emma did not linger to await the outcome.

"What is going on?" demanded De Bressuire. "Who are these men? What are they to you?"

She ignored him and turned to lead them back up the slope until she was well away from the sprawling melee. Then she slowed her mount to give it some respite.

She went to Anne. "My lady, you have a choice now. If you come with me you will be safe, protected at my brother's castle nearby. Or… you can go with the Comte

De Bressuire and the queen… perhaps try to reach Jasper Tudor. But if you do that, I can't protect you and I think you'll be taken by the king- if not now, then very soon."

"Come!" urged De Bressuire, "Lady Emma has won us only a little time."

"Dear Emma," said Anne, "you've proved a loyal servant once again, but how I can leave my husband's mother - not when she is so crushed by events? And for what? My father is dead - the Neville cause is lost... I should be glad if you would come with me…"

"No, my lady, for my future lies with another… Take care on the road and trust no-one."

"If we are taken then I still have my sister, Isabel… and I believe the royal dukes, Clarence and Gloucester, will help me to face their brother, the king."

"Ladies!" insisted De Bressuire, "we must go!"

Anne put a gentle hand on Emma's arm. "I still have something precious that I took from you. Though it has brought me great solace, Emma, it rightly belongs to you."

Anne started to retrieve the velvet pouch but Emma stayed her hand.

"Come, Lady Anne!" urged De Bressuire.

"Please keep it," said Emma. "It's more fitting for a princess or even a daughter of the Earl of Warwick than for a lady of such a dubious family as the Elders. Keep it - and perhaps, sometimes, think of me… as I will often think of you. But De Bressuire is right: you must hurry now."

Emma watched them head north until they reached the forest edge then she turned back to see how Robert fared. With relief she saw that he had driven Cullen's men off and was hurrying towards her. He looked unhurt and she breathed more easily.

"You saw them off speedily, my lord," she said with a smile.

But Robert was not smiling. "That was not my

intention," he said. "I'd hoped to gain a little more time for your brother to free Eleanor."

"It was Cullen himself then?"

"Aye, I almost had him trapped but there were just too many of them to hold. Pray God, Ned has enough time."

"What about the queen… and Anne?" asked Emma.

"We can't just let them go, Emma. I've a couple of men tracking them through the forest. They may lead us to Jasper Tudor but, if not, then we'll pick them up in a day or two at most."

70

4th May 1471 in the afternoon, by the ruined house in Bussheley

Hal crouched nervously at the breach in the wall where he could see the hall entrance and a little of the courtyard. The others were spread out along the wall where they could watch several approaches to the house through the forest.

It was quiet for a long time, just the reassuring song of the woodland birds. After a while though, he noticed that the birds sounded more distant. By the time he noticed the birds were gone, his attention was elsewhere. There was a sudden cry and he was certain the name Ralph was shouted. He stood up and saw several men moving across the yard. Tom appeared at the hall door and Hal almost cried out when an arrow struck him.

He moved through the broken wall and scanned the yard, but wherever the bowmen were now, they were well hidden - perhaps in the store houses. He strung his bow nonetheless and waited. Then a cry came from somewhere behind him further back along the outer wall.

"Oh, no," he breathed and crept back along the outside of the wall towards where the horses were tethered. To his relief there were still two men there.

"Did you hear that, Hal?" asked one.

"I heard. There's trouble at the house too, so stay watchful," Hal replied, "I'll go and check on our comrades."

They looked nervous, he thought. They were excellent men at arms: put them in your battle line and they would hammer away at your enemies until they dropped - no matter what the odds. But put them in a forest, where the trees grew close and dark shadows played tricks on the mind, and it was a whole different matter.

He moved slowly, careful not to disturb the undergrowth more than he had to. His eyes, always sharp, focussed and refocused on the trees, looking for traces of movement. He found one all too soon: a small wiry branch of birch quivering as it sprang back into place in a narrow shaft of sunlight.

Where was the man posted at the far end of the wall? Perhaps his man was just going for a quick piss. Hal returned to the line of the wall and continued along it to the end where he found his man. His man wasn't having a wander. His man had two arrows in him.

Hal sighed deeply: Cullen was here and he was approaching with care. Perhaps he too had heard the shout from the house or more likely he had stumbled across this poor fellow, the first of Hal's watchers. Hal retraced his steps back to the horses where his two comrades still waited. They almost died when he ghosted out of the trees before them.

"Sweet Jesus, Hal!" hissed one. "Don't do that!"

"Peace," whispered Hal. "Cullen's men are here. They'll be too many to stand and fight so we'll need to get Lord Elder and the others out and then ride hard for Quenhull. Be ready to leave as soon as I come back!"

They nodded, distracted, checking their weapons - no doubt for the hundredth time.

He left them and headed back to the breach in the wall to find an ashen-faced Croft staggering through it.

"Hal! Thank God!" wheezed Croft. "We need... some

help… to get out…"

"It's worse than that: Cullen's here," said Hal.

Croft stared at him blankly then fell forward into his arms. His comrade had two arrows in his back and one in his thigh. The wounds in his torso alone might have killed him but the spiked artery in his leg made it certain. Every step he had taken pumped out his life's blood and he had run to find Hal, run until there was barely a drop of blood left.

Hal wept. Croft had given his life to reach him, yet he could do nothing to help those in the hall. Lord Elder was trapped, Cullen was coming at them through the forest and Hal had at most three men and one bow. He laid Croft's body gently on the ground by the wall and studied the house and yard once more. If Croft could not get out alive, then neither could he get in to help them. Lord Elder had told him not to rush in like a fool. He had left him outside because he trusted him to do what was best.

Hal picked up his bow and headed back to the others but a strangled cry stopped him ten yards short. It was too late for them and now it was too late for him to reach the horses. It mattered little since a horseman would leave a shattering imprint in the forest; they would hunt him down all too easily. On foot though, he had a chance - a small chance - and he decided that his lord would want him to take it. So he made off into the trees, away from the manor, away from Cullen and away from his trapped comrades.

There was still enough light to make his way through the forest and once he was clear of the hunting chase and out into the open fields he ran hard. He was forever looking behind for signs of pursuit but saw no-one. He fell more than once and had to wade across the brook which lay below Quenhull but seeing the castle's familiar towers spurred him on.

§§§

Robert was consoling Emma and Maighread when Hal burst into the solar. He looked exhausted and gulped in breaths as if starved of air.

"Sir Robert, if we leave now," said Hal, "we might still save them!"

"Hal?" said Maighread uncertainly.

"Where's Lord Elder?" asked Robert.

"Trapped," said Hal, panting between words, "but… if we go now… at once… with a dozen men… we can help them!"

"Catch your breath, lad," said Robert. "Tell us what's happened."

Robert though could guess all too well what had happened. He had not, it seemed, bought Ned enough time.

"If we delay even an hour, they'll be dead: Lord Elder, Lady Eleanor, Bear, all…" cried Hal desperately.

"But it's almost night, Hal," said Emma, "what can be done in the darkness?"

Death, thought Robert, death could be done all too easily in the darkness.

Hal knelt before Maighread. "Please… my lady - if they have any hope, this is it…"

Maighread turned to Robert and the scars on her cheek seemed to draw him in.

"Sir Robert?"

He looked at Hal. "Can you find your way through that damned forest in this light?" he asked.

"Yes." Hal replied at once.

"Robert, you don't know it well enough," said Emma. "We passed through some of that thick forest today, in bright sunlight, and it was difficult. To go there at night, would be foolish."

Robert sighed. "This morning, my love, your brother and I pledged to be brothers in arms. Can I desert him the first time he needs my help?"

"You've nothing to prove to Ned... or to me," she replied.

"Hal, how many men at arms does the garrison have left?" asked Robert.

"Men at arms... none - only about a dozen archers."

"And how many mounts, however poor?" asked Robert.

"I can find a dozen..."

Robert shook his head. "Very well, get your archers mounted in the yard. I'll be down shortly. They'll need their bows - crossbows if they have them - and torches."

Hal dashed out of the chamber and Robert wondered if it would be enough. God knows, Sir Roger Cullen must have raised men from half the county to take to Tewkesbury. How many of them would he have at Bussheley?

"Thank you, Sir Robert," said Maighread. "Pray take good care of yourself."

"I'll bring him back to you, my lady," said Robert, forcing what he hoped was a confident smile.

Maighread went to the door. "I'll see that... they have enough torches..." she muttered, leaving him alone with Emma.

"Come then, my lady," he told her, taking her hand in his, "you can wave me farewell."

"Why are you doing this?" she asked. "Don't do it for me. Please don't do it to prove you love me - because you don't have to..."

"I'm doing it for your sister... and I'm doing it for Ned."

"Why?"

"Because it's what brothers do..."

"But you're not his brother..."

"We're brothers in arms and soon I'll be his brother by marriage..."

"Aye, you will... so take care that you come back," said

Emma softly.

"I'll make sure I'm surrounded by many men, my love. You know me: I don't take chances."

She smiled. "I won't come down to the yard but… just… come back to me."

He left her and hurried down to the yard where his horse awaited him and the men were already mounted. He noticed Hooper on foot by the gate and went to him at once.

"Well?" he asked.

"The queen's lodged locally - at a house in Bussheley."

"By the saints, how did they get there? We sent them in the opposite direction!" said Robert.

"I think they rather lost themselves in the forest - we got dizzy just following them," said. Hooper

"Well if they're in Bussheley, I fear they might have a rather disturbed night ahead."

"Trouble?" asked Hooper.

Robert nodded.

"Do you want me to come?"

"Very much, my friend," replied Robert, "but I also need you watching our fugitives - I made a promise that we wouldn't lose them. So keep a close eye on them for me."

"Fair enough," grinned Hooper, "but who do I report to if you're dead by morning?"

"I won't be… but William Stanley's the man you'd need to find. Now go!"

Robert walked back to his horse, mounted swiftly and turned to Hal.

"Ready, Hal?"

"Yes, my lord. Men armed and mounted - all bows strung ready."

Robert gave him a nod. "Let's see how good a guide you are then. Light the torches!" he shouted and around the yard pages took lighted torches from one rider to another and within moments the courtyard was ablaze with light.

"Lead on then, Hal," said Robert.

529

71

4th May 1471 in the late afternoon at the old manor at Bussheley

They had put her in a dovecote - a dovecote! She had light at least and a pot to piss in, but little else. She sat on the earth floor, oblivious to the accumulation of bird shit and feathers that lay there. She had lost track of days but her head was starting to mend, though she gave no sign of it to her captors, feigning dizziness when they came to feed her. It was just as well that her skull was carved from solid oak with the amount of punishment it seemed to be taking. A brief smile flitted across her lips as she recalled Ragwulf's jibe that her thick skull explained why she thought so little before she acted.

She heard a sudden cry of 'Sir Ralph!' from the yard and sat up straighter. She was alert now, listening. Then another voice, Ned's voice, brought a wave of joy until she made sense of what he was saying: offering a parley. Then came the unmistakable sounds of a struggle, then silence.

She eased herself up onto her feet, glad that they had removed the hobble. She did not feel much like a fight just now but Ned had come; her brother had come for her. She retrieved the piece of tile she had patiently honed against the brickwork. Then she took a deep breath and puffed out her cheeks before rapping on the wooden door. Aside from hurting her knuckles, nothing much happened. Perhaps there was no-one outside. She made a fist and banged harder on the door.

"Keep quiet," said Thomas. She smiled and her spirits were lifted. Thomas, thank God it was Thomas.

She leant against the door. "Thomas," she whispered, "My head hurts still…"

"Please, my lady, you must keep quiet!" hissed Thomas.

"Would you keep quiet, Thomas, if you were in such pain?"

"Sir Ralph will hear you," whispered Thomas.

"Good!" cried Eleanor, kicking against the foot of the door "He needs to if you won't help me!"

"But he'll blame me, my lady… if you make a noise."

"But, Thomas, I think I'm dying. I feel so weak… I…"

Then she said nothing more. The long pause, she knew, was the key. Silence was her most powerful ally now. So she waited… and said nothing. She was never very good at waiting and leaning there with her head resting against the door, was excruciating. It was hard to keep silent, but she must.

After a while, Thomas softly called her name: "Lady Eleanor, are you alright?"

She gritted her teeth and did not answer.

"Lady Eleanor?" said Thomas again.

She said nothing, almost beginning to feel sorry for him - almost.

She drew away from the door as she felt the bolt being drawn back then she sat down again on the filthy floor. The door swung open. She kept her head down and her body still.

"Lady?" whispered Thomas.

"Help me, Thomas," she breathed without moving a muscle.

He bent down to her and she gave a little whimper.

He took her arm and lifted her a little - he had such a

gentle touch, poor boy.

She held onto him for support and then pressed the shard of tile against his neck. Once she would have cut his throat without a thought, but now she hesitated.

He felt the prick against his skin and stared at her in disbelief.

"Aye, Thomas," she said softly, "women can dissemble as well as men - only perhaps a little better…"

She swiftly explored his belt until she found the hilt of a dagger and drew the weapon out to exchange it with the tile.

"I came to help you, my lady," he said miserably.

"Aye, and you are helping me, Thomas," she replied. "But can I trust you?"

"My lady, I don't think I can let you go…"

"Aye, I thought not," she said, almost laughing out loud at the honesty of his response.

"My lady…"

"Stand up, Thomas, but… for your own sake have a care and make sure this blade stays at your throat."

"My lady…" he pleaded.

"I like you, Thomas." She withdrew the knife from his throat. "Stay here and keep safe," she said and slammed his head hard against the dovecote wall. His knees buckled at once and in seeking to break his fall she banged her head yet again.

"Good Christ!" she moaned at the sharp pain. "Why did I do that?"

She was tempted to relieve him of his sword but it looked far too heavy for her; the dagger would have to do.

§§§

Ned leant against the wall and looked down at the crossbow bolt in his chest.

"It doesn't hurt much - and there's a fair length of it

sticking out," he said, "that's a good sign, isn't it?"

Bear nodded solemnly, keeping his eyes fixed upon the hall door which still lay wide open.

"Not deep," murmured Bear, "but don't pull it out."

"Fine, if I leave it long enough, perhaps it'll work its way out like a wood splinter."

"You passed out, my lord," Pinner informed him from the kitchen doorway.

"What have I missed?" asked Ned.

"Well, no-one's died in the past few minutes," said Pinner.

"Did Croft get away?" asked Ned.

"I think so," said Pinner. "He might have been hit though."

"He's tough is Master Croft," said Ned. "William…?"

"He's watching the kitchen door, my lord," said Pinner.

"Good, good."

He heard the horses in the courtyard then a sound that was all too familiar: riders slowly coming to a halt and dismounting. That was not so good.

"Cullen…" he said.

"And some friends, my lord," said Pinner.

"Well, however many friends he has, we need to hold out till Croft gets back."

"It sounds like many…" said Bear.

"At best Croft will have half a dozen men - and Hal's bow," said Pinner.

"God's blood!" grumbled Ned. "Listen to you two miserable sods! I've been in far worse places than this - and so have you, Bear. Have a little faith!"

Bear looked across at him and Ned suddenly realised the great warrior was wounded.

"You're hurt?" he asked.

"Won't die of it," said Bear, "but I don't move so well." He smiled and laid a mailed glove on Ned's arm. "I always have faith, lord…"

"Any good news anyone wants to share?" asked Ned.

"If they come at both doors now, we're dead," said Pinner.

"I don't know you very well, Pinner, but is that your idea of good news?"

"No, my lord, just saying…"

William called from the kitchen. "They're moving, my lord!"

"Stay with him, Pinner," ordered Ned. "Bear and I can defend here."

Pinner nodded.

Bear heaved his bulk up off the floor and picked up his pollaxe. "Right arm still good, lord," he said with a grimace.

"Well then," said Ned, "I knew there'd be some good news. Perhaps they've all gone…"

He crawled across to the far side of the door and an arrow skidded past him along the stone flags. "And then again, perhaps they haven't."

He got carefully to his feet and drew out his sword. It was like an old friend but its blade looked dull and neglected, for he had not used it either at Barnet or Tewkesbury.

They must have been massing by the door because the suddenness of the attack caught him off guard - but not Bear. The first man through was dead before he took a pace into the room, his head half removed by Bear's axe. Ned hurt another enough for him to fall back but more filled the doorway.

As the numbers at the door increased, the pair met them head on with less concern for stray arrows or quarrels. The two of them filled the doorway, thrusting and hacking at the attackers as they pressed forward. Flecks of blood splashed onto their arms, chests and faces. They fought as one, as if harnessed together, hammering stroke for stroke, despite their wounds. It reminded Ned of countless times in the past, when only Bear kept him alive. If Ned's sword faltered, Bear's axe blade filled the void. The man fought with only one arm but he outmatched all and soon their adversaries crawled back into the yard, bloodied and beaten.

"Down, lord!" warned Bear and they dropped to the floor - easy enough in their utter exhaustion. Arrows and crossbow bolts once more snapped against the wall behind them and they dragged themselves into the shadows beside a doorway that was now half-blocked by corpses.

"Pinner?" called Ned. "William?"

There was no reply but the noise from the kitchen told him there was a struggle going on.

"Shit," said Ned, looking at Bear's blood-smeared face. "Think you can hold this door on your own for a while?" he asked.

Bear nodded, with a grin. "You just get in my way, lord."

"Aye, thought so," said Ned and got up to stumble over to the partitions.

§§§

Eleanor ran around to the rear of the house to the service yard where the work of the house would have been done. There she found stables and several outhouses. She dashed into the first one she came to and collided with an archer coming out. It was instinct that drove her knife through his leather jack and into his breast. He simply looked stunned and fell back onto the floor. She seized his bow and arrow bag and peered out of the doorway. She could hear horses approaching and within a few moments the yard was full of men. It would not be long before someone discovered the dead archer - and her.

Ralph Teller's voice sounded close by and she held her breath.

"Welcome, Sir Roger," she heard him say. "We have

them all, shut tight in the hall and Ned Elder took a bolt in the chest."

"Well done, Ralph," replied Sir Roger. "Get his sister."

"At once, my lord," said Sir Ralph.

Eleanor froze by the door. Ned wounded, perhaps worse. Her thoughts were only of revenge. Sir Roger must be standing only a few yards away from her. Could she plant her blade in his neck before they took her down? Would it make any difference? She'd have to kill Ralph too. She might get one, but not both… but she would have avenged her brother.

She looked down at the bow in her hands and smiled. Then she tested the bow string and found to her annoyance that it was very tightly strung, perhaps too tight for her. The distance would be nothing though and she might manage one arrow.

She heard Ralph return and report to Sir Roger what she already knew: his little bird had flown.

"She can't have gone far," said Sir Roger, "but you'd best find her before dark!"

He didn't sound pleased. Well she would see how pleased he looked wearing her arrow.

In her youth she was no stranger to the bow and used a lightweight hunting bow in the forest of Yoredale, but she had not picked up such a weapon for many years. She found she was shaking - it must be the cool air. She selected a straight shaft from the bag and smoothed the goose feathers carefully. Then she nocked the arrow and stood on the threshold, composing herself: breathing shallow and even, relaxing her muscles.

She checked again that the arrow was lodged correctly and took some strain on the bow. Just one arrow, she told herself, just one arrow. The voices had come from her left so she took two swift paces out of the door to her left. Sir Roger was gone.

She turned the other way and saw several men at the far end of the yard - no doubt searching for her. They had their backs to her now but she would have to move fast. She drew back inside as several more men at arms appeared in the yard and headed for the door into the kitchen at the rear of the hall - the servants' entrance. She let them pass but her eyes followed them thoughtfully. Even as she realised they were going to attack, there was a roar from the front of the house as an assault was pressed home there at the same time.

She peered out to watch as the men at arms battered the kitchen door in with their axes. In the gloomy light she could not make out who was on the inside but, whoever they were, they were putting up a brave fight. Two of the attackers drew back nursing wounds, but another harried the defenders with a long spear or pollaxe. There was a cry from within as he thrust it repeatedly through the shattered door. Then he too fell aside and more took his place.

Eleanor stepped into the yard and held the bow ready. She had a good eye but even a gentle pull on the string was hard work. Her back muscles screamed mercy as she pulled back harder on the bowstring. She was shaking with the effort but she could not stand in the open forever. Any moment one of the others would see her. She prayed she had drawn it back enough and let the arrow fly.

"Well, well, Lady Eleanor," said Sir Ralph from close behind her. "Hidden talents, I see."

She felt his blade slice under her ribs.

§§§

Ned saw Pinner by the kitchen door trying to pull William aside. The lad was parrying a pollaxe with his sword but Ned could see that he was already badly hurt.

"Move away, Pinner!" cried Ned, knocking him aside as he lurched towards the door. He brought his sword hard down on the pollaxe shaft and split it. Then he pulled

William away and lifted his sword once more to meet the attacker. The man facing him looked surprised and then dropped the useless shaft of his weapon. Ned cracked him on the helm with his sword and the man fell back, dazed. Two others took his place but Ned assessed them at a glance: one wore only a leather jack and the other had no helm. He crushed one man's skull with a weighty blow but the other raised his mace to strike. The mace paused in mid-air and his assailant dropped forward onto his knees to reveal an arrow through the back of his leather jack.

He shoved the man away and took a step forward into the yard. The wounded men there backed away in fear. Then he saw Eleanor, with a bow in her hand, hair fluttering as she stumbled towards him. Ralph Teller was close behind her. He could defend the door for her, but he knew she would not get there.

"Ellie!" he shouted.

She heard him and scrambled towards him.

"Where's an archer?" bellowed Sir Ralph.

Eleanor cried out to Ned as Ralph caught her arm and pulled her down.

Pinner appeared at Ned's side and his arm moved in a blur. Ralph would not have seen it coming and, though Ned might have wished him a slower death, who could argue with a knife in the throat? He stepped forward to help Eleanor up and half-carried her into the kitchen, still clutching her bow and bag of arrows.

Pinner looked at the broken door. "We can't defend this place now, lord," he said.

"Aye, we'll pull back into the hall," said Ned, helping William along the passage.

Eleanor followed him in with Pinner.

Bear took one look at William and shook his head.

"Pinner," said Ned, "See if you can staunch William's bleeding."

Pinner gave a bleak nod, knowing an impossible task when he saw one.

Eleanor hugged Ned tightly. "Thank you."

He yelped. "Have a care, little sister," he complained.

She looked at the quarrel in his breastplate then pointed to her bloodstained side. He stroked her face gently and kissed the top of her head.

"Cullen planned this - he wanted you to come for me," she said, unable to keep the sadness from her voice.

"I know," he said.

"And so many are dead…"

"Aye, but you didn't ask for this," said Ned. "At least there'll be no more treachery from Ralph Teller."

Pinner came back in.

"William?" asked Ned.

Pinner gave a shake of the head. "The lad's ordeal is over," he said.

"He was a good lad. Can you do something for Lady Eleanor?"

"It's not so bad," said Eleanor, but she allowed Pinner to bind the wound nevertheless. Then she gave him a kiss on the cheek. "Thank you," she said, "in case I don't have the chance to say so later... even though I did tell you to stay with my children."

"I only wish I had, my lady," complained Pinner.

72

4th May 1471, early evening in the forest at

Bussheley

They covered the short distance to the forest edge in a matter of moments and there Robert drew his mounted men at arms to a halt. Hal and the archers dismounted at once and put out their torches.

"Make sure you give me enough of a start, Sir Robert," Hal told him.

"Just get moving, Hal, or we'll still be here at dawn!"

Hal gave him a curt nod and set off into the woods with his comrades. Robert dismounted his men and waited in the low scrubland. Impatience, he decided, could be the death of him. He must give Hal enough time. All the same, he could feel the tension amongst his men and he didn't blame them. Not only were they waiting on the edge of a large, dense forest with night fast approaching, but they were lit up as if they were going off to sing a mass. No, they were right to be worried - in fact, they should be terrified.

The last vestiges of light had almost gone when he finally gave the order to remount and took them into the forest to carry through the plan he had devised with Hal. Without torches they would have lost themselves utterly on the ride to the mill. But though the torches were essential, they also gave Cullen ample warning of his approach. They took a broad, clear track to the mill and dismounted there, planting their torches in the soft ground around it.

Anyone nearby would see only the flaming torches against the outline of the mill but very soon, Robert knew, men would be hurrying to investigate. They came almost at once, peering through the line of torches for a sight of the men they knew must be there. Some were men at arms, others carried loaded crossbows as they headed towards the light… like moths to a candle flame.

When he reckoned there must have been a score or more men trudging across the ground that sloped up to the mill, Robert decided it was time to get their attention.

"Listen!" he shouted. They stopped in their tracks.

"I am Sir Robert Radcliffe and I have three score men and archers with me this night. Your lord, Sir Roger Cullen, has acted unlawfully, but I freely give you the chance to lay down your arms, leave now and go back to your hearths, wherever they are. After that, any man bearing arms against me will be treated as a traitor, so make your choice now."

He paused and, through the flickering torches, he saw a few men throw down their weapons and scurry back down the slope but, as he feared, most remained. These men did not care that Roger Cullen was acting outside the law, for who was the law in Bussheley but Roger Cullen?

There was a shout from one of the men and suddenly they moved forward as one. Robert hoped Hal was in position or in the next few moments he was going to appear very foolish and, most likely, very dead. Just as the doubts began to crowd in on him, he sensed a slight disturbance in the night air. He felt it somehow and then he heard the cries of the wounded and dying. Still some men charged on towards the ring of torches and a second volley of arrows from Hal's archers struck them.

"Hold!" cried Robert and pushed his horse forward

through the ranks of his men. The mare gave a little shudder as it passed between two torches. Behind him, his men retrieved their torches and remounted.

"Now," declared Robert in a grave voice, "take your wounded, leave your weapons and go."

The remnants of Cullen's small army fled into the forest night. Robert raised his arm aloft and led his riders down towards the house. At the outer wall they stopped, dismounted and readied their weapons. Most of the torches were now extinguished and tossed aside.

"Keep a few of those burning," ordered Robert. He stared at the dark shape of the manor house as he waited for Hal and the archers to catch up.

Hal soon arrived, breathless. "Pray God we're not too late, Sir Robert," he said.

"Aye, it's very quiet," said Robert, "and that's a worry after all the noise we've been making… We must be careful, Hal. Those we've just put to flight were not Cullen's best men - they'll all be here."

Hal suddenly seized his arm. "Look! What's that?" he said, pointing at the house.

Robert could see nothing. "Where, in God's name?"

"There's a little red glow - and look, another over there…"

Robert sighed.

"Shit!" said Hal. "That's not good…"

"No," said Robert, "You'd better get your archers busy and quickly, Hal!"

But, even as they watched, a torch flared alight at the hall door and was thrown inside. The tiny pricks of red light followed it into the building.

§§§

"Very well," said Ned, "we have a bow and four arrows. That's good, but who's going to use the bow?"

They all looked at each other and slowly they

understood.

"Indeed," said Ned. "Ellie, you've that knife wound. Bear can only use one arm and Pinner... well... So that leaves me and as long as I've got this quarrel sticking out of my chest, I'm not going to be able to use a bow very easily."

Eleanor was dismayed to see that her prize asset would be useless to them.

"So," said Ned, "someone needs to pull it out."

"No, lord. Better leave it in," advised Bear.

"It's only a slight wound, more of a nuisance - the plate took most of the impact. Now pull it out for me, Bear - or I will."

Bear held up a hand. "I do it, lord." He took a grip on the shaft of the bolt and pulled gently. It hardly moved.

"Come on, Bear, you must be the strongest man alive, get it out!" said Ned.

"You bleed more if I do..." muttered Bear.

"Well, I'm used to that, aren't I? Just do it - oh, Jesus!"

"It's out," said Bear, tossing the bolt onto the floor.

Ned gave him a nod, but said nothing. Eleanor could see that he was taking short breaths, waiting for the pain to subside.

"Are you bleeding more?" she asked.

"A trickle only," he murmured, "and nothing I can't cope with. Give me the bow."

"At least it's dark," said Pinner. "So they'll not be able to see us."

A moment later, as if in answer, a burning firebrand was tossed through the open hall door, illuminating the whole chamber.

"Pinner," chided Eleanor, "I forbid you to say any more!"

"Pinner," said Ned, "stay with Lady Eleanor by the screens to the kitchen. Bear and I will be at the main door."

Each moved to their position and made ready. Eleanor

composed herself. She was ready for death, as she had been for a day or more now. She looked down at the knife in her hands, stained dark with blood. It was all she had. She saw that Pinner still had two throwing knives in his belt. Bear would use his pollaxe and Ned the bow, with an arrow nocked ready, but all she had was a narrow piece of steel…

There was a sudden roar of noise and men burst into the hall from both doors.

"Oh, shit!" cried Pinner, throwing one of his knives.

"Down!" shouted Bear.

Eleanor dropped onto the floor, bruising her knees as she landed.

There was a thunderous blast of sound and flame as several handguns fired over her. She opened her eyes to see Ned crawling across the floor under a haze of smoke. The bow was still in his hand but not the arrow, though she couldn't recall seeing it fly.

"They must reload," said Bear.

"Ellie?" shouted Ned.

"Alive!" she cried out and went for the gunners. One was already down on his haunches, contemplating Pinner's knife and the growing stain of blood across his chest. The other had taken a few paces back to reload behind the screens. She sprang up at him and her blade glinted in the flickering light as she stabbed at his leather-clad breast. Torn between letting the gun fall and defending himself, he reached for her dagger with one hand but only succeeded in seizing the blade. She twisted it out of his grasp, slicing through several fingers. He snarled at her then and relinquished the gun but he was too late to avoid her final thrust. She staggered away from him and leant against the screen, weeping with the pain.

"Pinner? You hit?" called Ned.

Eleanor quickly looked around. "He's down!" she cried, her voice hoarse.

The smoke was clearing to reveal Ned on his feet putting another arrow to the bow and Bear hacking down a gunner by the door. Eleanor went to Pinner, who lay moaning on the floor. He had been shot in the first volley and the stump of his left arm was shattered. She used the knife to cut away part of her kirtle and bound it above the wound. Pinner passed out as she pulled the band of cloth tight. She winced as her own wound tore yet again and she felt new blood seeping from it.

The burning brand just inside the door was guttering.

"Crossbows!" warned Bear.

Eleanor looked up to see the wounded warrior wrestle the first man down. He crashed the man's head against the floor repeatedly until he lay still. She gasped as another flaming torch was thrown in and two more crossbowmen clambered over the bodies on the threshold. Ned's arrow accounted for the first but the second released a bolt which struck Bear in the leg.

Eleanor, still down on her knees, watched Ned cast the bow aside and draw his sword to cut down the crossbowman before he could escape back through the door. She sighed with relief, but Bear shouted a warning and she glanced up.

The last of the gunners, having reloaded, appeared a yard away from her by the partitions. Bear started to limp across the hall towards him but she knew he would not get there in time.

The gunner took aim at his chest. "This'll bring down even the biggest man," he laughed.

"Aye, so will this!" screamed Eleanor, plunging her dagger up into his groin. The gun discharged over her head but she kept stabbing until the gunner's tormented screams faded to a whimper. Finally it was quiet and only the smoke remained with a glimmer of torchlight playing upon it. She rolled on the floor with her hands on her head but could not stop the ringing in her ears.

Ned came over to her and picked her up. Bear went to Pinner and dragged him over to prop him against the wall. She leant there beside him and looked up at Bear. His armour was blackened, his breastplate knocked askew and the skin around his neck burned raw. The gunner had not missed entirely.

They rested for a moment whilst Bear bound up Pinner's wound once again. Pinner looked ashen and she thought he could not last long. Her big brother slumped down beside her. He was, as ever, battle-scarred but confident.

"That wasn't too bad, was it?" he said.

She shook her head and punched his shoulder gently.

"Anyone seen Cullen yet?" he asked.

"No," replied Eleanor, "but you can still hear his men outside. Good Christ! He must have scores more of them... Where shall I stand?" she asked.

He shook his head. "Just stay here with us," he said.

"But they'll come in through the kitchen door," she said.

"Let them," said Ned gently. "We're not going to stop them getting in, Ellie. The best we can do is to give a good account of ourselves. Perhaps he'll spare you..."

"You know better, Ned. There'll be no survivors here..."

"Then say your prayers, my friends," said Ned, "for it's the last chance you'll have."

After a moment, he stood up and Eleanor too got to her feet. She embraced him with tears in her eyes, crushing herself against him, remembering Ragwulf and hoping he would not judge her too harshly.

"Is this hurting you as much as it is me?" Ned breathed in her ear.

She pushed him back and brushed her tears away. "You make so light of everything..." she murmured.

THE LAST SHROUD

Footsteps echoed on the stone flags by the main door and she turned to see the best part of a dozen well-harnessed men entering the hall.

"Sir Roger Cullen," said Ned, "I've been waiting for you for hours. See how many men had to perish before their brave leader was prepared to put his own life at risk."

Cullen stepped further into the hall and his men spread out to flank him.

"Not much risk now, Ned," he said with a broad smile. "Your friends are close, though - very close, but they'll come just a little too late."

"Don't be fooled by our apparent weakness," said Ned.

Cullen gave a hollow laugh. "I'd like to have savoured this moment a little longer, Ned - perhaps taken your head to Clarence - I'm sure he'd still welcome it. But alas, it's not to be."

Bear suddenly threw down his pollaxe and stepped away from them. "I'm not his man," he shouted at Cullen. "I fight for silver - so, if you have silver, I am your man!"

The men at arms facing him watched him carefully, all too aware of the raw power he still possessed. Cullen stared at him and smiled. "Very well," he said, "you're hired. Now, be a good giant and wait outside."

Bear gave him a nod and limped towards the main door.

"Bear! No!" Eleanor screeched after him. "You coward! May you rot in purgatory forever!"

Ned looked at her, impassive, resigned. Did nothing shatter his belief, even the betrayal of his most loyal man?

"No matter what happens," Ned said softly. "Stay with me and watch my back."

Eleanor nodded and gripped her knife more tightly so that she would have it in her hand when she died.

"Take him," ordered Cullen and all of his men stepped forward, swords raised, maces poised.

A sudden blast shook the hall and scattered the men at

arms. Eleanor had no idea who fired but Ned was already moving and she went with him. He carved his way through the bloody mass of men and steel, making for Cullen. A mace brushed past her head and she stabbed at an exposed armpit. Her opponent grunted and took a step back, his arm hanging limp by his side. She was tempted to stab him again but Ned was moving forward so she backed away, keeping by her brother. The wounded man came after her but then came to a halt, his good arm reaching round to his back. He went down slowly and she saw one of Pinner's knives lodge there.

"Good Master Pinner!" she shrieked, but when she looked across at him he lay still.

She glimpsed Bear then, bludgeoning a man at arms with a smouldering handgun. She heard a gasp behind her and glanced around in panic. Ned was wounded, blood trickling down his breastplate.

"Run!" he told her, "out through the kitchen."

"No, never!" she cried and hurled herself upon one of his assailants. Surprise gave her a moment's advantage but Ned could not help her as Cullen and another took it in turns to batter him into submission. She clung to her victim's neck. He tried to knock her away with his mace. She prised up his visor to ram the knife into his face but the blade slid from her grasp and she screamed in frustration. His weapon flailed about her, pounding her back, its sharp spikes cutting into her flesh, but she pressed her thumbs hard into his eyes and kept on pressing until he dropped the mace and she fell down with him onto the floor.

She twisted around to see how the others fared, but only Bear was left standing. He was surrounded, three bodies already at his feet. Even his one good arm was not enough. A mace slammed into his shoulder, he seized the weapon and rammed its shaft back into the owner's face. Then a sword clattered into his back and he went down.

She screamed and picked up the mace that had been used against her, meaning to go to his aid, but another man fell onto the floor beside her and she found herself looking into Ned's eyes. Above her, Roger Cullen stood poised to drive home his sword.

§§§

At once Hal and several others launched torches through the night air into the yard. One died as soon as it landed but others remained alight. Dark figures scrambled for cover and Hal's archers took some toll. Nevertheless, orders were barked across the yard and Cullen's men responded with arrows of their own and a few crossbow bolts.

"Keep down!" shouted Robert.

Then from the hall came several small blasts. It was as he feared: handgunners. Screams splintered the darkness.

"We've got to get in there!" cried Hal.

"Aye, I know, I know!" said Robert. "Mount up!" he told his men at arms. "Throw in a few more torches, Hal, and watch for targets - and especially watch out for us! Then follow us in."

Hal nodded.

Several more torches blazed through the sky and Robert's horsemen followed them into the yard with a roar. The brief glare of light gave Robert a clear enough picture: several men at arms were strung out across the yard with one or two crossbowmen before them. Massed in the doorway was a larger force of men at arms.

He slashed his sword down across the shoulder of the first man he came to, dimly aware of a quarrel flying past him from somewhere. Men were shouting and crying out all over the yard, but the horsemen made their impact count and pressed them back. The men at arms by the hall door split up then and half disappeared inside.

No, thought Robert, no. He needed to get in after them

but the remainder stayed at the door and were experienced enough not to be drawn further out into the yard. They were no fools: they knew he could not take the horses to them where they stood.

"Dismount! Dismount!" he bellowed, leaping from his horse. At once two armoured knights set upon him, but one was driven back by an arrow in the throat and Robert thrust his sword at the other. His men were with him now and a fierce melee broke out in the doorway. The torchlight was waning though and it was hard to tell friend from foe.

"More torches, Hal!" he cried, wondering then whether there were any more. But two more came, soaring into the melee itself and breaking up the lines so that all those fighting took a sudden pace back.

"Yield!" demanded Robert. "Yield, and, by Christ, you'll be spared!"

"You yield!" came the answer, "Cullen men don't yield!"

"Aye," said Robert, "but they do die - and that's the choice you've made!"

The two sides came together again with a crash and Robert took a blow to the head. He fell back, dazed and found Hal beside him.

"Sir Robert?"

"I'll live but by Christ, Hal, this is bloody work. Cullen's already in the hall. Take some of your archers and see if there's another way in."

Hal set off at once. Robert was angry now, angry at the futility of it. They had all just fought two bloody battles to win a kingdom, to win peace, and here they were killing each other for the greater power and glory of one man. Madness!

There was a sudden blast and he caught a glimpse of the giant man at arms, the one they called Bear, in the doorway. Then he disappeared back into the hall leaving Cullen's men at arms in shocked disarray.

Robert sheathed his sword. "Give me that!" he told one of his men and snatched a pollaxe from him. Madness could only be cured by extreme measures, he decided, and pushed his way forward into the fray. He looked at his men. Aside from Hooper, they were his best men.

"Give me that door!" he roared at them and with a shout of "A Radcliffe, a Radcliffe!" he drove into the midst of Cullen's men at arms. His axe ploughed a bloody furrow through his opponents and they fell back before him, flanked as he was by other equally determined men. The defenders retreated back into the hall and he pursued them with more bullish strokes from his axe, oblivious to the blows he received.

"You should have yielded!" he bellowed angrily as they fell before him. Finally he was on the threshold, clambering over dead men to embed his axe in the helm of one of the last men standing against him.

Torches were guttering inside the hall as he stood there, exhausted, drinking in the bloody carnage. Bear was being beaten down and Lady Eleanor lay in a pool of blood on the floor. And Ned? Ned was falling even as he looked on and Roger Cullen's sword was raised. Robert took a step forward and a sword thrust at him from the shadows inside the doorway. He grunted and leaned back against the door post for support, staring at Ned in vain.

§§§

Hal hurried towards an archway with four comrades, each clutching their bows with arrows nocked. The man next to him was suddenly plucked away by an arrow and they took shelter behind the arch.

"Wait," Hal ordered and scampered back across the yard to pick up a torch, only barely alight but it would have to do.

"Ready?" he said and tossed the torch through the arch.

At once his men loosed their arrows and they all hurried

through before their opponents could react. They found only a solitary bowman, already skewered by two of their arrows.

"Come on," urged Hal.

"I've no arrows left," said one.

They inspected their bags and Hal gave the man one of his last two arrows.

"One arrow each," he said grimly. "Make them count."

They found the shattered servants' door to the kitchen and edged inside, expecting a bolt or arrow to fly at them out of the dark interior. Nothing flew at them, but there was a mighty struggle going on in the hall.

"Arrows nocked," said Hal. "Have a care and choose your targets well. There are friends in here, remember."

They nodded and he led them in single file through the kitchen and into the hall. They blinked in the wavering light but there was no time to delay. They let fly at once. Two arrows thudded into the men who stood over Bear. A third caught the shoulder of Robert Radcliffe's assailant. But Hal hesitated, his eye drawn to the floor, to his lord's battered body. Ned Elder saw him and his bloodstained face creased into a smile.

The last arrow, Hal's arrow, flew straight and true, piercing Roger Cullen's eye with such force that all but the goose feathers burst right through his head.

73

5th May 1471 at dawn, on the ramparts of

Quenhull Castle

Maighread stared out across the sea of dawn mist spreading up from the river, enveloping half of the slope below Quenhull Castle. The village of Bussheley, always cloaked by forest, seemed now even further away. The ramparts were crammed with all those who remained at the castle, mostly women and children - John and Will were both there. They stood still, like stones... their prayers done, but their vigil not yet over. All that was left was the waiting.

"You're shivering, my lady," said Becky, draping a cloak around her shoulders.

"It doesn't matter," said Maighread. She felt empty to the core for, in the depth of night, the cool hand of death had chilled her soul and numbed her heart.

"They'll be coming," said Becky, "you'll see. They'll come soon - it's lighter now."

"I can see them!" John's voice shattered the calm. There was a murmur from some of the other women, keen-eyed wives and mothers, living on hope and straining to see what John saw.

His young eyes were sharper than most and he pointed

now to the mounted men who were slowly emerging from the shroud that lay upon the valley floor.

The assembly fell silent again as the column came nearer, cowed by the knowledge that fewer men were returning than had set out.

"There's two wagons," announced John, and others slowly nodded.

Indeed there were two wagons and that did not fill anyone with hope. Sir Robert had not left with any wagons and they all knew, though no-one said it, that wagons meant dead and wounded men.

"Can you see your father, John?" asked Maighread, squeezing his hand so hard that her nails dug deep into his skin.

"No."

"Can you see your aunt Eleanor?"

"No."

"I can't see Robert," breathed Emma, bowing her head to rest it upon the damp stonework. "He would surely be leading, wouldn't he? Who's leading, John?" she whispered.

John said nothing more but stared at the distant column as it continued its slow advance across the fields. At first only the heads and shoulders on the horsemen were visible above the mist but yard by measured yard they came on.

Maighread knew why they came so slowly. Emma, beside her, was shaking, the tears rolling down her cheeks.

"I can't see Ned," said Emma. "And I can't see Robert or Eleanor…"

"Hal," said John abruptly. "Hal's leading, my lady…"

Becky thrust herself forward against the low wall to catch a glimpse of him. All strained to see, mothers lifting children up to the wall.

"He promised to come back to me," groaned Emma, "he promised…"

Maighread turned away, still gripping John's hand lest

God should wrest the lad from her.

"Open the gates!" she ordered. "We must go down and greet our men," she said, willing her voice to be strong and calm.

"No, I can't," said Emma. But Becky took her arm and together they followed Maighread and John down the many steps to the smoke-filled hall, where a fire had been kept burning in the hearth all night.

"Tables! Put up the tables," cried Maighread, "and cloths, bring cloths! And draw water from the well!"

"We may need hot irons," said someone else.

By the time they reached the yard, the gates were already open. Maighread stopped to wait with her stepson at the head of the crowd.

Hal led the column in. The men looked exhausted, as men look after a crushing defeat.

Hal dismounted and Becky rushed forward to hug him, but it was Maighread he looked to, and John.

"My lady…" he choked on his words, unable to speak. "I'm sorry… and we've been so long… We'd to wait for more light, to treat the wounds, find men who had fallen… and then it took so long to find two wagons - you'd think it would take no time at all…"

"It's alright, Hal," said Maighread softly. She understood that he could not tell her about Ned, could not find the words.

Both wagons had now come to rest on the cobbles. Men dismounted swiftly to find their loved ones, women's voices broke in delight then all fell silent again as the wagons were unloaded. Emma and young Will pushed past Hal to get to them. John let go of Maighread's hand and followed them.

"Oh Robert, Robert," Emma cried as she clawed at the wagon.

"Blood of Christ, sister!" growled Eleanor. "Stop your mewling! God knows what you'd be doing if he was actually dead!"

"Eleanor?" whispered Emma. "Robert?"

Will flung his arms around his mother.

"Gently, Will, please," moaned Eleanor.

Emma scrambled onto the wagon and found Robert.

"You're alive…"

"No thanks to Roger Cullen!" he grumbled.

Emma crushed his hand in hers until he cried out. "Damn me, woman, am I not wounded enough?"

Around them the cries of grief began as the bloody work proceeded of tending to the injured and laying out the dead.

"We've tables set up in the hall," announced Maighread, wiping away a stray tear. "Take the wounded in there. Becky, fetch shrouds to cover our loved ones."

Maighread was determined to keep busy, to put off the moment. If she did not see him dead, perhaps he would not be dead. But Bear led her away from the rest into a corner of the yard.

"You're hurt badly," she said, but he shook his head and knelt before her, weeping.

"This soldier begs forgiveness, lady," he said and his gruff tones demolished her resolve and she too wept. After a while, she wiped away her tears and took his hand.

"Get up," she said. "See your wounds tended - no forgiveness is needed between friends."

§§§

In the first wagon, John found his father, took his hand and held it tightly. It was stiff and cold but even so he was glad to hold it. He stood by the wagon, holding the hand until Hal and some other men came to lift up their lord and bear him into the hall. John walked with them and watched as they gently laid Ned Elder on a table. He felt empty to the core, the newly forged bond between father and son severed so soon.

THE LAST SHROUD

The hall echoed with the agonies of the wounded and the shrill cries of the grieving, so he gave his father one more long look and then wandered back up to the ramparts. No-one saw him. No-one followed, but he preferred it that way.

§§§

In the evening Maighread went to the chapel where Ned, his body washed, lay shrouded on a bier, almost filling the tiny nave. She did not want him to lie in darkness and lit candles everywhere, filling the small chamber with light.

Emma came in, supporting Eleanor.

"You should be in your bed, Eleanor," said Maighread.

"I wanted to be with my brother and my sisters, at least for a while."

Maighread nodded and they sat down together in silence.

"Robert insisted on seeing Hooper," said Emma, "though he should be resting. He's lucky to be alive!"

Indeed, thought Maighread, staring at the bier, but she bit back the words that came to mind first.

"The queen will not get far," she said.

"No," said Emma, "she'll be overtaken soon by Sir William Stanley - but she's a broken woman now."

"Not broken enough," said Eleanor, "and whatever they do to her, it will never be enough…"

Maighread looked into Eleanor's grief-hardened eyes, a pair of shimmering emeralds.

"The anger in you," murmured Maighread, "will surely consume you… if you let it."

Eleanor stared back at her - a bleak, unforgiving stare.

"Ned is gone," said Maighread, "as Ragwulf is gone and many others besides... and men have paid the price."

"The price is not yet high enough for revenge," insisted Eleanor.

"Revenge? Does the queen not mourn as we do?" asked

Maighread. "I want no more talk of revenge. We will have no more feuds. And if I - who have lost my lord, my one love - can say that, then it is not for others to question."

Eleanor opened her mouth to speak, but Maighread disarmed her with a sudden smile.

"Dear sister, let us remember the men we loved. But let us remember the hope they gave us… not the wounds they suffered or gave."

She noticed that John had crept unnoticed into the rear of the chapel and now stood, silent and still, in the shadows. She took Eleanor's hand in hers and then Emma's too, gripping them tightly.

"We may rail against God or fortune, but above all we are mothers and we must strive to see our children grow and flourish. Ned was not a perfect man, but all of us were thrust, young and unknowing, into a world of blood and treachery. The anger of youth drove him to strike out blindly… and folk died because of it. Yet always he fought to save us and time upon time the sheer force of him threw death aside.

"In times to come, when I remember my husband, your brother, I'll remember his courage and his steadfast loyalty when all seemed lost. I never loved another man and I never will…. and I'll sing masses for his soul until the day I die."

"As will I," said Eleanor.

"And I," echoed Emma.

"And so will I," said John and the three women turned to see him standing behind them, his clear, grey eyes fixed upon his father's shroud.

§§§ §§§

THE LAST SHROUD

Author's Note: The Last Shroud

So, if you have read all four books now - and I thank you kindly if you have - you'll have followed the Elders from September 1459 to May 1471. You'll have had the whole story and I hope you'll feel that you have seen development in all the major characters. When the story began the three Elder siblings were young and brash but also rather innocent and unaware of the powerful forces that would shape their lives. Experience teaches them much!

Do they in any way really represent a lesser noble family of this period? I think so. Inevitably I've written much about the intrigue and fighting because they were important during the Wars of the Roses, but I've also tried to present Ned Elder as the head of more than just a family. His affinity embraces the servants in his household, the archers and men at arms who fight and sometimes die for him and the humble tenants on his lands.

Young Ned is almost oblivious to the carnage he wreaks upon foes and supporters alike but, as time goes on, he begins to understand that his responsibilities require more than that: he starts to think more about the people involved rather than just the outcome he hopes to achieve. All three siblings, in their own very different ways, come to realise that life can be complicated. Loyalties and alliances can be tenuous. The one you love may not represent the perfect ideal you had in mind.

Children play a significant part in the story, for what else is everyone fighting for in the fifteenth century but the fortunes of their families. Family is above all, but it is often qualified by ambition: as with Richard Neville, Earl of Warwick. The Elders demonstrate a lesson: things don't always turn out as you intend, or as you would like. Thus, in my stories, people die - sometimes people the reader rather likes. But that's what happens in life - whether now or in the fifteenth century.

To find out more about the series and my next project, or if you would like to contact me, you can go to my website: **www.derekbirks.com**.

My blog is at: **www.dodgingarrows.wordpress.com** and you can follow me on Twitter as **@Feud_writer.**

My Facebook page is: www.facebook.com/feudwriter.

Thank you very much for reading my stories about the Elder family and I certainly hope that you have enjoyed them. As an independent author, I must market my own work and one thing that helps me enormously is the response from readers. Please feel free to get in touch by using the contact form on my website.

If you have enjoyed my work then you might like to give it a favourable mention either in the shape of an **Amazon** or **Goodreads** review or on another site of your choice.

Either way, many thanks for reading.

Derek Birks
August 2016

THE LAST SHROUD

Historical Notes

The Wars of the Roses

Everyone knows about the Wars of the Roses – or do they? The range of historical opinion is so broad and varied on this whole period that I could not hope to do more than follow a consistent thread of narrative through it. Besides adhering to an accurate chronology of the events, I have also tried to set the events between the Elders and Warwick within an appropriate late fifteenth century context.

In this final book Richard Neville and his family, notably his daughter, Anne, again have an important role but we also see a little of both of King Edward's brothers, George and Richard. Whenever the story encounters an actual person I have attempted to create a character that would at least be recognisable to students of the period. I have endeavoured to make them as believable as possible, though of course their actions in this story as they relate to the Elders are completely fictitious. Below I shall try to unravel for you some fact from the fiction.

Edgecote and the Rebellion of 1469

There is enough evidence to show that Warwick was behind the revolt in the summer of 1469 and such a revolt could not have been spontaneous. What is described in the book must have been planned for some time. The rebellion was orchestrated from Calais by the Earl of Warwick and the Duke of Clarence, who had just married the earl's elder daughter, Isabel.

The Yorkshire rebels, who formed the basis of the army of rebellion which fought the battle of Edgecote in July 1469, were led by a man who was known as 'Robin of Redesdale'. He was certainly one of Warwick's affinity, probably Sir John Conyers or his brother, William, but certainly not the fictitious Robert Radcliffe.

As with most Wars of the Roses battles, there is some controversy about exactly where and how the battle of Edgecote was fought. I have described what I believe happened, based on the current evidence. Some facts are known for certain: the archers of Humphrey Stafford, Earl of Devon, played little or no part in the battle; the fighting was fierce; the outcome was in doubt until the arrival of what we believe to be Warwick's vanguard; and the Herbert brothers were executed by Warwick afterwards, despite the fact that their only 'crime' was to fight for their lawful king. The king was captured at Olney though of course Ned Elder was never there! King Edward was taken to Warwick castle and from there to Middleham.

During the summer of 1469, Warwick ruled through Edward, but the country was confused about who was actually in control. Warwick did plan to call a parliament but abandoned the idea when it became clear that his takeover was not popular. Clarence must have thought that he would assume some sort of power, but in the end Warwick could not countenance regicide and stepped back from the precipice. The king summoned lords to him and managed to get away to return to London. On the face of it there was a reconciliation between the king and his leading subjects, but neither side was fooled.

Warwick's flight and return in 1470

In the spring of 1470, Warwick and Clarence tried revolt again but their support trickled away: the Stanley brothers, powerful in Cheshire and Lancashire and the Earl of Shrewsbury all stayed at home and even Warwick's own brother, John Neville, Earl of Northumberland, did not rise up to support him. So Warwick and Clarence were left isolated and forced to flee. As described in the book, they headed south to Warwick's ships, picking up the heavily pregnant Isabel on the way. They eventually took ship from Dartmouth and set sail for Calais where Warwick - as commander of the garrison - expected a friendly welcome. The journey must have been a nightmare for all of them because King Edward had sent word to Warwick's deputy at Calais and the earl was denied entry. Cannon were fired at Warwick's ships to drive them off. Poor Isabel's baby was delivered aboard ship and perished. Finally Warwick's entourage made landfall in France but it was a bitter experience for Warwick.

The events described in the book after Warwick's flight follow the history fairly accurately. Defeat forced Warwick to consider other options and the French king, the wily Louis XI, facilitated an unlikely agreement between Warwick and surely his most bitter enemy, the former Lancastrian queen, Margaret of Anjou. It was an uncomfortable alliance and, though cemented by the marriage of the Lancastrian heir, Prince Edward of Westminster and Warwick's daughter Anne, I doubt that Margaret ever trusted Warwick. But for her he was a lifeline and the Lancastrian cause was alive again.

Battle of Barnet

Again there is doubt about some aspects of this pivotal battle - not least the exact site. I have gone with the traditional siting of the battle and the events are described as accurately as one can. There are doubts, for example, about whether young Gloucester led the left or right 'battle' of Edward's army. I have decided upon the left, but there is no conclusive evidence either way. The battle is famous for the fact that it was fought in fog, as described, but also because Warwick was killed, thus removing one of the major protagonists. We do not know the exact circumstances of his death, but what is known fits the story I've told.

Battle of Tewkesbury

Tewkesbury was a last throw of the dice for Queen Margaret and the House of Lancaster, though it was not fought at a time or place of her choosing. Who knows how things would have turned out if she had been able to cross the Severn and join up with Jasper Tudor? Yet, Edward IV was difficult to beat in battle...

As in previous battles I have used the essential known ingredients with my own fictional characters - thus there was a force of mounted men in the deer park though of course it was not led by Ned Elder. The story of the Duke of Somerset's attempt to outflank the Yorkist army relies on the best guesses of those who have made a close study of the battle and I believe my account is quite feasible. The death of Prince Edward has been argued over and attributed to several men. There is also some question as to whether he was killed on the field of battle or later. I think the account I've given is possible and fits what is known - that does not of course make it true!

Margaret's escape

The details are sketchy but it appears likely that she did cross the river at Lower Lode and certainly journeyed north-west into Worcestershire - by what route, however, is only the stuff of legend. It seems to have been Sir William Stanley who apprehended her a few days later.

The Stanley Brothers

The brothers, Thomas and William, are key figures in the Wars of the Roses and their growing power in the northwest makes them influential in the events that occur. Thomas Stanley in particular is often regarded as a man who sits on the fence a lot and does not commit himself to either side until he can see which might triumph. However,

THE LAST SHROUD

I have some sympathy for his position. Many families were made or ruined depending upon which of the main protagonists in this struggle they supported. He survived by hedging his bets and I don't really blame him. His brother William, equally ambitious, appeared to commit himself rather more rashly and thus is the perfect lord to whom our Robert Radcliffe might switch his allegiance.

The Middleham Jewel

As some readers may know, this jewel, a reliquary, was discovered near a footpath not far from Middleham Castle in Yorkshire. It is a very high status piece of jewellery as described in the book and must have been made for a woman of royal or the very highest noble rank - a queen or a duchess therefore. It is known to have been made in the period but I have probably stretched its earliest date of manufacture a little to 1468/9 and I have suggested that King Edward had it made for his queen, Elizabeth Woodville. He is known to have spent lavishly on items of clothing and jewellery so it would not have been out of character. Nevertheless, it is fiction, I'm afraid. It could equally well have been commissioned by Richard III or the Earl of Warwick - or someone entirely different.

It's presence near Middleham suggests that one way or another perhaps the recipient was either Anne, Countess of Warwick, or her daughter Anne, as I suggest. The jewel is currently held by the York Museums Trust.

The Shrine of Our Lady of Caversham

The Countess of Warwick had a close association with Caversham and the famous shrine of Our Lady of Caversham - as did her mother, Isabel Beauchamp, Countess of Warwick. The shrine was a very popular place for pilgrimage for several hundred years until the reformation when it was utterly destroyed in 1538.

It is now not even known for certain exactly where it was situated, though its original site is said to be on the northern side of an earlier Caversham Bridge. Its memory lives on in a shrine at the local Roman Catholic Church. It is all too easy for us to forget the great importance of such places to many of the people of earlier centuries. Thus it would be very appropriate for the Warwick ladies to visit the shrine on their return to England, with young Isabel now newly married and made Duchess of Clarence.

The manor house near Caversham, where Robert Radcliffe catches up with Emma was in the now lost hamlet of Esthorpe. It was owned by Warwick and made a perfect staging post on the journey north from Southampton to Warwick.

Coverham Abbey and the Praemonstratensian Monks - the White Canons

Coverham Abbey did exist but remains now only in a few ruined fragments. The order took a more pragmatic approach to their worship than some other orders and believed in going out into the community to fulfil pastoral roles in parish churches. The abbey, and the fictional Canon Reedman, play only a minor role in this book.

THE LAST SHROUD

About the Author

Derek was born in Hampshire in England but spent his teenage years in Auckland, New Zealand, where he still has strong family ties.

For many years he taught history in a secondary school in Berkshire but took early retirement several years ago to concentrate on his writing. Apart from writing, he spends his time gardening, travelling, walking and taking part in archaeological digs at a Roman villa.

Derek is interested in a wide range of historical themes but his particular favourite is the late Medieval period. He writes action-packed fiction which is rooted in accurate history.

His debut historical novel, Feud, is set in the period of the Wars of the Roses and is the first of a series entitled Rebels & Brothers which follows the fortunes of the fictional Elder family.

The sequel to Feud, A Traitor's Fate, was first published in November 2013 and Book 3, Kingdom of Rebels, in September 2014. The final book of the series, The Last Shroud, was published in the August 2015.

Derek is now working on a new Wars of the Roses series which is set about ten years after Rebels and Brothers ends.